Love UNDERCOVER

TRACEY BARSKI

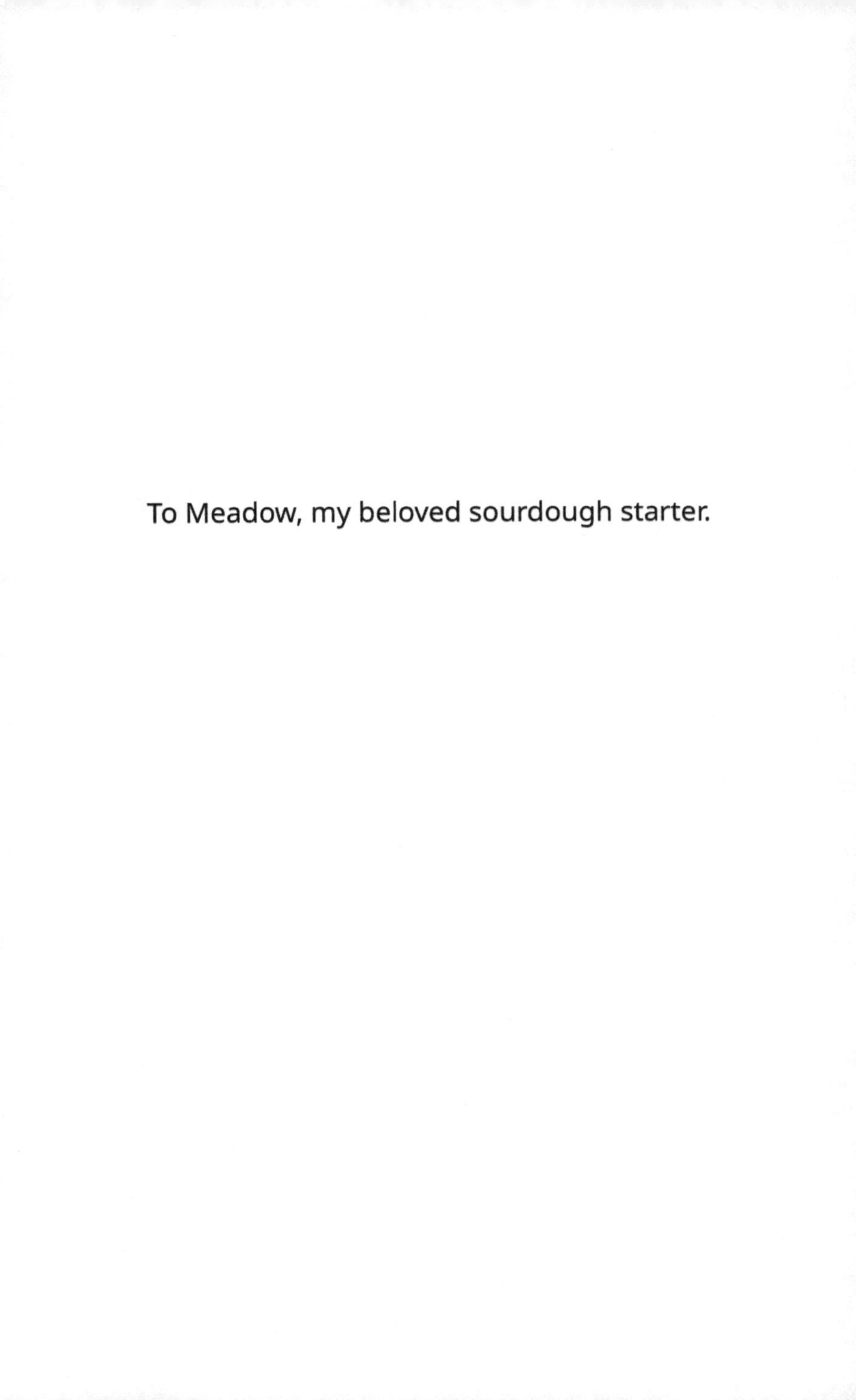

To Meadow, my beloved sourdough starter.

Contents

1

Crimes Against Coffee

There were plenty of signs that should have tipped Sadie off. First, the fire alarm that woke her up before five in the morning. Its blaring chirps sent her shooting straight up in bed, heart a jackhammer against her ribs.

Jerking awake in a panic well before she'd planned to be up and having to stand outside in her rattiest pajamas for forty-five minutes was definitely an omen of things to come. If Sadie put stock in that sort of thing, she would've crawled back into bed for the day.

The spilled coffee was the second sign. Because she'd been rushing—even more than usual—she didn't make sure the freshly poured mug was securely on the counter when her hand left its sides. Not only did she lose the precious caffeine, she broke her favorite mug, and there wasn't time to brew another cup after cleaning the mess. She hadn't even had time to secure her bronze-colored hair into its usual braid.

She found the rip in her favorite pair of linen pants as she walked into the library where she worked over the summer. The frayed edges of the hole along the seam in the fabric tickled against her thigh, drawing her attention and a huff. She could sew it later. Or—the more likely scenario—she'd toss them into the laundry basket and forget all about them until the next time she wore them.

Looking back, that third strike should have set her quaking in her organic hemp sandals. But that was still before the proverbial you-know-what hit the you-know-what.

The overly air-conditioned library created a constellation of goosebumps along her skin, and her shoulders drooped. She'd, characteristically, left her sweater in the car. It was ninety-five degrees outside already, and of course, she knew the air-conditioner was necessary in the middle of July in Maryland. But needing a sweater inside during the height of summer was a little ridiculous. Whoever was in charge of the indoor temperatures overcompensated, and it made her want to send an anonymous hate email. Maybe she could pretend to be a patron.

Greg had always harped on her for complaining about being cold wherever they went inside buildings during the summer.

"Just bring a fucking sweater, Sadie. How is that so hard to remember?"

High quality, that one was, she thought with a curl of her lip. Definitely no qualms about the end of that relationship, though she regretted the fact that there had been a relationship in the first place. Unfortunate she'd stuck it out as long as she had.

"Why are you frowning?" Roberta Jenkins pulled a stack of books off a cart she'd wheeled to the counter.

Sadie blew out a sigh, her whole body deflating. "I forgot my sweater in my car."

Roberta was always early and liked to get a jump on the holds people placed overnight on the website for pickup. She was in her late forties, single, a little sour, and she *loved* books. More than anyone Sadie had ever met. Roberta often said doing the holds made her feel connected with readers and helped her learn about the patrons who checked them out. She would smile in fondness over the volumes she, herself, had read at one point or another and wrote down titles she hadn't yet gotten to.

"Ah. Well, you could go get it before you clock in if you're quick. Or during your break." Roberta looked down at the cover of a hardback novel and pursed her lips. "Not sure you have enough time before your shift starts, though."

Following the rules was one of Roberta's favorite things, outside of books, of course. Not that Sadie was a rule-breaker. But she also knew how to be flexible. Being a kindergarten teacher made it a necessity.

Instead of responding, Sadie gave her a sarcastic thumbs up—which she missed—and headed for the back office to dump her stuff. She pouted a little when she spotted Roberta's travel mug of coffee sitting on the desk, lamenting the lost time that morning and the fact that she hadn't been able to stop on the way for a replacement. To be fair, her particular preference and brand of coffee were harder to find, and there were very few cafes that carried it. Not to mention it was much more expensive—ethically sourced and organic tended to be.

She was starting to think it was a splurge worth making in this case.

But since Roberta was doing her a favor by letting her work the summers between school years, she had to play by the pedant's rules. It was kind of a dream side gig for a teacher, really. Many of her friends took jobs in retail or coffee shops over the summer.

Hmm, being a barista would have come in handy right about then.

"First toddler time is in fifteen minutes," Roberta called, and Sadie ground her teeth at her saccharine sing-song voice.

Not that she didn't like what she did. But sans caffeine and over-tired didn't mix well when dealing with a room full of toddlers. She needed energy and verve.

"Got it!" She tossed a wistful look at the travel mug and briefly considered stealing a sip before she came to her senses. She was more desperate than she realized, though she had known for some time that her coffee addiction was borderline out of control.

She tucked her purse into the drawer of the second desk in the office and straightened to brush her hair away from her face. She forced the biggest smile she could manage in anticipation of exaggerating the voices and cadence of storytelling to a bunch of one- and two-year-olds.

Back-to-back sessions brought her right into her break. After all that time doing dances and hand motions, she regretted not flouting the rules and arriving a few minutes late in favor of brewing another cup or stopping somewhere for that caffeine fix.

She rubbed at her cheeks to soothe the soreness from smiling so much during her toddler reading times and headed toward the office.

"Roberta, I have to run over to the coffee shop," she said as she passed the older woman.

Roberta looked over the rims of her reading glasses as Sadie came back through the front desk area. Her eyes narrowed ever so slightly, but she dipped her chin instead of reminding Sadie that her break was exactly fifteen minutes.

Small miracles.

The summer sun was sweltering outside, but its attempt to blister her skin only resulted in a pleasant shiver as it chased away the cold from the library. She even looked forward to the baked innards of her car for the few minutes it would take for her to warm up before overheating.

Trapping her lip between her teeth, she looked up her favorite shop that adhered to her strict requirements for coffee just to be sure she'd have enough time to get there and back. It would be a close shave, but she knew exactly what she wanted. If only they had online ordering so it would be ready the second she arrived.

Keeping a wary eye out for cops, she considered the speed limit a suggestion and made it to her destination in record time. Nothing unsafe, but she'd definitely been liberal with her acceleration.

As she headed in from the parking lot, Sadie dug into her cross-body purse for her homemade lip balm, feeling the cylinder slide out of her grasp several times within the depths. She finally stopped to look inside the chaotic pit, biting a lip. Probably needed a good clean-out. But she knew herself enough to know she'd add it to a to-do list she would never check again.

"Sadie?"

Her head snapped up as if someone had yanked her hair from behind and found that her ears hadn't deceived her. It was Greg sitting there at the wire outdoor table. One hand was resting on its surface next to a to-go cup, and she could see his leg bouncing through the holes in the iron basket weave that formed the top.

He smiled at her, but it struck her as wolfish. He could probably see all the muscles in her body seizing up. Another reason she should have grabbed her sweater. She didn't like that he could tell she was bothered.

"Greg," she said, forcing a smile that bordered on a grimace, trying to talk her body into relaxing, into believing that there was no reason to be tense. "How are you?"

"Well, definitely better now that I get to see a pretty face." His grin widened.

Her chin shifted forward, eyes narrowing. He rarely doled out compliments without something else being behind them. The narcissistic jerk usually wanted something from her.

"Can I buy your coffee?" he offered, leaping to his feet so he could grab the door for her. Not a single lock of his dark-brown hair fell out of place in the process, which just felt unfair.

She tucked her tongue into her cheek as she walked past him. Letting him buy her drink wouldn't hurt anything. Unless some sort of string was attached. She'd just order the largest size, and say no to whatever it was he wanted. She might have been too forgiving most of the time, but she did have her limit. When she hit it, there was no budging on her side.

She gave him a honeyed smile. "Sure. I'm pretty low on fuel today, so I was planning on getting a large."

His smile tightened just a smidge. "Feel free. Want a croissant too?"

"If you insist," she replied, even though she could tell he was being mildly sarcastic.

His smile disappeared entirely. "Of course."

The line was short, so she ordered and stepped aside to let him pay, his lips forming a thin line as he handed over his card.

It was barely ten dollars, but he obviously wasn't happy about it. Which gave her a little thrill of pleasure. It was his own fault. He'd offered.

She moved to stand by the counter to wait for the drink instead of giving him any hope that she would sit with him outside. It was not smart to open that door.

Greg hovered awkwardly nearby, seeming to forget that he was trying to charm her for a moment. Even his annoyance with her appeared to have evaporated. Three lines formed on his forehead as he delved into some introspection, his brown gaze distant. Doubtful he was ruminating on his shortcomings and all the ways he'd done her wrong. She certainly wasn't going to ask what was bothering him.

He took a breath, shifting like someone had nudged him with an elbow as a reminder to be polite. "So how are things?"

She cocked a brow and couldn't help a suspicious tone. "Fine."

"Right. Right." He rubbed his hands down his thighs, unusually ruffled and preoccupied. "Well."

He moved toward her to envelop her in the most awkward hug. She stiffened as his arms went around her, his weight jostling her, and she took a step back to steady herself.

"You take care, then." He pulled away, knocking her sideways—literally—as he rushed for the door.

Was it her imagination, or was he looking around a little too nervously? So odd.

Whatever. She'd gotten a free coffee and pastry out of it. And he hadn't stuck around to try to weasel his way back into her life.

They called out her iced latte, and she lurched forward to snatch it from the counter, giving the barista a smile and offering her thanks before heading back out into the sunshine.

She checked her watch, the thin gold thing a relic of her grandmother's that she needed to wind regularly to keep it working. But that was a habit she rarely forgot these days.

She released a tight breath through her teeth and speed-walked to her car, texting her bestie about the weird interaction with Greg.

In typical Fiona fashion, she jumped immediately to him having an agenda.

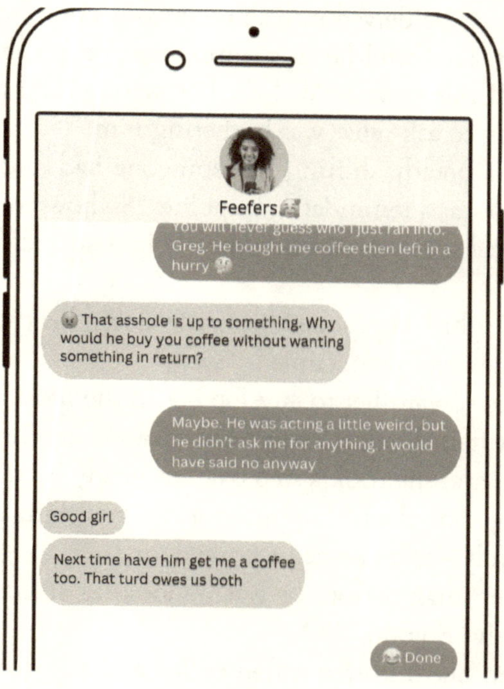

Sadie smirked and, with the giant iced coffee in hand, rushed into the library with only seconds to spare, her eyes scanning for Roberta's sour face. Even though, technically, Sadie wasn't late, in Roberta's book, not early *was* late.

The coffee got her blessedly through the morning and another toddler time, the STEM activity for the elementary kids, and the ear-full of chit-chat from the adult conversation-starved stay-at-home moms. That last one made her late getting back to the office computer to clock out for lunch. Sadie hurried across the library, hoping to sneak by her boss.

Not only did she fail to avoid the older woman's eye, but it wasn't Roberta's austere glare that made Sadie slow her step and clutch the empty to-go cup in her hand a little too tightly.

Two men in suits stood with Roberta, and it was the staring contest of the century. Anyone who could dish back what Roberta doled out deserved a prize, and Sadie assumed that these men were hardened against such tactics. One had his hands on his hips, his blazer tossed back in the process, revealing the gun in a chest holster.

Law enforcement, then. Feds if she had to guess, but that was based on the shows she watched on TV rather than actual experience. If they had been wearing sunglasses, she would've expected an alien to bust out of the Roberta-suit she'd come to know as her boss. It would explain some things, actually.

But there were no sunglasses, and Roberta was just naturally that weird.

The two men were older than Sadie, but maybe not older than Roberta. It was hard to tell exactly. One had a slight paunch compared to the wiry frame of the other.

Sadie approached with trepidation and plastered a polite smile on her face. It wasn't hard since her muscles were used to holding it in place by this time of the day.

"Here she is now," Roberta said, gesturing with jerky displeasure.

Sadie's eyes widened, and her smile turned brittle. They were here for her? "Is. . . there a problem?"

The two men turned simultaneously, like they were puppeted by the same master. The paunchy one pursed his lips and looked her over. The lean one narrowed his eyes, his frowning mouth dipping even farther.

"Ms. Powell?" The paunchy one had a surprisingly smooth and pleasant voice, like a butterscotch candy that slowly melted on the tongue.

It unsettled her even more. "Yes, that's me."

"I'm Agent Hicks, and this is Agent Richter." He flashed his FBI badge before slipping it back onto his belt without looking. "May we have a word with you?"

Even though she had expected as much, given the greeting, she couldn't think why they'd want to speak with her and struggled through her response. "I—yes, of course. Um, Roberta, can we use the office?"

Roberta lifted a sharp eyebrow but dipped her chin once in assent.

Sadie swallowed and spun on her heel, leading them behind the check-out desk and into the office as tingles ran through her entire body. Would straight-laced Roberta fire her for this?

It wasn't like it was *normal* for her to be questioned by the FBI, but Roberta didn't necessarily know that. This was only Sadie's second summer here, and two months hardly gave enough insight about a person. She still half-believed Roberta slept here.

Heading directly to the desk trash can to throw away her empty cup gave her something to do as she searched wildly through her recent activities. Was there anything she potentially got herself into without knowing it? She certainly spent a lot of time bingeing serial killer documentaries and podcasts, but who didn't? That was, like, the second-most popular American pastime.

The two men walked into the room with overly casual movements. Richter, the lean one, stood with his legs slightly spread and stared at her while Hicks surveyed the room with a hunter's slow deliberation.

Their silence filled the room like a physical presence, sending prickles of panic along her skin.

Oh, God, she thought. *I looked up how serial killers evaded capture the other day. They probably think I'm a murderer and a danger to my students.*

Her breaths came in little spurts, and she felt the heat creep into her cheeks. Richter's head tilted very slightly, apparently noting the change. Could he hear her galloping heart?

"I'm sorry, gentlemen," she blurted, her voice tight. "Can we cut to the chase? Have I done something wrong?"

Hicks glanced over, his expression mild. "I don't know. Have you?"

"No!" She held up her hands, shaking her head vehemently, though she shuffled through mentally again. Speeding to the coffee shop wouldn't bring federal agents into her sphere. Maybe rolling through that stop sign, but that would be small potatoes for the FBI.

"Hicks," Richter warned with an eye roll.

Hicks' mouth tilted up on one side. "You haven't done anything wrong. That we know of," he added with a wry grin.

She looked at Richter, whose expression hadn't changed. It was hard to get a read on the situation if one was teasing her and the other wasn't. "I don't understand."

Hicks's expression turned a little more serious. "We have some questions about your boyfriend, Greg Calloway."

Her stomach torqued in a way reminiscent of that time she got food poisoning after a seafood dinner. The one that put her off lobster bisque for life.

She swallowed the sensation down and tried to keep her voice even. "Greg? Why? Has he done something wrong?"

"How long have you known him?"

Hicks sauntered toward the window, and she wondered if his movements were supposed to put her at ease. But it was impossible when Richter stared at her so incisively. It felt like his gaze would cut right through her.

She shifted, folding her arms across her chest as if he were seeing through her clothes, which reminded her that she wasn't wearing her best bra. Not that he could actually know that. She mentally slapped her forehead, flinching as if she'd done it in real life.

Answer the question, Sadie, she scolded herself.

"Um, two years? But he's not my boyfriend. Not anymore."

Hicks turned, raising a brow. "But you have been in contact with him."

"No. I—" She stopped when she realized that wasn't actually true. The memory of their earlier interaction flashed into her mind. "I mean, yes. But not really *in contact*. I ran into him on my break."

Hicks and Richter exchanged a look, a sense of doubt simmering between them.

She thought back to their conversation, wondering if there was anything out of the ordinary, aside from his feigned altruism in the moment and his nervousness. "I don't get it. He's an accountant. What could he—"

Both men stared at her as she worked through what exactly an accountant *could* do. With the kind of information he encountered, he had access to a lot of financial records and accounts for some big names.

He made decent money, but he had expensive taste. Definitely a bit hoity-toity for her. He'd been bothered that she was merely a kindergarten teacher even though she held a master's in psychology and had been about to start her doctorate. But it was what she enjoyed. Her undergrad in child development and education had led her to teaching, so she'd opted to pass on the doctoral program.

"You could have been a doctor, Sadie," he'd once said.

She shook her head as if someone had repeated the words aloud. Sadie never put stock in his snobbery. He'd found her lack of waver infuriating. There was no doubt in her mind that he'd hoped to convince her eventually.

"It was random." She shook her head. "He was at a coffee shop I go to sometimes."

"What shop was that?" Richter asked, while Hicks pulled out a notepad.

She gave them the name. "He didn't act like he'd done anything wrong." She wasn't sure why there was a defensive note in her voice. It didn't matter that he wasn't her boyfriend anymore, or that he'd been a crappy one in the first place. She apparently felt some twinge of loyalty.

He had told her he loved her once.

She clenched her teeth together. Looking back, she could see how it might have been insincere, though. There was no need to protect him.

"Actually, he did seem a little nervous," she amended, subdued.

"In what way?" Hicks this time, his pen hovering over the page in his notebook.

She shrugged, face twisting as she thought back. "Just anxious. Like he was waiting for someone to arrive, though he followed me inside and paid for my drink. All he did was ask me how things were and then left."

"Did he mention having a meeting with someone?"

Her eyes were on the glossy surface of the desk, her mind reeling back to two hours before, so she didn't register who had asked the question. "No, I don't think so. I honestly didn't care. We didn't exactly end our relationship on the best terms."

She pictured the way he'd fidgeted, his eyes traveling everywhere but her face for a few minutes. He hadn't even said anything biting like usual. So maybe he'd been more nervous than she thought.

Blowing out a breath, she shook her head. "I'm sorry. I can't give you much more. We barely talked. Just the usual pleasantries exchanged between acquaintances."

"Or exes."

She jerked to look at Hicks' wry smile.

"Do you know where we can reach him?" Richter asked.

She turned a questioning look on him. "What do you mean? Don't you have his number? His address?"

"Yes."

She stared at him for one long moment before it dawned on her. "You can't find him? He disappeared in the two hours since I saw him?" She tried to laugh, but it came out choked, so she covered it with a cough.

Richter's brows quirked. "That was his last known location, yes."

"I-I'm sorry," she stammered. "I don't have any secret information for you. I don't know where he would hide if he was on the run. He'd be stupid to go to his parents or anyone you would connect him with that I'd know. And he'd be stupider still to come to me for help."

Hicks slipped his notebook back into an inner pocket of his blazer, nodding. Richter didn't take his eyes from her face. As if he thought she was lying. But if that butthead of an ex showed his face at her apartment now, she'd kick him down the stairs.

Her steely expression must have given him a hint of where her thoughts had gone because he finally broke eye contact and relaxed his stance.

2

A Tale of Two Kidnappers

Chase leaned into the shadows of the hallway, draping himself in darkness to keep spectators and cameras from spotting him. He slipped into the corridor to slink up the stairs to the second floor.

He'd scoped the place after tracking Greg Calloway to the apartment multiple times within the last two weeks. He never would've found himself in this little suburb of Baltimore otherwise. The ex-girlfriend's place.

Ex, Chase thought as he crept along the wall toward the door. If he didn't know better, he might have thought the guy was going back for a little post-break-up booty call. It was a fine booty, to be sure.

He may or may not have taken a peek. And by peek, he really meant in-depth survey. If he was going to sit for hours on end doing surveillance, he might as well enjoy what little nuggets he could.

It would've given him pause that Calloway was visiting his ex's apartment so frequently, but he'd noticed something about the unusual timing: he only showed up when she was gone. Which meant she probably didn't even know he was spending time there.

And that meant her apartment would be of particular interest to Chase.

The metal of the knob was warm along his palm as he worked the lock. Most were easy to jimmy—flimsy, at best. Largely useless against someone who had a basic knowledge of what they were doing and really wanted to get in. And Chase *really* wanted to get in.

Which was why he had it in ten seconds flat and without much noise. He slipped inside at an angle, so he wouldn't open the door very wide and was careful to shut it softly.

He knew the ex wouldn't be back for some time. Her routine usually followed the same pattern: leave by seven forty-five a.m., home by five p.m. every weekday. She arrived home closer to 8 on Friday evenings, so he knew he had some time. The last two weeks had afforded him a glimpse into the flow of her life. Dinner every Friday with the same friend.

Because he was nothing but thorough, he'd confirmed by following her from the library when she got off this evening to the same restaurant a block away and watched her hug the friend outside before he'd headed to her apartment building.

His gaze swept the space. It should have been tidy. It had that feel—minimalist farmhouse chic. Or whatever they called that popular style of home decor.

He'd caught an episode or two of that design couple in passing. Okay, so he'd never admit to anyone—even himself—that he actually enjoyed the show and made a mental note of when episodes would air so that he could "catch" one.

It was clear she watched it too based on her decor choices.

But someone had been here before him, and they'd gotten in when he'd been out looking for Greg at his usual haunts. Which sent a prickle of irritation through him. If someone else was looking, that meant there was more here than he'd been told.

Which also meant that this little ex-girlfriend was in more danger than she probably knew.

Her books, once stacked on bookshelves next to tiny potted plants, were strewn on the floor, little pictures and scribbled notes she'd tucked inside spilling from the pages like hidden secrets. The two large-frame black and white photos above the couch were knocked sideways, and her throw pillows had been tossed on the floor and gutted, feathers streaming onto the cockeyed beige rug.

Cupboard doors in the kitchen were left open, bowls and mugs haphazardly strewn across the counter. There were plenty of dirty dishes in the sink already, but a potted plant had been knocked over, its soil pouring into the basin and onto the plates. So the intruder had even searched in there.

He found more of the same throughout the two-bedroom apartment. Drawers hung open, clothes half-dangling out and dragged around on the floor. All of the articles of clothing were neutral, soothing colors that matched interchangeably with other pieces. Though he paused to consider the fact that the underwear drawer, which had been ransacked more thoroughly than the others, contained a variety of neon, bare-ly-there numbers that had him reflecting again on the appeal of the booty.

Another stirring of anger churned because someone had turned this place upside-down with unnecessary savagery. He fought the urge to right as much as he could. It wouldn't be hard to figure out where it all went. If it had been him, no one would've noticed he'd even looked through everything.

But not everyone was as fastidious as he was.

He turned to slink through to the second bedroom, which she had converted into an office and a pottery studio of sorts. The sun was creeping toward the western horizon, gilding everything with its golden touch. It gave the room an ethereal glow, and it was clearly where she totally let loose because it was significantly less orderly. Maybe orderly wasn't the right word.

Even viciously combed through, he could see the chaos that reigned here. The drop cloth under his feet had ground-in slashes of clay and stains that made him wonder if this was where she was most at home. He started to think maybe the minimalism that kept the rest of the house contained was her attempt at disguising the disarray that threatened to rule her life.

He contemplated the trace of a clay footprint on the drop cloth, the curve of her bare foot stirring something within him. Maybe it was one of the pieces fitting together to give him just enough of a picture to be intrigued.

He stepped carefully around spilled plastic bins containing what looked like a child's craft supplies. His eyes froze on the strip of alphabet tracing pages. Maybe she was a teacher during the school year. The library must have been a summer gig, which made sense considering a teacher's wages often didn't cover all the expenses a person might have.

Two college degrees were stuffed into a discreet corner. The bachelor's in elementary education and child development made sense. But the master's in psychology made him pause. Neither were on display. In fact, it seemed like she meant for them to stay hidden.

He moved on, assuming that everything that had been searched wasn't worth double-checking. They'd been fairly thorough, if absolutely barbaric. He checked the vents for recent removal and other seemingly undisturbed, but possible, hiding places.

It was as the sun was half in the embrace of the horizon, orange fingers scraping the sky, that he heard the footsteps outside of the apartment. She was home early, and he'd spent way too much time checking every nook and cranny.

He moved to the darkened corner of the room next to the only window, thinking he could sneak out that way. In the dusky light of rapidly descending evening, he saw two men walking toward the apartment building, which set his stomach rolling. There was no question whose goons they were. Santiago was easy enough to recognize on his own, but his sniveling little shadow, Travers, was a dead giveaway.

The real question was if they were the ones who'd tossed her apartment in the first place. It was likely, and he could guess why they were on their way back: they hadn't found anything either and thought she might have answers. The Suits were probably not far behind. No doubt the feds would be all over this by now, considering Calloway had given them all the slip. Which was exactly why Chase had made his way back here.

He ducked under the windowsill and pushed himself against the wall in the dim light of the hallway, creeping closer. A key jiggled in the lock, and he reached into the back waistband of his pants for the hidden holster clipped there, pulling out his nine mil and palming the weapon. He brought it in front of him in one fluid motion as he moved forward.

The door swung open and blessedly obscured him from her view, but he was still able to peruse the feminine body as she walked into the room and froze, her hand tightening on the knob.

As he snuck toward her through the shadows, he took in the shock that threw her eyes wider and her brows toward her hairline. His gaze traced her profile, a twinge of familiarity niggling at the back of his mind. The caramel-colored hair, the short, button nose above full, unlipsticked lips.

"Oh my. . . " The truncated phrase dissipated into a huff of air as her head swiveled slowly to take in the mess. "What the fizz?"

Chase stopped moving for a second, tilting his head at the odd lack of vulgarity in the exclamation, thrown off by the wholesomeness it embodied.

The way she shifted, as if to step back outside—likely realizing that the mess meant danger—spurred him to action, though he regretted his next move for the way it was about to send both their lives on a new trajectory.

"Don't," he said, just as she was reaching into her purse for what he assumed was her phone. His voice came low and gruff, just as he'd intended, though he inexplicably hated the way she stiffened.

Those pouty lips parted just slightly to release a tremulous exhale.

"Shut the door quietly," he told her, holding the gun where she could see it without pointing it directly at her.

She didn't turn, but the dark lashes that framed her eyes fanned down twice in quick succession as she blinked in response. She pushed the door slowly closed without turning. Just a stretch of her arm behind her.

He waited until he heard the click to step forward and twist the deadbolt, the *snick* of the lock sliding into place lowering his anxiety a touch, though he imagined it spiked hers.

"Please, take anything you want. I won't even look at your face or call the police. You can just go." Her words tumbled out quickly, but they were less shaky than he would've thought they'd be.

"I'm not here to rob you."

She released a breath that bordered on a sob. She thought he was going to do something worse, no doubt. "Then w-why did you go through my stuff?"

"I didn't ransack your place," he said, gesturing with his gun for her to move further into the room. "I found it like this."

She took a few steps forward, and he drew up behind her, leaving only a hand's width between them. He was surprised that her height brought the top of her head to his chin. Very few people, let alone women, were tall enough to hit that point standing next to him. He hadn't realized because the sensuous curves of her body gave the illusion that she was shorter. And that particular detail was not something he wanted to dwell on at the moment.

Shaking the thought from his mind, he urged her toward the couch so he could glance out the window to check for Santiago and Travers. He didn't see them, which meant he probably only had a couple more minutes.

"Do you know what they were looking for?" he asked her, the urgency tightening his voice.

She turned her head then, perfectly shaped brows folding low over her honey-colored eyes, and he felt it like a blow to his gut. Not just because she was beautiful—damn, there was that to add to the list under *nice ass*—but because he felt that inkling of recognition again, like they'd met somewhere before. He just didn't know where or when.

"Looking for?" she asked, bringing his mind back to the situation at hand. He'd forgotten he'd asked a question. "Weren't they just robbing me?"

He focused his thoughts and lifted a brow, jerking his chin toward the eviscerated pillows on the floor. "If they were only robbing you, why would they gut your throw pillows?"

She swallowed and looked around at the feathers strewn about the floor. "Wait." Her eyes darted back to his, narrowing for a second as she scrutinized the planes and angles of his face.

Shit, did she recognize him from somewhere too?

"Do *you* know what they were looking for?" The accusation in her tone was surprising and shot straight through his chest.

A teacher, he thought dryly.

A sound outside her door sent a bolt of adrenaline through him, electrifying his muscles. They were out of time, and he still needed answers.

Because Calloway had disappeared, and she was the only lead. And not just for him.

Chase raised the pistol in his hand, pointing it vaguely in her direction, though still not *at* her, to discourage an attempt on her part to use his distraction to her advantage. "We have to go."

She blinked. "What?"

He gestured toward her bedroom, but she didn't move. He huffed a sigh. This girl was seriously less scared than she should have been. "You want to look like your pretty throw pillows in about five minutes? *Move.*"

She tsked as he bum-rushed her toward her bedroom. "If we're leaving, why are we going to my room?"

He didn't answer as he shut the door behind them and moved toward her bedroom balcony. It was small, and he'd gauged the distance between hers and her downstairs neighbor's when he'd scoped the place earlier. He could reach easily. But she was at least five inches shorter, and he'd have to catch her.

Still, he opened the slider as quietly as he could and took her by the arm.

She resisted, digging in her heels, then flinched when a thud came from the other room like the front door had banged against the wall. Her hair flew around her head, slapping him in the face as she jerked to look in that direction. Still, she worked against him.

He gritted his teeth. "If you want to die, by all means, stay here."

She turned back to him, those amber eyes turning a chocolate color in the quickly diminishing light. "How do I know *you're* not planning to kill me?" she hissed.

He stepped closer to her, clamping both hands around her arms, the sense of urgency igniting his nerves, making it feel like his palms were on fire from the touch of her skin. "If I was going to kill you, I would've done it already," he growled.

She relented only after hearing a rumbling voice from the other room and let him drag her toward the balcony. They both stiffened as the sound of someone moving toward her door carried to them. It lit a fire under her, and she willingly scrambled out with him.

He slipped his gun back into its holster and planted his hands on the railing of the balcony, swinging his legs over and dropping onto the railing below.

"Jump down. I'll catch you."

He heard a frightened little squeak then caught sight of two sandal-clad feet, followed by a firm, round bottom. Lifting his hands, he forced his mind through rounds of skip counting to distract himself as her butt fell into his palms.

His hands slid over her hips to her waist, and he lowered her to his chest so he could brace her weight against him. As he helped her slide down, her entire back side rubbed down the front of him. He started the alphabet backwards in Spanish as his mind sputtered over the full-body touch.

Instead of releasing her when her feet hit the ground, he slung them both over the railing onto the sidewalk on the other side, and she let out a surprised gasp as he pushed her forward into the parking lot.

Street lights flickered on with the sun now gone, though the sky held that orange glow in the distance that kept the stars invisible. Thank God he'd parked away from any light, tucking his car into a discreet corner.

She willingly weaved through vehicles with him, and it made the guilt and regret tangle in his gut to think what he had to do next.

He dug around in his pocket, not bothering to hide what he was doing as they approached his car. She might think he was just going for his keys, and she had reached the point of trusting him—at least partially.

He made a show of jangling the key chain to keep up the ruse until they reached the passenger side of the car, where he unceremoniously pushed her against the frame, whipped her purse from over her head, and yanked her hands back to zip-tie them.

She gasped, having no time to prevent the move.

He flipped her around, using his body to pin her. She looked like she was about to scream. So he did the first thing he could think of to silence her. It didn't hurt that it was a question he needed an answer for.

"Where's Greg Calloway?"

She balked, momentarily thrown off-balance. "Uh, what?"

"Your boyfriend, Greg."

Irritation sparked in the glowing amber of her eyes. "He's *not* my boyfriend."

He grunted to cover his laugh. The fact that she could be irritated instead of scared blew his mind. "You saw him today. Did he tell you anything? Give you something?"

She snorted. "He didn't give me anything but a migraine and a free drink."

Either that was confirmation of what he suspected, which was her ignorance of what her ex was up to, or she was a lot more steely than any of them expected. Regardless of the answer, he needed to get them out of there while he still could.

Without preamble, he whipped out a bandanna and placed it over her mouth before she could react, praising himself for using the distraction well. She fussed and grunted, jerking her head back and forth as if it would keep him from being able to tie the back. It made it a little more complicated but didn't slow him much.

Her eyes, huge and frightened and angry, begged him not to do what he was about to. He hesitated for a fraction of a second before he dragged her resisting form toward his trunk.

"I'm sorry to have to do this," he murmured, popping the lid open.

She tried to plant her feet as she shook her head hard enough that he worried she'd knock her brain loose.

Her stance wasn't much help as he backed her up, the trunk bumping behind her knees. By then, it didn't take much to throw off her balance, and she tumbled in with a muffled yelp. He made sure to situate her in a way she might be most comfortable as he drove.

"I can't have you seeing where we're going."

Why was he explaining? As much as he hated what he was putting her through—and it was, in fact, much kinder than whatever the goons back at her place would do—he didn't owe her a reason or an excuse considering he had a reputation to uphold.

Once satisfied with some modicum of comfort on her end, he lowered the lid of the trunk on her glistening eyes as she continued to implore him not to.

He smashed her phone on the curb then snatched her purse and went for the driver's side door.

Damn it. This was not going according to plan.

3

Junk in the Trunk

That *was* Chase Lundgren, right?

Sadie hadn't realized it at first because the fear had shorted out her brain as soon as she'd heard his voice and seen the gun in his hand. All she'd thought in that moment was that she was about to die.

But then his eyes had widened, the gruff scowl on his face softening briefly. That split-second flash of utter surprise had lodged itself in her mind, tripping a chain reaction of mental gymnastics that eventually led her to a solid connection.

The giant man who'd bundled her into the trunk of his car was the quiet, brooding basketball star from that high school she spent only a year attending in Virginia when her dad had been stationed at Camp Elmore. They'd never interacted much, given how self-contained she'd been at that point. But she'd noticed him. Lots of people did. He was always ducking his head as the others cheered and slapped his back after a game.

The reluctant basketball hero.

And he'd just kidnapped her.

She'd been kidnapped! *Oh, cripes.* Stuffed into a trunk like a sack of groceries.

But she'd set out Meadow, her sourdough starter, to make some loaves later! She would die if Sadie didn't feed her again. She'd been cultivating that starter for years. Her stomach flipped at that realization.

"Where is Greg Calloway?" he'd asked in a gruff baritone.

It had sent tingles down her spine. Because she had been terrified, *obviously.* Definitely not because of the fact that his body had been pressed against hers.

And what a body. His lean basketball player's frame had bulked up, and he was all hard lines and muscle.

How was it possible to be thinking about *that* when the man had just fizzing kidnapped her?

It was keeping her from panicking. That's what it was.

Because if she dwelled on it, she *would* panic and stop thinking straight, and she would probably make some grievous mistake that would get her killed before he had a chance to take her out himself, and that would just be ridiculous considering she had a glimmer of hope that he might *not* actually kill her, even though she knew next to nothing about him or his intentions, but he'd said he wouldn't.

Panicking.

She grunted in frustration, startling herself in the darkness of the small space with her own voice. But that snapped her mind from the stream-of-consciousness hysteria and back into focus mode.

Because she needed to do something!

She shifted, grimacing, and the bandanna around her mouth slid down a little. Inspiration struck. She could concentrate if she could breathe better, and getting that thing off was step *numero uno*. Already her lungs burned, making her chest ache as she heaved air in and out through her nose like a galloping racehorse.

It didn't help that it was so hot inside the trunk. The sweat already trickled along her hairline, soaking through her tank top under her arms, and down her spine.

She wiggled her head, rubbing along the carpet until the bandanna slipped off her mouth and down her chin. But still, her breathing was too close; the wet warmth of it blowing back into her face made her heart beat faster, even as she rested from her efforts. It was just so dark and tight.

The car drove over a bump in the road that jostled her, snapping her teeth together. She ran her tongue along the grooves to make sure she hadn't cracked one. If her hands had been free, she could pillow her head to keep from hitting the bottom on the next bump. But if they were free, she'd be doing a lot more than just protecting her skull.

She *needed* to get her hands in front of her.

There was that move she'd seen on TV: fold herself just right to loop her bound hands under her feet and bring them around. Then she could search for that trunk release button or pull that was standard inside most cars these days. But it wouldn't matter if she didn't have her hands available.

She shut her eyes, trying to calm her mind as she counted through each inhale and exhale, trying to ignore how heavy the air was.

And his name floated through her mind again: Chase Lundgren.

No doubt about it. But this wasn't Norfolk, Virginia, where they'd first interacted twelve years ago. And by interacted, she really meant a *very* loose orbital overlap in attending the same high school. Basically, she knew his name. But everyone did. He was the aloof, boyishly handsome star of the moment—the one who'd won them the championship.

By comparison, Sadie was the standoffish transfer student who spent most of her time in the art hall, practicing her newfound hobby of sculpting clay pottery. It had been a temporary assignment for her family, as her Marine father had been stationed elsewhere within a year, so she hadn't bothered to lay any roots.

Still, Chase Lundgren had never disappeared completely from her memory. Though his smooth baby face was more angular and now shaded with a full beard, his moss-green eyes were unmistakable.

Crackers, was she seriously thinking about the eyes of the man who'd just kidnapped her instead of figuring out a way to get out of his trunk?

Not that she'd entirely thought that one through. The car was moving at a decent clip and had made few stops. It had been a while since they'd even slowed. She assumed they were on a highway now. Which meant that if she got the trunk open, she wouldn't be able to get out without splattering her guts all over the concrete and getting run over by other motorists.

But that would come later. First things first: getting her bound hands in front of her.

She inch-wormed around in the tight space, grunting like a. . . grunting thing. Did badgers grunt? Aardvarks?

She made a mental note to Google it later—if she lived long enough, that is—and was reminded of a student who'd once pretended he was a caterpillar to get out of doing a math lesson.

Focus, Sadie.

She gritted her teeth, shifting her shoulders to try to bring her knees up as close to her chest as possible.

She wasn't sure if the amount of grunting and thunking was audible inside the car because—surprise!—she'd never had a person, conscious or not, in her own trunk before. But he probably wouldn't be shocked she was moving around. He likely expected it.

But it did make her wonder why he hadn't just drugged her or something instead. Not that she *wanted* to be drugged. Still, it seemed like the simplest way of handling a kidnapping victim.

Her breathing spun out of control again, so she shut her eyes.

"Kidnapped," she huffed. "You've been kidnapped. By a super hot guy you knew in high school." She shook her head. "By a really tall, buff guy from high school who is clearly some kind of evil criminal now. But you *can* do something about it."

She tried working her bound hands under her feet, but it was too hard to move her arms with her weight resting on one of them. Maybe her arms were too short? Or the rest of her was just too long.

Huffing again, she shuffled through other ideas. How much space was between her and the top of the trunk? Usually, trunks fit a couple of stacked suitcases. Maybe she would have enough room if she worked her way to her knees.

Using the momentum of the vehicle to get into a kneeling position, she rocked her body until she got onto her knees, crunching up in a demented version of child's pose like she was doing a yoga routine instead of maneuvering in a trunk. Pushing with an elbow almost toppled her sideways since she couldn't stabilize herself properly. She rested in that position for a moment and took the time to congratulate herself on making it this far as she puffed air in and out. It became clear, though, that she was out of vertical space; her spine brushed the top of the trunk.

Clamping down on a fresh wave of panic, she rocked to the left, landing on her other side so she faced toward the back of the trunk. The faintest light peeked through a crack along the backseat of Chase's car that blocked her from the interior. Her own backseat folded down in the event she needed to transport something that was too long. That was how she'd brought home a random two-by-four for a project she'd wanted to do with her students, the piece of wood stretching all the way to the front seat, hovering over the gearshift.

She tucked that info into the back of her mind. Kicking it in and attacking him from behind would've been an option if she had her hands available to actually do the attacking. Using her feet wasn't practical for that. All that would do is make him crash the car and kill them both.

Setting her jaw, she felt along the seam of the trunk lid behind her for the release latch. Of course, she wouldn't open it yet, not when they were clearly traveling on the highway. But at least she would know where it was.

A bead of sweat trickled down her temple as she groped around frantically for the release.

She grunted and scooted up, wincing as she lifted her bound hands awkwardly. All she felt at first was the rough carpet lining the trunk and that foam they put around the seam of the lid to keep moisture and debris out. Then her fingers fumbled over a little plastic pull, and a surge of elation bubbled through her chest.

Every muscle in her body relaxed, and she practically flopped down, breathing hard and laughing softly like a loon. Now she simply needed an opportunity. Maybe he would stop for gas or a bathroom break.

Or a bathroom break for her. She shifted as the pressure on her bladder made itself known at the reminder. With her mind settling a little, she was much more aware of her body's needs. Luckily, years of teaching had trained her to hold it for unhealthy amounts of time.

The consistent speed of the vehicle made her heart sink lower and lower, though, and the panic started again, an insidious chill that crept through her chest and squeezed like a frigid hand around her ribs.

She shut her eyes, focusing on slow, even breaths again. Like a kid having a meltdown, all she needed to do was count slowly.

In: *one, two, three, four.* Out: *one, two, three, four.* Again.

Moss green eyes.

Apologetic and concerned.

Attentive and focused.

It was his eyes that made her decide to climb over that balcony into his waiting hands. Some element of trustworthiness existed in their depths, and she was so sure that he didn't want to hurt her.

Then he'd shoved her into his trunk. To be fair, he hadn't hurt her, but why had he taken her?

She could think of no reason someone would want to trash her apartment or what any of them were after. It was clear Greg was in over his head with something, given that the FBI had questioned her earlier that day. But she didn't understand why anyone thought she would know anything about it.

Fizz you, Greg! she wanted to shout. It was *his* fault she was huffing and puffing inside this god-awful trunk with her shoulders screaming from her inch-worming around.

♥ ♥ ♥ ♥ ♥

The steady rhythm of the car engine and the wheels over the road lulled her into a half-sleep. She wasn't comfortable enough to truly drop into unconsciousness, but she was too bored to stay fully awake.

It was the slowing of the vehicle that snapped her into full awareness. Even though she didn't totally fall asleep, she was disoriented when she opened her eyes and couldn't see much of anything.

Stupidly, she tried to sit up and thunked against the roof, letting out a panicked sob when she tried to pull her hands free and found them still bound. The space tightened around her, and the urge to stretch her legs became unbearable. She heaved in gasping breaths that made her lips tingle as she yanked against the restraints and kicked at the walls of her prison.

Calm down, the rational part of her mind commanded—the one that dealt with tantrums on a weekly basis. But her thoughts continued to spin wildly until the car lurched to a stop, jolting her into motionlessness.

Instead of letting her rapid, panting breaths continue, she trapped the oxygen in her lungs, straining to hear movement outside of the car. Then she remembered: *the latch!*

She huffed out a breath and shifted, wrapping her hands around the pull to open the trunk. Without thinking of what came after, she yanked hard and heard the latch release, a triumphant gasp escaping her lips as cool night air breathed against her sweaty body.

But since she hadn't planned her next step, she recognized the dilemma of her back facing the outside world.

Not wanting to waste her opportunity, she twisted, throwing her legs out and using the momentum to roll out of the trunk. But there was no time to gauge the distance to the ground, and she wasn't able to get her feet under her. She ended up flopping into the dirt on her knees, hissing as the gravel bit into her shins through the thin fabric of her linen pants.

"What was your plan from here?"

She yelped at the calm, rumbling baritone and lurched up, whacking her head on the bumper of the car. Without her hands, she flopped back down toward the dirt, tucking her chin to avoid smacking her face on the ground.

"You know I could hear you moving around in there, right?"

She glared at him as he leaned over her, absolutely no humor in his face. A navy sky glittered behind his head, and she momentarily forgot about her predicament to marvel at how many stars were visible.

And then he slipped a hand around her arm to haul her to her feet. She stumbled, but he easily kept her upright, not even shifting his weight as counterbalance.

And it was no wonder. Now that she wasn't straight terrified out of her mind, she took in his sheer bulk. She was no tiny woman, and he dwarfed her.

Without much explanation or warning, he tugged her forward, drawing her attention to the building in front of which they'd parked. He reached back to shut the trunk, almost as an afterthought, and barely broke stride.

Meanwhile, her legs wobbled like jelly, and she stumbled to the porch steps of a small cabin-like home. The dark windows looked like many sightless eyes, and the opening scene of a horror film flickered across her memory.

This is where people go to die.

This is where I'm *going to die.*

Her eyes flashed to the surrounding darkness, and she could just make out the skeletal arms of an encroaching forest that surrounded the cabin. Who knew how deep and dark and remote those woods were? She swallowed as he urged her up the steps.

The third step up the porch was where her toe caught, and she started to fall. He yanked her upright before she did more damage than the stubbed toe that had her hissing in pain and limping up to the front door.

"You all right?" he asked.

She wanted to ignore him and his gruff manner, though she heard genuine concern in his voice. Which felt incongruent to the situation.

"Fine," she ground out.

The sound of his keys jangling sent a shiver up her spine, a reminder that she'd let that sound lull her into a false sense of security earlier, which was how she'd ended up in his trunk.

His gaze slid to her as she leaned away from him, the green catching a beam from the porch light, giving his eyes a horrific, otherworldly glow.

Was it an omen, a premonition of things to come? "Oh, crackers, you're going to kill me, aren't you?" she breathed.

He huffed, the sound bordering on a laugh. "Sure. Planning to kill you right after I saved your life."

Seeing little point in hiding her thoughts about the situation, she muttered, "This is a serial killer house if I've ever seen one."

He snorted and pushed the door open, then nudged her forward and flipped a light on.

Her expectation of a dim, creepy torture chamber was met with open-mouthed shock as she took in the contents of the cabin. This was no hideout for a criminal on the run. This was someone's home. And it was cozy. Bright. Airy. Sparse as far as personal touches went. But homey in a modern kind of way.

"I imagine you need to use the restroom," he said, urging her forward.

Her bladder flexed in response. "Yes."

He steered her toward an open door off to their right. It was set in the wall next to a row of other doors, and she tried peering inside the rooms as he guided her toward the bathroom, but they were too dark for her to see much.

She spun to look at Chase, not realizing how close behind he was, and they collided. She stumbled back a step. He didn't, but his lids lowered to half-mast.

Heat poured into her face, though she tried to convince herself it was stupid to be embarrassed to ask for free hands to be able to pee.

She didn't need to ask, though. He pulled her into him again, eliciting a surprised gasp from her, and cut the zip tie before she even had the chance. Feeling cascaded back into her fingers, and she clenched her teeth against the discomfort.

It took half a second too long for her to realize she could step away from him, a little flutter in her stomach temporarily shutting down brain function. She was distracted by the ache in her shoulders, the pins and needles in her hands. Or so she told herself. It might've also been the muscles straining against his t-shirt.

Her eyes shot wider. *Stop thinking about the muscles.*

"Thank you," she murmured, rubbing at her shoulders in turn, trying to loosen the soreness.

He dipped his head once as he stepped back, reaching forward to close the door for her.

4

Not Given, Earned

Chase's whole life flashed before his eyes because this. . . this was definitely going to kill him.

The toilet flushed, the water ran, and he'd schooled his features before she opened the door, but it didn't mean he was anywhere near in control of anything. Not his thoughts, not his body, not this damn situation.

Not for the first time—nor likely the last—he thought about how much of a mess he'd gotten himself into. But it wasn't like he could have left her to the wolves.

There was no doubt those wolves would have devoured her. She might not have been useful to any of them—she didn't appear to have any obvious information about Greg Calloway or his whereabouts—but it didn't matter. Calloway had put her in the crosshairs, regardless. Going to her apartment as often as he did had drawn a big fat target on her back, making everyone believe she knew something she probably didn't.

Even though those goons were Zimmerman's other guys, there was no love lost between Chase and Santiago, and there was no way he could've thwarted whatever Santiago might have wanted to do. They'd both started as muscle, but Chase had moved up in rank because of his skills with the financial side of the money laundering operation. And Santiago, who'd been with the crime lord for a lot longer, didn't like it. He wouldn't have spared Sadie much thought. He might have drugged her, taken her somewhere dark and unclean. He pictured Santiago's dimwitted sidekick's lascivious stares and roving hands and felt a stab of rage lance through him.

They would've had no problem using pain to motivate her, even if she had nothing more to offer as far as information went.

And because the final puzzle piece of why she'd seemed familiar had fallen into place on the drive here, he knew this was going to get even more complicated as time went on.

"Why are you staring at me?"

He almost jerked at her words, forcing himself from that train of thought, and pushed away from the wall. Instead of answering her, he placed his hand against her back to guide her into the main bedroom.

She recoiled from his light touch, and he clenched his jaw. He hated that she was afraid, that the idea of him hurting her in any way crossed her mind. It made sense, though. What was she supposed to think after he'd hidden inside her apartment and stuffed her in his trunk?

He flipped the light on in his bedroom, glad he'd had the forethought to change the sheets before this little mis-adventure, even though that had been for himself. Not like he could've anticipated such a deviation from the plan. But maybe if he offered the best room in the house, he could somehow convince her that he wasn't who he appeared to be.

He couldn't very well come out and say it, though he could see about petitioning Gibson for an allowance just this once. But until he got clearance, his explanation remained locked behind red tape.

"Is. . . is this your room?" she asked, cringing away from him as he filled the doorway behind her.

He didn't want her to feel trapped, though he couldn't just let her wander—or leave—until he'd checked the perimeter to make sure he'd truly lost the tail he'd worked hard to shake.

"Yes. There's another bathroom over there." He gestured to the left. "Make yourself at home."

She gave a mirthless snort as she looked around, her eyes landing on the windows briefly, then flashing to him.

As if he wouldn't notice her attention.

"Don't bother trying," he said flatly. "This place is old, and they're a bitch to open. Super heavy and real fucking loud."

He was surprised to see the skepticism in her eyes. "So you just never open them?"

"Not worth the energy."

"Well, that sounds like a fire hazard," she muttered, rubbing at her wrists absently.

He huffed a laugh, but the humor died away as she shot him a look full of distrust and uncertainty.

Good reminder, that. Sucker punch to his gut, though.

She wrapped her arms around herself as he backed out and shut the door between them.

He leaned back against the wall and ran his hands through his hair, fighting the urge to release a guttural groan that would likely freak her out more. Dragging his palms down his face would have to be enough for now.

He pushed away from the wall and went to the linen closet for a couple of blankets. He'd never had to sleep on his own couch before, so this was going to be an adventure for a man his size.

Tossing the blankets onto the arm of the couch, he settled in to wait for her to fall asleep before he did his sweep of the property. The house was fairly secluded, though it wasn't far from civilization.

It always gave him the solitude that he craved, especially in his line of work, but it didn't isolate him. The silence soothed his frayed nerves, and the nearby town eased him back into normal society after long jobs.

Right now, all of it made him feel jittery. The split-second decision he'd made earlier that day was definitely going to bite him in the ass. It already was because now things weren't as cut and dry as he was used to.

How would he convince her to trust him?

How was he going to keep from blowing his cover?

The pseudo-kidnapping was supposed to convince Zim and his other guys that Chase was the criminal he'd been pretending to be for two years. But that had likely damaged any chance he'd have to earn her trust.

He'd have to see what he could do about it.

Setting his jaw, he stood and went to the wall-mounted TV, pulling it aside to reveal the safe behind it. He punched in the code to unlock it. From inside, he pulled out his agency cell phone, turning it on.

His gaze shifted to the closed door as he stepped as quietly as possible in that direction. He stopped at the end of the short hallway. Close enough to be overheard but not seem like he was right outside the door. Or like he was doing it on purpose.

A coded message popped up on the screen from a blocked number, and he knew Gibson was expecting a check-in soon.

He coded in a response and sent it, waiting for the phone call that would shortly follow.

The screen lit up, the phone buzzing in his hand.

"Sir," Chase said by way of answer.

"Report," Gibson replied in his usual clipped tone. It wasn't just his role and this situation that got that kind of concise treatment. The man wasted no words, ever. He barely wasted oxygen.

"There's been a complication." Chase's eyes went to the closed door again, noting that the light had turned off, the crack beneath suddenly dark.

"What kind of complication?" It wasn't any more a demand than it might've been had Chase reported the usual.

"The girlfriend." He held his breath a moment. "She's here with me. At my house."

One beat passed. "Alive?"

"Yes."

"Unharmed?"

"Yes."

"She a target?"

"Seemed to be. Zim sent Santiago."

Another beat passed as Gibson re-calibrated. Zimmerman was on the top of the agency's list, a player they were still trying to get the goods on. Greg Calloway had been on Chase's radar as a possibility for nailing Zimmerman, but whatever Calloway had was big if Zim was sending Santiago in.

And since Calloway had put everyone's focus on Sadie, it meant she might have or know something—even unwittingly.

Which made her valuable to all parties. And if that was the case, then Chase figured it was worth a shot to ask.

"Permission to break protocol—"

"Denied, Lundgren," Gibson interrupted. "You've already gone off script by taking her. Until we know the extent of her involvement, she doesn't get to know squat."

"Sir—"

"No. Lie low until I give you the all-clear to check in with Zim. Got it?"

"Yes, sir."

Gibson clicked off, and Chase shut the phone down, staring at the screen as it went dark.

So he couldn't explain himself to her. There had to be some other way to convince her to open up and give him information he could use against Calloway. The little things would help—letting her have his bed and leaving the bedroom door unlocked was a start.

It was a matter of time and effort on his part. She'd already seen that this house was just that—not some creepy dungeon where he'd torture and kill her. But other than a very loose association in their youth that he wasn't even sure she remembered, he was starting from scratch.

So far, the first impression wasn't in his favor.

5

Man vs. Espadrille

After trying the windows—the effort Sadie put in hadn't budged them an inch, and she was afraid to try harder since that would cause a racket—she'd crept to the door, listening for movement. Turning off the lights was her effort to make him think she'd gone to bed in hopes that he would let his guard down. Once he was asleep, she would try to escape.

But hearing him talk on the phone, then his footsteps through the living room that sounded like he was pacing, noises from the kitchen—doing who-knew-what. . . all of it stirred a deeper and heavier dismay as time crawled by, and he didn't settle.

Eventually she got tired of sitting with her back against the door and curled up on top of the blankets of his bed to rest while she waited him out. She grimaced, wishing she had her purse so she could rub some cream into her shoulder muscles that were aching after the long ride in the trunk with bound hands.

Despite her discomfort, she dropped into a fitful sleep. She woke numerous times, heart hammering as she tried to orient herself to the facts. And she would still hear footsteps outside the room, a ceaseless activity that made her squeeze her eyes shut and clamp down on the urge to panic. Rest was her best friend until she could figure out a plan.

When the sun painted the woods outside with early morning light, she gave up on sleep.

And still, he was moving around before she'd even gotten her bearings. The bright side of the early wake-up was that it gave her the time to formulate a plan, even if her efforts were futile. After all, he was a big dude.

The grand plan came from a movie she'd seen once. It involved a hand towel, and an individual trained in martial arts, but still.   She tiptoed to the bathroom, snatching the plush cotton from the rack and snuck back to the bedroom.

Pressing her back against the wall and making herself as flat as possible, she turned her head toward the door. He was noisy as he walked, almost as if he wanted her to know he was coming.

Like a chain reaction of tension, every muscle in her body contracted as the footsteps drew closer. She tightened her grip on the towel, pulling it taut as she heard a tentative knock.

The knob twisted, turning her stomach with it, and the door opened slowly.

Chase's blond head appeared first, his eyes set on the unmade bed directly across from him like he expected her to be there.

Before she could second-guess or he could see her coming, she launched herself at him, whipping the towel around his neck, yanking the ends in an X across his throat, and pulling down with her body weight.

The bedroom door slammed against the wall as he lost his balance, knocking into it.

The thrill of success and adrenaline shot her eyes wider, and she jerked the ends of the towel tighter as Chase stumbled into the room. A wave of red crept up his face as she cut off his airway.

His big hands clamped around her wrists, yanking. Her grip loosened only a little, and they spun in circles like it was some sort of morbid death dance.

His eyes locked on hers, wide and questioning—and something else that made her falter a little.

A fraction of a second later, his foot was behind hers, making her stomach drop out as she tripped over it and fell to the floor.

His first gasp of oxygen punctured the silence as the towel slid from around his neck. He tossed it aside and came toward her.

She shrieked, scrambling away from him in a crab walk that reminded her of the game she had her students play when the weather was too bad for them to have recess outside.

"I'm not going to hurt you," he rasped, but his face was still red, and he was lumbering toward her like a drunken bear.

"Like heck!" she hollered, kicking her sandal-clad foot at his head.

He pulled back slightly to avoid the bludgeoning by espadrille. "Sadie!" he bellowed.

She froze for a second. He remembered her name? Or had he done research?

"You kidnapped me!" She bumped into a small table, feeling on the top for the digital clock she'd seen there earlier, and yanked it down before flinging it at him.

He ducked, letting the clock sail over his head to crash against the wall. "I was trying to keep you alive!"

"Yeah, right!" She twisted and scrambled to her feet, running headlong for somewhere to hide or something else to use as a weapon since he was between her and freedom. She should've thought the towel thing through a little better. It seemed like her only option at the time.

His hands landed on each side of her hips, and he yanked her backward. He was so much stronger than she was, and she tumbled back into him. The unexpected collision threw off their balance, and they both went down.

Sadie landed hard on his abdomen, and all the air expelled out of his lungs with an "oof," and her brain fritzed as she registered the ceiling above her.

They both lay stunned, her panting, him working to pull air back in for a second time. She scrambled off of him, forgetting that his momentary incapacitation meant she could get a head start. The door was open, but instead of taking off, she was urging him to take a breath like he was a hurt student.

He rolled to his hands and knees, the sound of his lungs re-inflating a comically cartoonish sound that made her burst out laughing.

She was insane. She was delirious. She was in shock. She was having a nervous breakdown. Something.

He looked at her from the corner of his eye, gasping for more oxygen now that he was breathing again.

"Why aren't you running?" he croaked then coughed. "The door is wide open."

Her laughter died suddenly, and she pushed to her feet, her wary eyes on him.

He sat back on his heels, his thick, chiseled chest rising and falling with effort like he'd just run a marathon.

"Is this a trick?" She took a few steps toward the open doorway.

He shook his head. "It was never locked."

Her mouth dropped open. That had to be a lie. But she hadn't even checked. Like an idiot, she'd just assumed. Not that it mattered. She'd heard him prowling out there all night.

"Why stuff me in your trunk if you weren't even going to bother locking me in here?"

He got to his feet with a grunt, and she stumbled a few more steps toward the door, even though he simply sat down on the end of the bed, bracing his weight with hands on his knees.

"I want you to trust me."

She scoffed. "Trust you? After you pointed a gun at me?"

"I never pointed it at you."

She opened her mouth, shut it, opened it again, shut it. Thinking back, she realized it was true. He had never once actually pointed his weapon at her. But that didn't mean much in the grand scheme. Not when she considered everything else.

"You're keeping me here against my will," she insisted, her voice weaker than before. Shocks of adrenaline were still firing all over her body, but she'd stopped moving toward the door.

"I *brought* you here against your will," he amended, one big hand going to his throat where the towel had rubbed the skin raw. He apparently hadn't noticed the red mark on his cheekbone. "You can leave if you want to. There's a town about six miles from here. Northeast." He coughed, swallowed, winced. "Damn, you have a tight grip."

She narrowed her eyes at him. "I work out," she deadpanned.

He gave one raspy bark of laughter, wincing again.

"You didn't explain why you had to stuff me in your trunk."

He raised his eyes to her face, and this time, his grimace was deeper. "That is. . . a complicated story. I suppose telling you it was for your safety wouldn't be enough?"

She squinted at him.

They stared at each other for one long moment. She read in his eyes that he was asking her to stay, though she didn't truly understand why. Nor did she get why she seriously debated on doing just that.

Was she suffering from Stockholm Syndrome? Could that set in this quickly? Or was it some misguided sense of familiarity because of her prior, albeit loose, connection with Chase Lundgren?

It doesn't matter, she told herself.

She backed toward the door, spun, and sprinted for the front of the house. She tried the front door, found it unlocked, just as he'd said, and left it open as she rushed toward the porch steps and down. Her sandals against the wood felt loud in the stillness outside, the sound bouncing against the trees and back to her.

Ten feet past the car, she slowed, letting her mind take in the thick forest around them. The narrow, dirt driveway wound around through the trees and disappeared a few hundred yards out, swallowed on either side by green.

Her heart thundered against the cage of her ribs, and her stomach sank.

Chase could murder her out here, and no one would know. Not one person would hear her even if she screamed.

Someone would eventually report her missing, but they would never know where to look. Even though he'd given her the direction and the miles to the nearest town, she wasn't sure she believed it. For all she knew, they were farther than that.

Or the town was in a different direction, and he was trying to trick her.

But she still didn't understand the end game. What if he was a psycho who simply liked to keep her guessing? He might want to keep her for days, luring her into trusting him, then torture her until she begged for death. Who knew an old high school acquaintance would turn out to be a serial killer?

Admittedly, it was a little coincidental that he would kidnap her the same day she'd run into Greg, been questioned about him by the FBI, had her place ransacked, and then someone else had shown up to her apartment to do who-knew-what.

She walked forward a few more yards, getting to the edge of the woods, and a chill ran through her at the shadowy darkness within. Despite the growing summer heat of mid-morning, fingers of cool air reached her where she stood.

She turned back to look at the cabin. A veritable horror house if she ever saw one. Except the inside didn't match the outside.

And Chase was there on the porch, leaning against a post with his hands in his pockets. Something told her the impression she had of the house was a metaphor for the man.

The way the sunlight limned his imposing, muscular frame made her catch her breath. This moment, the bright sunshine glowing over the house and the man, surrounded by lush forest, was the perfect ending scene for a romantic movie.

City girl meets taciturn outdoorsman.

The way he stood, waiting for her like she was finally coming home after the main conflict had been resolved, a faint, self-satisfied smirk pulling at the corner of his mouth. As if to say *I knew you'd be back*.

It was absurd that some unfurling of warmth spread in her chest, like a lazy cat stretching out in the sun. Somebody call Hallmark.

But she could *not* let her guard down. He still had a gun, had still broken into her home, had still shoved her inside of his trunk. With her hands tied behind her fizzing back!

But she set her jaw and walked back toward the house, her steps slow with doubt.

"Northeast is that way." He tipped his head over his right shoulder, but his eyes never left her face. His voice was still scratchy from their scuffle.

She held his gaze. "What does it matter to you if I go in the wrong direction?"

He lifted one shoulder, and they stared at each other for a stretch. Then: "You hungry?"

She didn't answer.

"I'm making eggs."

Another beat went by.

Then he turned toward the door and went inside. He either expected her to follow, or he didn't care if she did.

She sucked her bottom lip between her teeth, casting her eyes in the direction he'd indicated as northeast. It just looked like more trees to her. But based on the morning sun's position, he actually might've been telling the truth. She took a couple of steps that way, half-convinced that six miles wasn't that far, but her stomach grumbled, and she realized how long it had been since she'd eaten.

Maybe after breakfast.

She peeked just inside the door.

He was already slapping some butter into a warm pan, pulling out the egg carton. He tilted his head slightly so he could look at her from the corner of his eye. "How do you like them?"

She eyed the carton, frowning at the label as she came closer. "Pasture-raised and organic," she answered without thinking.

He snorted. "I'll make a note for next time."

"Not just cage-free," she insisted, despite his sarcastic tone and the warning that shot off in her head. Most people didn't like lectures, and he was her kidnapper. And yet, she continued. "That just means they're all locked in a building together, still in too tight of quarters, even if they're not in cages. Even free-range doesn't mean much."

He turned to look at her, the spatula raised in the air like a question mark. "So, do you want the eggs or not?"

She slid onto one of the bar stools tucked under the island, grimacing. "Over easy is fine."

"This isn't grass-fed butter either," he warned, and she could tell he was messing with her.

"Heathen," she accused playfully.

He turned to her with a grin, and it stopped her heart. And then she realized how ridiculous it was that she was reacting to him. She was actually flirting with the man who'd abducted her!

Her returning smile disappeared, and she looked down at the marble countertop, tracing the vein of gray in the glittering white.

He cleared his throat and opened a cupboard to get plates for the eggs.

"Want some coffee?" His voice was cautious, overly polite, as he set the food in front of her.

She stabbed her fork into her eggs and shook her head, feeling the warmth creep into her cheeks.

He narrowed his gaze on her face, suspicion sharpening his features. "You don't like coffee?"

She shoved a forkful of eggs into her mouth to avoid answering.

"Free-range coffee isn't a thing," he said mildly, raising a brow.

She choked on the eggs as she laughed. "Um. No."

"But?"

God, he was going to make her say it. And, admittedly, it sounded so absurd, and it made her seem so high maintenance because of all of the things she'd said already.

Given her situation, though, she shouldn't be complaining about anything he was giving her. Because he'd kidnapped her.

Maybe if she said it to herself enough times, it would stick. "Sadie?"

Her name on his tongue sent a jolt through her. It was so bizarre because he'd never once said her name in high school. They'd never had a class together and hadn't run in the same circles.

"Coffee is one of the most heavily sprayed crops with pesticides," she said around a mouthful of egg.

He pressed his lips together against a threatening smile as he nodded slowly.

He thought she was stupid. But he'd asked, and, sure, she could have just said she didn't like coffee and left it at that. But that wasn't even true, so why bother lying? Especially when his opinion literally did not matter.

Except that it did.

Which made zero sense considering the situation.

This absolutely unbelievable, unreal, *insane* situation.

"Can really taste the cage in those eggs, huh?"

She jerked to look up at him.

He'd leaned back against the counter, arms folded over his chest while his coffeemaker sputtered and bubbled behind him.

"No, I. . . " She looked down at the eggs. "I'm just trying to wrap my head around being abducted by the nicest and most accommodating kidnapper that probably ever existed."

His expression tightened at the same time the corded muscles of his arms contracted. Her words bothered him, but weren't they the truth?

She tilted her head. "And it's the most confusing situation because you clearly want me to think you didn't, but then why would you tie my hands and stuff me in the trunk?"

He ground his teeth together, but he stared very intently at her like he was willing her to read his mind. Which she would absolutely be down for if it were possible.

But she couldn't. And so they stared at each other.

He'd claimed it was to keep her alive earlier, but the fact remained that he wasn't telling her why.

She'd overheard his phone conversation the night before. He'd asked about breaking protocol, and part of her hoped that meant he was not the bad guy his actions would lead her to believe.

She dropped her fork with a clatter and held her head in her hands. "This is so confusing."

"Sadie, listen."

She lifted her eyes to him, and an intensity vibrated off him that made her fingers want to curl into her palms. The effort it took to hold back while wanting to tell her was obvious as he moved toward her cautiously.

"Those guys that broke into your house—"

"*You* broke into my house!" She stood abruptly, moving a few feet away from him, and notably toward the door again.

He watched her, his expression open and contrite as he leaned forward on the counter as if to make himself smaller, less intimidating. "Yes, I did."

But it was true that he'd never aimed the gun at her. She hadn't realized it until he'd pointed it out. And he'd apologized before shoving her into his trunk. What kind of kidnapper apologizes before kidnapping someone?

"Those men," he said, quieter this time, "work for someone named Zimmerman. What you'd call a white-collar mobster. He's got his hands in corporate America. None of the street stuff you're probably used to, what you see on TV."

She said nothing, but she was overly aware of the way her lungs filled with air, how her heart rushed as she absorbed his words.

"They followed us."

The fear that flashed through her made her flinch.

"I had to make them believe you were being abducted. And I had to take the circuitous route from hell to lose them."

She barely took a breath. "Why did you want them to think you'd kidnapped me?"

His mouth flattened into a line. "So they'd believe I'm on their side."

So they'd *believe. . .*

"But you're not?" The words came out haltingly. "On their side?"

"I can't answer that."

But he wanted to. He hadn't moved, but it was like some invisible force strained toward her with every fiber in his being, and she felt it like it was corporeal.

She took slow steps back to the chair she'd vacated, a desire to trust him winding inside her, but the logic wouldn't fully relinquish its hold.

So she settled on finishing the eggs. It's not like she could get far with him right there watching her, anyway. And sustenance was necessary if she wanted the stamina to run.

If she got the chance again.

6

Spill the Beans

Sadie ate her eggs silently while everything in Chase fought to tell her the truth. Never had he felt the compulsion so strongly before.

Sure, there'd been others who needed help to escape the clutches of whatever organization Chase was working for undercover. But he'd never felt such a need to make them understand his intentions.

Usually, they'd figure it out, though. Those desperate to escape were already poised to trust someone who promised to get them out.

Sadie wasn't connected to this life, to what her ex-boyfriend was mixed up in. The man had gotten a taste and dug deep, though Greg was a more recent player in this game. He'd been tapped as a low-level peon to help cook the books in Zimmerman's schemes. But it didn't appear that Sadie had been aware of any of it.

He wondered if maybe because they had this random overlap in their past, he felt the need to explain it all to her. It didn't help when that gaze of hers drilled him with wariness. He inexplicably wanted to see her unmitigated trust.

They were only a couple of feet away from each other since she'd come to sit again, and he was still leaning over the counter. But he found himself drowning in the depths of her honey-colored eyes, and he had to look away.

"Does it hurt?"

He swung his gaze back to hers as she reached to touch his cheek. He sucked in a sharp breath when the tender spot sang with pain under her fingertips.

"Only when someone touches it," he said wryly, frowning. He hadn't even realized it was there. He'd been too busy catching his breath after their tussle that morning.

"I have something for it," she offered, her voice taking on a husky shyness he found simultaneously confusing and enthralling. "It's in my purse."

He nodded his head toward the table next to the couch where he'd set her bag.

She slid from her chair and walked over to grab it, digging around in its depths like it went on for miles.

"Here," she said, pulling out a white tube as she came to sit back down.

He squinted at it. "What is it?"

She lifted a shoulder. "Arnica cream."

As if that would mean anything to him. "What-a cream?"

She smiled. "Arnica cream. It's a homeopathic pain reliever. It reduces swelling and bruising."

He wrinkled his nose. As if he needed to be doctored with baloney medicine. "That's not necessary." He drew back when she started to unscrew the lid.

She glanced at him from under her lashes with a smile. "How about you just trust me?"

He almost choked on his own tongue. "Okay," he said, the word falling out of his mouth. He would have said yes to anything she'd asked of him in that moment. He barely knew what she'd said. He'd even forgotten what they'd been talking about.

She put her hand on his arm to pull him closer again, and he rested his forearms on the counter so they were at eye level. With gentle fingers, she dabbed the cream onto his cheekbone, which sent jolts of pain through it, and he winced.

"I know it hurts now, but it will feel and look better sooner." Her breath fluttered over his face. "I've gotten rid of bruises this way."

He just stared at her, struggling to process her simple words in order to respond. But she was so close, and she was quite stunning, and his body was reacting to her in a way that he was totally unprepared for.

She was looking at him oddly too, like she had lost her own train of thought.

It made him start to come back to himself because he was in very real danger right now as he watched her eyes flicker down to his mouth.

"Clever idea this morning, using that towel to choke me out."

She blinked and pulled back. The wariness returned to her eyes, which was good. He wanted her to trust him, but he also wanted her to keep her guard up. He was protecting her, but that didn't mean she was safe.

"Well, I knew it was my best shot for bringing you down. You're so much bigger than I am."

He acknowledged that with a small smile. He was so much bigger than most people, which worked to his advantage in a lot of situations. It was because of his naturally intimidating stature that he'd been an early pick for this job. And why people didn't often mess with him, even when he was still working up the ranks in his undercover roles.

"You remembered my name," she said softly, still with that caution that was the wall between them. "Do you make a habit of kidnapping women you went to high school with? Or was that just research?"

He'd forgotten about that. It had snuck out. He never planned to let her know that he remembered her from high school, let alone that he knew what her name was. But because of her attack and, in his desperation to calm her, he'd let it slip.

It was all shot to shit, anyway; he wasn't sure why he'd figured on sticking with any kind of plan. But it had always been his way. Now he had to figure out a new path forward. He could run with the idea of it being research, as she'd suggested. But he didn't see the point.

"I don't make a habit of kidnapping in general," he replied.

Her eyes narrowed in skepticism.

"But I do have a pretty good memory." He tipped his head. "I take it you remember mine?"

She tipped her chin down as pink blossomed in her cheeks. "No one forgets Chase Lundgren."

His mouth tilted as he tried to hide his dark amusement. "I wish everyone would."

She brought her incisive gaze back to his face. "You did always seem to want to fade into the background. But even being at that school for one year, I remember how they'd chant your name in the halls."

Chase pushed away from the counter, his expression tightening. Most people talked about their glory days as high school royalty or celebrated athletes with pride. But he'd rather forget it all.

The spotlight was never anything he'd wanted. At least not for that reason.

The corner of her mouth lifted a little as she watched him. "Still trying to fade, seems like."

He shifted, the discomfort like an ill-fitting suit against his body. He didn't like the direction of the conversation.

She placed her arms on the countertop, shifting forward a little. "Why did it bother you so much to have the attention?"

He backed up to lean against the counter again, folding his arms across his chest. As if he could put as much space between himself and this topic, the memories, as possible. He lifted a shoulder to give the impression it didn't bother him, though it made his stomach churn.

"I wasn't really the all-star everyone thought I was and made me out to be. I was just a tall kid, and the game came easier for me than those other guys."

She rested her chin in her hand. "I saw you play. I think you're selling yourself short."

He gave his head a decisive shake and grabbed the empty pan he'd cooked the eggs in, bringing it to the sink. It was what people often said. The sport came naturally to him, and because it's what his dad wanted at the time, he was pushed to be something he wasn't. And then all of that stuff happened with his dad, and Chase pushed himself even harder.

There was so much baggage tied to that time in his life, and because he felt so much, he buried so much, shoving it all deep down, throwing as much dirt on top of it as he could.

Now that was a skill he was proud of. One that had served him for the last two years working this job.

Which he was now putting in jeopardy by making the choices he had the day before. Woman before job, before the bigger picture. Pretty woman, to be sure. And a woman tied to his past, which had inexplicably called to him. But she was innocent, too. She didn't deserve to be left to those wolves.

"I'm sorry," she said, breaking into his thoughts. "I didn't mean to pry. This is. . ."

He turned when she didn't finish. She looked away, tucking her caramel-colored hair behind her ear, and his eyes tracked the movement and then traced the curve of her neck with a hunger that surprised him.

He forced his gaze back to her face. "You have nothing to apologize for. I just don't like to think about it."

"Okay." The word was so soft, and she kept her eyes from his face, which made him feel like shit.

He wanted to smooth the awkwardness. "So, since my bed and breakfast is not up to standard for you, what with my non-organic eggs and my poison coffee, should we make a list of what you'd like me to have on hand?"

She jerked to look at him, and he appreciated the color his words brought back into her cheeks. Why she'd be offended by what he'd said, he had no idea.

She must have quickly talked herself down, though, because she seemed torn on what to say for a moment, and the flame in her eyes died.

"This kidnapping situation definitely isn't going the way I would expect."

He bristled, but he beat back the automatic rebuttal he'd started to form until he knew he would speak calmly. "I know what this looks like, Sadie. But it's not the kidnapping situation you think it is." He stopped himself from saying anything further because he would end up telling her something he wasn't supposed to.

Her brows pulled together as she tried to parse his words and watched his face. He didn't know how much of his thought process showed in his expression, but if it looked anything like there was some kind of evil curse keeping him from spilling the beans, it would be close to accurate.

"I don't get this. I don't get you." Her mouth pinched as she squinted at him, and he had the absurd thought that she was trying to read his mind.

If only.

Having her know everything might make her more willing to keep a low profile, and it would make his life a lot easier.

"I want to give you the answers, but I can't. Not yet," he murmured, pressing his palms flat on the counter, the cold stone leaching warmth from his skin.

His bluff about her escaping earlier had paid off, though he'd been all twisted up inside about the possibility of her leaving the seclusion of the property. It was a gamble he'd willingly taken to get her to at least start trusting him.

Because he couldn't let her leave. Not alone, anyway. And not until he knew the coast was clear.

And based on what he knew of Zimmerman, it was far from over. His "boss" was a dogged individual who had a lot of skin in this game. Not to mention the FBI and the whole reason Chase was even tangled in this mess.

"Why can't you?" Her eyes bored into him, and it was another gut punch. "Is it because of that phone call last night?"

He fought to keep the relief from his face that his plan had worked. Maybe she would figure it all out on her own, and he wouldn't have to keep it from her. He said nothing.

"You asked permission to break protocol," she continued, watching his face for any change in expression.

He held himself very still, but every cell in his body was straining to communicate with her, to confirm what she was clearly working out in her mind.

Trust me, his mind begged.

"Are you. . . FBI?"

He rolled his lips inward, feeling the vibration in his muscles as he clamped down on himself.

"You asked me about Greg," she said slowly, her big eyes narrowing on his face.

Was he sweating? He felt like he was with the effort to keep his mouth shut.

"And I'd just been questioned by the FBI about him earlier in the day."

The muscles around his eyes contracted, the only betrayal of his self-control.

And she leaned forward in response. "What exactly is my ex-boyfriend into?"

That, he had no issue keeping locked down. It had nothing to do with her trust. But the fact that she'd gotten to this point in her mental process gave him a hope that electrified his skin.

"You want someone to think you've kidnapped me." The words were drawn out, stretched like warm molasses. "Are you working undercover?"

7

Tomato, Tomahto

Chase dropped his head, a sigh rushing out of him in obvious relief, and all Sadie's mind focused on was how she could see rippling muscles along his shoulders and upper back through his thin t-shirt.

Crackers.

She forced her thoughts back to the conversation, back to what she'd just spoken aloud, and the way he'd suddenly relaxed after holding his body so tightly she thought he'd snap his bones.

He lifted his head, the first real smile on his face that she'd seen, and that full grin was the sexiest thing she'd probably ever seen in her life. Which was not what she should have been thinking about.

Even if he was an undercover FBI agent who acted to protect her, she still didn't have any proof his story was true, and she'd be remiss if she didn't verify it in some way.

She folded her arms over her chest. "Do you have a badge I could see?"

His face fell. "No."

Every expression was so genuine and so sharp all of a sudden—more expressive than anything he'd shown in his face before—that she struggled to find a reason not to believe him.

Trunk, her rational mind said. *Bound hands. GUN.*

"It's too dangerous to keep it around during these kinds of jobs."

He didn't break the intensity of their locked gazes while he waited for her to accept his answer. And she really wanted to. It made sense that he wouldn't have a badge on hand. Someone could easily find it, expose him as an undercover agent, and possibly get him killed.

But it would go a long way in securing her trust right about now.

She bit her lip, and his eyes dropped briefly to her mouth. His Adam's apple bobbed with a swallow, his gaze slowly rising to meet hers again.

The urge to speak, to fill the silence and break the tension, forced the words out because she didn't trust what was happening here.

"Okay," she said softly. "Say I believe you."

The strain in the air deflated like a balloon with that one concession. Still, his gaze sharpened on her face like he knew she wanted to say more.

"What is the next step?" The question feathered up her throat, not nearly as strong as she'd hoped it would be.

He pushed away from the counter, a restless energy rippling off him. She didn't miss how he glanced out the window over the sink like he was checking for something.

"We lie low. There are too many unknowns right now." He turned back to her, his gaze weighty. "I need to identify why you're on everyone's radar."

Her stomach clenched. The men in her house, Chase's presence, even the questioning by the FBI the day before meant it was all tied back to her prior relationship with Greg putting her at risk. But she knew nothing, had nothing.

"Why was I on *your* radar?"

A heavy beat passed. "Your connection to Greg Calloway."

A flash of anger sparked inside of her, and she stood to pace away from him. "And we're back to this, again. I don't understand. We broke up. He's a jerk, and I want nothing to do with him. How much clearer can I be?"

He hadn't broken her heart, but he'd been a toxic leech on her life. One she wished she could scrub from her memory.

Chase straightened to his full height, and she was reminded how large of a man he was. It was no wonder he was believable as a criminal. She fought to keep from shrinking back.

"You saw him." His voice was a low rumble that vibrated through her. "Talked to him yesterday. Right before he disappeared on all of us."

His entire argument hung on the thread of a chance encounter?

She released a mirthless laugh at the absurdity. "You mean when I *ran into him* at the coffee shop?"

His expression didn't change.

"I told the other FBI agents that was nothing. I haven't talked to him in months. It was just random," she insisted. "I don't know how or why or where he's gone."

A steadily rising panic built in her chest when Chase's expression remained dubious. Especially when the fact that she'd run into Greg at her "hippy coffee place" really solidified in her mind. He'd turned his nose up at it on more than one occasion, had even given her flak for it. Had Greg been there on purpose? To specifically run into her? Her heart thundered. What had he done?

"He's been making visits to your apartment," Chase said, his tone clinical.

His words took a second to slide home. But then they finally sailed past her mental acrobatics about his appearance at the coffee shop.

"He what?" *When? How? Why?* Hadn't she gotten her key back from him?

Chase tipped his head ever so slightly at her tone. "I tracked him there at least half a dozen times in the last couple of weeks. And if I did, so did Zimmerman's other guys."

Her stomach wound tight, twisting like someone wringing out a wet washcloth as she thought about not only Greg going inside her apartment without her knowledge but also those other men.

And Chase.

She looked at him watching her, his expression inscrutable. "Do you think I'm working with Greg?"

He was so still as to be a statue, but she saw his chest expand with breath, reminding her that he was flesh and blood. "I don't now."

The relief she felt at his answer surprised her. It shouldn't matter what he thought.

"Not after watching him sneak into your place over and over when you weren't there." His head shake was almost imperceptible. "But he dragged you into his mess, and that puts you in danger, whether you know something or not."

She straightened her spine, though her knees felt weak from the fear his words inspired. "So you kidnapped me."

His expression pinched. "As a ruse."

"Tomato, tomahto," she shot back, failing at infusing humor but not quite managing censure either. It was too difficult to commit to either when she wasn't sure she believed him yet.

He sighed, apparently accepting that. Maybe he thought he'd done as much as he could for the moment and planned to wait her out. Or prove it some other way.

And maybe the whole thing was a ploy, and she was falling for it. Which meant she was an idiot. Her eyes flashed away from him, and she wanted to hide her discomfort.

Distance was what she needed. She pushed out of her seat. "I, uh, need to go freshen up."

He waited a beat before nodding, taking the plate from her before she could bring it to the sink herself. It wasn't clear whether he sensed her uncertainty or not, but she had always been an easy read.

Even more reason to get some separation while she analyzed her thoughts and feelings about this bizarre situation.

Once in his bedroom, she shut the door, leaning against it. With the distance, her mind started whirling through all the reasons she could not trust him. And she certainly shouldn't let her guard down.

She hurried to the windows, hands hovering above the warped-looking wood. She'd tried them before, and they'd been hard to budge. But maybe she needed to put more muscle into it. He might've been lying to her, and she'd just given up too easily.

She placed her hands differently than the night prior, when she'd been desperate and juiced on adrenaline. It was hard to find a spot to get her fingers in to lift, and she broke a nail trying the new angle, hissing as she stuck the finger in her mouth. She glanced at the closed door before deciding on a final attempt.

It really couldn't be that hard.

Repositioning her hands again, she ground her teeth as she squared her stance, giving it another try, muscles straining to lift the pane.

A raucous scraping sound ground out as the window slid maybe half an inch upward. It sounded like a bull elk during rutting season, and Sadie backed away from it so quickly she stumbled. Her heart jump-started into a panicked gallop as she looked to the door again, waiting for Chase to come charging in.

He didn't.

"I heard that," he said from the other room, sounding more amused than angry.

She pressed her hand over her heart, blowing out a breath, then wiped the sweat that had gathered at her hairline from the effort. So he hadn't been lying, once again. But it was worth the effort to be sure.

A low annoyance simmered in her stomach as she shot a glare at the offending and uncooperative window, so she stomped off to the bathroom to find a washcloth to scrub her body clean of the dried sweat from her trunk adventure.

It was pointless to shower since the sweat had leached into her clothes, but she needed to do something to give her some semblance of control, even if it was small. At least freshening up was within her power. It wasn't likely he had the kind of shower accouterments she was used to and preferred, so she wouldn't bother with that.

Offering to get some things at the store was likely a scheme to lure her into trusting him when she shouldn't. She couldn't see the purpose in that. Other than getting her to give away whatever information everyone thought she had. If he still thought she had any info about Greg, he'd be sorely disappointed. The only thing Sadie could tell him about Greg was that he lasted longer schmoozing at corporate events than he did in bed.

She paused in the act of getting the washcloth wet, her gaze shifting to her grubby reflection in the mirror. If she let Chase believe she trusted him, she could use the time he'd be at the store to make her escape. Surely he wouldn't tie her up when he left. That would definitely crack the thin trust she considered extending.

She washed her face first, gently scrubbing the dried sweat and dirt from her skin, then focused on the sweatiest places on her body, her top lip curling as she settled her shirt back down over herself. It was probably a wasted effort with how dirty her clothes were. Who knew what had been in that trunk before her?

A clown suit. Yikes. Taxidermied animals. Ick.

Dead bodies.

A shudder ran through her as she rubbed at her wrists, feeling where the zip tie had bitten into her skin. If she had her purse, she would have sprayed something on it to help the pain and to heal it.

But her purse was still out in the kitchen where she'd left it when she'd gotten the arnica for Chase's face. What exactly had possessed her to offer that? He'd clearly thought she was a loon when she pulled it out. But he'd let her apply it.

Greg always called it her witch doctor voodoo and refused whenever she offered. Then she'd stopped using any of it in front of him since he liked to bring it up around his friends just to poke fun at her.

She caught her own scowl in the mirror and forced the expression smooth, finger-brushing her hair to see if she could get it into some manageable state.

How did she end up here? Bitter at a man she should have dumped way sooner than she had and kidnapped because of her affiliation with him. It was not something she'd ever anticipated adding to the list of reasons Greg was a sucky ex-boyfriend.

Fiona would have a field day adding such a solid black mark on her very real list of *Why We Hate Greg*. In case Sadie ever had second thoughts about ending things, she'd said. Not that Sadie ever would.

She sighed thinking about her best friend. No doubt Fiona would be worried by now. They rarely went so long without checking in. If only Chase hadn't taken her phone.

But no self-respecting kidnapper, undercover FBI or otherwise, would let their kidnappee keep a phone that could be traced and tracked. Her true crime podcasts had told her that.

The sound of the front door opening and closing startled her. It was loud, like it took a good yank to break it loose of the jamb and required an extra hard pull to settle it back into place.

Or maybe he was just agitated.

She crept to the door and listened for movement on the other side before venturing out of the bedroom. The silence was too heavy for there to be anyone else in the house.

Still, she moved carefully out into the living room and toward the kitchen. The window above the sink didn't reveal anything different about the sweeping front yard that extended down to the treeline.

She bit her lip. Did she dare venture outside to investigate?

It made her nervous to even try, so she moved around the island to a small side window in a little nook behind the couch, pulling back some gauzy curtains.

She jumped back when she caught movement and dropped the curtain over the glass before her mind registered that Chase wasn't jumping out at her. She held herself out of view and pulled the curtain just enough to peer out without being seen.

He was full-out sprinting to the tree line. When he got there, he spun quickly and flew back up toward the house. Without stopping, he ran through a series of obstacles. Sweat had already begun to slick his t-shirt to his torso, so it was probably getting hot out. No surprise this far into July. But he was also running the obstacle like a madman, and she swallowed at the kind of intensity infused into the process.

How a man as big and muscular as he was moved with such fluid energy, she had no idea, but he was a sight to behold.

8

Unsettled

The shadow of unease loomed over Chase, threatening like a rising wave. He rarely functioned without a plan—even one he constructed while on the move. But so much more hinged on him now. Namely, someone else's life. Protocols that normally didn't apply to him put a pressure on his mind.

Gibson had been clear about his instructions to lie low, but Chase felt like a sitting duck when he didn't know what steps his enemies were taking out of sight. He could try to guess because Santiago was not exactly prolific in his methods, but he still had seen no sign of him and had heard nothing from Zimmerman.

Because of the relationship Chase had cultivated with Zimmerman, he would've thought the crime boss liable to give him a call before making a move. A courtesy, really, given all the things Chase had been entrusted with in the business.

Had Santiago fed him a story that led to him getting cut off? For all Chase knew, they were gearing up to eliminate him. Or they were waiting to see how the whole thing played out.

He didn't trust Santiago, and, given their history of barely tolerating each other, he didn't put it past the man to feed Zim some story that was likely to get Chase—and Sadie—killed.

And Sadie. . . just having her in the same room electrified his nerves in a way that was so shocking and foreign, so pleasant and so *very* bad.

It felt like it had come out of nowhere, even though he eventually figured out they had a past. He remembered her from high school—her name and face, mostly. She'd been one of those flash-in-the-pan events—the coveted new girl—for a bit. Every guy had been half in love with her for the first few weeks. But she'd fallen out of grace pretty quickly. That tended to happen with fragile teenage male egos when a pretty girl turned them down.

Chase had been too entrenched in the drama his life had turned into by that point, so he'd put his head down and focused on what he could control—his basketball career and getting the hell out of dodge to a college as far away as he could get.

The window in his bedroom made its telltale groan of protest when Sadie tried to open it, alerting him that she was still testing this new situation—and his honesty. Which was expected, but it still made his gut twist.

And then his mind wandered to the possibilities of what she might be doing in there to "freshen up," and he suddenly needed something to redirect his thoughts.

Nothing emptied his mind like a brain-melting workout, and he bolted out the door, skipping the five steps from the porch to the ground entirely, and started on a full sprint around the side of the house. He took a straight shot from there down to the treeline and back.

The absolute misery that came with the oppressive, sticky heat that enveloped him drove thoughts of Sadie and this whole mess from his mind as his singular focus became pulling oxygen in and out of his lungs in a practiced rhythm.

He hit the rows of tires behind his house at full speed, practically slamming his knees into his chest as he lifted them in quick succession. Back and forth he went, pushing himself harder and faster until his lungs threatened to rip from his chest and his legs wanted to give out.

It wasn't until he went back inside, after almost an hour, soaked in his own sweat, that he came back to himself, half-startled to find Sadie curled up on the couch. He stiffened just inside the door as her eyes shifted up to his face.

Her arms were wrapped around the legs she'd pulled in close to her body, making her look young and small.

"Want a snack or something to drink?" he asked breathlessly as he walked to the fridge for some water. "I know I don't have much that's free-range or organic."

She watched him as he chugged a glass of water and poured himself another.

He fought the urge to let his expression mirror the twist he felt in his gut. "Tell you what: I'll go take a quick shower. You at least come look and see what you might like for lunch."

She gave a slow nod, her eyes tracking him to the bedroom, and he was grateful for the door he shut between them.

Even though the separation did his nerves good, it didn't settle his mind. She could take the opportunity to run, though she wouldn't get far. He doubted she'd think to erase her tracks, so he'd catch up pretty quickly.

Still, he hurried through his shower and getting dressed just in case she decided to use the time to her advantage.

She wasn't in sight when he came back out, and his heart shoved itself up into his throat. It didn't take long before he found her on the porch, leaning against the railing. Her fingers fluttered endlessly along the worn wood.

Even though he knew they were mostly safe here, it was still possible that Santiago and Travers would figure out where they were. He'd worked hard to lose them, but there were no guarantees. He fought the urge to order her inside, reminding himself that his knowledge was not hers, and he was just extra on edge when he had no way of knowing what was going on out there.

And because everything felt so out of control, especially when it came to what was happening between them.

"Did you even look at what I've got?" he asked.

She didn't look at him, but the muscles in her back seized when he spoke, telling him that she hadn't heard him come out.

"You have so much space out here," she said. "You could do so much with it."

He padded forward and stuffed his hands into his pockets. "Like what?" Even though he could guess what ideas she'd probably have, he wanted her to tell him. Maybe it would help her relax.

She shot him a sideways glance, reluctance holding her captive for a moment. "An epic veggie garden, for starters."

He pursed his lips against a smile, having expected that answer. "Mm. And where would you put it? In front here?"

She shook her head as her fingers stopped fluttering. She pointed where he'd indicated. "I'd plant flowers for bees and butterflies and to add a little curb appeal. Might help with the serial killer vibe." Her eyes slid to him again, the faintest smirk cradling her mouth.

"I'll remember that the next time I kidnap someone."

She squinted at him like she was trying to figure out if he was joking, and the fingers fluttered again.

His head dipped in encouragement. "So where would you put the garden?"

She lifted her hand to point to the side of the house. "Over there. It gets a good mix of shade and sun."

He grunted, trying to picture it. Who knew what an epic vegetable garden actually looked like? But he could imagine her, kneeling in the dirt, digging while she hummed nursery rhymes or something. Maybe in a tank top and a floppy hat.

He cleared his throat and looked down, toeing a loose board where the post met the porch. That was not something he should let run rampant in his mind's eye. What he should've been doing was keeping an eye on their surroundings and convince her to come back inside.

"You could have chickens too," she continued, not picking up on his discomfort. There was a determined bent to her expression now, like she was mapping out every square foot of space around them. "There's enough room for a nice coop and a big fenced-in area for them to roam safely."

She'd stopped wiggling again, and it spread a web of warmth through him, distracting from his worry. His mind filled in more images of her working the land around them, feeding and tending animals, watering plants.

"Where would the goats go?" he asked with a smirk.

She started like she'd forgotten he was there, and the suspicion was back in her eyes. For a different reason, he suspected.

"Or would you rather have cows?"

Her mouth pinched, and she turned back to stare out at the tree line. "Maybe someday. A dream for far in the future. I'd love to have a little homestead." One shoulder lifted and fell. "Nothing totally off-grid, but something self-sustaining."

No surprise there. He had a hard time imagining himself making it into that kind of oasis, but he could see her there. Planning it, building it, channeling all that restless energy and spunk into something life-giving.

"I could bring students out." Her voice was soft and cautious, drawing his attention back. "Teach them about caring for animals, plants, the environment."

He tipped his head, filing away that secret passion he heard in her tone. "Like a wilderness school."

Her brows crashed low over her eyes, then she turned to stare at him. Suspicion again, now twofold. He felt the weight of her skepticism about him entertaining her ideas, and her general wariness of the situation.

It killed him to know she still didn't trust him. In giving these tiny tastes of who she was, she created an insatiable craving for more, and the desire to earn her trust was a sharp demand inside him.

It sliced almost as keenly as the renewed awareness of how exposed they were out on the porch. He'd never felt so ill at ease in this place. It was supposed to be his safe haven, his escape from the life he pretended to lead in the city. He didn't come back often just for the sake of keeping it secret, which was probably blown now. Up until this little adventure, the forest had provided a sense of privacy for him, but he realized that it also afforded good cover for anyone scoping the place.

His attention went to Sadie as she shifted, watching him like she sensed his unease. No doubt taking in the stiff silence that had enveloped him as his eyes scanned the trees. It might have been easier for someone to remain concealed in the woods, but they still would be hard-pressed to sneak up on him at the house.

Everything was wide open and clear surrounding the cabin, and any vehicle coming down his drive gave itself away with a dust trail that rose above the tree line like a smoke signal.

"What is it?" she asked, breaking his concentration.

He brought his gaze back to hers, nearly drowning in the depth of her amber eyes, the magnetism inexplicable, even to himself. He cleared his throat. "How about lunch?"

Instead of ordering her inside, he figured he could lure her in, maybe keep building the foundation instead of obliterating it. As long as she was back in the house, he could rest a little easier. Maybe she'd tell him more, unfurl some of the layers he'd begun to see beneath.

Standing, he extended his hand to her, which she took after a moment's hesitation, apparently accepting his lack of answer to her question.

She trailed behind him as he went inside to investigate his supplies. To be fair, there was not much to choose from, so it probably didn't matter if she'd looked for something suitable. He'd have to cobble something together and make a run to the store later.

"I could make chili," he offered after inspecting his supplies in the pantry. It was dismal at best, but there were cans of beans and he always had a stash of meat in the freezer. "Wait, you do eat meat, right?"

When he turned, she was just sliding onto the same bar stool she'd used that morning, though he didn't miss the subtle eye roll.

"I eat meat," she confirmed. "Even if it's not organic or grass-fed."

She didn't smile, and it wasn't even her dampened mood he sensed as the culprit. She was almost sheepish.

"Like if your choice is to eat poison or starve?"

Her lips twisted to the side, and it was real humor he detected. "I'll just do a detox when I get home." Then her face fell. "If I get to go home."

He caught his wince before it took hold of his expression and turned, setting to work quick-thawing the meat. Pulling out all the seasonings, he ignored the way his skin tingled with her eyes following his movements.

It was almost more unsettling than worrying about someone watching the house from the woods.

He thought again about how this split-second decision was going to kill him.

9

Crunchy Lady Staples

It was astounding that by the end of the meal, Chase's kitchen was in the pristine condition it had been in before he started. Like he actually finished a task prior to starting on the next. And then he cleaned up immediately after they were done eating. *Like a crazy person.*

Sadie's kitchen always looked like a bomb went off every time she cooked. Part of her wondered if there were little kitchen nymphs that played in the ingredients, splashing it all over when her back was turned.

Like when she made sourdough. It only took three ingredients. And yet, she ended her baking endeavors with flour in places she swore she never went.

Her minimalist style had been her attempt at organizing the chaos her apartment always became with more things to leave around the house. But that only sort of worked.

Of course, he wouldn't know that the trashed state he'd found when he'd broken in was only marginally worse than what it looked like on a regular basis. Especially during the school year when she had less time and energy to devote to it.

He appeared to favor the same minimalist style, but she figured it was because he wasn't there often, or at least not much recently based on what he had in his pantry and refrigerator.

After they ate, she wandered over to a small bookshelf, perusing his very limited selection of tomes. She only picked one and sat because she didn't know what to do with herself while he settled in on the opposite side of the couch with a laptop, but she barely registered what she read. No surprise, really, though. It was on some history of the area, which might have interested her if it was a little less dry and if Chase didn't keep sneaking looks at her.

His heavy gaze always stole her attention, even when her back was turned. It was like a caress, a warm, wandering hand against her skin.

It made it hard for her to sit still. Not that being still was ever her modus operandi in general, but this felt like more than her usual restlessness.

As if he sensed that she was unsettled, he closed his computer and gave her his full attention.

She tried not to acknowledge him, pretending she was too engrossed in the book, but he wasn't having it.

"Teacher," he said.

She inhaled deeply, then shut the book, setting it aside to meet his gaze head-on. "How'd you know?"

A faint smirk pulled at his lips. "The degree in the corner of your pottery room, your teacher craft supplies."

He'd seen her pottery room. Heat blossomed in her cheeks. Of course, he'd seen it. He said he'd been through the whole place, but that room was *her* space, the one area she truly let loose without any thought of someone seeing it.

He didn't seem to notice her reaction. "What grade?"

She lifted a brow. "So now you're interrogating me?"

He actually smiled at that, and it nearly stopped her heart. "I'm trying to get you to relax."

She caught her gasp before it escaped and worked to harden her expression. "What makes you think I'm not relaxed?"

His amusement grew. "Your leg hasn't stopped bouncing since you sat down."

She looked at the leg he indicated, and she concentrated on making it stop. She narrowed her eyes at him. "So you're only asking about my teaching to distract me."

He pulled back a little. "No, I actually want to know. I wasn't sure you'd open up, but since you're getting more anxious, I figure I might as well give it a shot."

Her brows slammed down. "How do you know I'm getting *more* anxious?"

His gaze didn't waver, and again, it was like a touch along her skin.

"I can feel it." His voice was a low rumble. Almost wistful. "I'm trying my best to make you more comfortable. I don't want you to be afraid."

Her breath stopped, the sense of being seen making her feel like a trapped animal for a second. Having him put it into words helped her to recognize the truth—that she *was* scared. Scared of this situation, of how she'd gone against her instincts and stayed with a man who ended up putting her in this position. She was scared of what came after, of what would happen if they didn't find Greg.

She didn't know how long this would be her reality, how long she'd be away from her family and friends, her students.

Maybe she should let him distract her because it didn't appear that anything would be changing any time soon, and her heart torqued behind her ribs like it wanted to rip in half.

"Why kindergarten?"

Apparently, he was undeterred.

She sighed. "I like the noise and the chaos, the challenge of making things fun and interesting. Kids have this amazing way of seeing the world with fresh eyes, and I like that fresh view to be as positive as possible."

He tilted his head. "Is that your favorite part?"

She drummed her fingers along the closed book in her lap. "No."

A soft smile tugged at his mouth in response to hers. "What is?"

"You know those really tough kids you see on TV or that others talk about? The ones that just drive people crazy?"

He squinted at her.

"What?" She laughed, the sound oddly nervous, though she couldn't figure out why there were flutters in her stomach.

A little bit of color crept into his cheeks. "I might've been one of those kids."

She sat back a little. "I should've known. I was too, though probably for different reasons."

"What reasons?" There was a bit of a playful challenge in his tone. "You weren't willful and defiant?"

She suppressed her grin. "I have always been walking chaos. I was a talker, distractible, *distracting. . .*"

"Distracting is definitely the word for it," he murmured, and she froze. Even looking at his expression didn't tell her if he meant it positively or negatively. "So teaching five-year-olds is the perfect place for chaos?"

It wasn't a conscious decision to rein herself in, but she saw it like she was watching a movie, imagining herself wrapping a blanket around her body and tugging it tight. Holding all those bits in and protecting herself with her own warmth and comfort.

"Controlled chaos," she amended. "There is a method to my madness."

"And what's that?"

Was he really interested in this? Or was it what she suspected—a simple distraction, or diversion to get her to let her guard down? Either way, it was an opportunity. Because two could play that game. She could convince him she trusted him, make *him* relax his guard and make her escape.

So she told him about it all, not even feigning the joy in her voice, the passion she felt welling up inside her about the ways she got creative to pull in even the most difficult kids, who were truly her favorite to teach because they needed more of her love and attention.

And the more she talked, the softer his expression became. He transformed from that brooding, intimidating man to someone who could settle in and chat about mundane things.

He encouraged her to keep going, asked her probing questions about why and what and how and who.

It had been a long time since she'd had that kind of rapt attention, to have someone validate the work she did as rewarding, not just a waste of her mind and talent and time. Like it was some hobby until she got a real job. And she found herself believing that maybe he was actually interested in what she had to say.

She only stopped when she realized the light in the room was diffused, the sun having made its trip from one side of the house to the other, signaling the end of the day. And she noted how calm she was, sitting on the couch instead of pacing, the nervous energy in her body quieted by the constant flow of words.

She felt the heat in her cheeks. "Oh, crackers, I've been talking for a really long time. I'm sorry."

He looked relaxed too, his arms stretched over the back of the couch, one foot up on the coffee table. "Don't be sorry." His smile was soft, almost affectionate.

And, jeez, that and the way it felt sort of natural to be sitting together, chatting, made a warmth build in her chest.

"Are you getting hungry?" he asked, leaning forward.

"A little," she admitted. "I feel bad that you're always cooking for me." The words were out before she could stop them.

He laughed. "Like I'd give you access to the knives."

She smiled a little. "That would fly in the face of kidnapper protocol."

"You're familiar with the code," he said, raising a brow.

She lifted a shoulder. "Podcasts are my thing."

"Is it a How To Successfully Kidnap Someone podcast?"

She sputtered a laugh. "No. True Crime."

"Same thing." He shrugged, walking around the island to open a drawer. Out came a pen and a pad of paper, which he set on the counter.

She stared at the items quizzically.

"My limited supplies are dwindling rapidly," he said. "Write down anything you'd like me to get at the store. I plan to go in the morning."

He couldn't be serious. She was an idiot for complaining about his non-organic, non-pasture-raised eggs, non-grass-fed beef, and his pesticide coffee.

Even though those things absolutely mattered to her, she wasn't sure what had possessed her to even say anything to the man who'd kidnapped her, honorable intentions or not—was that even a thing?

But, depending on what the plan was moving forward, she might need only a couple of things, or she might need a lot. A chill swept through her at the reminder about the big question mark that loomed.

"How long are you going to keep me here?"

His body went rigid as if she'd shot a bullet of accusation at him instead of a subdued and completely valid question. He was apparently bothered that she might think of the whole thing in even a remotely negative light.

"I'm not sure yet," he said through a tight jaw. "This was not exactly part of my plan. But it will at least be a few days while I gauge the level of danger."

She struggled to stand with the heaviness that settled over her, but she managed and then padded to the counter, rolling the word "danger" over and over in her mind. When she passed him, only a few inches between them, she swore he sucked in and held a breath. Her eyes shot to his as his heat pressed into her, but she tore her gaze away, focusing on her task.

Picking up the pen and tipping it back and forth in her fingers, she directed her thoughts. Deodorant and soap. Because she already stunk, despite her attempts at freshening up. Being in the trunk in the middle of summer, scared and trying to break free, had drawn out a nervous sweat that felt tattooed into her skin.

Toothpaste. There was no way she was going to use the poison-filled popular brands. After her mom's bout with cancer and the things they'd learned about environmental toxins, she'd done her best to avoid them. Teeth and mouth health flowed to the body, influencing so much more than just the commonly known heart issues relating to gum disease.

Lotion.

He moved closer, the heat at her back unmistakable. "I have a lot of this stuff here already."

She turned a little, and he was much closer than she'd anticipated he'd be. Inches. Centimeters. Just a breath between them. Her lips parted, and the muted green of his eyes flashed brighter, emerald jewels in his handsome face.

She blinked, totally derailed from logical thought. "What?"

"I have lotion, toothpaste, deodorant." At least he'd kept the thread of the conversation, though there was a buzz of tension coming off him. Muscles pulled tight, jaw feathering as his teeth clenched, like he was fighting himself for control.

For a second, she wished he didn't lock himself down, the irrational part of her responding to the song her body was singing—lust and want.

Her common mantra, the phrase she'd heard thousands of times growing up ghosted through her mind: *Focus, Sadie.*

She shook her head. "But they're—"

"Not organic and free-range?" he interrupted, one corner of his mouth tipping up.

"Something like that," she said, her voice barely above a whisper. Not that she'd need the volume with him so close.

His eyes narrowed on hers for a second, and that tension wound tighter, wrapped itself around her, pulling her in.

She forced herself to turn back around and scratch the deodorant off the list. "You know what? If you have some of the right ingredients, I can make my own deodorant."

He gave a soft snort. "Like what?"

"Coconut oil, baking soda, and arrowroot powder."

"Um." He moved away from her, and she finally took a full breath without the pressure of his presence so close, so stifling, so magnetic.

She looked up in time to see him searching his pantry.

"Coconut oil. Baking soda. No arrowroot. Whatever the hell that is."

She clicked the pen twice before writing it down, tucking her tongue into the corner of her mouth. "I'll add that to the list. Maybe some shampoo. Unless you have apple cider vinegar?"

He turned toward her, letting out an incredulous laugh. "Sadie, what the fuck?"

She scrunched her shoulders, locking her eyes on the paper in front of her as her next words tumbled out. "I know I sound like I'm being obnoxiously particular, or I'm a snobby princess who's too good to use normal beauty products. But your skin is your largest organ. It absorbs everything you put on it, which then assimilates into your body. Every toxic fragrance and ingredient can become an endocrine disruptor. . ."

He stared at her, and the heat poured into her face. Her spiel had always felt important to her, but right now, it sounded absolutely ridiculous and embarrassingly privileged.

She shut her eyes, pinching her lips together.

"Okay," he said, no judgment in his tone. "But what does apple cider vinegar have to do with shampoo?"

She released a slow breath and opened her eyes. "It's a natural cleanser. It works great as shampoo in a pinch. Cheap too. Especially since a lot of the more 'natural' shampoos can be expensive."

His mouth quirked. "And you can't suffer through with whatever I have here for a few days?"

She swallowed. Of course, she could. It wouldn't be the end of the world. But she'd cultivated these habits over the last ten years, and she believed in living a life as free of toxins as possible.

She lifted a shoulder, brushing a hair behind her ear. "Like I said, I can make the deodorant myself. If you have corn starch, I can compromise and use that. Apple cider vinegar?"

"This is really important to you, isn't it?"

She raised her gaze a fraction, noting the crystalline glimmer that came into his eyes again. Looking at him like this had an impact on him, and his eyes changed every time she did it.

He sighed, turning to look in the pantry. "Yes for both cornstarch and vinegar."

"Thank you," she murmured, the embarrassment still like fire in her cheeks.

"Anything else?"

As if this conversation hadn't made her feel humiliated enough already, she was going to have to ask for more. But her silence simply stretched, and she pulled her messy hair over her shoulder to give her something to do, an excuse not to look at him as she inspected the frayed ends.

He noticed though. "What is it?"

She cringed. "Well, I need to shower. And change."

"Okay," he said slowly, not understanding. "I can get you a change of clothes while I'm out. Unless you need handmade organic cotton or something. Not sure how much of that the local Walmart carries."

Her cheeks flamed hotter. "No. . ." The word dragged out, almost a question. She picked at the hem of her top, finding a loose thread she was tempted to yank on. "I only have one set of. . ."

Oh crackers. She was a grown woman. She could say the word *underwear.* Nothing to be embarrassed about. But maybe because of the way she felt around him, the way he reacted to her, it felt inappropriate.

It must have finally clicked, though, because his eyebrows shot up when realization dawned, and he straightened as if someone had jabbed him in the spine.

"Oh." The one-word answer dropped into the air like a stone into still water, the ripples of silence enveloping them. "What, um, kind? Um, size?" He cleared his throat and rubbed the back of his neck, which had turned a nice shade of crimson.

It oddly made her feel less embarrassed about it. Seeing him uncomfortable gave her a shot of satisfaction, like she had the upper hand for once in this scenario. One of those urges came over her, the impulse to play with fire.

"You don't want to guess?" she teased.

His gaze jerked to her face, and that emerald edge came into his eyes again.

It sent a thrill through her down to her toes, and she laughed.

10

Spontaneous Combustion

Chase muttered to himself as he looked at the list in his hand, grumpy as hell after barely sleeping the night before. He'd been incapable of shutting his brain off after they'd chatted during dinner and afterward, like they were old friends.

At least he'd gotten *her* to relax, falling into an easy pattern as she'd told him about moving all over the country and even overseas while her dad was in the Marine Corps.

The way she lit up while talking about going to new places and meeting new people, the constant adventure of it making her smile and laugh. It had kept him from thinking of that one little flirtatious question. But as soon as they'd settled in for the night, his mind rolled each of those words around until he knew the edges and angles, the subtle dips and curves in her tone. Which only made him think of the ones on her body.

Big problem.

He was almost glad to be out of her presence, the miles from his house to the town a much-needed buffer between them. Not to mention the tangible task the list presented.

Except. . .

He didn't want to read past the first two items—the toothpaste and soap he needed to hunt down. It was bad enough that he already knew what else was there on the paper.

She'd written her sizes for new underwear and a bra with specifications on style and color in her chaotic, looping handwriting—so like the woman he'd begun getting to know. But he didn't want to think about the details any more than he needed to.

Because he was going to combust. Go up in flames right here in the middle of a Walmart. Thank God they had a clothing section, so he didn't have to go to a lingerie store or some shit. That would have been a kind of torture he wasn't sure he could endure.

As it was, he was in a special level of hell already.

And, damn it, Sadie knew it. She'd teased him, sending his mind down a path that was a veritable death trap, riddled with hidden pits he would surely fall into. He was going to break his neck.

He'd absolutely made the wrong decision here. He should have left her in her apartment, focused on the job, and moved on.

No. No. He couldn't have done that. Any time he thought about what might have happened if he hadn't gotten her out of that apartment, a twisting sense of dread filled him.

Santiago wouldn't have been gentle with her, let alone stuck to any sort of moral code. Because she was pretty—too pretty—and shapely. The kind of curves that made Chase forget there was a protocol, could make a man forget his own name.

But those goons had no rules to follow. Zimmerman wouldn't care what they did with or to her in their search for the information he wanted. When they found out that she didn't know anything at all, there would be even less holding them back from doing any and everything their twisted, black hearts desired.

And that set Chase's blood on fire, his rage at the hypothetical scenario chasing out the remaining lust he'd been trying, unsuccessfully up until then, to extinguish.

He snatched the toothpaste off the shelf and grumbled his way down the aisle to the soap, finding that one easily enough.

He'd already scoped the rows and found foods that probably would suit her—organic, non-GMO, etc—and briefly wondered what was wrong with him that he was catering to her this much. But he could admit as he swung down the coffee aisle, scoping the bags for something organic and fair-trade, that he was stalling.

Did he want to pick out underwear and a bra for a woman staying in his home? Absolutely. But under the right circumstances. Not like this. Not when he knew he couldn't do anything about the way his hands hungered for the feel of her bare skin, the contours of her hourglass figure.

He gritted his teeth, knocking the bag of coffee into the basket he held, and practically stomped his way to the intimates section.

She'd said comfortable. Cotton. But he was met with too many choices. Sports bras, underwire, no underwire, cotton, lace—fuck. That wasn't a mental image he could have in his head and remain sane.

"You look a little overwhelmed. Do you want some help?"

He jerked to look at the shriveled old lady who'd approached. The panic must have been apparent on his face.

"Ah, yeah. A bra for. . . my girlfriend. Something comfortable? These things don't seem comfortable," he said, holding one up that was stiff and structured, labeled as an underwire.

"What's her size, sweetheart? Sometimes it doesn't matter that it doesn't *seem* comfortable. A certain size requires a little more support." She gave him a wink.

He held the paper for her to see.

"Yes, she'll want the underwire. But you are right that this one isn't as comfortable." She took the one he held and set it back on the hook, reaching for a different one. "This one is popular with the young ladies."

"Sold." He took it from her. "How about underwear?"

She led him to a different rack and pulled a pack of six off the hook and handed it to him. Good enough for him.

"Thanks," he said, squinting at her name tag, "Edna."

"Sure thing, honey. It's very sweet of you to shop for your girlfriend, but you know, it's a lot easier for a lady to pick her own undergarments."

"Yeah. Believe me, next time she will." He dipped his head because it seemed like something a gentleman would do, and she grinned like a fiend, showing off her overly white, unnaturally straight dentures.

He felt something tickle along his hairline and swiped at it, surprised to find that he was sweating. Damn, what this woman was doing to him in a mere forty-eight hours.

Breaking plan, putting his entire undercover operation in jeopardy, making him think thoughts he'd left little room for, had him buying her freaking underwear, organic coffee, all-natural toothpaste.

And all he could think about suddenly was the way she'd bitten her lip and looked up at him from under her lashes. The first few times hadn't been intentional on her part, but it still slammed into him with the force of a freight train.

But that last time. . .

Oh, this woman. She hadn't known it then, but she knew now.

"Sir?"

Chase jerked out of his thoughts at the prodding of the woman behind him and walked to the available self-checkout register.

He yanked everything across the scanner, practically throwing every item into the grocery bag. Several shoppers glanced over at him, mildly alarmed.

He was used to being gawked at—being as tall as he was. He was foreboding in stature alone, but his years of work building a muscular physique and his naturally broody expression sometimes made him look downright dangerous.

And here he was grumbling and grunting, angrily throwing stuff around. He needed to chill out before he drew unwanted attention to himself.

As he tossed the bags into the passenger seat of his car, he began to wonder why lace wasn't comfortable. And then, realizing just what it did to him to think about *that* image and how uncomfortable it made him, he decided it wasn't a thought worth pursuing.

He checked the clock as he turned into the long, winding drive, gauging that he'd been gone about an hour, maybe a little more.

The house came into view, and his gut suddenly twisted with nerves. The relief he'd felt at her guessing the truth had been so consuming, it nearly knocked his knees loose.

But he knew she wasn't one hundred percent certain he was trustworthy. Still, it was a start, and he'd take what he could get. Especially if it meant she wouldn't attack him again.

He put the car in park and absently rubbed at his throat where his skin was still a little tender to the touch. He had to give her some serious credit for the effort and what she'd accomplished against him—a much larger opponent who had more hand-to-hand training.

He slid all of the bags onto one arm and trudged up the porch steps to the front door. Jangling the key into the lock and turning was easier than it should have been. The deadbolt usually stuck and took a little finesse. But it made the telltale click that told him it was already unlocked.

He'd instructed her to lock the door behind him. Had heard the deadbolt after she'd slammed her weight into the door to get it to go.

He threw the door open, pulling out his gun as he stepped inside. He dropped the bags onto the counter and moved to sweep through the house, all senses on high alert.

Nothing and no one.

He kept his weapon pointed down and went back outside, searching the ground for unfamiliar tire tracks in the dirt. Nothing but his own, the fresh imprints from his departure and subsequent return scarring the gravel.

Had someone come on foot? He glanced toward the trees, scanning the forest for anything amiss but could find nothing. If someone had come, the most likely direction would be from the town he'd just left. It was the closest and easiest to get in and out of.

He jogged down the steps and veered left, angling north-east.

11

Escape From Kidnap Mountain

S adie waited exactly five minutes after Chase's car disappeared down the drive before searching the house for a phone or the computer she'd seen him use the day before. If she could just get contact with the outside world—the police, Fiona, her dad, anyone. Even Roberta. Because then she could apologize for being a no-show at work the last three days.

Oh, cripes, would she get fired over this? Was there an "I was kidnapped" excuse in the handbook for missing work without a call?

Even though she sort of believed Chase, she couldn't just sit there twiddling her thumbs. But her frenzied search netted zero results, and she groaned in frustration before a new plan formed in her mind.

He'd said the town was six miles northeast. Six miles. She could jog that many in, what, an hour, right? Maybe a little more. She didn't think it was smart to go sprinting into the forest in wedge sandals, but she could manage a brisk hike, right?

Without another thought, she hurried into the kitchen, rifling through cupboards for a water bottle of some sort. She was fine without food, but she'd need water for her trek. Especially if she accidentally got lost.

She found a cloudy plastic Nalgene in the depths, deciding not to be picky about it not being glass or stainless steel, considering her situation, and filled it, chugging half, then filled it again.

She hesitated only briefly before leaning her entire weight against the door as Chase had instructed so that the deadbolt would slide loose.

A weird sense of guilt washed through her that she was leaving the house with an unlocked front door. It felt so unnatural, but it wasn't like anyone would randomly come all the way out here and break in, right?

It was a few hesitant steps forward before she shook the sense of responsibility off and took the stairs at a jog and made her way toward the tree line. She pointed herself in the direction he'd indicated as northeast the day before, checking the position of the sun to be sure—though she admitted directions weren't her forte—before diving into the dim depths of the trees.

They were less tightly packed than they appeared from the outside, but she still had to pay attention to her footing since there was no obvious path and roots rose up out of the ground at unexpected intervals. It made it feel like she had two-by-four blocks strapped to her feet every time she had to navigate the tripping hazards.

Once she got a good rhythm, a surprising peace settled over her as she walked, the sound of her breaths puffing in and out with the exercise muted by the dense trees that surrounded her. The air was cooler since a lot of the sunlight was blocked by the overhead branches.

Mottled patches of light cropped up occasionally, and it helped settle her mind that nothing about the outside world had changed. The sun was still there, reminding her that there was a possibility of normalcy soon.

She was careful not to veer from her path, though she had to weave around some trees that stood in the way, hoping it wouldn't pull her off track too easily.

When she glanced behind her, she was no longer able to identify any distinction between what lay at her back and what was before her, and she wondered how long she'd been walking, checking her watch belatedly. She mentally berated herself for not looking at the time *before* she left. That would have been the smartest move.

Too late now.

The going wasn't as smooth the deeper she got, so her pace slowed. Initially, she'd figured her journey would take about two hours, but at this rate, it would likely be longer. To cut time, she stopped only a few times for sips of water and to wipe at the sweat beading along her brow before pressing on.

Would Chase have gotten back to the house yet? Would he be mad to find her gone? Resigned? Worried? Maybe she should've written him a note, so he would know she'd left of her own free will.

The thought was so absurd. To leave her kidnapper a polite note so he wouldn't worry. . .

But if what he'd said was true, maybe he'd just let her go. She could go hide out at her dad's house until this whole thing blew over instead of remaining Chase's pretend kidnapping victim indefinitely. Surely that would be enough to keep her out of harm's way.

Or maybe she should go on a month-long European vacation. She'd always wanted to go back.

The cry of a bird above her sliced through the peaceful silence as it took flight, and she jerked at the sound, heart hammering against her ribs as she looked up. It blasted from the branches above her, soaring up through the leaves, taking her attention with it.

The distraction kept her from seeing the root in front of her, and she caught the toe of her sandal. Her inhale whistled through her teeth as she lost her balance and staggered forward, hands automatically shooting forward in case she fell. She didn't. Until her ankle dipped sideways, and she went down with the pain that seared up her leg like lightning.

On hands and knees, her pulse throbbing in her ears, she shuffled around, ignoring the bite of pine needles in her palms as she pushed herself back onto her bottom. She winced as she moved her legs in front of her.

Probing around her ankle with shaky fingers pulled a hiss through her teeth, the pain slicing under her touch.

"Oh, no, no, no." She felt along her ankle again. "Ah." Her shoulders fell. "Great."

She pulled her purse forward to rummage for the arnica and rubbed the cream over her injury, suppressing the urge to wince again. Hopefully, it was just a mild sprain. She'd rolled her ankles before, not always watching her footing during runs or when she'd played volleyball in college. Usually, it only bothered her for a few days if she took it easy. But she couldn't take it easy now. She was in the middle of the woods, and her only way out was on foot.

Chewing her lip, she looked in the direction she'd been heading. How far was she from town? No answer magically came to her, of course. And there was no way to tell how long she'd been walking to get a gauge on distance.

It was poor planning on her part that she hadn't checked what time it was when she'd left. If she knew when she'd set out, she could figure out whether the town or the house was closer, assuming she'd stayed on track the whole way.

Maybe she could walk on the ankle. It might make her recovery time longer, but it would be worth it in the end. She could add ankle injury to her kidnapping excuse for missing her shifts at the library.

Using a nearby tree to leverage herself up, she was careful to keep her weight on her good foot and set her mind on pushing through the pain. She puffed out several deep breaths and started forward with a limp. But even trying to use that foot as little as possible, hot stabs of agony stabbed through her with each step, and eventually, she crumpled to the ground again, a steadily climbing rage bubbling through her.

It was times like these that she was tempted to break her rule and let a stream of curses loose. But she was nothing if not committed to her students, so she clamped her lips against the urge.

She scooted back to a tree and leaned against it, counting each forceful inhale and exhale until her frustration lowered to a simmer.

Okay, now she needed to make a plan. Maybe just resting for a while would do her good. Give it fifteen minutes and try again.

Opening the water bottle, she took a long pull of hydration, glad she'd thought to bring it. Not grabbing a snack was now looking like a terrible decision since her adventure would be taking longer than anticipated.

Should've known better, she thought. How often did she go through the day with her kindergartners and see that always having a snack on hand solved a multitude of ills? Sure, they were children and she was an adult, but the basic logic was there. Always have a snack for unforeseen delays.

The bark was against her head as she leaned it back and tried to focus on the way the leaves of the deciduous trees fluttered in a breeze far above her. She could easily pretend this was just an exercise in connecting with nature instead of an attempted—and thwarted—escape from a probably-good-guy-disguised-as-a-bad-guy-kidnapper-inn-keeper.

Except that her whole foot now throbbed. And she still smelled like dried sweat. And her hair was a ratty mess. And the pine needles were poking into her butt through her thin—and still ripped!—linen pants.

Sitting wasn't doing her much good, considering the negative thought patterns, so after a few minutes, she tried again to get to her feet and walk.

"Suffer through the pain," she told herself, the words coming through her teeth. "People walk with gunshot wounds. They swim after shark attacks."

With all her focus on walking through the pain, she didn't catch the noise at first. Then she heard a twig snap and halted, her muscles pulling taut. Putting a hand against a tree trunk to steady herself, she listened for another sound, hoping it was just her imagination. Or a cute woodland creature. Not a mountain lion getting ready to attack.

Please be a squirrel.

Heart punching against her ribs, Sadie turned to look behind her, eyes searching the trees that suddenly felt like reaching skeletons instead of protective pillars.

A thrill of nerves cascaded over her, and the impulse to run came on so strongly that she took off, the pain in her ankle disappearing beneath a rush of adrenaline. It pumped in her veins like a drug, making her feel invincible. And drop the water bottle.

"Sadie!"

Chase's voice sent an electric bolt through her, halting any mental capacity for half a second. She faltered, stumbled, then went down.

12

Piggyback

In hindsight, Chase realized he should've approached things differently.

He'd come across Sadie as she rested against a tree. She didn't look scared, so she probably hadn't been brought out against her will. But it didn't mean she was alone. So he'd circled the area, checking the ground for footprints that didn't belong to her, oblivious to what he came to realize when she tried to flee—that she'd injured herself.

When he shouted her name, the way she'd stumbled and fallen had pulled his eyes to her leg, which had folded under her. She cried out, the agony in her voice cutting straight through him.

He jerked forward as if he could catch her, then took off, hurdling over the roots that lurched up from the forest floor, then slowed just in case he would scare her again. But she was apparently not concerned because she stayed on her hands and knees, puffing air in and out through clenched teeth.

She was in a lot of pain but she wasn't afraid of him.

He crouched beside her, his hand extending to touch her back, but he stopped himself before he made contact. "What hurts?"

"My ankle," she ground out. "I twisted it a little while ago, and I might have just made it worse."

Shit. His fault for sneaking up on her. Definitely should've handled that differently.

"Sit back. Let me see," he murmured, apologetic.

Her eyes sliced to him, but she didn't move her head, that split-second debate making his chest constrict. Then she pushed back, grimacing as she settled on her butt and stretched her leg out carefully.

The difference in size between the two ankles was obvious at a glance. "You're sure it's just twisted?"

Her brows scrunched. "Well, I don't have my portable x-ray machine on me, so. . ."

The sarcasm bit harder because it came through her teeth. He pressed his lips together.

"It's hard to tell how bad it might be with the way it's swelled up." He leaned forward to examine it closer. "Not discolored though. Can you wiggle your toes without pain?"

She gave them a flutter then met his gaze, a sheepishness to her expression. "Are you mad I left?"

He took a breath. No, it wasn't anger. Worry, maybe. Spiked with something like frustration—not quite so sharp but definitely heated.

"Why would I be mad?" he asked, his voice even. The feeling still roiling in his stomach didn't feel quite so innocuous.

"Because I ran out on you."

Those words though. . . they burned through him. He kept his gaze on her ankle for a moment longer. "Sadie, anyone in your position would've done the same." He looked at her then. "Honestly, I should've known. Because it's the smart move."

All entirely true. Whether his intentions were good or not, the smart person wouldn't take his word for it and would try to escape. It's what he would've done.

She narrowed one eye, the corner of her mouth tipping up a little bit.

He couldn't keep that gaze though, couldn't deny that it did bother him that she hadn't trusted him enough. Shifting his attention, he gingerly felt along her lower calf, just above where the swelling started, checking the bone's integrity.

"I just wish you hadn't tortured me with the underwear task if you were planning to bolt anyway."

She tilted her head to the side. "Tortured you?"

He gave her a wry look, lifting a brow. He wouldn't spell it out for her, and he needed to concentrate on checking her ankle. The added distraction of her skin being soft as velvet under his palms was enough to make a slow heat spread through him.

"Oh." She gave one nervous laugh. "Um, sorry."

He glanced up again, watching her face as his hands moved down toward her foot.

She jerked her head back, sucking a sharp breath through her teeth when he probed around the ankle.

"We need to get back to the house and get some ice on it." He tamped down any intensity in emotion, keeping his face clear. "You okay coming back with me?"

Their gazes locked again, and he wondered, hoped, she'd understand the question beneath his words: *Do you trust me now?*

She held his eyes, a determination taking shape in the honeyed depths. "I can't walk on it."

His heart beat a little faster, a tingle surging through his body. "You won't have to." He turned his back to her while staying in a crouch. "Can you climb on?"

A burst of laughter shot out of her, and he glanced at her over his shoulder.

"A piggyback ride?" Her fingers hovered over her incredulous smile.

He shrugged, unable to hold back an answering smile. "It's the easiest way for me to make the trek back."

She bit her lip and rolled herself forward, sliding slender hands over his shoulders, leaving behind a trail of flames at the touch. He tried not to dwell on that as he tucked his hands under her knees, hoisting her up. Her fingers dug into his chest a little, and he felt the tension in her body.

It made it harder for him to walk with her so rigid, and he racked his brain for a way to relax them both.

He latched onto the first thing that came to him. "Tell me about your summer job."

He sensed her surprise in the way she pulled back slightly.

"We have a bit of a hike ahead of us. Might as well fill the time," he explained.

"Right. Um. Well, I like to stay busy, as you know."

He chuckled.

"I do the story times, summer activities, and programs the library puts on. It's a nice way to earn money when I'm not teaching."

As he'd suspected. "You don't want a break from dealing with kids?"

He felt her shrug. "It's still something different. Plus, I like being around kids. Except when I don't get my coffee or I run into my ex-boyfriend," she added.

"And get questioned by the FBI."

She tsked.

He couldn't help his smile. "Explains your active avoidance of curse words of any kind, though. You're quite committed with your alternatives."

"I'd rather stay out of the habit than slip accidentally." She sniffed, sounding offended.

"It's a commendable effort."

She had gone rigid again, almost like she wanted to pull away. Did she think he was making fun of her?

"I mean it," he assured her. "I'm sure the parents appreciate it, too."

She softened a little. "I don't care that much if other people curse. But I've always been put off when adults use language in front of children, especially that young."

He hadn't thought about it before, but he also wasn't around kids a lot. "That's fair. My habit has been pretty un-breakable."

"How hard have you tried?" she asked, and he heard the smile in her voice, felt her doubt.

"Not very," he admitted. "The kind of people I'm around are a lot worse than the occasional curse word. To fit in, I have to speak like them." *Among other things. . .* Now he was getting tense. "Do you like teaching or the library better?"

She took a breath. "Good question."

He felt her relax a smidge, and it made him want to know more. Not just because it brought that passion out in her voice again.

"If you had to give one up, which one would you choose?"

Her hands had softened against his chest, one finger tapping along his collarbone as she contemplated.

"Hmm. I'm not sure." She paused, her silence holding a weight and shape that he desperately wanted to hold in his hands. Her next words came more slowly, halting, like she struggled to form them. "I've been told before that I'm *too much*." A soft laugh. "Certainly for a librarian. But you know who doesn't think I'm too much? Kindergartners."

He laughed, imagining what maybe was "too much" and realized it really wasn't. Sure, it was ridiculous at first to hear her list of requirements. But she also backed off and capitulated on the ones she could compromise on. Like she was used to push-back. And, really, what was the big deal with a few items that settled her mind? If it made her feel physically better, too, why not?

"Tell me about your hippie ways," he said, and that stiffness snapped her muscles tight again, like she was preparing to defend herself.

She took a while to answer, and he wondered how often people gave her a hard time about it. Of course, she didn't know him well, but that was twice she believed he only intended to judge her.

After a couple of minutes, her tension eased a little, though the rigidity in her body didn't fully loosen. "My mom got sick about a decade ago."

She stopped again, though he didn't think it had anything to do with him and his reaction—or lack thereof. It was more like she was giving that time in her life a moment of silence for the difficulty it must have brought.

"Cancer," she finally continued. "Things like chemo, radiation. . . that was the treatment path. We saw what those things had done to my grandmother. How it extended her life just enough for her to be absolutely miserable. She suffered, and then she died anyway." She swallowed. "My mom wanted something different."

Her fingers dug in just below his clavicle, the intensity of her emotions evident as it vibrated through their connected bodies.

"We researched everything you could imagine. Diet, environmental toxins, hormone-stuffed foods, pesticides. There are poisons in so many everyday things that make our bodies fight so hard just to function.

"We switched out all of our conventional products, cleaned up the house, what we ate. Her doctors thought we were crazy to refuse the chemo and radiation." She scoffed. "It was so stupid, though. I remember when we had a consult and discussed the scans. They specifically mentioned the fact that sugar fed the cancer. They could see it in real time when doing scans on cancer patients. And in the same meeting, they were telling her to eat cake to gain the weight the sickness made her lose."

He tipped his head to the side, amazed. None of her requests seemed ridiculous now. She had a very valid reason that twanged his heart.

"Did it help?" he asked softly.

The silence stretched again, and he got the impression she'd forgotten herself, forgotten he was even there, though her arms and legs were still wrapped around him, and he was still moving through the trees. She had fully relaxed against him.

"Yes. She got better," Sadie finally said, subdued. "She felt well, thrived even, for a long time. Her scans looked good; the tumors shrank. It was pretty amazing. So my parents went on the trips they'd often talked about, took those dancing classes she'd always wanted to take, and enjoyed some focused time with us."

That weighty silence hit them again, hemmed in by the grief he could already feel. It was so at odds with the brightness of sunlight that shoved between the trees ahead of them, which meant they were almost back to the house. Part of him was sad that this physical connection would soon end.

"It was an aggressive form of cancer though." Sadie's voice was just a breath along his neck. "We lost her a couple of years ago when it came back. We were all much more at peace with it by then. She'd outlived her prognosis and with more joy and dignity than she would've had otherwise."

Neither spoke for a few minutes, the only sound permeating the heavy air in the depths of those trees was his breathing. She wasn't hard to carry, but adding that much weight to his back had his heart pumping harder, his oxygen needs more demanding.

But it might have been what her story pulled out of him, memories of what he'd witnessed, so very different than her experience. He thought back to his dad's illness, the way he'd wasted away, become a shell of the man he'd once been.

"My father died of cancer too."

Her hands flexed against his chest, and he felt distinctly like she wanted to hug him, to offer comfort or a sense of understanding.

And as they emerged into the late afternoon sunshine with the house before them, he felt even that waning light was too harsh against his eyes, its heat biting at his skin.

13

Forest by the Sea

A sense of desolation stole through Sadie when Chase deposited her on the couch, like the disconnection from his body was a physical ache. Even as he arranged her leg up on a stack of pillows and went to retrieve some ice packs, there was this nagging sense of abandonment.

Which was absurd. She'd just tried to escape not a few hours ago.

And it really had been hours. It had taken them more than an hour to get back to the house, which meant she'd trekked for at least that long into the woods. And considering her rest after injuring herself, the day was half gone already.

With a stirring embarrassment bubbling through her, she watched Chase move around the kitchen, retrieving a sandwich bag to put ice cubes in. Then he drifted back over to her, draping a towel over her foot before arranging the ice on top of it.

Her face was hot with humiliation. Not only had she sent him on the errand to get all of those things—which had made her sound demanding and persnickety. But then she'd taken off and hurt herself in the process, rendering the whole thing utterly pointless.

He went back to the kitchen to put away the items he'd haphazardly tossed onto the counter before taking off after her, organizing them on shelves with labels facing out. For easy readability, probably.

Nothing changed in his expression, but there was something in the air, a tension that wasn't obvious unless she was paying close attention. His shoulder muscles were tight, his movements less fluid than they should be. If she hadn't seen him move through the trees so quietly and swiftly, she never would've thought twice.

"You probably think I'm an idiot for taking off the way I did," she said, desperate to get it to release.

He glanced at her from the corner of his eye. "Honestly, I'm just glad it wasn't one of Zimmerman's guys forcing you out there against your will."

"Nope. Just me, looking to break a bone," she muttered darkly.

He eyed the sandals sitting by the front door. "Yeah, those aren't exactly hiking boots."

She ignored the flush that crept into her face again. "Well, when I was being kidnapped, I didn't have the forethought to plan my escape footwear."

He huffed a laugh, the smile forcing the lines to fan out around his eyes, and it sent a web of tingles through her.

His forearms flexed as he rolled the empty grocery bags and stuffed them into one. "I'll warn you next time, so you're packed and ready."

"That would be a win-win," she said as he bent to stuff the bags in the cabinet under the sink. "Then you wouldn't have to go buy me underwear."

His eyes flashed to her face as he straightened, flickering like a flame in the dark as he placed his palms on the counter before him. Was he doing it to steady himself, or was that just in her head?

"Speaking of," she hurried on, swallowing past the dryness in her throat, "I know the ankle presents a problem, but I really would like to shower. Especially after that adventure."

His expression was stony. "Sure. I'll get you a fresh towel and stuff." He pushed away from the counter and headed for the hallway.

She stewed in uncertainty, was heavy with it as she watched him gather everything she'd need.

"I assume you'll need to borrow something to wear while your clothes are in the wash?"

She blinked as understanding settled. She could've let him get her clothes when he was at the store. He'd offered, but it had felt extra demanding. Especially considering she'd been planning to run while he was gone anyway.

"I might be able to find something you won't be swimming in," he continued when she said nothing.

She pulled a lock of her dirty hair forward, running her fingers through it nervously. "Oh. Yeah, that would probably be good."

He gave one swift nod and disappeared into the bedroom—*his* bedroom, which he'd now let her use twice.

She hadn't realized it was the only bedroom until she'd investigated earlier. There was one other room, but it was much smaller—really only big enough for the desk and shelves that dominated the space—and it was currently filled with boxes, which she'd discovered on her rabid search for a phone to contact the outside world.

Chase emerged from his bedroom, and she couldn't help the way her stomach clenched when their eyes met, stirring something entirely foreign inside of her.

"I laid the clothes out on the bed."

He came over to the couch and took the ice off her foot. Before she could say anything or guess what his intentions were, he hoisted her up and into his arms. Her hands scrabbled to grip around his neck, and she swore she saw him smirk.

"*Crackers*," she breathed.

"The hall bathroom would work better since it has a tub you could sit in, but I figured you'd want the privacy of the primary," he murmured, carrying her effortlessly into the bedroom.

Cripes, her heart was pounding so hard, like a maniac fighting to get out of a bone cage. If he heard it, he gave no indication as he walked toward the bathroom, setting her on her feet just inside the door. There wasn't enough room for both of them unless they were pressed against each other.

Which gave her quite the image. A delusional part of her mind threw itself into that fantasy with enthusiasm. Him showering with her, those big hands tracing all the lines of her body. Her eyes shot wider as the flush burned into her cheeks again. She swore she'd be getting a sunburn just from how often her cheeks flamed with embarrassment.

He tilted his head sideways as he took in her expression. "Do you need anything else?"

She put her hand against the wall to keep her balance, and her response shot out in fits and starts: "Um. No. Thank you."

He hesitated for another few seconds before scooting around her to turn the shower on. He cleared his throat. "It's a little finicky," he said by way of explanation. "And just to save you the process of doing it yourself. You know. With your ankle."

The way his voice contracted made her smile. Seeing him as discomfited as she was by their proximity made her feel less like an idiot.

He straightened, and it put them only inches from each other. They were both frozen as he stared down at her, and her heart throbbed again, calling, calling for something. His chest moved like he'd just finished a sprint.

She started to lift her hand, that fantasizing part of her brain goading her to place it against his chest, to ask him to join her. Forget the circumstances that had brought them here because she craved the way his strong arms could hold her, and she pictured them together, slick with water and desire—consequences be damned.

And then she jolted. She hadn't even thought far enough to realize that there would even *be* consequences. And while she didn't always think consequences through in general, she was usually better about the long-game when it came to physical intimacy because she knew herself. She may have been a little indiscriminate about who she dated, but she never got naked with a man before they'd known each other a few months, when she felt she could afford the emotional attachment.

She dropped her hand, and the sound of it hitting her thigh was like a bullet to his concentration because he blinked and backed away, never taking his eyes from her face. Then he was gone, and the tension seeped out of her. But it was replaced by a sense of disappointment that made her bones ache.

She took a cleansing breath and hopped to sit on the closed toilet to undress instead of trying to balance on one foot.

It was absolute insanity that thoughts about Chase like that were running through her head. Not only had he kidnapped her, but he was an undercover FBI agent, and that meant unending complications she really shouldn't mix herself up in. Especially since she'd already unintentionally gotten herself tied up with the criminal element.

She pulled her shirt over her head and wondered if there was something wrong with her. She had clearly never really known Greg, even after dating for over a year. A waste of time, but still. And now she was having *thoughts* about a man she barely knew, even if she was sure now that Chase was a good guy in all of this.

At some point during their trek back to the house, she'd finally allowed herself to believe his story. Everything had been pointing to him being trustworthy, but she'd been fighting it as hard as she was fighting herself. Even if he was pretending he was a bad guy for the benefit of other people, he'd shown himself to be completely different.

Her experience with Greg had been the other way around. By the time things had ended with him, she'd realized how terrible of a boyfriend—of a person—he'd been. But it had taken so much longer for her to see it.

She stood cautiously to shimmy her filthy pants down her hips, gritting her teeth against the pain in her ankle when she touched her toes to the floor, and then mentally cursed Greg for putting her in this position.

He'd been sneaking into her apartment, tying her to his nefarious activity so she'd be thrown into the path of mobsters and criminals. Not to mention the feds. Unbelievable.

The process of showering was awkward as she balanced herself, but it went quickly as she stewed and simmered over the ways that Greg had screwed her over, had messed up her mind and her heart. But even before she knew about all of this nonsense, she'd had the strength to walk away. If only it had severed all ties like she'd thought it had.

She shut the water off and pulled the towel from the rack, drying off slowly, vacillating between sadness and anger that everything had culminated to this moment. But she reminded herself that she was at least safe.

Cared for, she added, thinking of how Chase had carted her back to the house after buying her the items she'd requested, then had helped treat her ankle, lent her clothes. Catered to her, even after she'd tried to run. What a strange turn of events, really.

She shook her head as she hobbled toward the bedroom to put on the new set of underwear then the clothes Chase had lent her. They smelled clean and so like him that she paused to take it in, almost knocked sideways by that mix of scents. She hadn't realized she'd discerned a distinct fragrance that was quintessentially him, but it hit her full force as she stood in his room, in his safe house in the woods, and now in his clothes.

He was woodsy and salty, a forest by the sea. It stirred that want in her bones that she was still grappling with, still so shocked by.

There was a tentative knock on the door, and she spun as if she'd been caught stealing.

14

Control and the Hippie Life

Sadie's strangled voice called for Chase to enter, but the odd tone made him hesitate.

He pushed the door open slowly just in case he'd misheard her, but she was already turned toward him when he peeked around, an attractive shade of pink coloring her cheeks. He was finding how easily she flushed with embarrassment incredibly appealing. As if she needed anything else to draw him to her.

She fiddled with the hem of the shirt that belonged to him. It fell almost to her knees, which were totally obscured by the basketball shorts that bagged around her, coming halfway down her calves. The clothes were wearing her rather than the other way around, but it stirred a weird heat inside of him.

A sudden flash of another life played like a movie in his mind's eye. A life outside of undercover work, away from the seedy world he'd known for far too long. A life where he came home to someone every day—someone who loved him, who wore his clothes for comfort as she lounged around the house they shared.

When he snapped out of the vision, he was standing in front of Sadie, reaching with starved hands before he came to his senses and stopped himself.

Her face tipped up in anticipation, her lips parting the perfect amount that equated to invitation, and he was ready to devour that mouth. He resisted—barely—but his face was only a few inches from hers, their breath mingling. He had to be sure he wasn't reading her wrong.

"Why did you stop?" she whispered. Her fingers brushed against his stomach, and his senses reacted like she'd shot currents of electricity through him.

"I. . ." He couldn't form the words after that. And maybe because he'd felt so out of control when he found himself right in front of her. Being out of control was one of his least favorite things.

Tentatively, her hands began to travel over his stomach, feeling along the rigid muscles there. She never took her eyes from his, but her mouth formed a little "O" that called to him, luring with a pulsing need for more.

And so he relinquished control, releasing every lock he'd ever had in place, and let their lips collide. To his shock, every part of him sailed into a new plane of existence as her lips parted to let him in for exploration, and her taste, minty like she'd just brushed her teeth and something else he couldn't name, almost knocked him to his knees. His greedy hands slid under the shirt that was practically a dress on her, craving the feel of her skin under his palms.

The way his body had been crying out for hers hadn't been obvious to him until this moment, when he was finally getting a taste, and he worried it would never be enough as the ache built deep in his blood, lighting every nerve ending on fire.

Her skin was as smooth as he thought it would be, warm and silky, and her curves dipped and rounded under his hands as he explored her. She tipped her head back to give his mouth access to the sweetness of her throat, and he willingly consumed, drowning in the thirst, the hunger, the absolute urgency scoring him from the inside.

More. He wanted more. More of her body exposed, more of her hands on him, more of his on her. He wanted to savor, to dive deep and never resurface.

That feeling like he would combust came over him again, an unrelenting heat that blazed bright and painful and intoxicating.

He swept her off her feet—literally—gripping the back of her thighs so that he could lay her back on the bed and settled himself between her legs, careful to keep his weight from crushing her.

She moved restlessly under him, her hands twisting in his shirt like she didn't know where to hold on as he slid a palm along her rib cage, brushing the side of her breast. Her breath came in short, hot gasps against his ear as he continued feasting on the skin of her throat down to her collarbone and back, tasting her like his body begged.

He cupped her breast, running his thumb over the nipple through the bra he'd bought her, and she arched into him, hands twisting tighter in his shirt.

His groan came out like a growl against her throat, and his teeth skimmed along the soft skin.

More, more, more, his mind, his body chanted.

He rolled, pulling her on top of him, and his hand shot down her back, under the band of the shorts she wore to grab a handful of her butt. He'd wanted to do that since he'd first gotten a backside view.

Her mouth was hungry for his, and he eagerly accepted it, overtook her enthusiasm, sending his other hand into the shorts and started shoving them down, thinking only of getting *more*.

And that's when he felt her start to come back to herself. The very slightest retreat in her body, which had been rippling with need only a half-second before, warned him that he'd best start locking things down.

"Chase," she said against his mouth.

"Hm?" He took one last taste of those pillowy lips and tried to pull back.

But she was having a hard time slowing the train because she sighed and laid into his mouth again. "Ugh," she said, placing her hands on his cheeks as if he were the one, not her, diving in again. "I—we—can't."

"Okay." He accepted another of her kisses, but otherwise made every other part of himself as still as possible. Difficult when one part really had quite the mind of its own.

She brushed her lips along his one more time, then finally pushed against his chest to sit up. He winced at the way her pelvis shifted over him, and his hands landed on her thighs.

It took all of his concentration to keep from moving.

She shifted her face away, tucking hair behind her ear. "I, um. . . I'm not on birth control."

He blinked. Birth control? Shit. He hadn't even gotten that far in his thought process. She wasn't the only one responsible for that, but he certainly didn't have anything on hand either.

He propped himself up on his elbows, trying to understand why she would be ashamed to admit this to him. Could it be. . . ?

"Wait. Why not?" he asked, suspicious. "Is it a hippie reason?"

She laughed, though it was strained. "Yes."

He reached up to touch her damp hair. It felt good to do it, to give in to the impulse instead of fighting himself on it like he had been all this time. "It's okay. This got a bit out of hand, and I'm honestly not really prepared myself." He cleared his throat.

She looked at him from under her lashes, a self-conscious smile tugging at her lips.

"You're not the only one in charge of *that* anyway. Even if you were on birth control, the wise thing to do would be using both."

She chewed her lip and looked away again. Did her chin tremble?

He sat up, shifting his weight carefully so that he didn't knock her off of him. "Hey. It's fine."

She shrugged one shoulder but said nothing.

"Who made you feel like it wasn't okay to not take birth control?" He gripped her arms lightly.

"Well. Greg."

He should have known. The flash of rage was acidic through his blood, stinging and sharp. This guy was an unlikable prick on paper, but the picture Chase was getting on top of that really drove the point home.

She released a soft sigh. "He's just one of many who's given me a hard time for my 'hippie' ways."

"I'm sorry if I've made you feel bad for it," he murmured. Because he still felt that new freedom to touch her, he brushed a hand along her face and tapped his lips against hers briefly.

"It's all right. I know how it all sounds."

"Ridiculous at first," he admitted. "But now that I understand—well, partially. Tell me about the birth control thing. And I'll get the laundry started with your own clothes. That was the whole reason I even came in here."

A genuine smile peeked behind her chagrin. "Who knew wearing *your* clothes would be such a turn on for you?"

He laughed to cover the way the thought unsettled him. "Not me."

Was it some weird macho, territorial thing? Because he'd had some sort of feral reaction to seeing her in his clothes, smelling his own scent on her. Even now, a primal tug was there under his skin.

He needed to steer his mind from that line of thinking because it would derail him, and he wasn't sure he'd survive it.

Remembering her ankle, he shifted to lift her and bring her back into the living room. Like before, her whole body tensed with surprise, and she clung to him like she thought he'd drop her.

"I can't believe you can just whip me into your arms like that," she said breathlessly. "Well, looking at you, I can. But it still shocks me every time."

He smirked. "Not the scrawny basketball guy I was in high school."

She tilted her head. "No, you're not."

Discomfort crept through him as he sensed her desire to press that topic again, to bring the conversation back to those days he'd rather forget. His reluctance to talk about it earlier would maybe deter her, but still, he decided he'd better say something to curb the possibility just in case.

"So the birth control," he prompted, lowering her onto the couch. He tucked the pillows under her foot again and moved to the freezer for another ice pack.

She took a deep breath, and he wanted to see her face, to make sure she wasn't still ashamed of the topic.

"There are lots of reasons." She paused, the weight of her silence pressing against him. "But particularly because it messes with the body's natural function. Playing with hormones, masking health issues, forcing the body to think it's pregnant, causing weight gain, messing with mood."

His brows lifted as he walked back to the couch. She wasn't looking at him, and it confirmed that she was still feeling ashamed of her own convictions, even though he heard the passion in her voice. Subdued, but there all the same.

"Those are all valid reasons," he said softly, setting the ice on her ankle again.

She looked up at him, her face a little flushed, a twinkling of admiration in her eyes as she took him in. "You don't have to be so nice about it."

Her words, spoken mildly, made a little spot in his chest pinch. She didn't think he was taking her seriously, and that made him angry again. Not at her, but at whoever had made her so cynical about it.

He opened his mouth to say something, but she spoke before he could: "I probably should put some more arnica on my ankle."

He blinked, thrown off.

"Would you mind getting my purse?"

He spun on his heel, walking stiffly to where he'd tossed the bag onto the counter earlier, trying to shove the anger and confusion down. He snatched it from the island and brought it to her.

She dug around for the tube she'd produced the day before to treat his face. He hadn't even checked it, but just feeling around the spot on his cheekbone now told him how much better it was.

There was a knowing smirk on her face as she unscrewed the lid of the arnica, and he wondered what she saw in his expression.

"Your cheek feels better, doesn't it?"

He fought the urge to deny it. He'd already been trying to convince her that he wasn't making fun of her or dismissing her fondness for the hippie life, but it wasn't like he could explain the real reason behind it.

That he habitually denied help, denied that anyone or anything had an effect on him whatsoever, good or bad. The scene not fifteen minutes before would serve as evidence that she was the exception to the rule.

So he mentally pushed out his tension, the desire to act as if nothing had happened at all, and forced his smile.

"Yeah, it does." The smile became genuine as he took in her pleased expression. "Kind of amazing, actually."

Her fingers rubbed the cream around her swollen ankle, and his eyes traced the pained grimace on her face. He clamped down against his desire to fix it or offer something so he didn't feel useless.

And because it made him jittery, he went to the bedroom to retrieve the clothes she'd shucked before showering so he could put them in the washer, all the while wrestling his mind away from thoughts of her stripping them off.

15

Unexpected Visitor

It felt good to have her own clothes on again, but clean and fresh, and Sadie had to hand it to Chase that he'd chosen well on the underwear he'd bought at the store. If she'd sent Greg, he would've come back with something sexy and entirely impractical that wouldn't have been comfortable to wear.

Her ankle was sore this morning, still a little swollen, but she could limp on it now, which she appreciated. As swoon-worthy as it was to have Chase carry her, it also rankled to be so dependent on someone else.

And it made her mind travel down a dangerous path. One that involved his mouth and hands all over her. Even the memory of the way his touch felt on her body was like a brand along her skin.

Crackers, that was not something she needed to be entertaining. Even if he was a "good guy," he was still working a job that involved very dangerous people, and she was already on their radar. How much worse could it get for her—or for Chase—if they got involved romantically?

Would it put him in trouble with his bosses? And what about with the FBI? Surely it wasn't sanctioned—what was it he'd called it? code? protocol?—to date the person you kidnapped, even just to keep them safe, while working undercover for a major crime boss.

Roberta would faint at the flagrant disregard for the rules.

Not to mention it could never just be a physical thing for Sadie. She was well acquainted with her own heart to know how easily she fell into the land of feelings. It was her way. There were already stirrings heading that direction, and a physical relationship would forge something in her that usually got her into trouble.

She walked into the kitchen, and he must have sensed her presence because he turned to acknowledge her. He froze at the sight of her, taking in her appearance—the clean clothes that actually fit, her brushed and braided hair, her fresh face.

He turned back to the stove, making eggs again, though the carton beside him said pasture-raised, and she suppressed a smile. It did send a twinge of guilt through her when she thought about how she'd taken off when he'd so graciously taken her preferences into account.

It made her voice small when she asked, "Is it okay if I make my deodorant?"

He raised a brow at her. "Sure. What do you need again?"

She ticked them off on her fingers as she listed the ingredients: "Coconut oil, cornstarch, baking soda, a saucepan, and a glass bowl to make a double boiler."

He reached over to open the pantry that stretched to the ceiling for her to look. Even after his grocery trip, it didn't have much—just the necessities, a few canned goods, a bag of rice. How much time did he actually spend in this house? Was it *his* home, some kind of cover residence, or just an FBI safe house?

There was still so much she didn't know or understand about this situation, and part of her didn't want to find out. The little she knew was already overwhelming enough.

She bent to look deeper, finding a half-full box of baking soda and some cornstarch. She couldn't find the coconut oil, but Chase cleared his throat, and she turned to find him holding it out to her.

"Thank you," she murmured, accepting it.

He set to work getting the saucepan and the bowl for her double boiler, and they settled in next to each other at the stove. Their arms brushed as she scooped out the coconut oil and measured each of the other ingredients. It was an effort not to look at him, even though tingles of phantom sensation ran through her from when his hands had been all over her body. He'd touched her like a starved man.

Which he very well may have been. What did life under-cover actually look like? Lonely, probably.

She wanted to ask, but she had to wait until all the heat pouring through her ebbed because it was too distracting for her to form coherent sentences.

To give herself the chance to gather her thoughts, she moved to the sink to fill the small pan with water and set it on the stove to heat. Then she pulled back to lean against the counter as he was turning off his burner.

He frowned, looking down at her ankle. "Just because it's feeling better doesn't mean you should be on that ankle for long."

She looked down at it too, then gestured to the double boiler. "I have to watch this closely, so I know when to add everything."

He sucked his teeth, narrowing his gaze on her face. "All right." He shifted to stand in front of her and placed his hands at her waist, lifting her to sit on the counter before she even knew what he was doing.

She grabbed at his shoulders belatedly, a giggle slipping out as he slid her back on the smooth marble.

"Now you can keep the weight off your ankle and watch it. Though you really should keep your foot elevated."

He didn't release her, and she didn't take her hands from his shoulders. Time stretched, temptation tickling along her mind as they stared at each other.

"Are you hungry?" he asked after a moment, his voice very quiet. Still, it scraped the air with the gravel in it.

Very, she wanted to say as she looked down at his mouth for a split-second. His fingers flexed against her waist, and she wondered what exactly was happening to her.

She'd always been impulsive, her spontaneity leading her to kiss guys on a whim in her past, even testing the waters with ones who probably didn't deserve her time. Sometimes her brashness afforded her once-in-a-lifetime experiences and relationships that grew and tested her. Other times, she'd earned herself nothing but heartache.

But this didn't feel like impulse. Not really. It felt like inevitability, two stars caught in each other's gravity, pulled into a crash course. Even knowing that it could end in a burning, devastating collision, she still slid her hands from his shoulders, settling them behind his neck, fingers playing a little bit with his hair.

"We are really going to get ourselves into trouble here," he murmured as she pulled his face closer to hers.

"I can't help it," she said, pressing her lips to his, "with your hands on me like that."

"Hmm, like this?"

She gasped, dropping her head back as his hands shifted higher. "Chase."

He pulled back suddenly, his breathing ragged. His eyes flashed, sending warmth into her cheeks as his gaze roved her face.

"I have half a mind to go back into town so we can end this torture."

"I have half a mind to let you." She was ridiculously breathless, but she couldn't find it in herself to feel embarrassed.

He raised a brow, the edge of his mouth curving up. "How do I know you won't disappear on me again?"

"I can give you my word."

His jaw muscles rippled as he fought his self-control yet again. It gave her quite the thrill to see him struggle so much. To be desired that much was heady, and she let her smile break through.

"Your water's boiling," he said softly, pulling back. "And we're about to have company." His hands slid from her waist, his eyes on whatever vehicle she now heard coming down the dirt drive.

"What?" she squeaked, fear washing through her, sharpening with the grim look she saw on his face. "Who?"

"Zimmerman's guy," he said darkly. "Santiago."

She started to hop down, but he held a hand out toward her.

"I don't want them to see you. Not yet, anyway."

He chewed his lip for a second, then reached to turn off the burner. His hands went to her waist again. "We have to make it look like I actually kidnapped you."

"You did." The words were out before she could stop them.

He huffed. "I mean like you're actually afraid of me." He lifted her off the counter, setting her down gently. "I'm going to have to tie you up again."

Her fingers became claws on his biceps, the fear twisting in her stomach like a writhing snake. "Why?"

"They need to believe I'm holding you here against your will." He plowed on before she could say anything. "And, no, I'm not."

He shuffled her toward the bedroom, and her stomach twisted again because there was genuine concern in his eyes, ripples of anxiety coming off of him in waves. A part of her still wondered if the level of trust she'd extended toward him was wise. There was still no actual proof of the story he'd fed her, but his demeanor, the way he'd taken care of her, made her feel he was telling the truth.

So if he was nervous about who was about to walk through that door, she should be too. And she should do exactly what he told her to.

Once in his room, he scanned the space. "The bed," he said, nodding toward it.

While she sat, he walked out of the room, rushing back in with a zip tie in his hands.

He bared his teeth. "I'm sorry. I'm going to have to tie you to the bed."

She swallowed the rising unease. It would only be temporary, right?

"It's fine," she croaked, her throat tight.

He'd already said it, but his eyes said sorry again, the apology a glimmer in the mossy depths as he positioned her hands and pulled the plastic tie tighter.

She couldn't help her wince when it bit into her skin.

"Sadie."

She looked up at him, taking in the intensity of his gaze.

"It's important to remember that anything I say from here on out is an act. None of it is real or true. Okay?"

Her chest tightened, a little spark of panic igniting in her core, but she fought to tamp it down and nodded.

16

An Enemy Revealed

Chase went back into the main part of the house as he heard the footsteps on the front porch. Two sets. So it was Santiago *and* his little pet, Travers.

The question was if Zimmerman knew about this visit, or if it was Santiago's idea. He wouldn't put it past the big Spaniard, given that he had never liked Chase, even before he'd outstripped him in rank.

He opened the door before Santiago could knock, though Chase hadn't expected him to. Santiago probably knew that Chase was aware of his presence. His ready smirk when the door swung open gave it away, his obsidian eyes glittering with glee like he'd caught Chase with his hand in the cookie jar. He must have suspected something was off already. He'd always questioned Chase's motives, but the stakes were higher now.

It set Chase on edge.

"You have a pretty little present for us in there?" Santiago purred, craning his neck to see past him to the bedroom.

How he knew where it was, Chase had no idea. This place had been his secret hideout until now. But just as Chase did, Santiago had his ways of getting information. His methods usually didn't fall under the *legal* category. Bribing or threatening the right person was not out of the realm of possibility.

"Definitely not for you," Chase answered, working to keep his voice neutral enough to not seem defensive. The effort to not throttle the man snapped a rigidity into his muscles, and he clenched the doorknob harder.

"Aw, but she's so. . ." Santiago sucked air through his teeth. "Delicious." He brought his eyes back to Chase's face as Travers snickered from behind him.

The smaller, wiry man was lacking in the brains department, but he had his uses. Having no moral compass meant nothing kept him from doing whatever he was told. Unfortunately, he was entirely too devoted to Santiago.

"Aren't you going to invite us in?" Santiago asked, his faint accent landing heavier as any pretense of friendliness sluiced away.

Chase didn't move, but Santiago pushed forward anyway, holding Chase's gaze like a dog challenging another to see if he would charge or back down.

Chase did neither, though the image of taking Santiago down played in the back of his mind. That was a future reality he'd someday relish.

He was aware of Travers as the little man slunk into the house, allowing himself to be overly familiar with the sparse decor. Chase pretended not to care, though he didn't like seeing Travers running his slimy fingers over his stuff. This was his home, his safe haven. Irritation churned inside even as he kept his face stony. He couldn't give these two anything to use against him.

"I haven't told Zimmerman you brought home a little souvenir," Santiago said, drawing Chase's attention back to him. "I don't think you have either."

Again, Chase said nothing.

"It's our little secret for now." His smug smile widened.

Chase's gut coiled at the tone, at the charge that filled the air. Something was coming. Something he wasn't going to like.

"I haven't checked in because I've been busy trying to get information out of the girlfriend," Chase said, his tone belying nothing.

"Had much luck? You got to her before we could."

Chase caught the note of frustration and tried to shove down any sense of satisfaction he felt about the fact. It was hard not to want to provoke the other man. "Some of us move faster than others."

Santiago's eyes tightened, and Chase fought his own smile. He didn't have the upper hand yet.

"Interesting tactic, kidnapping her," Santiago continued.

Chase lifted a shoulder, the picture of nonchalance. "I figured it would give me a lot more time to work her over for information."

Santiago snorted, dark eyes raking him up and down with bawdy skepticism. "Work her over, huh?"

Chase tried to clamp down on his reaction to Santiago's implied meaning and the fact that Travers had moved closer to the bedroom. Santiago tilted his head, noting the way Chase went rigid.

When Travers looked to his boss, Santiago jerked his chin to offer permission with a small smirk.

Chase lurched forward, panic shooting electricity through his body, but Santiago snatched the front of his shirt. He shoved Chase back, his expression darkening until he looked downright hostile.

"You know this puts you in a tough position," he said through his teeth, his face inches from Chase's. "You can't just let that girl go. We were going to make it look like a robbery gone wrong. But you took it one step further. You're going to have to dump her body somewhere far, far away."

Chase held his stony expression, but his heartbeat picked up, his fingers curling into his palms. His gaze flashed toward the bedroom and back.

"Let us take care of her for you," Santiago suggested, his accent smoothing out again. "Wash your hands clean."

"And why would you do that?" Chase asked, knowing full well it wasn't an altruistic offer.

Santiago shrugged, giving him a grin that sent a spike of fear through him. "Because we're buddies."

The hair along Chase's neck stood on end. "I can handle it myself, but thanks for the offer. Buddy."

Santiago stared at him for a long time, and Chase worked to keep his expression blank.

"She's very pretty," Santiago murmured, one brow quirking. "Ol' Greg has good taste."

Chase narrowed his eyes, noting that implication in Santiago's words again.

"She would make a very nice distraction." The Spaniard's voice took on that signature purr. "I'd be liable to enjoy some time with her before ditching her, myself."

Chase's nails bit into the skin of his palms as he clenched his fists tighter. "I'll let you know how she is."

Santiago's chin shifted forward just slightly, and even though Chase's words made a sick feeling twist in his stomach, a sense of satisfaction flooded him at Santiago's obvious irritation.

Santiago's grip on his shirt loosened, so Chase broke away. A smug smirk crept back onto the other man's face as Chase shoved past him to the bedroom.

Just as he rounded the corner into the hallway, he heard Travers's grunt and then a thud. He sped up, skidding to a stop just inside the door.

Sadie's chest heaved with emotion, her face flushed, hair mussed. Travers was kneeling on the floor, his hands over his crotch, a greenish tint to his sneering face. She must have kicked the asshole in the balls.

Chase's blood ramped up in temperature just thinking what had precipitated the move. He grabbed the little man by the front of his shirt and yanked him to his feet. But before Chase could do anything further, Santiago called for him.

"Travers!"

The little man flinched, and Chase's lip curled back. His fingers itched to pop the little weasel's head off his toothpick neck, but he shoved him back instead. It was best to put as much distance between his hands and Travers's throat as he could before he gave in to the violence that prickled in his muscles like a poison. Murder sang in his blood.

Travers scrambled back, wincing as he hit the door frame in his haste to get out of the room. Chase stalked after him, making sure he crawled back out to Santiago.

"I'm thinking of being a nice guy and keeping your little secret," Santiago said, barely flicking a glance at his hobbling minion.

"I don't give a shit what you do," Chase growled, the danger he felt coursing through his body infusing his voice with a darkness that should have scared him. Normally it would have. "You get your mongrel on a leash and keep him there, or I swear I'll rip him limb from limb."

One corner of Santiago's mouth tilted up, and Chase knew the man was filing his reaction away. On some level, he knew he'd tipped his hand. But at the moment, nothing mattered except keeping Sadie safe.

"I'll be seeing you then," Santiago replied, heading for the door. He snapped his fingers at Travers, who slid a glare in Chase's direction before slinking after the bigger man.

Chase didn't move until they were out the door, and then he strode forward to lock it, his need to check on Sadie ramping up like a vibration under his skin. And once he knew she was okay, he needed to plan.

17

Fizzing Exes

Repulsion rolled through Sadie in buffeting waves, hot and stifling along her skin. And something else was building. Something like panic—oppressive and bubbling, a black energy that made it impossible for her to be still.

Because being bound meant that someone could touch her, do things to her without her permission, and it made her powerless to stop them.

With that manic thought, the fact that her hands were bound spurred the feeling on, and she couldn't handle it, couldn't keep the screaming need to break free at bay.

With a force that scared her on some level, she yanked against the zip tie, the sound making a thunk against the bed frame she was tethered to. Again and again, she slammed against the plastic, even as it carved into the tender flesh of her wrists, breaking the skin.

"Sadie."

She heard Chase's voice, but she couldn't stop, not with that rising panic flowering inside, billowing through her limbs like a thousand insects in her veins.

"Sadie, stop."

His hands slid along her arms, fingers wrapping around her wrists to still her efforts, and she realized she was crying—heaving sobs that burst out of her like cannons.

He cut the zip tie, and she scrambled backward on the bed and away from him, away from his touch. His skin was like a blistering fire along hers, burning while the panic scorched from under the surface. She bumped into the headboard and curled in on herself.

"I'm sorry," Chase whispered, crouching where he stood, right next to where she'd been a moment ago. He didn't move toward her or reach for her, maybe sensing how fractious she was in the moment.

And it did feel like she would splinter apart, her wracking sobs were so violent. Wrapping her arms around herself helped, and she squeezed tighter, trying to keep the pieces together.

It wasn't as bad as some people had experienced. And it wasn't like she'd never had a man touch her without permission. But she'd been able to fight back if she'd needed to before. That had been taken from her with her hands tied.

As that rat-faced little man's hand slid up her thigh, fear had galloped through her body, and everything in her had rebelled. She'd thrashed as his hand slipped under her shirt, managing to knock him back a couple of times. The second time, she'd had the opening she'd needed to jam her foot upward into his crotch and send him to his knees.

Not hard enough, she thought. He'd been able to walk afterward.

Her sobs had noticeably quieted, that sense of splintering abating, rolling away like a receding wave. Her arms loosened from around herself.

"I'm so sorry, Sadie," Chase said softly. He still hadn't moved.

She didn't flinch. Barely reacted, felt almost nothing at his words, but her eyes shifted to his face.

"Did he—" He broke off, a flash of fury distorting his features. "What did he do?"

She turned her face away.

"I swear I will tear him apart," Chase growled. "But I need you to tell me where he hurt you."

"I'm not hurt," she choked out.

"I beg to differ," he intoned softly.

She slid a glance in his direction again, took in his earnest expression, and knew that he was being serious. That although she had not experienced physical pain, she *had* been hurt. It made something loosen inside her chest to have it acknowledged that way.

She reached out for his hand, and he stood to take it, carefully sitting on the edge of the bed next to her. The warmth of his body seeped into her, providing more comfort than she anticipated.

The memory of the rat-man's poisonous touch faded the longer they sat like that—with Chase sitting watch over her like a sentinel. His steady presence helped the panic leak from her body as time crept by.

But even as that sensation faded, the questions pushed forward in her mind. What had Greg gotten into that put her in the crosshairs of men like this? Even though Chase was actually on the good side, he still had to get answers from her to justify what he had done in the eyes of the criminals who also wanted whatever Greg had, that they thought she knew. That they'd come here to get.

Maybe there was something she didn't realize she knew. But she didn't have enough information yet.

"Chase?"

"Hm?" The pad of his thumb stroked the skin on the back of her hand in a soothing pattern.

She pushed herself up to a sitting position so that she could look into his eyes. "What did Greg do?"

He inhaled deeply through his nose, but he didn't look away. "As you know, Greg is an accountant for some big companies."

She nodded. For an accountant, he was pretty braggadocious about what he did and for whom. The names were the flex, though, not the job he did. There wasn't much that was flashy about number-crunching.

"I don't know exactly how he got in with Zimmerman, but he's been working for him for a while. Zimmerman has quite the reach in that world, and not just cooking the books. He also extorts from a few upper-level execs for some Fortune 500 companies, uses his influence to sway elections, lobby for legislation that's in his best interests. Greg has access to all of the account information and tracked the cash flow for him. Turns out, Greg was not only skimming Zimmerman's scores, but he decided he wanted to get in on the game."

Her lips parted as the picture grew darker. it was impossible to reconcile the buttoned-up, status-obsessed accountant with the criminality Chase described. Even if it was less seedy with him hiding behind the computer screen, that was some serious stuff to be dabbling in. And worse, he'd apparently bitten off more than he could chew with Zimmerman by getting on his bad side.

"He recently took all of the account information and the list of names and took off, leaving no records for Zimmerman to keep getting his scores." Chase looked down at their clasped hands briefly. "We assume he was planning to set himself up as the new crime boss, but Greg Calloway doesn't have the reach, influence, or intimidation factor to get a legion of minions under him. I don't think he anticipated what kind of muscle Zimmerman has in his employ. Or how determined he'd be to keep this stream of income."

He watched her face for a reaction. "It's also the evidence I need to bring the whole thing down."

She shook her head in disbelief. It was hard to wrap her mind around the fact that he'd gotten involved in something like this. . . But if there was one thing he'd made abundantly clear to her, it was that he had a vision for what he wanted his life to look like, and he apparently had no compunctions about getting it in whatever way possible.

"It's obvious you knew nothing about any of it," Chase said, his eyes softening. "But you don't seem totally shocked."

She'd never had much of a poker face, but it was still annoying that her expression would betray her thoughts so easily.

She exhaled the mild irritation. "I never thought he would be capable of doing something like this. But Greg has always had higher aspirations than were easily achievable. He would cut timelines and corners where he could."

The muscles around Chase's eyes contracted while she spoke, like he was reading something under her words. So she figured she might as well tell him the rest.

"He was kind of obsessed with status, with being seen a certain way, living life at a level his finances didn't always support."

Chase clicked his tongue. "Yes, he was in quite a bit of debt. Until suddenly he wasn't."

Comprehension dawned, and she sucked in a breath. Debt to pay for the lavish lifestyle he craved. Then he used his access through Zimmerman to pay off his creditors, so he was free and clear. But then he wanted more. It all made sense.

She shook her head, giving a short, mirthless laugh. "He never liked that I was 'just a kindergarten teacher' when I could have done so much more. He hated introducing me to his friends and coworkers because it wasn't impressive or flashy enough for him."

Something formed in Chase's eyes. She realized it was anger.

"Especially when you had such a fancy degree from graduate school," he said in understanding.

She shot him a sharp look, and he managed to actually look sheepish.

"I did a full search of your place after it had been tossed by Santiago and Travers, remember?"

That made a chill roll over her. If she dwelled too much on the fact that more than one person had gone through every item in her house, she would probably freak out again.

Redirect, she commanded herself even as her pulse throbbed. "What were you looking for?"

"Greg was going to your place for a reason." He lifted a brow, waiting for her to piece it together.

She gasped. "The files?"

He tipped his head to the side. "That was my thought. Probably Zim's too. But I didn't find them, and neither did Santiago, or he wouldn't have gone back to your place or come here."

She shuddered, revulsion a threatening wave. Greg had thrown everyone's attention on her on purpose.

Chase sighed. "If I get those files, I can pass them to the feds, and there'd, hopefully, be enough to nail Zimmerman and his whole operation."

She felt like there was another piece to what he'd said. And the hopeful part of her thought that maybe Chase would be freed from this role he had to play if Zimmerman went down. And she could see it, though the wistful look in Chase's eyes was there and gone so quickly she might have imagined it.

Instead of bringing it up, though, she simply nodded. "And because he'd been tracked to my place and seen talking to me. . ."

"They think you know where it is. Or where *he* is."

She tipped her head back with the weight of the revelation, looking toward the ceiling for a moment. "That's why the FBI talked to me that day." She looked at him again. "Right before you. . ."

He smirked when she didn't finish. "Kidnapped you?"

"You keep correcting me, so I don't know what to call it!" She flapped her hands in irritation, and his smile grew wider.

"I mean, if we want to be technical, we'll call it that." His smile disappeared, his brow drawing together in concern. "Do you feel like that's what I did?"

It clearly bothered him if she did, so she took the time to consider the question seriously. It was a heavy certainty as she realized that she didn't. She could see how he'd been protecting her. Especially after what she'd experienced just a short time ago. She shivered at what might have happened had he not forced her out of her apartment that day.

His attention on her face proved how much he cared about the answer, and he didn't like whatever emotions flashed in her expression.

"No," she finally said. "I don't think that's what you did."

She wanted the tension to release from his shoulders, but they remained bunched. Maybe he didn't believe her. Or maybe he still felt bad about it.

She squeezed his hand when he looked down. "If I really thought you'd kidnapped me, I wouldn't have kissed you." Probably.

He raised his eyes slowly, a little glimmer of hope in the facets of the green prisms. Jeez, that green was mesmerizing. And the way they morphed and changed was endlessly fascinating. She could get lost in them so easily. She had already.

"Since we've established that it wasn't really a kidnapping," he said grimly. "Maybe you'll trust me with what we have to do next."

18

Rage Dragon

"We have to leave. Santiago knows where we are, and he knows you mean something to me. He will be back."

Alarm shot across Sadie's face. Chase wouldn't dare touch her again unless she explicitly asked him to, not after what had happened earlier, but he wanted to. He wanted to calm her nerves, do whatever he could to make her forget.

More than that, though, he wanted to wring that little lizard man's neck. Watch the dull light snuff out of his beady eyes.

"Where will we go?" Her voice sounded so small, and it punched him in the gut. It took all his effort to keep breathing through it.

"I haven't figured it out yet," he said on an exhale. "But we have time. Santiago is a slow mover when he's on his own, and I'm positive Zimmerman doesn't know about this little side mission."

Even as his mind shifted through what he needed to do to figure their next steps out, the rage simmered under his skin. It writhed, stinging and active, calling for him to do something. It made it hard for him to concentrate.

He wouldn't let Travers's behavior slide when he came up against Santiago again. There would be no pretending aloofness or some other agenda. It stirred a determination in him to make this whole thing end—the crime ring, his undercover assignment, and that sniveling miscreant's life. But first things first. . .

"Let's finish breakfast, then I can get some things in motion."

She nodded, worry creasing her brow as she chewed her lip.

Once he got her settled at the island in the kitchen with the cold eggs from earlier, he tried to focus on the details of getting them somewhere safe. But all he could think about was whether she was eating well, and if the color was coming back to her cheeks. She was starting to look more normal instead of like a whipped dog, which should have calmed the beckoning of his anger, the destruction it craved.

But just thinking about what had made her look that way threw fuel on the fire in his belly, and he had no choice anymore. He needed to do something to dispel the painful heat that blazed through him before he could even begin to plan their next steps.

He pushed away from the counter so suddenly, Sadie froze, her eyes flashing to him.

"I need to take care of something," he muttered, heading for the door.

His heart pummeled his ribs as he sprinted down the porch steps and around to the back of the house. He just needed thirty minutes to tame the beast, though his eyes shot to the sky above the trees to check for the telltale dust that would alert him that someone was coming. It wasn't likely anyone would. Santiago may have found his little hideout, but the man wasn't stupid enough to come back in broad daylight. Chase would see him coming, and Santiago knew he wouldn't get within an inch of the house again.

No, if Chase had to bet money, he'd put a hundred on the fact that Santiago wouldn't be back until nightfall. An inkling of where they'd go started to form in his mind—another undercover agent in similar circles who could be a stopping point. But that would come later. With so much time between now and then, Chase would be putting him in danger just by contacting him. The safest option would be to show up unannounced, just in case.

Satisfied that they still had a window of time, he stripped off his shirt and leaped up to grip the pull-up bar in one smooth motion. But he pounded through fifty dips and lifts and couldn't douse the raging fire.

It burned and burned, eating at his control.

So he dropped into push-ups, eyeing the rows of old tires, knowing that was his next step. But he realized he might have to go into the garage to pound the shit out of his punching bag instead.

With a grunt, he flung himself to his feet, running through the tires forward, backward, sideways, and again. Over and over.

He remembered his dad screaming at him during these drills as a teen, when he was scrawny from growing too quickly. He'd pound calories, but he'd grown handfuls of inches in as many months, struggling with energy, with pains in his legs, earning stretch marks like tiger stripes along his back.

His dad always had a hard edge, and he'd been a competitive man. He wanted to use Chase's height to an advantage, pushing him to join basketball, to win, to be the best. He supposed he owed it to the old asshole that he'd earned a scholarship through his efforts. That came in handy since his dad was in prison by the time he graduated high school.

Sadie had only gone there that one year, and he wondered if she'd heard about all of that, if she knew of his personal ties to crime. She, of course, wouldn't know the reason he was able to insert himself so easily into that world was because of his dad.

At least Chase knew he was taking the poison of his father's decisions and turning it for good, even if he himself couldn't be entirely good in the process. A means to an end. Do what you have to if it means you get the worse guy. That was his blank check from the feds. Though Chase tried to toe a line that he'd drawn for himself, knowing that he could easily go too far to bring himself back, the world in which he operated dealt him a lot of gray.

Kidnapping to keep someone safe definitely fell into the gray category, and the familiar twist of uncertainty about it churned in his core. Sadie had come around, of course. She'd shown the level of trust she'd placed in him, and he wasn't sure he deserved it. Sure, he worked for the good guys—ultimately—but he had done a lot of questionable things to earn the respect of the bad guys. And while that had given him pause at times, his knowledge that it was for the greater good kept him from seeing his actions for what they were.

Until now. When there was a woman—one whose life had been entangled unfairly in the mess. And admittedly one he was finding himself wanting for more than just the time it would take to get the answers he needed to close this case.

And that was bad. So very bad.

He stalked toward the garage, flinging the door open so that it banged against the wall, but he didn't flinch. Didn't even bother to shut it. Just walked to the hooks on the wall where his boxing gloves dangled. Instead of putting them on, he grabbed his hand wraps, jerking the straps around with barely contained aggression. He might regret the pain later, but he wanted to feel the bite and sting as he imagined Travers's face on the bag.

He threw out a few phantom punches to limber himself up, already feeling the tingle in his muscles from his efforts outside, then planted his feet for a moment, eyeing the bag with a baleful glare.

It was like slow motion when the nerves in his body ignited, telling his weight to lift to the balls of his feet as he shuffled forward, locking his core.

He stepped forward, using the momentum to twist his body—hips followed by shoulders—throwing all of his strength and rage into his arm as it flew. A sigh burst through his lips with the release of pressure inside of him, the energy leaking out like the bag sucked it from his body.

Taking the lightness it created in him and letting it run rampant, he laid into the bag with a succession of rapid-fire jabs and hooks, grunting with each strike. He felt it when his knuckles split, little slices of pain making him grit his teeth, though he had that odd sense of satisfaction he'd known would come.

"Strike from your core, kid." His dad's voice played in his head, rough and gravelly, edged with frustration, always.

"This is not what I was expecting to find out here."

Chase jerked, missing the bag completely, and nearly fell into it before he whirled to face Sadie in the open doorway.

Almost all of his rage had burned down to ash, and his stomach dropped out just looking at her. The way the late morning sun illuminated her from behind, limning her in golden light, stole the few rational thoughts from his mind.

Her eyes were wide as she took in his expression, and the only sound that filled the silence between them was the air jerking in and out of him and the chain that was secured to a beam in the ceiling jangling as it swung back and forth.

He caught the bag to stop its swinging and swiped at the sweat on his forehead.

"Your hands are bleeding," Sadie said.

He puffed at the air again, his muscles screaming from exertion, and looked down at his left hand. Sure enough, red was seeping into the white wraps.

"Isn't that why you're supposed to use gloves?" Her gaze went to the unused gloves on the wall.

He shrugged, still unable to catch his breath enough to speak.

She tentatively moved into the garage, the glowing sunlight sliding off of her as the shadows devoured every curve of her body, and he swallowed. He might need to punch some more.

"I'm sorry I interrupted you," she said, her eyes traveling the space, taking in the indoor workout equipment in the corner, the car on the other half of the garage, the yard tools that hung from the wall, the workbench and toolbox.

Everything he needed to care for this secluded house in the trees. The one that was no longer safe. He could barely make out the trees through the door. No dust. His assumption about nightfall still held, but he needed to get moving on the plan.

"It's fine. I was almost done," he finally managed, looking at her.

She turned her attention to him, gaze tracing his shirtless form. Exercising in jeans hadn't been his smartest move, but judging by the expression on her face, it wasn't his worst look. The stifling garage had wrung him out like a sponge, coating him in a layer of sweat. He'd have to pound water after this.

Impromptu workout sessions could do that. So could blazing fury.

"Are you okay?" Her voice was softer, genuine concern infusing her tone and making his stomach clench.

But his response was automatic, even if not totally true. "I'm fine."

She pursed her lips, dubious.

He shook his head and figured he might as well call it quits. And be honest with her. He began to unwrap his hands, wincing as the cloth caught and pulled at the torn skin on his knuckles. The pain kept the anger in check. It was subdued, a cowed beast, though he knew from experience that it was never gone.

That was his father's other legacy. An ever-present red dragon that lived inside of him, big and scary and dangerous. He'd trained it, channeled it, learned how to control it. But it never went away. Just another reason the direction his thoughts kept going was a bad one. He'd never made a good boyfriend. He shook his head again, feeling the warmth of her gaze on him.

"I'm fine now," he amended.

"But you weren't before."

Not a question.

He inhaled deeply through his nose, stuffing the wraps into his back pocket so he could wash the blood from them. Though he probably wouldn't get the chance; he had a lot of details to work out between now and sundown.

She was there in front of him before he even realized it, reaching for his hands to inspect the cuts. They didn't look too bad, but she'd obviously caught his grimace.

"You going to put arnica on them?" he asked with a smirk.

She shot him a lighthearted glare. "Not on open cuts. I do have something else, though."

He huffed a laugh. "Of course you do."

"Hey, you admitted that the arnica worked," she accused. The words were playful, but they still had an impact.

"I trust you," he murmured, no strength in him to pretend otherwise.

Her intake of breath was audible, and his stomach clenched again. Their eyes locked. That impact again—jarring.

"I was angry," he admitted.

She released his hand, and he immediately missed the feel of her skin against his. It had soothed, and now the sting of the cuts screamed louder than they had before her touch.

"About the sleazeball."

She didn't look surprised by the admission, though he caught the faintest flinch, and he regretted bringing it up. It renewed the sense of urgency for getting them somewhere new. But this first.

"I have an anger problem."

She tipped her head to the side. "Doesn't seem like a problem if you know how to manage it."

He kept his expression blank even as something stirred inside of him. "Who says I know how to manage it?"

Those lips parted for the ghost of a smile. "You didn't go on some rampage. You channeled it into something productive. That's a lot of what we work on in my classroom. Emotional regulation."

He squinted at her. "You're comparing me to five-year-olds?"

She laughed then, the sound dancing through him. "Age doesn't matter. It's just easier to learn the skills when you're younger. Everyone needs emotional regulation. Anyone ever tell you, Chase, that anger is okay? You're allowed to be mad. It's what you do with it that matters."

It was so simple, and knowing it was probably something she said to kindergartners on a regular basis made it more ridiculous that he reacted to the validation, but he did. It was like a shot of warmth to his heart, and he had to turn away, his eyes finding the shape of his car in the recesses of the other side of the garage.

And it was weird too, because it made the remaining energy dissipate, the dragon curling up and going to sleep, giving him one of the rare reprieves from the constant burn.

How was that even possible?

19

Catch and Release

When they got back inside, Chase was eerily quiet. The constant buzz of tension he always held was muted, and his movements were more fluid than usual. It was odd that she'd picked up on those things without realizing it. It was only clear to her now that it had changed.

All because of what she'd said. He hadn't told her that, but it had been a physical presence that shifted after she'd spoken. Just like with her students. She'd studied that in grad school—the tactics for emotional regulation, the developing brain, the way the amygdala processes environmental triggers, etc. And it still shocked her how effective the strategies she'd learned were.

Even on grown men.

"Are you going to finish making your hippie deodorant?" Chase asked, walking toward the fridge for water.

She looked at the stove, all the supplies still set up and ready for her. "Is that the best use of my time, considering?"

He glanced out the window over the sink. It was a straight-shot to the treetops that lined his long driveway. "Santiago won't hit until nightfall. I'm planning for us to head out right before he does." He met her gaze. "You're going to need it, aren't you?"

Her shoulders inched toward her ears with her discomfort. "I suppose so. But shouldn't I pack or something?"

He lifted a brow as he took a slug of his water. "Pack what? You're wearing the only outfit you've got."

She looked down at herself, frowning. With the hole already in the pants, she wondered exactly how much longer the outfit would even last. "Yeah, about that," she started.

"It's on my list," he interrupted, smirking a little.

A ball of warmth spread through her chest, and a soft breath escaped her lips. "You have a list?"

His smile deepened, then he turned to set his water on the counter. "I'll hop in the shower while you do your thing."

That was as much of a dismissal of the topic as any. But she sure as heck wasn't going to let him have the last word. *He had a list*.

She could do something for him, too. "Then I can take care of your hands."

He spared his knuckles a fleeting glance as he moved toward the bedroom. "They're fine."

"Chase," she warned.

He held up his hands in surrender. "Okay, okay."

Satisfied, she turned to the stove, igniting the burner so she could get the water boiling again. The coconut oil in the bowl had re-solidified, so while waiting for it to melt, she measured out the cornstarch and baking soda. Once it was ready, she poured the liquefied mixture into a small container she'd found in the cabinets, pleased to discover that he used glass instead of plastic for food storage. No doubt he'd roll his eyes at her if she mentioned it, though.

But his reactions didn't feel condescending like Greg's always had. Maybe because Greg looked down on most of the things she was passionate about. Which made her wonder why he'd ever wanted to be with her in the first place. Or why she'd stuck around as long as she had. It had been an exciting whirlwind at the start, and that thrill lured her in, as usual. But then she'd stayed in it.

Maybe because she'd always been labeled fickle, she'd wanted to show everyone that she could commit to something long-term, go with the stable guy for once. And that turned out to be the worst decision she could've made.

She put the lid on the container and set it aside to cool and solidify for later use, and turned as Chase came back from his room. His wet hair was combed back, and he wore jeans and a plain, green t-shirt. In his hand was a half-full black duffel bag, probably stuffed with his clothes and toiletries. He moved toward the extra room, casting his gaze in her direction like he didn't want her to see.

Rolling through the possibilities of what lay in that room and what he might need to pack for whatever came next made her stomach twist. So she focused on bringing the pot of water from her deodorant efforts to the sink, dumping the water, and then washing the measuring cups she'd used. There were spills all over the counter, proof of her endeavors, so she turned to grab some paper towels to wipe them down.

With only one square left, she went searching in the cabinets for more. There was an unopened roll under the sink next to a small trashcan that was full. So she set the paper towels on the floor, digging deeper in the cupboard to find the extra trash bags. Several bottles of cleaning products were knocked over, and she went to work setting them upright.

By the time, she finished, she'd forgotten what she had set out to do in the first place until she noticed the full trashcan again. She finally pulled out the roll of bags to change it, straightening as she yanked the drawstring tight.

"Are you doing chores?"

She started and dropped the bag on the floor, jerking her hand back like she'd been burned.

"Cripes," she hissed, placing a palm against her pounding heart as she turned to face him.

"Sorry." He'd brought the duffel back into the living room, setting it on the couch to situate the contents. His biceps pulled against the sleeves of his shirt as he moved, reminding her what was underneath.

She swallowed. "It's fine. I was just changing the trash bag out. It was full."

"I'll take it out in a few minutes," he said, distracted by the duffel in front of him.

But she was not distracted in the least.

Not when she let her mind wander to watching him pummel the living daylights out of that punching bag. The obstacle course in the backyard revealed just how he'd developed those very chiseled muscles she'd found herself admiring the day before. The washboard abs were the most surprising part. Something she'd only ever seen on actors and fitness models, not in real life.

And then the way they'd felt under her hands was. . . mind-blowing. A total out-of-body experience. Which contributed to the insane way she'd reacted to him in that moment, though she really couldn't account for it logically. She couldn't even blame it on her impulsivity.

Maybe it was that fiery passion she'd read in his eyes. But no, she knew there was more to it than that. A history of connection, an instant and inexplicable attraction. And she couldn't deny that his admission of anger at what had happened earlier that day contributed to a renewed pull she felt toward him.

She walked around the edge of the counter, stopping at her purse to dig around for her Active Skin Repair spray bottle while he adjusted whatever he'd packed and worked on the zippers.

Once she found what she was looking for, she headed his way, pulling his attention from what he was doing.

He grew very still, attuned to her movements as he tracked her progress. That strain from earlier was gone, but a different kind of tension held his body rigid. Almost like he was anticipating something he wasn't sure he was ready for.

"Now I can take care of these." She trailed her fingers just below his knuckles, the torn skin reminding her what his hands were capable of—destruction as well as tenderness.

She wasn't sure what prompted her to do it, but she lifted his hand to her lips and kissed his knuckles gently. To acknowledge what those hands had done to her and for her.

His intake of breath was sharp, and she looked up, afraid that what she'd done wasn't okay. Something in his expression told her that even though he was surprised, it wasn't unwelcome. His lips parted, a wonder shining in his eyes that triggered more of the impulses that always rolled through her in unending waves.

She wanted to push onto her toes, plant her hand on his chest, and dive into his kiss again. The greed with which he'd tasted her lips before stirred the wildfire of desire in her. He seemed to sense it, the need that sang in her blood calling to him. His other hand—the one she wasn't holding onto—slid to cup the back of her neck.

Tilting her face toward his, her body hummed with anticipation. She could hardly stand it as he hesitated, searching her face. For what, she wasn't sure, but she didn't want to wait any longer. She lurched upward to let her mouth crash against his, dropping the hand she'd still held.

Once released, that arm snaked around her waist, bringing her fully against him, and she almost groaned when every soft bit of her collided with every hard edge of him. This kiss was different than before, not the frenzied consumption of that first time. He was slow and deliberate, drinking deeply, savoring, memorizing. With their bodies connected, their lips moving in an enticing pattern, her blood ignited.

A growl rumbled in his chest. The demand that roared between them had him spinning her and backing her up until she bumped the wall. His body pressed harder into hers, trapping her.

And she loved it. Relished the reaction, the intensity, the way her own body responded to the feel of him.

But he pulled back abruptly, exhaling unsteadily against her mouth, and she felt the shudder go through his entire body, the spooling tension winding tighter as he fought himself. But she didn't want him to. She didn't want to fight herself, either.

"You're killing me, Sadie," he whispered roughly, his breath fanning across her face.

He was killing her too, but she couldn't speak, couldn't get the words past her lips when his hands had inched up from her hips, under her shirt. His fingers teased along the skin of her stomach like they had a mind of their own, had not heard his jagged words.

She dove in for another kiss, letting her tongue dance with his for another moment before he broke away completely from her demanding mouth and body, severing the connection between them as he turned away to run his hands through his hair.

He groaned, the sound dark, tortured, and laden with want. "We have to stop."

It was an effort to lock herself down, though she knew it was the better decision. But she wasn't always the best at the better decisions. She was good at diving in headfirst without knowing how far down the bottom was.

"Okay," she said, regret and rejection shooting through her in waves, burning embarrassment into her cheeks.

He turned back, maybe hearing it in her voice. "Please," he said, stepping back to brush the hair away from her face. "Don't be embarrassed."

She shook her head and forced a smile. "It's fine. I get it."

"I want. . ." He shut his eyes, bracing himself with his hands on the wall, bracketing her on either side. "I want this—you—so badly, but. . ."

He tensed like he was startled by that confession and dropped his head. It didn't make sense why at first. But she was coming to realize the hard-won admissions and honest confessions were against his nature to share. It made sense, given his job. She couldn't imagine how scary it would be to have any vulnerability in a world like the one he had to operate in. But he felt different around her, right?

Or maybe he didn't. Maybe she was a new kind of vulnerability, a liability he couldn't afford. But she wanted to hope that she was also his road out. He'd said that if he could get his hands on the information Greg had, he could bring the whole thing down. She already knew Greg's role in all of it, but what was Chase's? And how did he get here? Would he even want out if he had the choice?

The need to know, to understand why he was on this career path was a pressure against her mind. And Lord knew she needed something—anything—to distract her from the lust that was wreaking havoc on her system.

"Chase."

He lifted cautious eyes to hers, but she had a hard time holding his gaze.

"How did you get into this line of work?"

He took a deep breath. "Before we get into it, I need. . . I can't concentrate. . ."

He pushed away, stalking across the room and raking his hands through his hair again. She regretted the return of the tension in his body. But if she was this ready to jump into bed with him, she needed to know.

20

Confession

Chase tried to focus on the facts rather than the way her question made his insides twist. Everything in him fought against telling her, revealing this part of himself—his past. He never wanted to tell anyone, but the thought of telling *her*, of changing what she might think of him had a whirlwind of anxiety building inside he tried to banish with his pacing.

He needed to be open about it, owed her a measure of trust to match what she'd extended to him. Not just because of what would come next, what he would ask of her when he enacted his plan. But because this wasn't some random fling for him. Not any more. And he suspected it wouldn't be for her either. She wasn't the type.

She was the marrying type.

That stopped him in his tracks. Because it was true. She had this hastiness about her, a wildness that made her say and do things without a lot of thought. But she was also sweet and wholesome, committed to her passions. She was absolutely the

bring-home-to-mom type. The settle-down-and-have-ba-
bies type.

The realization knocked the wind out of him. Because
damn if he didn't find a part of himself wanting that life.
But that wasn't something he'd ever let himself dream about
before. Because of the job. Because of who he was. Who his
father was.

But he ached at the thought of denying himself a real life
forever. Denying himself what he could have. . . maybe with
her. Even now, his body craved to feel her for real, to know
what it was to see all of her, experience all of her. She'd opened
parts of her heart and mind to him, revealing what a passionate
woman she was. He realized that his world had shifted, tilted
by her honesty and warmth.

Especially after her words that afternoon.

He swallowed, remembering the way that felt—to be vali-
dated for once. Somewhere inside of him, a little child was
sighing in relief. After all those years of his father's berating
dismissals, pushing Chase to the edge of his capabilities, he
felt some small thing release in himself.

"Chase?" she said softly.

He cleared his throat and turned as she pushed away from
the wall. She'd been frozen like she'd been afraid to move until
now. Even still, she was cautious as she came to sit on the
couch, curling up and tucking her legs under herself. The way
she looked so much like she belonged there squeezed his heart,
and that flash of another life hit him again.

What was happening to him?

He kept his features neutral, but the storm had started
inside. Panic, if he had to name it. But years of practice kept
him from drowning under that feeling.

He sat next to her on the couch, slouching like there was no internal war going on.

She picked up his hand again, inspecting the knuckles. "I forgot about these."

"We were a little distracted."

She smirked at his reply and lifted the bottle she still held. How she'd had the wherewithal to hang onto it during their moment was baffling to him.

As she looked at the cuts on his hand, he remembered the tender kiss she'd placed there. He swallowed as a warmth spread through him. The storm inside him sputtered and died out. Which would've scared him more if her touch wasn't such a balm to his nerves.

"You're not talking." She glanced up from under her lashes, her golden eyes glittering. Then she frowned as she straightened his arms, resting his hands on her lap.

A tight ball formed in his gut, and it threatened to lodge in his throat, keep him from telling her anything. How did one lay out the entirety of their nuanced and messy history?

"Did you know much about me back in high school?" he finally asked.

"Other than you being the much-lauded but obviously very shy basketball star? Not much." She shrugged. "When I knew my dad was stationed somewhere temporarily, I tended to keep myself disconnected from whatever was going on around me."

"Did that happen a lot?"

She gave him a sly look as she pulled the cap from the spray bottle. "Uh uh. We're not talking about me this time. It's the Chase show tonight."

Unexpected affection pulled a smirk across his lips. "Remember that observation about me being camera-shy?" he countered, though the effort was useless.

She raised a brow, looking like the stern teacher she was. No sassing Ms. Powell. That look must have slayed in the classroom because it cut right through him.

His next words poured out of him because of it. "It was during that time that my father was indicted for racketeering and fraud."

She grew very still, the reaction he was expecting there in her expression. But surprisingly, it didn't bother him. Not like it usually did. Maybe because it was Sadie. Or because he knew she was trying to hide it. He could tell when she was attempting to keep a reaction in check. She was terrible at it, so it was more obvious when she did. Definitely wasn't equipped for undercover work. And maybe that was another element of her draw. He would never question her intentions.

"My dad was in and out of prison most of my life," he continued. "So, I don't know, I always felt like I had something to prove. I was a straight-A student, model citizen. I volunteered; I sure as hell never got in trouble."

She still hadn't moved, one hand limply holding the spray bottle in her lap as she watched his face.

"I didn't want to be him. Be associated with that life. But even a scholarship to a nice college didn't get me out of it. Studying criminal justice, applying to the FBI. . . it followed me. My dad's reputation, though he wasn't some epic crime boss, was prolific enough that the director of the undercover division of the Bureau contacted me. He knew my father's name and reputation could work in our favor for undercover work."

Her head tipped sideways, like she was trying to figure out how he felt about it. But he wasn't sure exactly how he felt. Not in this moment, anyway. Not with her sitting so close to him. Not when her hand moved absently to the back of his neck, slender fingers tracing lightly along his skin.

"Because it was my reality, and if it meant I could do my job and accomplish something worthwhile, I jumped in. I didn't need a fake identity. I'd been hired so recently that it was easy for them to set it up like I'd been denied the job because of my dad's crimes. I used that story and my father's name to get my foot in the door, and I went in deep."

God, did she know how good it felt to have her fingers brushing along his skin in such a casually intimate way? He felt like he was being unraveled, one tight coil at a time.

"And you've been doing this ever since?" Her voice was barely above a whisper.

It would be easy to forget what they were talking about, to fall into her and drown it all in the depth of feeling she stirred in him. But this was too important to omit.

"I've been working this particular case for a couple of years," he said after a moment. "I had a different assignment before. I've established a certain reputation among these guys, so switching from one ring to another isn't that difficult when you're low-level."

She bit into her full bottom lip. "What kinds of things have you had to do?"

Every part of him froze. Even his heart stopped beating for a minute. He only started breathing again because his lungs screamed in agony. She'd asked the one thing he hoped she wouldn't. What had he done to get here? Who had he become to do the job? His gaze ran from hers.

"A lot of things I'm not proud of." The rest of the admission refused to surface, shame holding it captive. "Lines get blurred. This kind of job forces you to let things slide because there are bigger problems to deal with, scarier people to take down."

Miraculously, she accepted that answer. "How bad is this Zimmerman guy?"

He waited a beat, lamenting because her fingers had stopped playing with his hair, and she'd pulled back. The loss of that small touch almost devastated him, twisted his insides with regret.

He had to swallow before he could speak again. "Pretty bad. We're worried just how deep and how far his reach goes. I don't think your buddy Greg knew exactly what he was getting into when he took Zimmerman on."

She flinched at the mention of her ex and shook her head, lifting the spray bottle as if to distract herself from the reminder. The level of concentration she infused into the process of treating his hand might have made him laugh if the conversation they'd just had didn't fill his gut with lead. Holding the bottle about an inch from his knuckles, spritzing the broken skin. He tensed for it to sting, but it was cool and soothing.

She did the same to the other hand, not lifting her eyes. "Just let that soak in."

"What is it?"

The corner of her mouth curved up. "It's sort of like the crunchy lady version of triple antibiotic, but in spray form."

"Ah." Not that he totally understood, but if it worked and she felt like she was helping, he'd let her do whatever she wanted. The arnica had worked, so why not trust her with this too? With how much trust she'd placed in him, he owed her so much more.

His eyes shifted to the duffel bag on the arm of the couch behind her, and he knew he'd be asking her to extend a little more in the next few hours. He looked at his watch and felt her stiffen next to him.

"What's next?" she asked softly.

21

Free to Flee

Chase moved the car not long after, driving slowly along the dirt lane to keep from stirring the dust and giving himself away. Sadie watched from the kitchen window to be sure, chewing the edge of her thumb. The plan was to park far enough into the trees to be hidden but close enough to his driveway for a quick exit once they knew it was clear.

Then he trekked back toward the house so they could wait until nightfall when Santiago would come. He was sure the property was being watched, and leaving right away wasn't a gamble he wanted to take. There would be no way to know where Santiago or his spies were, and it made it easy for their enemy to follow if they left in broad daylight. He claimed to know Santiago's style, felt confident this was the best course of action.

They ate dinner in silence, the ticking clock tapping against Sadie's mind and preventing her from forming coherent thoughts. It was all just anxious *what-ifs*.

After dinner, while standing in the kitchen, she tracked his path as he moved through the house to make sure everything was set while she simply held herself, trying to keep the shuddering pieces of fractious emotions as together as she could.

The closer the time got, the more he morphed. He became alert, focused, distant. It made his movements seem more calculated and tactical and reminded her what his job truly was, who he always had to pretend to be.

A despairing sense of isolation stole through her as his eyes slid to the clock then to her and away. She didn't realize how much his tension set her on edge until she tasted the metallic tang of blood on her tongue and realized she'd chewed her thumb a little too hard. Even as she turned to look out the window at the fiery sunset, nothing soothed as the time crept closer like an incoming ocean tide. The inevitability threatened to drown her.

She flinched when Chase's big, warm hand brushed her hair back from her neck, kneading at the tight muscles there for a moment. The reassurance did as much as it was capable—letting her know that he was thinking about her, that he knew she was nervous. But it went no farther in actually dispelling the anxiety simmering inside her.

Especially when he went to retrieve a gun from the extra room. His eyes shot to her as if he thought she'd freak out at the sight before he tucked it into a holster at his back that made the sleek, black weapon practically disappear. He flipped the back of his shirt over it to cover the part that was still visible. Then he checked his watch, a bulky, black, tactical thing that would have dwarfed any other man's wrist.

"Is it time?" she asked, squeezing herself tighter.

His mouth tipped down. "Almost."

Her anxiety had rippled, an unpleasant tingle that billowed and coiled until she was so uncomfortable, she had to say something.

"We could stop on the way to get condoms for when this blows over." Her face flushed with heat as soon as the words left her mouth, and she started to curl in on herself. She wasn't sure what possessed her to say it at all, why that was the thing she chose to use as the tension breaker.

But Chase blinked and looked at her, his face cracking into a disbelieving smile. "Sadie. Good Lord."

She laughed, the sound wobbling with nerves and embarrassment. "I'm sorry. That was stupid. I shouldn't have said it."

He gave his head a shake as he chuckled softly. "No, it might be a good idea. We'll see what happens."

She nodded, dipping her head to hide how red her cheeks still were.

And then her unease buzzed like an annoying bug in the dark, tight space of the car's cab as they sat. She fought to keep her leg from bouncing, her eyes from dancing around the woods surrounding them.

And that's what her mind went to as a distraction, reminding her how idiotic it had been. She'd like to believe it was her rational side winning out, but she knew it was more of her impulsiveness shining through—that she would think about that instead of the practicalities of survival.

They'd hiked out to where the car was parked before darkness set in to wait until they spotted Santiago's vehicle coming down the driveway. Chase felt it was the only guaranteed way to sneak out and know exactly where Santiago would be. But it was taking longer than she'd anticipated, and she just wound tighter and tighter.

Chase must've been able to hear how her breathing came faster than normal because he reached over to take her hand.

"He's waiting for us to settle in for the night. Thinks he'll get the drop on us while we sleep," Chase murmured, though his soft words still punctured the silence like a needle to a balloon, and her whole body seized.

He squeezed her hand, sensing the reaction.

He'd explained earlier that as soon as Santiago headed around the bend, Chase would pull out of the trees and onto the road to their destination—the home of a friend of his, a fellow undercover agent he swore was trustworthy.

Another long, anxious stretch of time scraped along her skin. Then her stomach torqued, and she couldn't help her gasp when the sleek, black SUV pulled slowly from the road onto the dirt driveway with its headlights off. Moonlight bounced off of the shiny black paint and the darkly tinted windows as it rolled past their hiding spot.

Sadie sucked in a breath and didn't release it, thrown about the fact that Chase didn't react at all. But he'd had more practice in these kinds of situations.

Chase released her hand and reached for the keys hanging in the ignition, pausing as the brake lights from the SUV flashed back at them, jolting Sadie's heart. The red faded as the car rounded the bend, and Chase turned the key, throwing it in drive the second the engine turned over.

It was a process to maneuver the car out of the trees, but as soon as he cleared the line, he gunned it onto the road. Sadie twisted all the way around in her seat to check if anyone followed as his foot pressed more heavily into the gas pedal.

When no vehicle showed up behind them, she spun back around. Her hands gripped the armrest and the center console, an attempt to anchor her amid a spinning sense of panic as they bolted down the road, headlights off. The roads were empty of other cars and it ran pretty straight, but the worry wound around her gut as Chase kept his speed dangerously above the limit. The car flew past the dark trees that continued to flank the road for miles and miles.

She needed to channel her thoughts into something, anything, productive if she wanted to keep her sanity. "Does your friend know we're coming?" she asked, her voice strained.

Chase's eyes shifted to the rearview mirror. "No." His hands were tight on the steering wheel, knuckles so white it looked painful.

So he wasn't as untouched as he appeared to be.

"How do you know him again?"

"Kyle has been in the undercover game for a few years longer than I have. He showed me the ropes when I was just getting started, got me some connections."

She tried not to make a face. Chase had proven himself trustworthy and good, but that didn't mean it was true of every agent undercover.

"Does he work for Zimmerman?"

He shook his head. "Not specifically, but our circles overlap." He winced. "I haven't talked to him much in the last year. More responsibility with Zim means I haven't had time to maintain contact."

That didn't sound promising, and her stomach wound tighter until he finally flipped his lights on and reduced their speed. They'd started to encounter more cars as they got closer to the outskirts of Baltimore, its buildings flaring up against the darkness.

Chase's eyes went to the mirror again. For the first time in their thirty-minute flight, headlights flashed behind them, but he didn't speed up. "I think we're in the clear for now."

Streetlights popped up along their route as they got into the main drag of the city, the glow flashing over his face in waves, alternating between light and shadow like moving tiger stripes.

She released her grip on the armrest and console, dropping her hands into her lap, but they twisted together there, her panic replaced by the hum of her latent fear. Chase reached over to hold her hand in his again, and her fingers interlaced with his automatically.

"Kyle's is just a stopping point," he said. "Somewhere safe while I figure out my next step. I've gotta check in with my boss, Jared Gibson. He might have some insight for me."

She pulled her bottom lip between her teeth and nodded as they turned into some of the more rundown parts of town. Not the most dangerous but definitely not wholesome. It was the kind of neighborhood you might not worry about drive-bys but you would worry about break-ins.

It was late enough that some of the barred front windows were dark, while others still blazed with activity. Chase released Sadie's hand and parked. After he turned the car off, he waited, silent and motionless, maybe to see if anyone prowled down the street after them.

Minutes ticked by, each one building Sadie's anxiety higher. His focus jumped from house to house as if to check for nosy neighbors or lurkers on front porches.

Finally, he got out of the car, and she took it as her cue to follow, though she moved more slowly, weighed down by uncertainty and inexperience.

He walked to the trunk to retrieve his black duffel, shutting the lid softly, then rounded to the sidewalk where she stood. He took her hand and led her down a few houses. He'd probably parked in front of a different one on purpose.

The neighborhood was older, and the narrow sidewalk was barely wide enough for the two of them. The slabs of concrete were pockmarked and buckled along its cracks every few feet. In contrast to the aged homes and shoddy upkeep, there were beautiful, mature trees that shivered in the heavy summer breeze. They provided some manner of normalcy that lessened the anxiety inside her.

She matched Chase's light tread as he led her up the porch steps, assuming there was a reason. His edginess wasn't obvious, but it buzzed through their connected hands.

He rapped softly on the front door and released her hand. The silence snapped tighter, and she strained to listen for footsteps inside the house. There weren't any, but the door jerked open a fraction, and she almost jumped back.

She did take a step in retreat when the barrel of a gun caught the smallest sliver of moonlight.

Chase's hands came up. "It's Chase."

"Lundgren?" came the tight reply.

"Yes."

"Who's that with you?"

Chase turned to Sadie, and she practically folded in on herself. "Someone I'm trying to keep safe."

Kyle muttered a low oath and pulled the door open all the way to let them in, though he didn't quite lower his gun. He took Sadie in quickly as she shuffled by behind Chase, then his gaze swept the neighborhood before he shut the door and locked it behind them.

The entire house was dark, and the uncertainty crescendoed inside her. She missed the reassurance of Chase's hand in hers, but she didn't know what was acceptable in this situation, so she wrapped her arms around herself. It didn't do much to calm her.

"You're taking a big chance coming here, Lundgren," Kyle said as he walked past them to switch on a floor lamp against the opposite wall. His voice was gravelly and menacing—definitely not happy to see them.

The frail light illuminated the room just enough to show there wasn't much in it. Just a rickety TV stand and a beat up leather couch. The stereo and gaming system were pretty fancy, though.

"I just needed a safe place for the night until I figure out what to do," Chase said, drawing Sadie's attention back.

Kyle turned, dark brown eyes almost black in the dim light. He was a shorter, squat guy who was clearly packed with muscle. On top of the tight muscle, there was a layer of padding, giving him a menacing bulk. His hair was cropped so short, the sheen of his scalp was visible under the brown fuzz.

"What'd you get yourself into?" His gaze raked over Sadie again, this time with slow deliberation, and the faintest light of understanding glimmered in his eyes. "Doesn't look like a whore."

Chase stiffened.

"Excuse you," she growled. Or at least tried to. She was shocked to find she could feel offended in this situation. Were prostitutes their usual idea of female company?

Kyle's mouth twitched at her response.

"She's not a whore," Chase said through his teeth. "She's a kindergarten teacher who's caught in the crosshairs because of an ex-boyfriend."

Kyle squinted at him, brief humor dying. "Whose crosshairs?"

"Right now, just mine and Santiago's. But Zim will catch on soon enough."

"Fucking A, man." He shook his head, one hand curling into a fist. Then he jabbed a sharp finger in Chase's direction. "You have one night. I got a meet in the morning with Casper. You better be gone before I'm back from that. I'm not interested in this kind of trouble." He appraised Sadie again, jaw muscles working.

Chase held up his hands. "No problem."

Kyle's lips flattened, but he jerked his head for them to follow him down the hall. "I only have the one extra bedroom. You can have the couch."

Based on the way Kyle glanced back with a brow raised, it was apparent they weren't fooling anyone, but she kept her urge to touch Chase for reassurance in check anyway. It felt like a test, and Chase had put a distinct distance between them since they'd arrived.

Kyle stopped and gestured to a dark room, waiting. Sadie scooted past them both to go inside, and Kyle reached in to flip the light on, revealing a smallish bed on a wrought-iron frame. A worn quilt was spread neatly over it, but there was not much else to the room. She felt herself shrink.

"If, uh-if you need a change of clothes, there's some stuff in there." Kyle gestured to the closet. "Not much. Stuff I've been meaning to get rid of." His face had softened. "Ex-girlfriend left some shit."

Sadie nodded and turned to shut the door, that familiar sense of desolation snaking through her as her gaze locked with Chase's before the door was a barrier between them.

She faced the room again, fighting the urge to cry.

22

Over Your Head and Above Your Paygrade

Kyle pushed past Chase to head back down the hall to his living room. "You must be out of your damn mind," he hissed as soon as they had distance from the bedroom.

Definitely am, Chase thought as the compulsion to turn right back around and go to Sadie plucked at his self-control. She'd looked ready to burst into tears, and his arms ached to hold her.

"Your stoic fight to stay put is commendable. But I know exactly what this is." Kyle snatched a throw blanket from the floor in the corner and threw it at Chase with jerky aggression.

Though Kyle clearly knew what was up, Chase would never openly admit how far over his head he really was, so he grasped for the first verbal jab he could find.

"Ex-girlfriend, huh?" he said, dark humor in his voice, though he didn't smile. "She must have done a number on you."

The glare Kyle shot him was a weapon that would have dropped him dead. "I know a smart guy making dumb-ass decisions when I see one."

"I know a bitter bastard when I see one," Chase shot back.

He shook out the blanket to give himself something to do instead of letting the anger flare into a full on inferno. It wasn't Kyle's fault Chase was all wound up, or that he'd gotten himself into this. Or that Kyle might be right about him being out of his mind.

Kyle stopped moving, straightening to his full height—a good ten inches shorter than Chase—to give him a serrated stare. He'd always been rough around the edges, an easy pick for undercover work.

"You don't know what you're talking about, anyway," Chase said before Kyle could form his comeback. "This is about keeping an innocent woman alive."

"Doesn't hurt that she's drop-dead gorgeous, does it?" Kyle bit out. That edge of his had sharpened in the last year.

Chase kept his face from giving him away, though his stomach flipped, and his gaze threatened to pull away from Kyle's. He spread the blanket over the nearly defunct couch.

"Look, I get it, man." There was a rare softening in Kyle's demeanor, and Chase wondered exactly what had happened with that ex-girlfriend. "When you're the good guy, and there's a pretty girl that needs help, you feel like you're the only one who could offer it."

Kyle's intention fell flat with that last part, and the flame burned brighter, the dragon shifting inside of Chase. He stepped in Kyle's direction, knowing how much of a threat was laced in the movement.

"I *was* the only one," he growled, danger in his voice. "Santiago and Travers were on their way to her apartment. You know what those guys are capable of."

Kyle just crossed his arms over his barrel of a chest. Chase might have almost a foot on him, but he was a scrappy guy. "Yeah, and then what happened? You kept her with you. You're here instead of passing her off to the Bureau."

Based on Gibson's reaction when he'd called, it hadn't seemed like an option. But he hadn't asked and Gibson hadn't given him the choice. The mention of Gibson was the reminder that Chase needed. He walked his anger back, knowing it was misplaced.

"I need to check in with Gibson," Chase muttered. "You got a garage or somewhere I can park my car out of sight?"

Kyle's jaw shifted forward as he stared at Chase. Then his chin lifted. "Pull around back. I'll open the garage for you."

Chase made his way outside, though being out in the open gave his anxiety a little boost. Despite the night being heavier under the shade of the trees, he knew he would stand out to anyone watching, thanks to his height and bulk.

He breathed a sigh of relief when he got into his car, pulling out his phone at the same time he put the key in the ignition. He could fill Gibson in while driving around to the alleyway between rows of houses.

The conversation wasn't long, but he turned off the car and sat in the dim illumination offered by the overhead light while Gibson berated him.

"Quite a mess you've made, Lundgren," Gibson muttered, and Chase pictured the man running a hand over his face. "I'll see what I can do, but it's your ass on the chopping block."

"Noted, sir."

"Don't get smart with me, dipshit. Check in tomorrow."

When Gibson hung up on him, Chase sat for a few minutes more, brooding until the overhead light flicked off. He needed to shut the garage to keep his car hidden, so he forced himself out. The button to shut it glowed faintly so it could be found in the dark by searching hands, and the noisy machinery whirred to life when he pressed it, triggering the overhead light again as the door shimmied down.

He made a mental note of the gym equipment tucked into the far side of the space, and walked out to the backyard that divided the house from the garage, feeling less exposed because of the way Kyle had it landscaped. Large trees and bushes lined the fence on all sides, boxing him in and blocking all sound. It muted his footfalls along the curved stone path and trapped an extra measure of sticky summer heat.

The back porch had creaky stairs he couldn't combat with a light step, but he figured it didn't matter much. Probably better so that Kyle knew he was coming.

He shook his head. He'd hoped Gibson would have a protection option for Sadie, though Chase hadn't gotten any information from her that would label her as valuable in the Bureau's eyes. But surely having Santiago on their tail would've warranted some kind of guard.

He didn't like the flash of jealousy it inspired when he thought about no longer being the one in charge of her safety. And it likely wouldn't get her anything more than someone stationed outside her apartment, which didn't feel like enough. Not when he knew what Santiago was capable of, even if strategy wasn't his strong suit. Though his viciousness was legendary, he didn't think well on his feet, which was why he'd been playing second-fiddle to Chase for the last year, staying firmly in the "muscle" category.

And why he hated Chase so much.

Now Gibson was pissed at him for this turn of events, and not just because it was almost midnight. The verbal beating Chase sustained might have knocked him down in the past, but no part of him felt the heat now. Not when he thought of what might've happened if he'd done absolutely nothing.

Once Chase got back inside, he settled in on Kyle's couch as the other man headed off to bed with a tired wave, the old wood floors groaning as he walked down the hall. The adrenaline rush of having Chase show up on his doorstep had likely drained him considering that, in this business, nothing good showed up on your porch at midnight.

Chase tucked his arm behind his head since he had no pillow and Kyle's only extras were currently in the room with Sadie. Staring at the ceiling, he worked to ignore the lumpiness of the couch and the fact that his feet hung off the end. In the quiet and stillness, the unease slithered through him. Although he had no regrets about doing what he could to keep Sadie safe, he didn't like not having a plan laid out.

Strategy was one of his strong suits, but he'd taken some unanticipated steps, throwing himself onto a path that was only lit behind him. He could feel his way through the dark, find that thread to get onto a mapped-out course eventually, but it had seemed wisest to tap the higher-ups. Operating as an island meant he could only do so much to keep Sadie safe. With that as his priority, his determination to bring the whole thing down solidified.

A sound reached his ears, snapping him to full alertness, and he sat up. A shadow moved against the heavy darkness in the room, though he felt it more than saw it.

"Chase?" It was Sadie whose whisper danced through the shadows toward him.

"Are you okay?"

"I can't sleep." She stopped uncertainly before him like she was waiting for an invitation.

He lifted the measly blanket, lying back so she could she climb in with him, lay her body along his, and burrow against his chest.

"I'm worried."

He sighed, hating and loving that her worry drove her into his arms. Lying on the couch with her snuggled into him was like the fruition of a fantasy he never knew he had, and a flash of uncertainty about handing her off to his bosses burned through his veins. The only way to guarantee anything was to have her right here with him.

"I'm sorry." His words dropped into the darkness like a weight, heavy with all the things he was and wasn't responsible for but felt regret about anyway.

"Don't be sorry."

He took a breath, ready to argue.

"Just hold me." The words were so soft, he barely heard them.

That he could do.

Sometime in the wee hours of the morning, she stirred. He slept only in snatches but the warmth of having her in his arms kept him content, even if he got little actual rest.

She must've been worried about Kyle catching them because she wordlessly pressed her lips to his and snuck back through the weighty darkness to the hallway.

Kyle had covered every window in his house with blackout curtains to keep it dark when he slept and to prevent prying eyes from getting the drop on him. He was a paranoid guy, having been in this game longer than he probably should have. Add to that the fact that he'd grown up on the streets of inner city Chicago, gotten blown up in the army by bombs in the middle east, and spent most of his time these days around thugs and mobsters, it made sense.

It was similar to why Chase had set himself up with the cabin. He needed an escape from that world to shake the grime before it perforated his soul and took root.

It wasn't long after she left that he gave up on elusive sleep and got up, peeking out the curtain over the front window. Sunrise was leaking into the inky sky with a faint orange glow. His unease still shimmered inside him like the dying starlight.

Kyle would sleep a few hours more, and Chase hoped Sadie would as well. He should probably run to the gas station to fill up his car. There was no telling how quickly they'd have to get up and go as soon as Gibson had a place for them, and he was only a few gallons away from the light popping on. It didn't hurt that he could take care of their barrier problem, which she'd unexpectedly reminded him about the day before, the reason behind it tumbling endlessly in his mind.

Because the need still simmered under his skin. The demand to feel Sadie in every possible way, especially after they'd lain together half the night on Kyle's couch. That had felt more intimate than anything they could have done sexually. She had become more than just a physical thing though, not just a presence in his space, a reminder that he'd gone wildly off path.

He headed toward the back of the house and nimbly leapt from the top step to avoid the noise. He wanted to do this as quickly and quietly as possible, without alerting the others.

Kyle kept his garage remote clipped to his sun visor, and he left the car unlocked while it was parked inside. So it was a matter of opening the driver side door and snatching it so that Chase's exit would be quick and easy.

He'd made a mental note about the nearest gas station on their drive in. It was only a mile or so down the road, which was convenient, considering his gas light blinked on right before he pulled in, confirming his earlier guesstimate.

The city was starting to come to life, the early morning workers already about their business, though he felt fairly confident about the hour being his temporary protection against the possibility of Santiago finding him. They'd be long gone from Kyle's before Santiago could even think about where they were.

He might not even think Chase had sought out Kyle. He was way outside of the Spaniard's circle. It was Casper, the man Kyle was set to meet later that morning, who'd been his actual connection point for Zim's operations. He was a networking guy among these kinds of syndicates, the go-between for the various rings who sometimes worked together when need arose.

Chase was in and out of the gas station in a matter of ten minutes, the sky alerting him that the sun would soon blaze the remaining night away, and headed back toward Kyle's.

Instead of going inside though, he took the opportunity to pound out enough of a workout to burn off some of the residual nerves that continued to fire off throughout his body.

He knew Kyle wouldn't mind and figured it would get his day started right.

When he came back inside, it was still dark and quiet, but the sense of time slipping by without traction chased away the relief the workout had given him. He took a quick shower and came back out to a slice of sunlight bursting from the small, boxed-in kitchen.

When he rounded the corner, he spotted Sadie at the stove, reaching to turn on a burner, a mixing bowl cradled in her arm.

It stopped him dead in his tracks to see her, barefoot and with her hair piled in a bun on top of her head. A mess of pancake mix was scattered on the counter, and he had that out-of-body experience again, like he was seeing another version of his life, and he couldn't keep himself from moving in behind her to slide his hands around her waist.

"Are you hungry?" she asked, and he heard the smile in her voice, was soothed by how loose and relaxed she was in his arms.

He looked over her shoulder to inspect the pancake batter. "You're breaking the kidnapper/kidnappee code."

"What about the middle-of-the-night flight to protect the woman you kidnapped code? Surely there's a caveat in that one that allows for me to make a thank-you breakfast?"

He huffed a laugh and forced himself to break away, moving to the sink as he snatched a paper towel, getting it wet so he could wipe the counter down. Kyle had never been a particularly fastidious guy, but Chase figured since they were trespassing on his begrudging kindness, they could at least make it feel less like they'd ever been there.

"Are you thanking me or Kyle?" he asked.

Her tongue slipped out between her lips as she carefully poured batter into the pan, the soft sizzle of heat permeating the air. "Both." She grinned at him, and his chest pinched.

A search through the cupboards and fridge yielded the cache of maple syrup and butter they'd want for the pancakes.

He set both on the counter and leaned back against it, bracing himself on either side. "How's your ankle?"

Her brows furrowed, and she looked down at the offending joint like she'd forgotten it existed. "A lot better."

"Good." Good because it meant she would be able to run if the need arose. Tension pooled in his gut at the thought. Hopefully it wouldn't come to that.

He busied himself with making coffee, knowing Kyle would want some, and wondered if their circumstances had gotten her to relax her standards at all.

She eyed the bag he scooped grounds from, her mouth twisting to the side, which told him she was wavering. "I'll just have a sip of yours. To ward off a caffeine withdrawal headache."

He chuckled, adding some extra scoops, figuring she'd drink half of his.

23

Flash Drive

After finishing breakfast, Sadie snuck back to the guest room. They'd left some pancakes for Kyle, and she hoped he'd soften a little at the gesture.

She was grateful even if she'd been unable to sleep on the hard bed that sagged in the middle and had that musty smell that came with old houses and hand-me-down linens. The whiffs of strong fragrance that gave away his use of popular, toxic laundry detergent had mixed with the dank smell and given her a headache.

Sleep had been nearly as hard-won in Chase's arms, but her mind had been more settled because of his familiar warmth and scent. He must have used an unscented detergent because she'd only ever smelled his quintessential fragrance in the linens of his bed.

He wasn't the least bit conscious of those sorts of things, but maybe he didn't like strong scents. Or maybe it was just the cheapest option at the time. She didn't know him well enough to guess at his purchasing motivations. All she knew was that she'd already grown accustomed to that unique foresty scent of his that lingered in his bed sheets and tried to distract herself from the weird sense of homesickness it inspired.

She could make a list of less toxic detergents for his next purchase. There was a running list of brands and prices in her purse, among many other things, that she could share with him.

She shut her eyes, trying to still her mind. Because this line of thinking was absolutely absurd under the circumstances. No longer just kidnapped by an undercover FBI agent, but now on the run, staying in the house of another undercover agent with rougher edges than the first.

And she was thinking about laundry detergent.

Probably better than thinking about what would happen next, though. If she dwelled on any of it too long, she'd start to freak out, and she needed to be as calm as possible. She couldn't make this any more difficult for the people currently involved.

Her eyes lit on the closet across from her. She should let her curiosity take over and search the contents of the closet for the extra clothes Kyle had mentioned the night before. A shower and fresh digs sounded nice.

She was careful to slide the doors open quietly, not sure how to read Kyle's feelings about the fact that they existed or that she might wear them.

There wasn't much she would pick for herself. A lot of flashy, revealing pieces that weren't practical. But she managed to find a white v-neck tee and a pair of jeans that were probably too short, but she could roll them up at the hem to make them look intentionally that way.

When she came out of the room, she glanced back and forth down the hall and practically sprinted across to the small bathroom for her shower. Washing her hair was unnecessary since it hadn't been that long since the last time. Plus she didn't want to use any products she couldn't pronounce the ingredients in.

Crackers, she sounded like a snob.

After her shower, she found she had to shimmy the jeans on, grateful they had a little give in the fabric. Otherwise, she would've had to stick with her linen pants that still had that little hole along the seam.

As she suspected, the jeans were too short, but they would do for now, so she left the bathroom in search of Chase. She wondered if there was any news from his boss—Gibson, he'd called him—about their next step. Regardless, they'd have to leave sometime that morning, as promised.

She found Chase in the kitchen, leaning against the counter with a mug of coffee in his hand. A picture of calm, though she knew his natural tension was there below the surface almost always. It pulled tighter the second he saw her, though it eased after a moment.

It was like her presence was a shot to his system until he leveled out, those eyes going flaming bright. Or maybe it was that he was thrown by her change of clothes. The jeans were a little tight, after all.

She walked across the small kitchen to inspect the contents of the coffee pot.

"It's not organic. Might even be laced with coke."

She jerked to look at him, but he was smiling at her, that muted, sexy grin making her insides flip. "I'm just going to have a sip of yours, remember?"

"I drink it black with a whole mess of sugar."

She wrinkled her nose. "Maybe not, then."

A few sips though. Because of the headache thing.

She took a mug from the cupboard next to him and poured two fingers of black liquid inside, then moved to the fridge to check for milk or half-and-half. She grunted when the waist of the jeans jabbed into her stomach, reminding her that she'd all but stuffed herself into them.

Chase muttered a curse under his breath, drawing her questioning gaze.

He shifted uneasily. "You in those jeans."

Apparently, they were just tight enough. She tried to hide her smile. "Karma for the coffee comment."

He shook his head and turned to set his coffee mug on the counter, likely to keep his eyes from her backside as she searched the fridge. She found the half-and-half and pretended not to notice it wasn't full-fat or organic. The pickings were slim, and she was not exactly in a position to be fussy.

She pulled it out, straightening. "Maybe you should do a grocery run as a thank you to Kyle."

Chase snorted. "Please tell me you're not going to suggest I buy you more underwear."

She grinned as she turned to add the cream to the coffee. "Nah. Just jeans that fit."

"Please, God, no." He hooked a finger in a belt loop to pull her flush against him.

She laughed, but the sound was breathless as every part of her threatened to catch on fire. "You might have to cut me out of these, honestly."

A growl rumbled deep in his chest, and it vibrated through her. "This is a terrible time to put that image in my head."

Shuffling footsteps sounded in the hall, and a thrill of panic danced down Sadie's spine as she pulled away. Not just because of the possibility of Kyle catching them, but also because she was wearing his ex-girlfriend's clothes, and she still wasn't sure how he might react.

Chase released her with reluctance then reached for his mug of coffee as Kyle padded into the ever-shrinking kitchen. Sadie moved as far from Chase as she possibly could, though it only put about three feet between them.

Kyle's dark eyes shifted between them, and he grunted. She realized it was a greeting only after Chase uttered a "good morning" back.

"Coffee's ready," Chase added, taking a sip of his sugared, black brew.

Kyle grunted again, reaching into the corner for the pot, which was right behind Sadie. She leapt from her spot, shuffling toward Chase again. The sense of being trapped was a flash through her before it dissipated.

All it took was a reminder that she was safe, if uncomfortable.

"I, um, made pancakes. If you're interested." She brushed at the wispy bits of hair that never stayed in her buns behind her ear, feeling the flame of Chase's gaze on her face.

Kyle turned, holding his mug. "Thanks," he muttered, walking past them back to his dining room.

Chase pushed away from the counter and followed.

She turned to grab her own mug and went out too, feeling awkward about staying in the kitchen alone. She felt nearly as awkward about lingering in the dining room while Chase addressed Kyle, who clearly was not ready for a full conversation.

Chase asked about the other man's meeting with "Casper," and they launched into details that kind of went over her head.

Kyle asked about news from Gibson, which Chase replied to in the negative.

"Don't worry. If I don't hear from him in the next hour, Sadie and I will head out anyway."

Kyle did another one of his grunts.

Sadie licked her lips and made her way back to the guest bedroom to find her purse and the lip balm hidden in its depths. Her lips were dry, but it was mostly to put some distance between herself and the conversation the men were having that had started to twist her stomach up.

Because they were talking about the world she'd never truly understand—the one she'd been pulled into against her will. Indignation and anger mixed into a toxic poison in her veins when she thought about what had brought her to this point. Greg and his stupid ambitions, his half-cocked ideas, his what? revenge against her?

She didn't want the reminder of why she was in this stranger's house, cut off from her family, her job, her life. Thoughts of that made her heart stop dead, the pain constricting her ribs. Surely they were all worried.

Was her family in danger now that Santiago was zeroed in on her? And would she even have a job at the library when—if—she got back? Roberta might not want her around if she disappeared the same day that agents of the FBI had come to question her about her ex's shady dealings.

She held her floppy purse against her chest, lip balm forgotten as she thought about the possible ramifications of what had happened to her. All because she'd stuck around too long with a man unworthy of her time.

It was a reminder to her of what happened when she went against her instincts. Sure, she was accused of being fickle at times, which was why she'd forced herself to stick with Greg, but she had a decent read on people and situations. Why waste her time?

Never again, she decided.

"Hey."

She jerked at Chase's voice, dropping her purse to the floor as she spun to face him. He was ducking sheepishly through the door, nearly filling the space with his broad shoulders and height.

"Sorry." He came in, his eyes going to the floor where her purse had landed, spilling its guts on the hardwood floor.

They both crouched to clean up the items that had escaped.

"Kyle headed out, and I wanted to make sure we were all set and ready to leave."

"Right." Her stomach flipped as she scooped the random knick-knacks that had no business being in her purse back into it. She really needed to clean it out. It was a little ridiculous to find the still in-package toothbrush she'd gotten at her last dentist appointment almost four months ago and, not one, but two half-filled boxes of crayons.

At least she'd found her lip balm. Her fingers closed over it and something else that had skittered under the bed, and she pulled it out while Chase shoved the rest of her spilled stuff into the purse.

She palmed the lip balm and held up the other object to get a good look in case it was more nonsense or something she could throw out.

A flash drive? Tipping her head to the side, she tried to remember when the last time she'd used a flash drive was. Her new laptop didn't even have a port for one.

Every muscle in her body snapped tight as she sucked in a breath. Chase must have thought she was in pain or something because he reached out like he was going to yank her to him.

She just shook her head to ward him off and held up the innocuous-looking flash drive for him to see.

His brow wrinkled. "What?"

"This isn't mine." Her pulse throbbed in her ears.

She thought about the people who were looking for her, the feds who'd questioned her, and the way Greg had acted when they'd run into each other that day. He'd been nervous. But he'd also been uncharacteristically friendly without asking a thing of her. And he'd given her that really awkward hug.

"Sadie, what are you saying?" Chase's voice was edged with apprehension, cracking on the air.

She cringed as it bit through the slowly building panic stirring in her chest. "I-I don't know. I just. . . It's not mine. And Greg hugged me that day." Her shoulders inched upward at the memory. "Like, wrapped his arms around me so oddly."

They both lifted their eyes, green locking with hazel, and she felt a twang down to her toes.

He snatched the drive and slipped a hand under her arm to help her to her feet. "You got everything?"

She nodded, but he wasn't looking at her, his mind already turning things around. The vibration of energy rolling off him as he turned toward the door was palpable, and she hurried to follow him out to the living room.

He yanked his duffel from behind the dilapidated couch, sliding out a bulky, black laptop, different than the one he'd used before. This one was heavy-duty.

He sat on the couch, looking up at her with a quirk of his brows like a question, as if he were asking if she was joining, and she sat, his hand going to her thigh for the briefest of reassuring touches. A spot in her middle warmed to have him take the time despite the circumstances and his tension.

One of his fingers tapped against the edge of the computer screen, which was the only real indication that he was anxious about what they might find on the flash drive. His expression remained unreadable otherwise.

She felt her own stress inside, but it bubbled and simmered down deep because she still didn't know the depth of the implications associated with it. Her job—her life—didn't depend on it.

Or maybe they did because that was the whole reason she was here, forever changed after a chance encounter with an ex she'd had no intention of ever talking to again. He'd pulled her into this with his idiotic attempts to get ahead in life. It made her angry that even though she'd wasted all that time with him, she *had* cut ties. And still he'd pulled her back in, put her in danger. He'd specifically chosen to go to her apartment, intentionally putting that target on her back. He'd waited for her at the coffee shop, one he'd scorned in the past. It wasn't a chance encounter. Fiona had been right.

She shoved the anger down as Chase plugged the drive into the port and a file appeared on his desktop, popping up brazenly like it wasn't possibly life-changing for both of them—the reason for the tangled situation they were in.

It was in slow motion that he moved the mouse to click on it. And when it opened, none of the letters formed comprehensible words. Then she realized it was a list of names, though none of them meant anything to her. At first.

And then she started to recognize some of them. Names that sent darts of shock through her. Seeing these people who shouldn't have been on a list that belonged to a corrupt white-collar criminal hammered her with dread and fear.

She glanced at Chase, and the speed with which he was reading through the names concerned her. Especially because of the way his muscles bunched and tightened.

Then he abruptly stood from the couch, setting the laptop on the coffee table. He stared at the screen, breathing hard, his fists clenching and unclenching.

She leaned forward. "What is it?"

He spared her the briefest of glances before he turned to his duffel bag, pulling out his gun and checking for ammo.

His reaction scared her. But so did the stiffness in his body, his silence, the length of the list on the screen.

Obviously she didn't know every name on it, but the ones she saw, the ones that shocked her, gave her a small inkling of what they might be dealing with. A district attorney she'd met once, a couple of judges who'd presided over some major cases she'd heard about in the news.

That alone meant this was bad.

But someone on that list had upset Chase enough that he was spinning, and that made her stomach torque. If he was thrown off, surely she should be.

"Chase." His name shot out of her mouth, fear tripping over itself in her mind.

He finally looked at her, chewing the inside of his cheek, and a hardness settled in his gaze. "Casper is on that list."

She blinked. She'd missed it, but she hadn't known what she was looking at initially. Plus the name meant very little to her. "The guy Kyle is meeting with?"

Chase tipped his head in acknowledgment, pulling out his cell phone to scroll and click through it until he brought it to his ear. After a few seconds, a curse rattled through his teeth as he hung up, and he looked like he wanted to throw the phone across the room.

The implication alone was terrifying, but maybe it was something else. God, she hoped it was something else.

"Are you sure this isn't just a hit list or something?"

His lips flattened, becoming a colorless line. "Some of these others are known Zimmerman associates."

She fell back against the couch like she been shoved.

He stared down at the floor, breathing hard for three full seconds. "I have to go find Kyle. If Casper is on this list, he's been compromised. And it's my damn fault for coming here and dragging Kyle into this."

"Maybe he doesn't know anything." Doubt wrapped itself around her voice.

Chase jerked to look at her. "Casper is who connected me with Zimmerman, got me into that ring. And he knows we're FBI."

Panic lit like a flame in her core. "Crackers," she breathed.

"I need you to stay here. Lock all the doors and wait for me to come back."

He started toward the back of the house, but then he spun abruptly and came back toward her, pulling her from the couch and into his arms in one swift motion. His kiss came hard and fast against her lips before he set her back on her feet.

"Be careful," she whispered.

And then he was gone.

24

Attacked

Tension rippled down Chase's spine as soon as he left Kyle's house, his eyes repeatedly going to his rearview mirror. How long had it been since Kyle left? Did he have time to sweep the street for anything unusual?

He drove slowly around and decided the extra two minutes wouldn't be wasted if he checked the cars lined up at the curb in front of the houses. No one was just idly sitting in any of the few vehicles on the street, and he noted that the front window of Kyle's house was still obscured by a black curtain.

When Sadie had left the dining room earlier, Chase finagled information from Kyle about his meet with Casper, some premonition of things to come urging him to cover all his bases just in case his dumb-ass decisions got Kyle into trouble. He sent little prayers up that Casper didn't know a thing about Santiago's little side mission and that Zim had yet to be informed of Chase's recent extracurriculars. It was just to be on the safe side, to make sure nothing had happened to Kyle because of his choice to seek asylum at his house.

The drive wasn't long to the seedy motel where Kyle said he was going. It was only a few miles, and soon enough, Chase was pulling into the parking lot. There was no fancy entrance, no building with a big lobby where anyone could see you coming and going. It was just a string of dilapidated rooms attached by flimsy walls. Each had its own door to the outside world, offering a discreet entrance and exit to those who wanted to lie low.

Chase swung the car around to the back corner where the afternoon sunlight didn't reach, solidifying the impression that this was a place where dark deeds were done. He spotted Kyle's car, and the disquiet crept through him.

He threw the car in park and did a sweep of the parking lot before he set his eyes on that door in the corner and got out. The tension kept twisting, and he was ready to crawl right out of his skin. The feeling coalesced and sharpened as he pulled out his gun, and he stopped dead in his tracks for a split second before he reached for the knob.

Then he took a breath and turned it, swinging the door open to a dark room that immediately felt wrong. Even before he spotted Kyle on the bed, he knew he shouldn't go inside, experiencing that ripple of instinct right before the fist swung at his head. He ducked back just in time. But he wasn't expecting the second guy who yanked his gun hand, knocking it from his grasp as he went staggering inside.

He caught himself on the edge of the single queen bed where Kyle was lying casually as if he were sleeping. Except his eyes were wide and unblinking, and coagulated blood trailed down the side of his face from a bullet hole in his temple.

Chase made some quick calculations. Two guys, neither of them Casper. Probably Santiago's. And if Kyle was dead, and these thugs were here, that meant Santiago was either on his way or already at Kyle's house. And wherever Santiago went, his greasy shadow followed.

"Welcome to the party," a gravelly voice said, menace infiltrating the layers.

Chase spun away from the bed, kicking the legs out from under the man, who uttered a string of curses as he went down with a thud. Chase searched the dark room for the other guy, and, most importantly, his gun. But his eyes hadn't adjusted to the dim light yet, and the second attacker had an opening to pick up a chair, slamming it into Chase's side. A spider web of pain shot with lightning speed through his rib cage.

He took a wheezing breath and mustered the strength to spin away again, catching sight of the dark shape of his gun on the floor close to the door. Scrambling to his feet, he lurched for the weapon, grappling for the handle. He turned and fired off the first round at the first guy, who jerked sideways and caught it in the shoulder instead of the chest like he should have.

"Son of a bitch," the man muttered, lurching back.

The move cost Chase, and he wasn't able to prepare for the lamp the second guy used against his face. He caught it square against his cheekbone, the skin spearing open on impact as his teeth rattled together.

The other man chuckled darkly as the hot copper taste of blood blossomed inside Chase's mouth. Must have sliced the inside of his cheek on his teeth. He spat red onto the floor, trying to calculate his next step when another blow landed against the back of his head. Something hard.

Spots clouded his vision, and when it cleared, he was starting to topple face-first into the carpet. The image of Sadie's terrified, panic-twisted face filled his mind, and he remembered that she was alone and defenseless against that asshole and his slimy underling.

Thinking about Travers putting his hands on her again filled Chase's vision with red. The rage poured into his body with a blinding heat that was beyond his ability to fathom, that he quickly lost control of. It was like his soul left his body the minute he gave himself over to it, and he watched himself from above as the dragon took control.

His huge frame pushed up from the floor, releasing an inhuman roar as he plowed into the second man, ramming him into the opposite wall like a linebacker. Chase pulled him forward by his throat and slammed again. The guy's head snapped back against the surface, making a crater in the drywall, and he flopped down to the ground, unmoving.

There was a small sound from behind that reached Chase's ears, and his full consciousness slid back into his body just in time for him to catch an arm around his neck as the other guy attempted to trap him in a headlock. He could tell the man was losing strength because of his gunshot wound, and Chase was able to block him from completing the move.

Planting a foot behind the other man's, Chase forced the guy backward, and he tripped and went down. Chase's breaths shot in and out of him in rapid succession as he pawed the floor for his dropped gun. He barely managed to aim before he pulled the trigger once, twice, and the guy dropped in a heap.

There was only space for one moment to catch his breath and his racing thoughts before he lumbered to his feet and staggered out the door. He would have sprinted if he could get enough air. But every breath hurt, and he wondered if he'd broken a rib. His cheek was swelling, too. He could see it as the puffiness infiltrated the skin around his eye on that side. Swinging into his car, he grunted and panted as he yanked the door closed. He didn't bother to buckle up as he whipped out of the parking space and sped through the lot to the street, steering one-handed.

He wouldn't tempt fate, though, and kept his speed at a reasonable level above the limit, cursing his way through two red lights and punching it as soon as he came to Kyle's neighborhood. His tires screeched on the pavement, and gravel pinged against the undercarriage of his car as he barreled down Kyle's street.

They'd hear him coming, but he didn't care. He had no capacity for planning, for strategy, for stealth.

The sick feeling twisted in his belly that they wouldn't be at the house anymore, anyway. Still, he sped through the tunnel of trees, his breathing continuing to come fast and painful as the house came into view.

No other vehicles out front. No movement in the window. He stomped on the brakes, the back end of the car fishtailing as it lurched to a stop at the curb in front of the house.

He threw it into park and practically leaped out of the car, sprinting up the steps, ignoring the way his body protested. There was no wondering if the door was unlocked, no need to ring the bell or knock. It was broken, shards of wood on the porch at his feet, and he slowed only long enough to pull his weapon.

He walked through the house cautiously once, then slammed through the whole place again, looking for any kind of clue, praying that his instinct was wrong. That she'd gone for a walk, that he'd imagined the broken door, that this was all just a nightmare he would wake from.

But the constant throb through his ribs reminded him that he was awake and living the nightmare.

He caught sight of himself in a mirror, wincing. His eyes were wild, his hair mussed, his cheek swollen and bruising. Blood dripped from the corner of his mouth. It didn't matter though. He lurched toward the door before he thought better of it. He needed to regroup, figure out his next steps first. Figure out where Santiago had taken her.

When he turned from the door, he spotted his laptop half-hidden under the couch. *Hidden*. Like she'd done it on purpose.

He stalked toward it and hissed when he bent to retrieve it, the pain ricocheting through him again. He flipped it open and unlocked it. It was still open to the list of names from the flash drive, but it was scrolled to the end, and his heart slammed down to his toes.

Jared Gibson, his boss. Had she recognized the name? Maybe she'd seen it and run. God, he hoped that was the case and not that his boss had sold him out and told Santiago where to find them.

He was such an idiot. Except he was *supposed* to trust his boss with his safety, was required to check in. But he hadn't taken the time to go through the whole list that first time, his worry for Kyle, founded but too late anyway, had blinded him. He forced himself to look at the other names now, to make sure he didn't go off half-cocked. If he'd known Gibson was compromised, he never would've left her alone.

But his mind whirled as he kept reading, noting the other names that made his stomach twist so tightly, he thought he'd vomit. Hank Jeppesen. Larry Fink. Upper-level agents.

Good God.

He shut the laptop with barely contained rage, the snap making him pause to wonder if he'd broken it. He inhaled deeply, curling his fingers into his palms.

Maybe she'd just gone for a walk.

The thought reverberated in his mind, empty and hollow. He looked at the front door where the wood had splintered off, the light color of the interior a contrast with the dark green it had been painted. Implausible. Not possible with the way that door looked. Someone had kicked it in.

Chase's phone rang, and he hit answer before looking.

"You got out faster than even I anticipated," Santiago said. He didn't sound irritated. More like amused.

"Where is she?" Chase demanded.

A dark, husky chuckle filled his ear. "Right here with me."

Chase's fingers became a fist at his side, air shooting out of his flared nostrils. Pain ran along his ribs like little fissures of agony with every breath, but his fury relegated it to background noise.

"You want her?" Santiago said, a smile in his voice. "Come get her."

"Where?" Monosyllables were all he could manage. He wanted to rip something—some*one*—apart. His body shook, his blood screamed with the need.

Santiago rattled off an address. "You have a time limit," he added. "Get here before the boss does, and you can have her. Seven p.m., Lundgren."

Santiago hung up before Chase could respond. He chucked the phone into the cushions of the couch, stalking away. His hands ached from being clenched so tightly, from fighting the urge to destroy something.

A plan. He needed a plan—something productive to channel the rage into.

There was a time limit.

A quick search of the address and for any info on the web to help him get his bearings yielded little more than a few images of a warehouse in the middle of nowhere. Everything in his duffel bag seemed insufficient against it.

He prowled through the house, looking for any secret stashes of weapons or supplies, finding hardly anything but a couple of extra handguns. Then he realized it would probably be the garage where he'd find anything that might be of use.

He wheeled back toward the living room, snatching his bag and the laptop, and strode to the back door, out, and to the garage.

The space was expansive when no vehicles sat inside, but it was cluttered all along the walls like Kyle had wanted to create too much visual noise as a distraction. It was a smart way to discourage people from looking through his stuff.

Chase took a coil of thick rope from a hook on the wall, figuring it would come in handy at the warehouse, then searched through the overflowing, disorganized toolboxes until he came across a crooked drawer. Pulling it out revealed a mess of dirty tools, but he felt along the lip of the drawer until he found a catch and pressed it.

A hidden panel slid out, and his eyes traced over the guns and knives at his disposal, a cold, calculation taking over like a computer program. Specs played through his mind as he perused. Which would be easiest to conceal and get to, which was most accurate, what was practical.

How many guys would Santiago have on his side? He wanted to believe that Travers would be an easy target. He was an idiot. But Santiago was no idiot, and there had to be some reason he kept him around.

And given that fact, Chase couldn't underestimate what he was walking into.

25

Stolen

Sadie couldn't stop staring at the laptop, even when the screen went dark. The names she'd recognized made her stomach churn. It didn't help that Chase was so thrown and that she was now alone in the house with a big question mark in front of her.

Maybe if they could figure out the end-game, like maybe what Greg's plans were, they could do something other than run and hide. She tapped the mouse pad lightly, wishing it would somehow make something that wasn't there appear in her mind. A clue about Greg's whereabouts, a hint about what would happen next.

But nothing would magically change about what she knew—or didn't know—because it simply didn't exist.

At least they'd finally figured out what Greg had done to pull her into his mess. A stupid, tiny, innocuous flash drive she never would've noticed because she never cleaned out her purse.

And she still had no idea why he'd dragged her into it, what his motives were. They'd broken up months before, and though it hadn't been exactly amicable, it hadn't been fraught either. At least she hadn't thought it was, despite her growing sense of his deficiencies as a boyfriend.

She checked the clock that ticked benignly from the wall above Kyle's TV, pretty much the only decoration in the room. Maybe his ex had taken all the homey touches when she'd left. If that's what had happened. It was as good a guess as any.

The need to feel useful, to do something vibrated through her, making it hard to sit still. She chewed her lip, stood to pace the room, simply held herself to still the thundering unease from shaking her apart. It was hard not to watch that clock. She knew from a lifetime of experience as the least patient person on the planet that sitting on the clock would make it move slower.

The laptop screen dimmed and one of her fingers tapped against her elbow. They hadn't scrolled through the entire list. How long was it?

The rest of the names would probably mean nothing to her, but she couldn't make her mind settle, couldn't figure out how to dispel the dread that moved like sludge through her body, giving her a sick feeling she couldn't shake.

Down she scrolled, names rolling past with no click of recognition. She swallowed and looked at the clock. Twenty-five minutes.

Still, the list went on. Then, at the bottom, a name that made her pause, a flash of familiarity blazing bright.

Jared Gibson.

Gibson.

Wasn't that the name of Chase's boss?

Almost the second the thought slammed home, she heard footsteps on the porch. The relief began to flood her in a warm deluge. That was faster than she'd hoped. Maybe he'd seen that Kyle was fine and headed back to her.

She was about to stand up when the knob jiggled, and her eyes shot to the door.

"Hey, pretty girl. I know you're in there."

The rat-faced man.

Nausea was a straight shot to her stomach at his sickly sweet voice. She slammed the laptop shut and shoved it under the couch just as a loud blast of sound splintered the door, and she dove for the floor with a scream as sharp wedges of wood sprayed in her direction. Scrambling to her feet, she staggered toward the back of the house. There was a back door, a backyard. Was there an exit? Was there an extra vehicle? She had no keys, though, and how far would she get on foot? Could she get to a neighbor?

She yelped and skittered to a stop when the back door burst open, kicked in by a booted foot, and banged against the wall. A big man filled the doorway with a smile on his face. He was probably the one who was in charge—Santiago. Although not as towering as Chase was, the dark and handsome part came right along after tall. A ripple of danger rolled off of him like a black aura.

Even knowing it was a wasted effort, she spun to go back the way she'd come, but the rat-faced man was there, sneering at her and blocking her way. He aimed his gun right at her.

Trapped like a scared cat. She shifted backward, keeping her eyes on the rat-faced man as he stepped closer. Her legs bumped into the table, and she placed a palm on its surface to steady herself.

"And here we find you. Alone. And left to roam free," the man behind her said.

She looked back at Santiago, his teeth glimmering garishly white against the tawny color of his skin. He shut the door behind him, the blatant sound of the deadbolt sliding home piercing the air, and she flinched. Maybe if she moved around the table, lured them closer, she could get to the door.

"Funny how he'd let you wander when you were supposed to be his captive." Santiago flicked his head as he prowled to her right, and Rat Face circled the other direction, effectively blocking any means of escape. They boxed her in on both sides.

Santiago stopped and rested one hand on the back of a chair, looking down at his fingernails as if this were the most boring interaction in the world. He had so many better places to be.

"He said he was still working you over for information." Santiago's almost black eyes flickered to her face, and a smile grew across his lips.

She shifted toward him because Rat Face was still coming from the left. She wasn't sure which was the safer option, but Rat Face gave her the creeps.

"But it looks like he's just gotten cozy and started playing house," Santiago continued.

She stubbed her toe against a chair leg, hissing with the pain.

Santiago chuckled. "We make you nervous, pretty girl?"

Don't respond. He's just playing with you.

"Where's Chase?" she asked instead, trying to infuse her voice with as much courage as she could. But it was flimsy, at best.

He sighed theatrically, rolling his eyes. "If you're worried about his safety, I'm sure he's fine. I didn't send my best guys."

Her brows knit in confusion, which appeared to be his aim because a pleased glint flashed in his eyes.

"I just needed to delay him a little. I want him to make it back just in time to find that you're not here anymore."

Her stomach clenched, ice filling her at his words.

Rat Face grinned as he crept closer. Even though he wasn't even as tall as she was, wild terror still galloped through her body. He may have been scrawny compared to Santiago and Chase, but she knew he could probably overpower her.

"Where will you take me?" she asked Santiago.

His brows quirked at her question. "Oh, we have a great place. You'll love it."

Rat Face got closer, and she blurted her next words without thinking them through. "I won't put up a fight!"

Rat Face froze, and Santiago managed to look borderline interested.

"Just call off your rodent," she continued, her voice feathery. "I'll come willingly if you make sure he doesn't touch me."

Santiago smiled, his eyes shifting to his little minion, whose expression fell like a child being denied a toy. A second later, Santiago gave a sharp whistle, and both Rat Face and Sadie flinched. She remained where she was, holding her ground until she was sure Rat Face wouldn't come near her.

The little man glared at her before slinking back over to his boss, though he kept his gun pointed at her.

"We have a deal," Santiago said, raising a brow when she still didn't move.

Her heart rattled against her ribs, and it felt like she couldn't get a full breath even as her chest heaved oxygen in and out. She took slow steps toward them, Santiago's sinister grin growing with each inch she covered. She may have just made one of the biggest mistakes of her life. But she hadn't stood a chance of fighting them off, anyway. Two grown men against her? With a bum foot? It was better, but she doubted she could outrun either one.

This was the better option, right? Cooperate until she came up with a plan or an opportunity presented itself.

Her eyes shifted to the door of their own volition, her mind calculating with the speed only panic and an influx of adrenaline could inspire. What were her chances of any escape plan working? If she screamed, would the neighbors even hear? And if they did, would they check who had screamed and why? Those psychology studies would say not.

"I wouldn't try it," Santiago warned. His expression showed amusement, but there was a darkness in his voice as he continued to smile at her.

She sucked in a breath, hating her face for giving her thoughts away yet again.

"Travers is small, but he's spry. Quick reflexes."

She looked at Rat Face, deciding she'd rather keep calling him by the nickname instead of his real one. It fit better.

"And don't forget that you have nowhere to run, pretty girl."

For the first time, the sound of real danger appeared in his tone. The way his voice had gone husky on *pretty girl,* and his eyes made a slow perusal of her body had her wondering if she'd misplaced a level of trust.

"I promise Travers won't touch you as long as you cooperate. Shall we?" He gestured to the door, and she swallowed.

He jerked his head at Travers, who scowled and went out the back door ahead of them. Santiago had her follow before he fell in behind her. The backyard was so closed off and secluded, she wasn't sure anyone would hear her if she screamed. With Santiago's presence a cloying heat that made the skin at her back tingle with awareness, she doubted it would do her any good anyway. His eyes raked over her, too, like a laser all down her spine, taking in the curves of her body like he was analyzing something.

She wiped her sweaty palms against her thighs, her breathing audible. She swore she could feel Santiago's grin behind her. He liked that she was scared.

Chase, where are you? her mind chanted as they led her around the garage and through a gate to the alleyway. The remnants of her hope died a quick and painful death as all she saw were high walls and hedges that blocked them from sight of the houses around them. No other cars sat in the alley.

Rat Face led them to a black SUV with windows tinted impossibly dark, and the anxiety writhed faster in her stomach, adrenaline flowing through her limbs, flooding her with the desire to run. It even cleared away the residual pain in her ankle.

"You said willingly," Santiago purred behind her.

She sucked in a breath. How had he known? Her face was an easy read, but was her body language so loud as well?

His body heat intensified, and she felt his breath against her neck. He'd moved closer, not trusting his words to hold her in place.

It was at the passenger side door of the vehicle when her heart rate jumped into erratic chaos, and she realized that this was real life, that she was actually in this situation.

She'd been scared when Chase stuffed her in his trunk, but not in the same way. Maybe some part of her had known he wasn't going to harm her. Not the way the knowledge that these two men would love nothing more than to hurt her was so solid and tangible.

Rat Face opened the door, his expression pinched, still grumpy about the deal she'd struck with Santiago. Knowing what he was sad about losing made her skin crawl, and she halted three feet away from him.

"I made a promise, pet," Santiago said, the humor obvious in his tone, and it was starting to become more and more obvious that she'd made a deal with the devil.

His hands danced down her arms, barely skimming her skin, and she spun, her whole body tightening up. He was grinning at her, and all of her insides froze.

26

Brewing Storm

Chase would have to be clever with his approach. Santiago likely expected him to come busting in, eager to play the hero. And he wanted to. He wanted to light that place up. But he needed to be smart.

He had no time to MacGyver anything clever, but maybe he could come in where they least expected it. If Chase knew Santiago as well as he did, the man was likely feeling pretty cocky. Probably only had a couple of guys with him.

As he'd seen when he'd looked up the address Santiago had given him, it was a warehouse in the middle of nowhere, and it almost made him roll his eyes. Like some sort of movie villain, Santiago had played to the stereotype. It didn't help that a storm was brewing overhead, adding to the vibe as he drew closer to the address his GPS led him to.

Chase mentally rolled through what he had in his black duffel bag. Rope, extra guns and ammo. Before leaving, he'd changed out of his bloodied shirt and into a black, long-sleeve compression shirt and black cargo pants, pausing long enough to inspect the blooming discoloration along his ribs and opt for some painkillers. He'd taken a moment to spray that hippie healing stuff on the slice along his cheekbone and tossed Sadie's purse into the car with the duffel and the rest of his supplies. He strapped his smallest pistols to the outsides of his thighs and slid two knives into the hidden slots in his boots.

It paid to work for a criminal. He and Kyle had access to weaponry not standard for agents of the FBI.

He'd spent the long drive rotating through all the facts. He wondered how deep this thing really went and how long Gibson had been under Zim's thumb, what his role was. Because all Chase had was that list of names, people who were compromised but not how. It made his stomach roil to think of the three men who should've been trustworthy, should've been "the good guys," and then he lingered on the one who had likely ratted him out.

He'd called Gibson and told him exactly where he was. Kyle was dead and Santiago found the house, and there was no way that would have happened if someone hadn't given them away. Had he been motivated by the fact that Chase had gone rogue? Maybe Gibson was worried Chase would find him out, so he preemptively acted to cover his ass. Did Santiago even know Chase was FBI? Or had Gibson simply put a bug in the Spaniard's ear?

Informing Zimmerman of the whole thing would've brought the heat down on Gibson because Zim didn't know Chase was FBI. Unless Santiago had outed him. But so far, it didn't seem like Santiago had brought anyone else in, and it wasn't clear if Gibson had told Santiago where Chase's loyalties really lay.

Whether or not Santiago knew, Chase didn't think he had any plans to keep Sadie alive. And he certainly had no desire to keep Chase alive. It was no secret that Santiago hated him, which meant that this might have been a ploy to draw Chase in and take him out. Maybe even to make him look bad to the boss, giving Santiago a boost in rank.

Chase flipped through various angles, focusing on the analytics. Because if he dwelled too long on what might've been happening at that warehouse, his blood would boil. He needed to channel every ounce of energy into calculated focus. He could not fuck this up.

His mind threatened to imagine what Travers could be doing to Sadie. The sick bastard had a special yen for her, and he was known for his appetite for women, a gluttonous and violent snake.

Chase's hands twisted on the steering wheel, and his foot pressed more heavily into the gas pedal. And then he steered himself away. He couldn't do anything about what was happening *now,* so he needed to use his time wisely.

He played the angles of the warehouse in his head. He had gotten a cursory idea from the images off the Internet, but he had no idea what the inside layout was. Warehouses typically had several doors along the sides and back in addition to the front. But they would have those covered, blocked, or locked. And they weren't worth messing with for time's sake.

He needed to get up high and get the drop on them that way. A higher vantage point would always play in his favor. So he needed to get to the roof or an upper window.

Sometimes these old warehouses had an upper level, usually where offices were located, so if he could figure out which windows led to that upper area, he would be golden.

He bit into his cheek, narrowing his eyes. He couldn't count on this going the right way, especially without any sort of recon. So he had to plan for the inevitable problems that would arise.

At least he would have the benefit of darkness. He took in the way the setting sun lit the summer thunderstorm clouds on fire in front of him.

Small miracles.

On these old country roads, he rarely met another car and knew the likelihood of running into the law was low, so he pushed his speed. He wanted to make it to the meet just early enough that they were on edge waiting for him, but he would still have the element of surprise.

When he came upon the drive to the warehouse, he slowed, shutting off his lights and pulling off into a stand of trees across the road. As he gathered his supplies and grabbed his bag, he squinted toward the building, a hulking shadow against the backdrop of twilit fields beyond.

27

Bad Road

Bad, bad, bad, bad.

It was all bad. All the wrong decisions. The sun crept toward the west as they drove out of the city, past some of the suburbs she'd yet to explore because they were on the other side of Baltimore from where she lived.

Sadie forced herself to pay attention to the route they took. If she was going to survive, she needed to try to get herself out of it.

With or without Chase's help.

"I know what you're doing," Santiago said, his smooth voice quiet. His faint accent was a soft trill.

She cut a look at him then at Travers, who was driving. His attention shifted to the rearview mirror at her face every few minutes. Santiago sat in the back with her, his body turned in her direction so he could keep his dark eyes trained on her.

"And what am I doing?" Her voice was strangely cool and alien-sounding. Almost imperious. Who was she?

He held no weapon on her openly, but she *knew* she shouldn't test him. Some instinct told her it was there, somewhere within easy reach. He probably made sure she didn't know where as protection since she might easily grab it.

In this small space, she might've been tempted to try taking it from him. Not that she trusted her ability to use whatever he had—probably a gun. Even though she'd grown up in a military family, her father had never insisted she learn much about weapons, and she'd never asked. She regretted it now as she cataloged the open, empty road outside the windows.

"You're taking note of where we are," Santiago said, smirking, bringing her attention back. "It's smart, but it's unnecessary. I'll tell Chase exactly where we are. No need to worry your pretty little head about it."

Oh, she would worry her pretty little head. Because that sounded ominous as heck, and a knot twisted in her stomach at the realization that she was to be the bait to lure Chase into a trap.

Santiago was smug, though it was hard to tell since it was his normal state of being. She had yet to see him ruffled or angry. But the smugness was magnified by the satisfaction rolling off of Rat Face in the front seat.

Regret about going with them surged through her again.

Though she figured going willingly or not wouldn't have mattered much in the long run. She probably would've ended up here regardless, so she tried to convince herself that she'd made the right choice. This way, they hadn't used force, and possibly pain, to motivate her—drug her, knock her out, whatever means they might've used to get her to come with them. She was alert, whole, unharmed, physically fit enough to run if it came to it.

Her ankle presented a problem, but she could push through. Right?

It wasn't until they were tearing down the highway in areas she fully didn't recognize that Santiago made the phone call to Chase, taunting him, though she didn't understand why he would give him the address to their destination.

To trap him? To trick him?

The dread grew heavier in her gut the longer they drove. Time crawled by, and like the disappearing sun leaching the heat of day, despair sucked all the hope out of her body.

She fought for the will, lugging the determination up to keep herself alive. Be sneaky, watch for opportunities, play them. Anything to survive and help bring them down, whatever that looked like for an inexperienced hippie kindergarten teacher who had a serious and unexpected passion for the undercover FBI agent who'd kidnapped her.

What a weird turn of events. She certainly would have something exciting to share when she started back to school in the fall. Assuming she'd even be able to tell them about this little misadventure. Maybe it would be one of those NDA deals, and if she told anyone, they'd have to kill her.

They didn't really do that, right? And this wasn't some spy ring.

Jail, then, probably.

As they tore down desolate country roads, she began to wonder just how far out from civilization they would take her.

The sun was nearly down when they finally turned off onto a dirt road.

There wasn't much to see other than the lonely stretch of land on one side and the smattering of trees on the other as they rumbled down the drive toward a squat warehouse. It was innocuous enough, but given her situation, it stirred a latent terror inside her that made her heart kick up a notch.

That building meant death.

She felt her impending demise so strongly in that moment, pulsing through her veins like a ticking clock, counting down the moments she had left. Each pump of her heart was numbered.

Santiago pulled out some kind of key fob, pressed a button, and what looked like a garage door rolled up, allowing the building to swallow the car. Her breath stuttered when the door shut behind them, engulfing the car in darkness. Only the dashboard's illumination lit the cab of the SUV, casting the faces of both men in an eerie, unnatural glow.

She swallowed as Santiago turned toward her, leaning forward in the dark. She pressed her back against the door as her heart climbed into her throat.

His hand brushed her breast—deliberately?—as he reached. For the door handle, she realized when the door fell away from behind her. She tumbled backward out of the SUV. Landing hard knocked the breath out of her, and Santiago's sadistic laughter permeated the blanket of darkness that was both terrifying and suffocating.

She choked on oxygen as she tried to suck it back into her lungs, and hands lifted her from the ground. The dark chuckle at her ear meant Santiago was sticking to his promise that Rat Face wouldn't touch her.

The feel of his hands on her still made a shudder run through her body. They felt too hot through her clothes, too charged with whatever intention he kept barely concealed inside of him. But she couldn't see his face or gauge what it might be in the darkness as he walked her through a door and into another frighteningly dark room.

The hands disappeared, and she was left standing alone in the room, her breathing too close against the living, writhing blackness that surrounded her.

And then a light flashed on, and she flinched. Even though it dimly lit the room, she still found herself squinting after being immersed in such a deep darkness.

The light revealed a medium-sized room and no windows. Very little was kept here, and she struggled to understand what its purpose might have even been. All she knew was that the air was stifled and likely toxic without having windows for fresh air. It was a situation where she'd start mentally shopping for air purifiers if she had to spend a significant chunk of time in it.

The thought was stupid and intrusive, but it was all she could think about as Santiago prowled the room, moving like a mountain lion along the far wall to the desk that sat in the corner, which she hadn't noticed before. There was also a small, black sofa that sat just to the left of it. It looked infrequently used and incredibly uncomfortable.

Travers hovered near the door through which they'd come, his beady eyes trained on her. Instead of a rat, he now reminded her of a hyena. It was like she was the gazelle that the lion—Santiago—had taken down and claimed, and Travers was the scavenger waiting for his turn.

But neither of them approached her. They'd given her a wide berth, and Santiago seemed like he was paying little attention to her at all.

Which made her feel more nervous than if he stared at her like she was his next meal as Travers did.

How long would Santiago keep his promise, she wondered as she looked at the creep again. The longer they stood there, the more restless he became. His eyes grew hungrier as they took her in. Over and over, his gaze traced her shape, and she wished for Chase's baggy clothes to bury herself in.

"Travers," Santiago snapped.

Rat Face was practically salivating, but he shifted his focus to the bigger man.

Santiago's gaze was heavy and dark as they rested on his minion. "I need you to take our guest to her room while I make a phone call."

She sucked in a breath and visibly recoiled when Travers's eager expression transferred back to her.

"Do *not* touch her," Santiago warned, a dark and sinister note infusing his voice. Because he sensed it too—Travers' desire to put his hands on her again.

She'd known it when he'd touched her before. His hands had been hungry and violent. He'd been rough, even in the few minutes he'd gotten, and she knew he liked to hurt others for his own pleasure.

She shrank back when he drew near to her. He obeyed his master, though his lip curled in frustration at the fact.

28

Tactical Advantage

Chase would have to hoof it with his duffel, clinging to the meager treeline of the copse along the drive to hide himself as best he could. He swung the duffel over his shoulder and crept across the road, down into a ditch, and back up to the cluster of thin trees. It wouldn't keep him totally invisible, but it helped.

Moving swiftly, he kept lower to the ground and stepped as lightly as he could. His eyes swept back and forth in search of another body in the growing darkness, then he checked his watch. Fifteen minutes before the time Santiago had demanded he show.

No sign of another person on the grounds. Seemed stupid on Santiago's part. But if this was unsanctioned, as he suspected it was, Santiago's resources were limited. He didn't have the endless supply of mercenaries that were on Zim's payroll.

Chase crouched at the edge of the trees when he drew closer to the warehouse and unzipped the duffel. He took out the rope and winced as he wrapped it over his shoulder and across his chest, eyeing the building. There were high windows positioned every few yards down the length of the building. He stood and walked farther down the treeline, hoping he'd find the window that had a fire escape ladder or something in place.

He spotted it on the back side of the building. The ladder stretched only half the length to the ground, so he'd have to parkour his way to the bottom rung. If he was lucky, that window led to a closed room or something. He could handle dropping into an empty office, but he needed a sneaky way in and an access point that would give him a chance to scope out the situation inside the building.

He stuffed his pockets with extra clips of ammo, his eyes tracing every shadow in the dark. The sun was entirely gone, and he caught faint flashes of lightning in the distance. Hopefully the storm would hold off until he'd gotten Sadie out of there.

He tossed his bag back into the trees a little, making a mental note of the location, and rubbed his palms together. One hand went to the ground, and he staggered his feet, imitating a sprinter's starting stance.

And then he stiffened, an electric pulse throbbing painfully through him when he saw the body, a black shadow against the brick wall. Someone *was* patrolling, but only by the ladder. Like they knew he might try to get in that way.

Santiago was more thorough than he'd thought.

Taking two slow, deep breaths to calm his heartbeat, he set his eyes on that window, wondering if there'd be another guy there. He'd have to chance it because it was still the best way in.

It didn't look like the ladder guard moved far from his position. He simply walked down the end of the building and back the other way, like a shark circling its prey in water.

If he played this right, he could sneak up on the guy. Chase's eyes traced the shape in the growing dark as he lowered back into his sprinter's stance, waiting until the man disappeared from view.

He exhaled a slow breath and launched forward, taking off at speed. He wasn't slow, but he was no Olympic athlete. He made it to the wall, fighting to tamp down his panting as he crept along its length until he reached the corner where the other man would be in a matter of seconds.

Pressing his back to the wall, he mentally prepped for taking the guy out. And then, for the second time, adrenaline rushed through his system as a voice squawked over a radio.

"*Five-minute check,*" the voice said.

"All's clear," the guard on the other side of the building returned.

At least Chase knew where he was. These guys sure weren't versed in subtlety. But what did he expect from an upper-level thug to a mobster? Santiago never needed finesse or stealth. He was the muscle.

Made it easier for Chase.

He slid around the corner of the building just as the guard had turned away, a grin sliding across his face at how easy this would be. Right after check-in, too. It was like someone was orchestrating the whole thing.

Chase pulled his gun from the holster and flipped it around so he held the barrel in his palm. Then he shuffled forward, pulling his arm back and angling it so he could bring it down against the guard's unprotected head.

The man made no noise. The only sound was the clunk of the gun against his skull, and then he was a heap of black clothing on the ground.

Once he was sure the man was down for good, Chase glanced up the wall toward the window. Gauging the distance to the end of the ladder, he felt along the concrete for any divots or spots where he might find foot or handholds, anything to help him in the process. He was surprised to find even rows of brick protruded about half an inch every few feet all the way up. He had that sense again that something was working in his favor.

Chase sucked in a breath and held it, backing up to get some momentum. He glanced behind and around, just in case there was another guard he hadn't picked up on, then set off at a run.

His toe landed on the lip of the row of protruding bricks, and his fingers brushed the bottom rung but didn't land. Slamming back to the ground sent a flash of agony through his ribs. He worked hard to release the tension that coiled his body in response to the pain. He straightened and backed up again, ignoring the radiating ache.

The longer this took, the higher the chance he'd get caught.

His eyes swung more wildly along the length of the wall as he geared up and let loose from farther back. The *thwong* that rang out when his hand slapped against the metal rung vibrated through him. He gritted his teeth as he whipped his other hand up to wrap it around the metal. His toes scrabbled against the concrete as he hoisted himself up, grabbing the next rung so he could get his foot on the bottom. Once he was settled, he took a steadying breath, setting his sights on that window.

One hand over the other, one step after another, he made his way up the ladder as quietly as he could manage. Slow and steady. He hated how long it was taking him to climb, but he didn't want to alert someone he was there by making a lot of noise. It didn't help that his body was working against him after the abuse it had suffered earlier in the day. He figured he could afford the time it would take him to be cautious.

It was still a few minutes until he was expected, and the window drew closer and closer.

When his fingers touched the ledge, he felt like he could take a full breath, though he was huffing and puffing from the effort of climbing. At first, he thought the glass was just dusty, making it hard to see in. But then he realized it was a dark room. Mercifully empty. At least he wouldn't have to worry about someone spotting him climbing in through the window.

29

The Ten Lives of Sadie Powell

Cold concrete bit at Sadie's back as she crouched in the corner, on edge in the small, empty room. Especially with the way Santiago was prowling, the gun he held hanging loosely at his side. He was agitated—odd when he was usually so cool and collected. It must have been because of Chase. But he was the one who'd lured Chase here, using her life as a bargaining chip.

The one naked bulb that illuminated the room carved deeper shadows below Santiago's high cheekbones as his dark eyes slid to her repeatedly, and her own nerves jumped endlessly, electric shocks that fired throughout her entire body. It was torture to stay still. But her worry about Santiago's jitters made her as cautious as a cat on its ninth life. She didn't want to set him off accidentally, and so she kept herself motionless.

And because she didn't know Chase's plan, she didn't know what would be helpful for him. She felt like the student who got lost on a field trip once. She'd explained to him that staying put and waiting was safer than wandering around to find the rest of the class. It was easier to hit a stationary target than a moving one. Still, she wished she could do *something*.

It was odd that Travers was the only one of them who wasn't bothered. He was so still in the corner of the room that she could easily forget he was there.

If only.

The closer they got to the time they'd set for Chase to arrive, the less attention Travers paid her, which was a small blessing. Maybe his stillness wasn't a good thing, though. Not being able to know wound her nerves back up.

And then she heard it. A faint, almost imperceptible thud. Like a sack of flour falling onto the floor from the pantry.

Santiago heard it too because his prowling stopped abruptly, every one of his muscles tightening. His head cocked to the side. Her heartbeat stuttered when they heard a man's shout.

It wasn't Chase's voice, though. She could never picture him shouting, anyway. But who was it, and why?

She flinched when Santiago took a step toward her, eyes pinning her in place, jaw shifting forward.

Was it possible for a cat to have a tenth life?

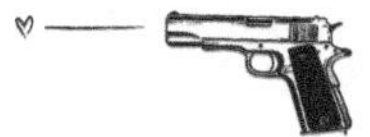

30

A Knife in the Dark

There was a gap between the ladder and the ledge of the window, and Chase thought about using the butt of his gun to break the glass. Then he decided against it because of the noise.

He scooted to the edge of the ladder, keeping a firm hold of the side rail, stretching toward the window. He felt around the edges, looking for some kind of emergency release latch. Once he found it, he struggled to get it to budge because of the angle.

Finally, it shifted, making a *shlunk* sound that had him holding his breath as if that would keep someone from hearing it. He waited a beat in case anyone came rushing in to investigate then pushed the window open when no one did. With it swung wide, he could make out the size of the room, if only vaguely. There wasn't much to look at, though. A few pieces of furniture, but it looked largely unused.

He sat on the ledge and flipped over, dropping onto his belly to dangle his legs. The floor was a bit of a drop, and he'd have to be careful not to break an ankle or make any noise.

He slowly lowered himself until he held the ledge just by his fingertips, face twisting with the effort of holding his own weight. He reminded himself to do more rock climbing when all this was over.

But he hadn't signed up for the CIA, and this was some CIA shit if he'd ever seen it. He'd signed up with the wrong agency. They were the sneaky bastards. Had better gadgets, too.

On his next exhale, his fingers released the edge. His feet hit the ground, and he rolled with the impact, swallowing back the grunt as his bruised–possibly–broken ribs screamed at him again.

He came back to a crouch and forced the air to come in and out as slowly as possible, though he wanted to hiss and curse through his pain. He had to pay attention in case he'd alerted anyone that he was inside.

In two strides, he was at the door, pausing to listen for movement on the other side before trying the knob and opening the door slowly.

The lighting was dim, so it was hard to see who was inside and where they were. Which had been intentional. But he could make out the metal railing that lined the balcony that extended from left to right and around like an L. There were other doors into what he assumed were more offices.

He caught movement to his left and heard the soft cough. His first target.

"*Two minutes.*"

His whole body clenched when the garbled voice crackled over a radio. Far enough away that he didn't suspect the guy on the upper part of the building with him had caught on to his presence.

At least he knew how much longer he had before they expected him.

He crept along the wall, praying the shadows would keep him hidden long enough to sneak up on the first guy. If only he could figure out where the rest of them were.

He slipped a knife from his boot as the silhouette of the first henchman came into view. His back was to Chase, still oblivious. But he was anticipating something. Chase could feel it radiating off the man's body.

Keeping low, he crept closer. To be on the safe side, he assumed the dude had a vest on, so he would go for the throat. It would be a quick death. But messy and brutal. Not something Chase *wanted* on his conscience.

But for Sadie.

The split-second before he reached the man, the cold detachment he needed to accomplish the task clicked into place.

He stood to his full height, a good four inches taller than Santiago's guy, and threw his hand around his neck, jerking his chin up. Pressing the knife against his throat, he dragged the blade across the scratchy flesh there as the man thrashed against him.

Chase had killed before, but never up close like this, and there was a part of him that squirmed as the man made a choking sound and teetered, lurching forward. Chase gave him a little shove, and he staggered toward the rail, bumped it, and tipped over, silently sailing to the concrete below.

He hadn't anticipated that and clenched his teeth when it pulled the attention of another one of Santiago's hired hands. And even though he was sure the guy couldn't see him, he yelled and fired off a few shots wildly in Chase's direction.

Chase flattened himself to the cold ground and belly-crawled his way toward the edge of the balcony. The other guy ducked back into shadow, but Chase could make out movement. The guy was panicking now, trying to stay a moving target, but it just made Chase's life easier.

Santiago would be pissed to know his henchmen weren't handling the situation well.

31

Unraveling Plans

Sadie flinched with every shot that rang out as if the bullets were striking her own body. Even her hands pressed against her stomach as if she would feel her life leaking out.

Santiago grew more and more still with each sound, his eyes on the barricaded door as if someone would burst through at any moment.

"Travers," he said through clenched teeth.

Rat Face emerged from the shadow in the corner, and she automatically recoiled as he drew closer.

"Find out what's happening."

Travers simply nodded, and Santiago moved to unlock the heavy, metal door. He practically shoved the smaller man out and slammed the door behind him, securing it again and spinning to look at her.

There was a fire in the depths of his dark eyes and a little bit of fear.

He'd already made the call to their big boss, but this wasn't going according to plan anymore. Not if she'd heard right.

He snatched her by the arm, and even though she resisted, dragged her to her feet. She pushed against him, fighting to make him release her until the cold muzzle of the gun pressed into her temple, and she froze. If she weren't so focused on keeping still, she might have vomited from the way her stomach contorted.

"If those shots didn't take out your little boyfriend, we're going to have a problem." The words came through his teeth again, and she realized how mad he was.

More shots rang out, and she flinched again. Santiago's fingers became claws against her arm, digging in painfully. She knew there would be bruises.

32

A Jaunt Out the Window

The slinking henchman in the shadows dropped where he stood; Chase's finger tingled from pulling the trigger. It only took him two shots to nail him. Two slow, deep breaths in and out.

He pushed away from the edge of the balcony and heard a heavy door open and slam shut, barely catching sight of the figure slithering out of the office in the corner.

He almost smiled to himself because now he knew where they were keeping Sadie.

But this was where Travers would be his problem. The smaller man moved more quickly than Chase ever hoped to. Even before he'd bulked up, he'd never been that agile. Already, he'd lost the little snake in the shadows and pushed back against the far wall to conceal himself within the darkness.

Learning a lesson from the guy downstairs, he didn't weave in and out in an attempt to make himself a harder target. It had only made him more visible in the dark. Instead, he moved slowly, creeping along to keep the cloak of darkness. Maybe he could just bust into the office where they were keeping Sadie and avoid Travers entirely.

"Your pretty girl is having the time of her life in there with Santiago."

Chase fought the urge to whirl toward Travers' voice. If he had to bet, it was the little man's attempt at flushing him out. It made his blood heat just thinking about Travers' words, but he remained motionless, gauging where the voice had originated from.

"We've each taken our turn with her. Even as your sloppy seconds, she was the best I ever had."

Chase almost growled. He didn't want to believe it was true, but it also wasn't out of the realm of possibility. Santiago's hatred for Chase could very well have driven him to those lengths. But Travers was goading him, trying to get him to mess up. So he was lying.

Instead of dwelling on it, he focused on where Travers's voice seemed to come from. Most likely a spot that would throw his voice effectively but keep him close enough to where his boss was.

Chase began to move.

He crept with a slowly building fury in his limbs, heat pouring like molten metal through him.

"She call your name like she called mine?" Travers continued.

Chase allowed a smile then, sure it was a lie now. She wouldn't have called out that rodent's name. But he knew he was close, hearing the voice like a breath over his shoulder. He drew flush with the wall, sliding closer to the corner.

He took the chance and peered around the edge of the wall, spotting the tiny man down the length of the concrete. The faint flash of lightning from the storm that was nearly upon them illuminated his thin frame.

Maybe the storm coming closer wasn't the worst thing ever.

Chase waited for another flash of electricity to light Travers's silhouette again, and several seconds later, a low rumble of thunder billowed above them. He took one quick toke of oxygen, then pushed away from the wall, charging toward Travers, who didn't catch on quickly enough to get his gun up.

He hollered at Chase's approach. Maybe he saw the fury in Chase's eyes. Or maybe he simply felt the heat of it just before Chase barreled into him. It didn't take much strength to move the smaller man, but Chase's rage ramped his speed too high as he slammed Travers back toward the window.

It was a half-second before the glass gave way under the pressure, and the little man folded up and sailed through. Chase caught himself before he went out with him, half hanging out into the night to watch Travers plummet.

Travers's scream chased him all the way to the ground until it abruptly cut off on impact. To be sure, Chase aimed his gun and fired off two rounds into the snake's body.

He worked to push himself back inside, then took stock of the situation to figure out his next steps. The door to the office where they were keeping Sadie would be locked.

But now that this window was gaping. . .

33

Only Cats Land on Their Feet

Sadie's stomach dropped out at the sound of Travers's voice. It was muffled, but she could clearly hear his words and the cocky way he was addressing Chase.

But it gave her hope. After hearing several gunshots, she'd had no idea if it was Santiago's men who'd been taken down or Chase.

Even as the flush of relief filled her, Santiago's fingers dug deeper into her skin, and she gritted her teeth. He yanked her back toward the window. She wasn't sure if he was planning an escape that way, or it was just to put distance between himself and the door. Chase wasn't likely to make it through that heavy beast, so the window was probably the liability.

A squawk made all the air slide out of her body, then she heard the crash of glass breaking.

The scream that came from outside drew their attention to the window in time for them to see Travers plunge to the concrete below, a puddle of blood billowing out around him like a grotesque halo.

Then two gunshots rang out, and the body on the ground twitched with the force of the bullets. She wasn't sure if he'd died from the impact, but there'd be no doubt now. Proof that scumbags didn't get nine lives, and only cats landed on their feet.

Santiago stared down at his little minion on the ground, disbelief carved into the smooth planes of his face. Then his expression twisted as he roared his frustration. He dragged her away from the window, pointing the gun toward it in expectation.

34

More CIA Shit

Chase hesitated before climbing up onto the ledge, grimacing as he took stock of his body. His bruised ribs, freshly mistreated during his climb up into the building then crawling around on the floor to stay under flying bullets, screamed for attention. His leg was bleeding. From what, he wasn't sure. A stray bullet, perhaps. He didn't remember getting it, but he felt the sting now, a burning slash across his calf.

He stepped up onto the ledge, the cool breeze buffeting him as the storm moved in closer, whipping his hair across his forehead and into his eyes. Turning his back to the sky, he stuffed his toe on top of the protruding bricks, hissing through a locked jaw when his leg muscles protested at having to work so hard again. Especially his calves, the one that still wept blood giving him the most feedback.

He dug his fingers into the protrusion at eye level, tensing to hold himself upright. The next window wasn't far. He just needed to hang on as long as he could.

He muttered a string of curses through a tight jaw, the audible sound of his clenched teeth grinding against each other sending chills up his spine.

As he shimmied along, he realized it didn't matter that it was a mere few feet. His muscles were about done, and it was agony crossing the distance as the wind continued to whip at him. The electricity in the air was palpable, making the hair along his body stand up.

His fingers slapped against the rounded corner where the window was cut in, his whole body shaking from the effort it took to hold his bulk against the wall. It was a quick process of discarding his initial instinct to kick in the glass. With how hard it was to hold on right now, he didn't have the leverage he'd need to swing his leg.

So it would have to be a gunshot. He just needed to aim it right to avoid hitting Sadie. If it got Santiago, that would be a welcome miracle.

One hand slipped down to his thigh where he'd strapped his second pistol. He wasn't sure he had any bullets left in the first one. He hadn't been keeping track in the moment.

He puffed air in and out through his teeth, quick bursts of oxygen, as he shifted to aim at an angle toward the glass.

35

Post-Traumatic Storm Disorder

Santiago pulled Sadie back toward the door, his gun hand raised toward the window.

He was expecting Chase to come barreling through any minute, but she wondered how that would even be possible. Was Chase secretly Spiderman?

Pop, pop, pop!

The window exploded into sparkling splinters, and she shrieked, turning instinctively into Santiago's chest as he twisted, pulling her with him in his attempt to shield himself.

The sound of the glass raining down onto the concrete only lasted a second, and the gunshots stopped almost immediately. Footsteps were crunching over broken glass before she'd even had enough time to process what happened.

And then Santiago yanked her hard, slamming her back to his chest, and the barrel of the gun pressed against the underside of her jaw. Every muscle in her body snapped tight, her eyes shooting wide as she took in Chase's face from across the room.

He was holding a gun, and it looked like he was aiming for her, though she knew it was trained on Santiago because that's where his narrowed eyes were pointed. Sweat dripped down Chase's temples in slow rivulets that caught the dim light in the room, and a cool breeze whipped inside through the broken window.

Santiago pulled her slowly backward, still practically dragging her because she wasn't making it easy for him, even if he had the gun on her.

"Boss is on his way. Should be here in a few minutes."

"Yeah?" Chase asked, his voice edged with danger. "And what are you going to tell him? Your guys are dead out there. And you got me here. What exactly was your plan, Santiago?"

The other man stiffened against her back. "I need what Calloway gave his lady friend. And if I don't get it from you, I'll use her to get it from him."

Despite the gun still pressed to her face, she found herself snorting loudly at the sentiment.

Santiago jerked her, fingers digging into her flesh again, and she hissed. Chase's eyes flashed to her face, a muscle near his eye twitching.

"What's so funny, pet?" Santiago asked, but his usual sinister purr was betrayed by the tension she felt in his body.

"Using me is a waste of time. Greg doesn't care about anyone but himself. Especially me. Obviously."

Chase turned his attention back to Santiago. "We don't have the information you need anyway. Thinking she had anything to offer was a mistake on my part."

Santiago gave one of his dark laughs, relaxing now. Something in what Chase said gave him a dose of confidence he'd been lacking.

"Then I don't need to keep her around," Santiago said, pressing the gun harder into the underside of her chin.

She sucked in a breath and stretched up on her toes to relieve the pressure.

Chase took one lurching step forward.

"Ah," Santiago crooned. "Not so cocky now, are you?"

Chase's jaw shifted just a smidge, eyes narrowing even further. A flash of rage ignited in his gaze.

"What a surprise that you'd fall for the pawn in this little game against Greg."

"Quit with the charade, Santiago." Chase shifted to the right, and Santiago took an equal step to his, keeping Sadie between them.

"What charade, Lundgren?"

"You think you're so subtle. Getting the info to Zimmerman would've just been a bonus. This whole thing was a ploy to make me look bad. That's why you jumped the gun and called him here, even though it's all going to come back to bite you in the ass."

Santiago stopped shifting like the process of understanding Chase's words halted his ability to function.

But she didn't understand any of what was happening or what they were saying, what it all meant.

"You think because you figured out my secret, and you know about my cabin that you've got this whole thing in the bag," Chase continued, his tone deadly. "But something you don't know about me is that I was top of my class in marksmanship."

"Wha—"

The sound of the gunshot was like an explosion in the enclosed space, and Sadie screamed, dropping straight to the floor.

She didn't know how tightly she'd curled in on herself until she felt fingers wrap around her wrists to move her hands away from her ears.

"Sadie." Chase's voice was soft, but she managed to hear it over the ringing when she lifted her head.

His face rippled before her, but she realized it was because tears had filled her eyes, obscuring her vision.

"We have to go. Now."

She nodded. Or thought she did.

He moved back to the window and took something from around his chest, messing around with it, but she couldn't make the pieces fit into any logical sequence.

He came back toward her and pulled her to her feet. "Take off your shirt."

She blinked, not sure she'd heard him right. "Wh-what?"

"Take off your shirt. We have to slide down the rope to the ground outside, and I want you to use your shirt to protect your hands."

She looked at Santiago's prone form at her feet and felt Chase dragging her to the window.

"Sadie."

She brought her gaze back to him, and a flash of lightning blazed behind his head.

"We don't have time for hesitation. Zimmerman will be here in a few minutes. He'll have a whole mess of firepower with him. We need to get out."

She nodded, but her mind still didn't quite compute.

He sighed then reached for the hem of her shirt, asking permission with his eyes.

She nodded again, and he was lifting it over her head, leaving her bare except for her bra. Goosebumps rippled along her skin immediately. He wrapped the fabric around her hands, then rushed to pull his own skin-tight shirt off and did the same.

"I'll go first. Come right after me. Okay?"

Her head bobbed again.

He stepped onto the ledge, lowering himself down and taking hold of a rope. That must have been what he'd been doing a moment before—securing a rope for them to use. He put his feet against the wall and walked himself down a couple of feet.

"Come on, Sadie."

His voice was soothing like he was talking to a scared child.

She followed his example, crawling onto the sill and turning around so that she could climb out. Gripping the rope and bracing herself against the wall, she sucked in a breath as the breeze and raindrops bit at her exposed skin. A little bit of clarity returned. Which was probably not a good thing as she saw how high up they were.

"Just walk yourself down."

She felt his hand on her hip as she did what he said, lowering herself into his arms.

"Okay." His breath tickled against her ear. "Wrap your legs around the rope."

She whimpered, looking down.

"I've got you," he assured her.

She took her feet from the wall and wrapped her legs around the rope, letting her weight settle into Chase's big body.

"Good. Now we'll loosen our grip just a little so we can slide down. Your hands will get hot, but hopefully, the shirt will protect them."

"Okay," she whispered, her heart hammering in her chest. She heard the tremor in the word.

His hand squeezed her hip. "All right. Let's go."

The heat of his body behind her disappeared and a gasp shot out of her. The rope trembled in her hands, but she didn't loosen her grip even as her muscles strained to hold her weight.

"Let go, Sadie," Chase called from below her. "Just a little bit."

She glanced down to see he was already at the bottom, a shadow on the ground.

Lightning illuminated his face, which was tipped up.

"Okay," she whispered again, taking several puffs of air.

Then she released her grip. The feeling of being out of control ripped a scream from her throat as she slid down, the heat building like a fire in her palms.

And then she felt him there, catching her with a grunt, and his arms went around her, the heat and dampness of his chest against her bare back. He pried her hands from the rope, then pulled her into a full sprint toward the trees as the rain pelted them from above. She tripped, dropping her shirt, but he dragged her forward.

"Leave it," he commanded when she tried to turn back, and she stumbled along, trying to get back up to pace with him.

They flew into the trees just as a pair of headlights cut through the darkness where they'd been only moments before, and he halted their progress to watch and let her catch her breath.

"Here," he said, panting. He held out his shirt to her, his eyes turned to the dark vehicle as it pulled past them toward the warehouse.

She didn't hesitate long as shivers wracked her body, setting her teeth chattering. She pulled the shirt on, and because it was so form-fitting, it wasn't that big on her. Long, yes. But it immediately helped with warmth, though the rain started to fall harder and faster. It probably wouldn't do much for long.

"Come on," Chase said, taking her hand again. "Move quickly, but watch your feet. We can't run full-on in here. My car is parked on the other side."

She nodded, then realized he wouldn't be able to see it, but he didn't insist on verbal confirmation as they shifted through the trees. They stopped once for him to grab his black bag, which he threw over his shoulder before pulling her along again.

He didn't seem to care how much noise they made, but it didn't matter with the wind rustling the trees and the raindrops as they splattered the leaves and ground around them. Plus, the thunder had gotten closer, letting out long, loud grumbles after every flash of light.

Time stretched, and she couldn't help glancing backward, worried that someone had already been sent to search the small wooded area for them. How long after they found the bodies would they wait before they'd come for her and Chase?

She stumbled over a fallen tree, catching herself against Chase, who slowed to help right her. He said nothing about her tripping, didn't scold her for not doing as he'd told her.

They just kept moving.

36

Grief and Guilt

They reached the edge of the stand of trees, and Chase pulled her to a stop. Her terror snapped on the air, vibrating like an electric shock that he felt through their connected hands.

He waited, watching the dark road for any other vehicles. He wasn't sure Zim wouldn't come flying back out or if a second vehicle might arrive with reinforcements.

Only a few seconds passed as the thunder rumbled above them, giving the moment an eerie sense of foreboding he couldn't shake. But he took a breath and shot out of the trees, pulling her across the road with him, his hand tight around hers. Until they were safe and away from here, the unease wouldn't dissipate.

He opened the passenger door for her, helped her climb in, and sprinted around to the driver's side, tossing the duffel into the back before getting in. He left the headlights off as they whipped around and went flying down the deserted highway.

It was probably ten miles before he felt safe enough to flip them on.

He glanced over at Sadie. One of her hands gripped the door, and the other was a claw around the center console, fingers digging into the fabric, just like the day before. Had that really only been twenty-four hours ago?

It gutted him to see how small and frightened she looked. Her lips were a colorless line across her beautiful, pale face, and her hair was soaked and dripping onto her shoulders. He turned the heat on full blast, angling the vents at her.

"How are your hands?" he asked.

She jerked to look at him, her already big eyes rounded in what could potentially be categorized as shock. Her delicate brows pulled low over her eyes as she looked down at her hands in question.

"Did they burn? Any blisters?" he prompted.

"Oh. . ." She ran her fingers over her palms. "No. They're fine."

"Good."

The way she continued to stare at her hands made him wonder what else had happened back there, if they had done anything to her. The thought alone stirred his fury.

"Sadie, I hate to ask, but. . ."

Her attention swung to him, her expression unchanged.

"Are you okay? Did they do anything to you? Did they—"

"No." The word came out on a breath. "They didn't touch me. I'm not hurt at all." Her head swiveled back to the window, and he made out the blank expression on her face in the faint reflection of the glass.

The rage had been hot and stinging through his body, but it lowered to a simmer now. He still felt the anger the whole situation had inspired like a poison in his veins, an unending burn in his blood.

If he'd had time, he would've done as much damage to Travers and Santiago as he could have. Caused as much pain as humanly possible. It was a partial satisfaction that the two were no longer breathing, dead by his own hands.

But now he needed to figure out what to do next. And he needed clarity to do that. They still only had half the information they needed, and he had to figure out who he could trust with what he had, or get the final piece of the puzzle—the evidence of how everyone was involved. After finding Kyle dead and getting jumped, he wasn't sure where he would turn next. Or if he should get help from anyone else. Any person he came in contact with would automatically be in danger.

So he was well and truly on his own from here on out.

His fingers tapped an endless rhythm on the steering wheel as the wipers dashed across the windshield. The rain was pouring so hard, it made it impossible to have a conversation over the sound of it hitting the car.

Not that it mattered. Sadie wasn't capable of having a conversation at the moment. Eventually, her head lolled backward as she fell asleep.

Waves of guilt buffeted him while a string of rebukes played like a broken record in his head. He never should have brought her to Kyle's. Never should have left her alone. Never should have let Santiago and Travers set foot inside his house that first time.

What Chase should have done was kept them moving as soon as they'd left, maybe going from one motel to the next, not going to his friend.

Kyle's blood was now on his hands.

He swallowed against the pressure that built in his chest. The guilt gnawed at his gut, reminding him that he wasn't allowed the grief that threatened because it was his fault.

He'd thought seeking an ally was smartest, that contacting his boss would help, offer safety. All it had done was get his friend killed, and taking with it any hope that he could drop Sadie off at home, let her go back to her life as usual.

It had died as soon as he'd seen that list. His belief in the good guys had perished just as swiftly. What was the fucking point?

If only it had just been Santiago and Travers. He could have taken her home that very night since things there were finished. But now Zimmerman knew about her, and whoever he'd send next and whatever he did would be another level of bad that Chase couldn't afford to ignore.

And that meant doing things alone. Otherwise, Kyle's death wouldn't be the only one on his conscience.

So one motel tonight. A new one the next night. And the next. Until he could decide what to do. Until he could figure out how to make the whole thing end. Because he couldn't go back to Zim now, pretend like he was still a faithful employee. Zimmerman would undoubtedly kill him. And if he didn't, Gibson would make sure of it to cover his own ass.

So the only option was for Chase to make it all end. Now.

He drove a circuitous route for two hours until he had to stop for gas. He pulled on a fresh shirt from his bag before going inside to grab a few snacks and supplies, then wound around until he found the most remote town that still had a motel.

At some point, Santiago had forced them all to cross state lines to get to his little warehouse, so Chase had to bring them back toward familiar territory, if not somewhere they actually knew or were known. The place he found listed itself as an inn, though looking at it proved it was a dubious label. He just hoped the linens were clean.

Sadie never stirred, even sleeping through his check-in process, only waking when he opened her door to carry her inside. She was groggy as she nuzzled into his neck, but she gripped and held on with a fierceness that made his heart ache.

They were both still damp, and she shivered in his arms as he brought her inside and set her on one of the queen beds.

She looked around dazedly, her mouth turning down as she took in the shabby details of the room.

"Want me to run a hot shower for you?" he offered, spying a robe hanging from a hook on the bathroom door.

She lifted a shoulder, her eyes unfocused.

He took that as a yes. The way she curled in on herself and continued to shiver, he figured it would be a good idea whether she agreed or not. Anything to help ease that look on her face.

He took a relieved breath in the bathroom as he turned the shower on. He couldn't stand seeing her in that state anymore. Not when he was part of the reason she looked that way. She'd been pushed beyond her limits. And sure, he had been too. But he knew how to handle it. Had been in similar positions before. Not normal. But *his* normal.

For too long.

He watched the steam billow and fill the room, and a shiver crested over his body as the heat seeped into him.

He didn't want this to be his normal anymore. He had to get out. He wanted it to end.

He no longer wanted to be the convenient choice for dangerous undercover work. It was inevitable now that he was in this position, knowing what he had to do to end this job. He'd have to go to the higher-ups to take everyone down, reveal who he was and who he really worked for.

But who and how? The reality continued to sink in that he didn't know who to trust.

He shook himself from his thoughts and turned to find Sadie standing in the doorway. She wasn't looking at him, but his skin flushed anyway. She barely seemed to register what was even before her, didn't move further into the room.

He took her hand gently. She didn't flinch as he'd expected her to, so he tugged her into the bathroom. She kept moving forward and crashed into him, burrowing against him.

He lifted his free hand to stroke her head in a soothing motion, finding more solace in the gesture than maybe she did. She didn't cry, but he felt the pressure of the need through her body against his.

"Just take a shower," he murmured. "Get warm. Put on the robe. You'll feel better."

"Thank you," she mumbled against him, hiding her face as she pulled away and moved around him.

He shuffled out of the bathroom, pulling the door shut behind him.

The duffel and the rest of his gear were still in the car, so he went out to retrieve it. He threw the bag onto the bed and stuffed the extra weapons he'd stashed on his body back inside to keep them out of sight then took out his extra clothes. He started to change then caught sight of the dried blood on his calf, sitting on the edge of the bed to inspect the damage. Maybe a bullet graze. Maybe broken glass. He had no idea, could barely tell, didn't much care.

Pulling out his first aid kit, he doctored and bandaged the wound then used some additional wipes to clean the blood that had trailed down his leg. His sock was sticky with it, and he pulled it off, followed by the other. He hadn't thought to bring an extra pair. So he'd have to wash them in the bathroom when Sadie was done.

As if she'd heard his thoughts, the shower shut off, moisture and warmth permeating the main room when she opened the curtain. He didn't mind as he sat back down on the bed, soaking in the heat. It felt good to be enveloped. Especially when his body ached as it did. He'd checked his ribs again, taking in the darker discoloration that mottled his skin and figured they weren't broken. Not that he was any sort of authority. But he'd bet money bruising was all the damage done.

Deep bruising, he thought with a wince.

A cloud of steam surged out of the bathroom as the door swung open, drawing his attention. Sadie's color was ten times better, cheeks flushed from the heat of her shower. Her hair was dripping wet again. Had she washed it? Using the poisonous motel shampoo?

She pulled the robe tighter around herself as if she felt self-conscious. That dead-eyed look had disappeared from her face, and a relief he hadn't expected flooded through him.

"Feel better?" he asked, his voice gravelly even to his own ear.

She nodded, biting her lip.

"Did you actually deign to use the motel's toxic shampoo?" he asked, trying for levity to break the uncertainty in her demeanor.

Her mouth curled up in the corner. "Of course not."

He chuckled, but his smile dropped away when she moved toward him, something in her eye and intention sending an electric current through the air that kicked up the rhythm of his pulse.

She kept that lip trapped between her teeth as she walked forward, still holding the robe closed over herself, and it slid home that she was naked under that thin piece of terrycloth. His body reacted to the realization, and he clenched his jaw, locking down every physical response building inside of him.

But she held that shy and knowing look on her face, like that had been her intention.

"Did you get condoms?" she asked, lowering her voice as she came to stand right in front of him.

He swallowed hard. That had been a purchase that felt like a lifetime ago, made by a wholly different man.

"Yes," he croaked. "You're sure?"

A shadow fell over her face, little lines appearing in her forehead. "Nothing about what happened today changed anything for me. And right now, after everything, I just need to feel something other than terror."

He exhaled, the guilt twisting in his chest. "I'm so sorry, Sadie."

"Don't," she whispered. "Just put your hands on me. Make me forget?"

37

Attention to Detail

Chase took a breath, nodding so slightly that Sadie almost missed it. It might have sounded like a manipulation, but it was a genuine need. Her skin was calling for the feel of his hands everywhere, to soothe and graze and warm and create a friction to scrub away the grimy feeling left on her by what she'd witnessed.

"As long as you want to," she said quickly, the sting of uncertainty making her wonder if she was being overly demanding. Maybe he didn't want to after all the things he had done that night. Like a real hero, he'd saved her life. She touched his cheek lightly beneath the cut that split his skin.

Air rushed out of him. "Oh, I want to."

A burst of warmth flooded her, and her lips turned up at the corners with her pleased, timid smile. "Okay."

Slowly, she pulled her other hand away from the robe. There hadn't been a belt to tie it, so she'd been holding it closed. And even though he was looking at her with unmitigated desire, a shyness fell over her. This kind of moment, the precipice before exposure, always stole a measure of her confidence.

The robe slipped open, though it didn't reveal her entirely, the edges catching on her breasts. But her damp skin was exposed from her throat, down her sternum, her stomach, and below for his eyes to rake with deliberate slowness.

He swallowed, then used both hands to carefully brush the robe open, placing warm palms against her sides, infusing her skin with the thrill of his touch.

She stepped closer, putting one knee on the bed beside him so she could hover just above his lap, then rested her hands on his shoulders. Moving them up, she wove her fingers into his hair, and he sighed, his breath fanning across the skin along her collarbone, sending tingles through her.

"Sadie," he whispered, moving his hands down slowly like he wanted to feel the shape of her, memorize the exact curve of her hips.

Another wave of chills washed over her, pleasant and rippling, and she couldn't help smiling.

She expected his touch to trail back up, but hesitation flashed in his gaze as he met her eyes. It was like he was asking her again if she was sure. But she'd never been more certain, the soft song of desire singing in her blood.

She nodded. "Make me forget, Chase."

It was apparently all he needed, and he pulled her closer, brushing the robe off to reveal her entirely to him, the terrycloth puddling on the floor. And even though she felt sure, it made her self-conscious to be so exposed while he was still fully clothed.

She curled in on herself a little.

"No, don't," he said, his husky voice bordering on a plea.

She brushed her damp hair behind her ear, glancing up.

"Every part of you is perfect," he murmured.

Heat blossomed in her cheeks. It had been a long time since a man had complimented her so earnestly. She'd always known she was pretty, and the few men she'd been with made it clear they'd wanted her.

But nothing compared to the way Chase looked at her now, the way his words burrowed deep within her chest and blossomed, spreading like lush vines around her heart.

As if he wanted to prove it to her, his hands moved over her skin, lighting off little fires in her body as he cupped her breasts then took each into his mouth in turn.

Her head fell back as she gasped, fingers tightening in his hair. She came alive with electricity. Like the lightning that streaked across the sky earlier, every nerve lit up with the power and sizzle. Her body was already begging for some kind of friction.

As if he heard that call, his hands made their way downward, fingers slowly moving and circling in a teasing pattern that built up more heat, more tension, more need. His tongue moved over her nipple, concentrating on that movement, and her consciousness left her body as everything focused in on this one thing that was happening to her.

She forgot they were in this questionable motel, that he'd rescued her from a psychopathic criminal only hours before, that she'd ever been in this mess in the first place.

Only his hands and mouth mattered in this moment, only the way her body moved without her permission, reacting to his attention by building higher and higher until her knees threatened to buckle. She went flying over the edge so suddenly, her muscles snapped tight for a split second before the first of the waves crashed over her.

She fell against him, even as the waves continued to pulse, hot and jarring.

His lips made a trail along her neck, gentle and tender like he was savoring her. She'd needed to forget, but it seemed he needed to be reminded. What it was to touch and be touched, to feel someone's careful caresses.

She was happy to be his reminder.

Slowly, she came back to herself, the shattered pieces of her knitting back together with every breath she took. Finally, she straightened, taking the hem of his shirt to pull it off, pausing to marvel at what she found underneath. The result of his obsessive cultivation was breathtaking up close. Muscle on muscle. Her fingers traced the lines and edges of every single one while her eyes admired and her lips murmured her appreciation.

She let her fingertips hover over the discoloration along his ribs, a frown pulling at her mouth. Before she could think twice about it, she gently placed her lips against the skin, and he sucked in a breath.

Looking at his expression told her it was not because of pain. Wonder shone in his eyes, and he took her face in his hands so that he could kiss her like he was thanking her.

But it was she who owed him her gratitude. He had those bruises because of her. It didn't matter that he was the one who'd taken her, brought her into his home. Because he'd done it to keep her safe, to protect her. Everything he'd done was with her in mind.

And he'd come to rescue her. He could have walked away at any point. But when Santiago had threatened to kill her, Chase had tipped his hand. That it very much mattered to him that she stayed alive, that she stayed with him.

She could have dismissed everything before this as simply physical attraction. He had been kind and accommodating, sure. But he was wired that way, even if he didn't show that side to everyone. Not with having to keep himself guarded in this line of work. But the things he had done *for* her, the way he'd fought to keep her safe, showed her this was more.

And so she let his mouth explore her naked body again while her hands worked over him.

Abruptly, he stood, picking her up and laying her back gently on the bed. He worked his pants off, revealing his entire gloriously built body, and she bit her lip as he retrieved a condom. He was mythic. Beyond comprehension as the muscles rippled and shifted with his movements, and she was suddenly even more self-conscious about the softness of her own body.

She worked out regularly, liked to build her strength, feel the improvement in what she could do and how she pushed herself. But she only had so much time, only so much motivation. Health was her biggest focus.

But Chase. His physique was the result of careful application, planned and precise cultivation of strength. There was nothing casual about how he came to look the way he did. She'd seen what built him in the elaborate setup he had at his house. And she'd seen how powerful his strength really was when he'd pummeled that punching bag like his life depended on it.

He climbed back onto the bed, his eyes such a deep green they looked almost black. He kept his gaze locked on hers as his lips skimmed her inner thigh, and she shivered in response.

He worked his way up her body with his mouth, and she began to feel feverish again, her core crying out for the feel of him.

"You're so beautiful, Sadie," he whispered against her stomach, peppering the skin with kisses.

Her hips moved under him as his mouth brushed her breasts again, still tender from his attention only moments before.

"I want to feel you," he breathed against her collarbone. "All of you."

"Yes," she answered, a begging note entering her voice.

His lips met hers as he slipped inside. She gasped into his mouth, the feel of him filling her to the brim, sending a shudder through her entire body.

"Are you okay?" he asked, holding himself very still.

"Oh, yes," she murmured.

38

The After

Chase braced himself on his elbows, and Sadie's slender fingers trailed along the muscles of his back as he began to move slowly. He didn't know how long it had been for her. But it had been way too long for him.

The women he encountered in his line of work hadn't been the kind he wanted to spend time with. High-end or not, he didn't like to pay for companionship. And those who weren't pay-to-play were immersed in a world he didn't want to sink any deeper into.

It earned him flak, but he didn't care. Not when it meant that he could have a moment like this—more powerful and life-changing than he'd ever thought possible.

Already his senses were on the edge, everything so sharp, he struggled not to take it hard and fast. It was agony to hold back, but he wanted this moment to last. He wanted to feel everything.

And it *was* everything. The way she reacted, her breath feathering over him, her body moving under him, her sighs of contentment, followed by gasps of surprise when he drove harder into her.

Even as he fought his release, he moved faster, unable to stop himself when she murmured her pleasure, caressed his name in a sultry tone, her breathing increasing with his.

And she cried out a split-second before he did, her second orgasm sharpening his own. It blasted through his body like a torpedo, blinding him momentarily with ecstasy.

He almost collapsed onto her before he recovered himself and rolled to the left, trying to catch his breath. His heart hammered against his ribs, but no part of his abused body was hurting like it had been. It was like their intimacy had healed him for the moment.

She sighed and turned toward him, so he pulled her closer, tucking her body against his. The warmth of relaxation poured through him, and his eyes drifted closed as she laid one hand on his chest.

After a moment, her fingers fluttered, tracing the muscles of his chest and abdomen with gentle exploration. It pushed him closer to the edge of unconsciousness.

"This should really be illegal."

It was a struggle to pull his mind back, and he didn't open his eyes. "What?"

"You are chiseled beyond belief. Like, I didn't even know there were that many muscles in the human body."

He barely had energy to respond. "I have a lot of time on my hands."

"Clearly." She sat up, and that side of his body immediately grew cold.

His eyes shot open, and he snatched her hand to stay her.

She gave a surprised laugh. "I'll be back."

He reluctantly let her go, then got up as well, removing the condom and shimmying his pants back on.

Sadie came out of the bathroom not long after, brushing her fingers through her half-dry hair, wearing only her underwear and bra. And for some reason, that was even sexier than when she'd had the robe half open.

She froze for a second, taking him in with a small smile on her lips, then shook her head. "I don't know that I could ever get used to a sight like that."

He huffed a laugh through his nose. "I'm sure you could. I'm not some rarity."

Not like her. She was sunshine and warmth. Funny. Quirky. Sexy.

She walked farther into the room, now effortlessly comfortable. She'd vacillated between self-consciousness and confidence earlier, but now, there was a level of ease in being undressed around him.

Everything about her called for his hands again, but he held back, fighting for control as he moved to his duffel bag to pull out his laptop. He needed to keep his eyes on something—anything—else if he wanted to direct his mind away.

But he wanted her again, couldn't stop that deep ache in his bones. Now that he'd had a taste, he felt insatiable. Worse than before because he'd gotten so much more, been buried inside of her, and a part of him wanted to lose himself there for the rest of time.

Because he sure as hell didn't want to come back to real life. But the reality of what they were facing came crashing back as he searched through his bag for the little pocket that held the flash drive. He still needed to figure out what he was going to do next.

"Why are you frowning like that?" she asked, coming up beside him, her hand sliding over his bare stomach.

It was so casual, so comfortable, and his chest ached when he thought about the fact that he'd put her in danger, that she was still in it by being with him.

Santiago was out of the picture now, but Zimmerman was a worse man to have on their tail. Chase didn't know how long they had until someone—Zim's guys or Gibson's—found where they were. If only he could sink into this with her, casually touching, discussing what this meant, what they were going to do next in this relationship that was so unexpected.

But his priority had to be figuring out what to do with the information they'd found on the flash drive.

"Chase?" Sadie's voice pulled him back, and he laid his hand over her arm across his stomach.

He took a deep breath. "I'm trying to figure out our next steps."

"You and me? Or. . . ?" Her voice trailed off as her brows pulled together, the faint flash of fear coming into her eyes.

He took her arms from around his waist, holding her hands to bring them to his lips. She'd already cut to the crux of his dilemma. There couldn't be a next step for the two of them, but his heart spasmed to think it; his stomach twisted when he realized this was the moment he had to say it, make it final.

"Sadie," he started, but her teeth flashed in a dark smile.

"You don't have to say it, Chase." Her voice was soft but unwavering. "I know there isn't a you and me."

He flinched. It was somehow more painful hearing her say it, even though it was exactly what he'd been ready to tell her. "Not until this whole thing is finished."

"I know. It's fine." She moved to sit on the bed, laying back against the pillows.

His eyes involuntarily raked over her, still just in her bra and underwear, as she pulled her legs in close to her body, sliding them under the covers.

He swallowed hard. "Are you sleeping in that?"

One side of her mouth quirked up, but she was still focused on arranging the duvet around herself. "Well, my pants are still wet, and I lost my shirt, remember?"

"Do you. . ." he cleared his throat. "Do you want a shirt to sleep in?"

She raised her eyes, and the sultry look she gave him slammed him in the gut. "I do get cold." She tipped her head, giving him that coy smile again, the effect like a midsummer day. "But I thought maybe you could keep me warm."

He stared at her, his very being erupting into a full-blown war. They'd just established that there wouldn't be a next step for them. Not right now. And he couldn't tell if she just hadn't been taking him seriously, or if she was really okay with letting it all go.

Because he wasn't. He *had* to let it all go, but he sure as hell wasn't okay with it.

Her smile grew, and she patted the spot next to her. Of course he'd rather sleep beside her than alone in the other queen bed. But he didn't want to blur the lines for her any more than they already were.

But he knew it wasn't Sadie who was having trouble with that. And he realized that was going to be a big problem when this all ended.

"Are you done?" she asked, raising a brow when he still didn't move.

His gaze followed hers to the bag his hands still rested on, the laptop and flash drive just out of her view.

The physical part of him wanted to be done with it. And the emotional side of him wanted to climb into bed and hold her, pretend none of the outside world existed. But it wasn't only illogical to ignore all of that, but it was also a dangerous game to play with himself.

"Sadie, I—"

She sighed heavily. "Chase, I know. This whole thing sucks. I want. . ." she turned her face to the side. "It doesn't matter what I want. Except for right now. I just want to be together while we can."

Her words reignited the war inside him, the battle raging between the fear that whatever came next would keep them apart and the relief that she was willing to just have this moment, right now, with him.

But first.

He sighed, regret stilling the conflict tearing at his insides. "I have to look at this list again."

She fought the reaction, but she still tensed up. "Do you have a plan?"

"Not yet," he admitted, booting up his computer. He felt the depth of his frown as he shoved the flash drive into the port.

Right now, all he had was that list of names. There was nothing on it about the connection they had, no account numbers, nothing to even tie them to Zimmerman in the first place. He checked as soon as he could click the drive open, scrolling through every last name to make sure he hadn't missed anything now that he had the time.

"No plan," she repeated, way too calm.

After their day, maybe that prospect was less daunting than it felt to him.

"No. I think I need Greg."

She made a face. "No one needs Greg."

He almost laughed at the look she shot him, reminded of that moment when he'd kidnapped her, how she'd taken the time to deny that the guy was her boyfriend despite the predicament she was in.

"In this case, I think I do need him, if only for the information he has." He rolled through the names again, wishing each one didn't make his stomach drop lower and lower.

"This isn't enough?" She nodded at the laptop, clutching the blanket closer to her chest.

He raised a brow at her, understanding that she hadn't quite grasped what he had. "Tell me: what did you see on this list?"

She pulled her hair over her shoulder, trapping the silken locks between nervous, stroking fingers. "A lot of names. Big names."

He nodded. "What else?"

She got that look on her face like a kid in school who was asked a question from the homework they hadn't done. "There wasn't anything else. . ."

He pointed at her, the truth of it clenching in his middle. "Exactly."

Realization dawned in her eyes, and her shoulders dropped. A breath rushed through her parted lips. "You don't have any proof."

"All I have are names." he shook his head. "If I bring this in, give them the story I'm piecing together, they'd laugh in my face. And worse, I'd tip my hand, and the guys on that list would make me disappear pretty quickly."

"Even if you went to someone above them?" Her tone finally held the fear he'd been expecting.

Frustration snapped at his muscles, but he clamped down on his reaction so he could try to explain it. "For all they know, I made this list myself. I haven't been in the Bureau long enough to build that kind of trust. Who would they believe? Me or my boss? Working undercover changes people, and he could spin a story about me turning to save his own skin."

She made a choked sound like she was about to cry. Because it did seem rather bleak. But he knew the guarantee for blowing the whole thing up and coming out unscathed: Greg.

He shut his eyes briefly. "Sadie, do you have any idea where Greg could be?"

She pulled back slightly, thrown off. "I–I'm not sure."

He took her hands. "Any bit of information could help. You were with him for, what, a year?"

Her lip curled back a little. "Almost two."

He searched her eyes, trying not to sound too desperate, too intense. "There has to be something. You met his family?"

"Yes, but—"

"A vacation home? A cabin somewhere?"

"I don't know." The strain was evident in her voice, and she looked heavenward as if the answer were written on the ceiling.

The desperation in her face struck him, and he scolded himself for pushing so hard after what she'd been through that day. What an insensitive asshole he was. Now was not the time, and she was not responsible for helping him. He could figure it out on his own. Maybe a night of sleep would clear his mind, and he'd miraculously get an idea.

"Hey." He lowered his voice, beating back his intensity. "I'm sorry."

She looked at him, very real despair in her eyes. The cogs of panic had already started to turn.

He brushed a hand over her hair, hoping to infuse the touch with soothing calm. While there was a level of fear that built inside of him, he knew how to control it. Just like his dragon of rage, he'd trained himself to channel fear into something productive. But this wasn't productive, especially not for her.

"Let's just get some sleep. You leave it all to me. I'll figure it out."

She slammed her eyes shut. "It was my fault. I asked."

He leaned forward to press a kiss to her lips, guilt a heavy stone within him. "It's not your fault. I was in the wrong."

She took a breath, released it, and opened her eyes. "Sleep?"

He dipped his head, tucking everything back into the duffel, and set it on the floor so that he could walk around to the other side of the bed. He slipped his pants off and climbed in beside her.

As soon as he was settled, she curled into him, her smooth, warm skin touching his and lighting his senses on fire.

He somehow found it in himself to turn off the light.

39

Rude Awakening

Sleep took Sadie eventually. But it didn't keep her. She'd dreamt, of course. Nightmares, really. Reliving the horrors she'd experienced already. And she knew it was nothing compared to what Chase had probably been through in his time undercover. Or what other victims of these men had endured.

Still, it was beyond anything she'd ever imagined going through in her life. It made her wonder what sort of horrors her Marine father had been through, what he kept hidden behind his aloof mask.

She knew he'd struggled. Her mother had hinted at it. But that had been something private between her parents, nothing she'd ever pressed to know, even since her mother's passing.

Chase's muscular back was to her. He'd turned over in slumber, and she wondered at the expanse, the defined muscles that were visible even in darkness and in his relaxed state.

She knew she wouldn't be able to sleep until she'd gone to the bathroom, so she slipped out of bed to take care of business, pulling the robe on.

Instead of climbing back into bed, though, she walked to the window where the faint glow of early, predawn light peeked from the top of the curtains. She held the robe closed over herself, a little chilled since the fabric was thin, and pulled the curtain back, hoping to catch the sunrise.

If she had to guess, it was somewhere around five in the morning. She had been so sleepy and out of it when they'd arrived, she hadn't picked up on many details, but it was clear their window faced east as the first orange and yellow bands breached the night sky with the impending birth of day.

She was only mildly surprised to see people outside, already packing up or leaving, cars driving along the road whose headlights cut through that small space between the wall and the curtain she held.

Chase stirred behind her, but she didn't turn. Not even when she heard him get up and come to stand behind her, the warmth of his presence seeping into her back.

His hands brushed lightly along her neck and rested on her shoulders, and he leaned forward, his body pressed against her so that he could look out from behind her.

Which was why she felt him tense up.

"What is it?" The question shot out of her.

"Get dressed, now."

She spun to see him already moving quickly to don his own clothing, throwing anything he found into the duffel he lugged from the floor. She rushed to turn on the lamp so that she could find everything she had, which wasn't much.

"Chase," she said, rushing to pull on her jeans, still shirtless.

"Zimmerman's guys are here."

His answer was not a surprise to her. It had to be something along those lines for him to react that way, but just having it confirmed set her stomach writhing.

"Do they know we're here?" she asked. It was a question that reminded her, absurdly, of something her kindergartners tended to ask—they often assumed she knew what other people knew or were thinking. Like she was a mind-reader.

"I'm not sure they know which room. But they know we're at this motel." He met her eyes just before yanking his shirt over his head. "I'm going to have to steal a car."

She should've had some kind of reaction to that. Guilt or something, right? But it was a relief that he had a plan of escape. And at the moment, she didn't give a flying fig newton about committing crimes if it meant they stayed alive.

"Okay."

He spun to survey the room for anything else they might have brought in and still needed, and she did the same. She had so little in the first place that there wasn't anything for her to leave behind. And certainly not anything she needed or could lead the men to them.

As a unit, they moved toward the door, though he swept his hand out for her to stay behind him. She didn't miss the gun he held in his other hand, pointed toward the floor as he eased the door open a fraction of an inch.

"Move quickly, and stay right behind me." He looked back at her. "Where's your shirt?"

She looked down at herself in just her pants and bra and held her hands up.

His mouth twisted to the side. "We'll get the extra one I have once we're on the road."

As if she cared at this moment whether she went out in public like this. It was not different than wearing a swimsuit top. And it was early enough in the morning not many people would likely see her. But she snatched the discarded robe from the floor and slipped it on. It was as good as it would get.

He gestured for her to follow as he led them outside, his gaze sweeping back and forth.

She crept along behind him, her heart pounding loudly in her ears. She was afraid she wouldn't be able to hear any instructions he gave her, so she tuned in extra tight to him, trying not to scan for whoever he'd seen that spooked him. She didn't know what she was looking for anyway.

He chose a car that didn't have any outstanding features, but that was probably intentional. It was older, beat up, and likely didn't have a car alarm that he would trip.

"Keep an eye out while I boost the car," he instructed as they crouched beside the driver's side door.

She nodded, not having the wherewithal to ask what she was looking for. Probably nefarious types who appeared to be looking for someone—namely them. But no one was near their side of the parking lot at the moment.

"Sadie," he hissed, and she jerked around to see him already climbing into the front seat, tossing a long wire into the back. It must have been what he'd used to unlock it.

She crept around to the passenger side as he pulled the lock up with his fingers. The interior smelled of stale fast food and marijuana smoke. That skunk-broccoli combo was unmistakable.

Chase gave no indication he'd noticed as he threw the duffel into the back and pulled the cables under the steering wheel to hot-wire the car, which he did in short order.

She stared at him as he sat up, pulling the door closed and looking almost comically large in the small sedan.

He must have felt her eyes on him. "My dad was a criminal, remember?"

He didn't wait for her response as he backed out of the parking spot, barely stopping at the entrance to the street, and gunned it to get in front of an oncoming vehicle.

She wanted to hold onto something to steady herself and her nerves, but she was too afraid to touch anything. How reliable would this rattling vehicle be in the long run?

Sadie twisted in her seat to look behind them. Had the guys seen them leave?

"We'll have to switch cars again."

She jerked to look at Chase, taking in the sharp edges of his face in profile. He looked too relaxed, too comfortable with this life. And she suddenly wondered how much this had affected him, how much it would carry over into real life.

"And by switch, you mean steal, right?" Her voice sounded small, diminished by the anxiety winding her up into a tight ball.

If they made it out of this, would he have the chance to get out of this life? Would he want to? Could he even live a normal life again?

Chase's eyes shifted from the road to the rearview, and his foot pressed more heavily on the gas pedal, making her heart rate accelerate in proportion.

"They're following?"

"Probably," he murmured.

The truth of what he'd said earlier—about there being no next steps for the two of them together—was solidifying in her mind, even as it made her heart ache. She had stoically accepted it when he'd insisted, knowing that her heart was tearing a little the whole time.

She did know herself, after all. Giving her body always led to her giving her heart.

But this life, this danger, his knowledge of this world made her wonder if there could be normalcy—safety—even if he got out of undercover work. Would she always be a target for his enemies? Would he always *have* enemies? Would he always be in danger of being taken from her?

Moisture stung in her eyes, and she turned to look out the window at the world flying by, fields catching on fire with the rising summer sun.

The reality was becoming more stark. She thought she'd have time before she had to process the fact. Like in the privacy and safety of her own home once this whole thing was over. She could have a good cry by herself.

"Hey." Chase's voice feathered along the air between them. "You okay?"

She wouldn't look at him, not until she had herself under control.

"Fine," she answered, annoyed that it was obvious she was crying. Maybe she could pass it off as exhaustion, shock, anything but the truth. Because it was stupid. They hadn't known each other that long.

But her little heart was so easily swayed.

"I'm so sorry you got dragged into this, Sadie." His voice was tight with some kind of emotion she couldn't place at first. Then it slid home. Guilt.

She looked at him, using her fingertips to press the remaining tears from her eyes. "No, it's fine. It's all just catching up to me. And I'm tired."

He blew out a breath, rubbing a hand down his face. "Let's end this."

40

The Exchange

The idea had started to form sometime during the night, when Chase had held Sadie pressed against his body, feeling the deep and even breathing that told him she was asleep.

With the faintest light sneaking through the edge of the curtains, he'd been able to make out the curves of her face, caressed by moonlight, her full lips partially open. And he'd ached.

Ached for more nights like that. When his only concern might be accidentally waking her when he turned over. Not worrying about whether someone was going to sneak in the window and slit his throat in the darkness.

He'd been desperately searching for a way forward, a way to end this job once and for all. Because unless he took out every player in the game, he would be at the top of multiple target lists.

The answer had come to him, and he'd planned to make the call first thing that morning.

And then Zimmerman's guys had shown up.

"Where are we going?"

Her voice sounded so small, still heavy with the emotion she was trying to pass off as exhaustion. He knew that wasn't it. Or not all of it, though he wouldn't pretend to know what she might have been thinking or feeling. But he sensed the depth, the well she was trying to send whatever emotions back into that stretched so far down, he might never plumb the depths.

"You remember what I told you about my dad?"

He caught her nod in his periphery.

"He was arrested by this old FBI agent who's retired now. And I think he might be our in for how to get around this list."

He felt her confusion envelop him.

"Did you become friends with him?"

He blew out a breath, thinking back to how they'd left that situation. "Not exactly."

She pursed her lips. "Why do I feel like *not exactly* means he might answer the door with a gun in his hand?"

A surprised laugh escaped him. He appreciated how the joking tone brought the life back to her face and voice. "I wouldn't put it past him, but I don't think it would play out like that. He'll be wary and skeptical. Might even shut the door in our faces," he muttered. "But it's worth a shot. I think I can convince him, and he might actually be able to help us."

"Okay," she said softly. "I trust you."

The words pierced him, a slice right to the bone, and he fought the grimace. Her trust made him want to live up to the expectation that he'd never intentionally put her in danger. But he felt like he'd already let her down.

They fell silent, and she turned toward her window again. At least she wasn't crying this time.

They pulled onto a road that led to a larger town he was vaguely familiar with. They could at least lose their tail temporarily, using the busier area to blend in and protect themselves.

Zimmerman had some powerful guys under his thumb, but he wouldn't want them to reveal who they were for a small fish like Chase. So it wasn't likely they'd open fire in public to take him down.

He suspected that Zimmerman didn't even know what exactly had transpired between Chase and Santiago or what information Chase had, let alone what he planned to do with it. Based on how much distance their tail had given them, they weren't in hot pursuit yet. Just a recon mission for now.

Thank God.

He drove toward the fancy resort he knew about on the edge of town, weaving into the summer tourist traffic that crawled by to gawk at the one-hundred-year-old swanky building.

The tension he'd sensed from Sadie had loosened during the last part of their drive, but he felt it winding her back up as she silently processed where they were going.

She didn't know what his plan was, but that was okay. She didn't really have to participate—honestly, the less she did, the better.

He followed the line of traffic winding through a round-about and took the exit that would bring them to the valet parking. Their use of valet would be dubious at best, given the state of the car he was driving, but he'd give a generous tip upfront.

Sadie straightened in her seat, and they pulled up under the portico.

"Chase. . ."

He didn't reply, his jaw tightening as he nodded for her to get out with him.

The frown on the valet's face told him exactly how the kid felt about the state of their car.

"Hey, buddy," Chase said, adding a smile as he reached forward to stick two one-hundred-dollar bills in the valet's hand. "Just dropping off for the day."

The valet's mouth twisted as he looked down at the money in his hand. "Okay. . ." He looked up at Chase. "Do you have a key?"

Shit. He hadn't thought about that. "Um, babe? Don't you have the key?"

He spun to face Sadie, hating himself for dragging her into his ruse.

Her eyes only widened for a second before she blinked. "I thought you had it."

He gave an entirely unfeigned nervous laugh. "It's a remote start," he said in explanation.

The kid narrowed his eyes and looked at the car, then back to Chase like he was ready for him to say *just kidding*.

"You go ahead," Sadie said, her voice just snooty enough that she legitimately sounded like she belonged. "It will turn off for you anyway after you park, and we can go back up to our room to find it. Pretty sure I left it when I ran back up for my sunglasses."

He twisted his mouth, taking in the robe she held closed over her chest. Maybe if he squinted, she'd look like she'd been at the pool. Or maybe that she'd been drinking.

As if playing to that character, she walked forward in a slight zigzag, grabbing Chase's arm to drag him toward the doors, stumbling just enough to make it believable.

In the reflection of the glass doors, Chase saw the valet scratch the back of his neck and bounce his gaze between them and the beat-up car. Finally, when they'd gotten inside the vestibule, the kid turned to get in and put it into drive.

Chase waited until the kid had driven far enough away before pivoting, pulling Sadie with him.

"What are you doing?" she hissed.

He ignored her as he checked the area for onlookers. There were probably cameras around, but that couldn't be helped. At least this would play in his favor for keeping his cover intact.

He snatched a key fob from the rows of hooks on the valet's stand and reached backward for Sadie's hand, yanking her forward when he felt her skin against his palm.

"Jeez," she huffed.

"Sorry," he muttered. "I want to make it look like I'm forcing you. Otherwise, they might think you're an accomplice in this whole thing."

"Aren't I?"

He glanced at her but said nothing. It was weird what the thought did to him.

They hurried into the parking lot, and he paced up and down the rows of flashy cars with her trailing behind, pressing the disarm button over and over again until they came to the one it belonged to.

A black Lexus. It was an expensive car, but it wouldn't draw the eye the same way a Mercedes or a Tesla might, which was as much as he could ask for at the moment. It was his fault for using valet parking as a means of procuring a new ride.

They both slid into the sleek sedan, and he tossed the duffel into the back.

Sadie let out a low whistle. "I feel like I'm going to contaminate this thing with whatever unseen germs I collected in the last car."

He smirked as he closed the door and started it, the engine emitting the softest purr. "Maybe you'll feel better about it once we get you some new clothes."

She looked down at herself with a frown. "You don't like my robe?"

He huffed a laugh. "I like you in anything." He made a face. "Scratch that. I like you in nothing. But if you have to be dressed, the robe isn't half bad."

She rolled her eyes. "Typical male response."

"Buckle up," he said, forcing himself to focus. If he dwelled too long on the fact that she was barely wearing anything, he'd do something that would cost them time and really contaminate the fancy car.

She pulled her belt across her body without another word, and he shifted into reverse.

41

Revelations and Remorse

They stopped outside of town, pulling into the parking lot of some kitschy tourist trap gas station.

Sadie looked for the least obnoxious t-shirt she could find and a pair of cheap leggings to change into. They were probably see-through if she bent over, but that was the least of her worries. She also managed to snag a brush and a tube of unscented lotion with less dubious ingredients. Dry skin after her second kidnapping and near-death experience was no joke. She brushed through her hair and braided it after she changed in the bathroom.

While she'd done all of that, Chase pulled around the side of the building. When she came outside, he was putting the finishing touches on a set of new license plates he apparently just kept in his duffel bag. She told herself she didn't want to know why he had them so readily available, whipping them out faster than she bought up the homemade tallow balm at the farmer's market.

She settled into the front seat, feeling a little refreshed, and a lot more comfortable without the muddy, borrowed jeans and the robe as a makeshift shirt.

Chase climbed in a few seconds later, eyeing her for a second before starting the car.

"I know. I flawlessly match the caliber of fancy this car embodies."

He snorted. "Like I said before: I'd prefer you in nothing. So it makes no difference to me."

She shook her head, working to ignore the way that sent a thrill through her. She was already in too deep here, her body still lit up by the brand of his touch. "Alrighty. Where to now?"

"Got the address for Carl Kesterson. We're going to drop in unannounced instead of asking for permission." He pulled out onto the road.

Her fingers twisted into the hem of her new shirt, but she was able to keep her voice evn. "You really think he will help?"

He took a deep breath, uncertainty filling the space. "We'll find out."

That sounded promising. "Does he know you're undercover?"

He tipped his head, grimacing. "He probably knows nothing about me."

The shirt twisted tighter in her hands, and she couldn't stop the flow of questions, each shoved out by the building anxiety. "Will he even know who you are?"

If Chase found it annoying, he gave no indication. "I mean, Kesterson tracked my dad for years, so he knew about my mom and me. My dad was a con man. They had to dive deep and follow every aspect of his life to nail him."

She felt like a starved dog reacting to every snippet of his past he was suddenly dropping for her. "So your dad was pretty clever."

Chase frowned like he didn't like her observation. "Yeah. Until he wasn't."

The way he said it. . . She tilted her head. "What do you mean?"

"My dad was methodical. About everything." He paused, the weight of the words he wasn't saying pressing around them. "It was almost like my dad wanted to get caught."

The weight grew heavier, sizzling on the air with intensity, like Chase's mind was slowly coming to terms with his spoken realization.

"He wanted to get caught," he repeated.

She didn't know how to read his reaction. The way his brows knit over his eyes as he continued to stare forward didn't give much away. It could have been anger, hurt, confusion. She didn't know much about his dad or their relationship, but she remembered that he'd said his dad had died of cancer, too.

"It wasn't long after he was locked up that he got diagnosed."

It was as if he'd read her thoughts, his mind going where hers had, though via a different path. She had no background information, no history to sift through. But those two things, without much context, still led her to a possible conclusion.

"Do you think he knew? And that's why?" The prompting questions crept out, like she was tip-toeing past a slumbering bear.

Still, he jerked to look at her. "You mean he made sure he got caught because he knew he was sick?"

She lifted a shoulder. "I didn't know him. I'm just throwing it out there. Your tone suggested maybe you were suspicious about the timing."

His jaw shifted a little as he stared at her. Then he slowly turned back to the road, rubbing his hand along his chin as he brooded. "But why would he rather get caught?"

A thought crossed her mind, but she waited a beat to say it, wary of his reaction, of what this conversation was already doing to him. "Did you and your mom get something out of him going to jail?"

His knuckles went white on the steering wheel. "My mom thought we would lose everything." His voice was so soft she almost didn't hear it.

"But you didn't?" she prompted when a full minute ticked by without another word from him.

She wasn't sure if she should stop, leave the topic alone, but he hadn't told her to mind her own business yet, even as his continued hesitation wrapped itself around them.

"No." He scowled toward the road. "I went to college. She moved away. I got a partial scholarship, a job so I could work for the rest. Except whatever was left over was always paid before I could do it, directly to the school. I only ended up paying for housing and my books." His lips flattened, and he shook his head. "She claimed it was an inheritance from her father. But. . . my grandfather was a two-bit mechanic. Where would he get that kind of money?"

There was very little emotion in his words, but each one was a shot to her heart. Because she saw it for what it was: his protection mechanism. Keep it all locked up tight until it exploded. And maybe this part hadn't come to the surface yet. Or maybe it had, and he'd battled it back, using the intensity of physical exertion to expel the fiery energy of his anger.

"Because I didn't want to know what my dad had been into, I wanted no part of it, no part of him, so I believed her." His jaw clenched at the same moment his hands did. "I should have. . ."

"What?" she asked when he didn't finish. "Denied the money? How could you?"

He threw one hand up. "I could have unregistered, transferred somewhere else, cut myself off from her. I can't believe she would use his dirty money like that."

As if a kid was responsible for what their parents did. How many kids did she see day in and day out who were hurting because of the decisions their parents made for them?

"Chase, you were young. And it gave you opportunities you wouldn't have had otherwise."

"But I was complicit by allowing her to use his tainted money." He huffed. "I'm no better than he was."

"You are," she insisted. "Look at what you're doing right now. You saved me. Twice. And now you're working as hard as you can to bring some of the worst guys down. Even if it means putting yourself in danger."

He shook his head.

"Chase, please." She put her hand on his arm, desperate to make him see, to understand. "Pull over."

He looked at her, a question in his eyes.

"Pull over," she said again, infusing the words with the authority she knew how to wield. Not loud but sharp.

He didn't make a move for a full minute, then he pressed his lips together and slowed, pulling to the side of the road on the desolate highway. She had no idea how long of a drive they had ahead of them, but it didn't matter. Not when it came to this.

He put the car in park, the engine still running, though it was so quiet, you wouldn't know it.

She unbuckled. "Look at me."

He stared at the dashboard, breathing hard.

She leaned over and put her hands on either side of his face, forcing him to look at her. She stared intently into his eyes, the green so like the woods that surrounded his cabin. "You are an honorable man."

His gaze shot down, shame warming his cheeks under her palms.

"Don't. Sometimes we're put in positions where we have to do the things we don't want to in order to contribute to the greater good. It makes *you* a stronger man that you make the hard choices, do the harder things. You are not your father. We do better when we know better."

She kissed him, pressing so hard against his lips with hers, it was almost painful. She put every ounce of her feelings into the kiss, not even hating that there was more behind it than there should have been, more than she even realized until that moment.

At first, he barely reacted to her kiss, but his brow furrowed after a second, maybe sensing what was underneath, and his hands went to her waist. He gripped so hard, the intensity his answer to hers.

Maybe she wasn't the only one feeling things to the depth that she was.

When they broke apart, she laid her forehead against his, and their breath danced between them.

"You're doing good, Chase. You hear me?"

He nodded, his eyes still closed.

42

Solicited Advice

Kesterson lived in an ancient brownstone that was as dated as it was meticulously cared for. That tracked with what Chase remembered about the man. He'd been old-school and thorough. Short and squat with a sour expression, it had surprised Chase to find he was as gentle as he was edged.

So when Kesterson opened his door with a glower, Chase assumed it was now permanently etched into his face instead of a grumpy mood.

The folds on Kesterson's eyelids obscured the color of his irises, but it was still obvious when he narrowed his gaze on Chase's face, recognition immediate.

"Son of Lundgren," Kesterson said with a grunt, taking him in from head to toe. "All grown up."

Chase waited while Kesterson tried to figure him out. The old man's eyes shifted to Sadie, doing the same once-over he gave Chase.

"Finding you on my doorstep feels a little bit foreboding, but I don't think you'd bring your girlfriend if this were a revenge visit."

Cocky old bastard, Chase thought.

"No desire for revenge on my part," he said. "I'm here for help."

Kesterson made a quick calculation then opened his door wider, jerking his head as invitation.

Chase took Sadie's hand and followed the old man inside. He led them through a narrow hallway to the back of the house where a cramped living room opened to a large back window. Despite the view, the room was dark. Dark-wooded furniture, dark-colored walls, and the light that tried to break through was diffused by the encroaching neighboring houses.

Kesterson moved with surprising ease. Chase had no idea how old he was, but he'd been well past middle age when he'd finally taken Chase's dad in. And that was at least a dozen years ago.

"Refreshments?" Kesterson gestured toward his small galley kitchen.

"We're fine," Chase answered, though he hadn't bothered to ask Sadie.

She remained silent, wide-eyed as she took in the space around them.

Kesterson frowned as he turned to sit in a well-loved recliner, flinging his hand out to invite them to the couch. He was remarkably relaxed about Chase showing up on his doorstep.

And anything that easy made Chase wary.

"So, son of Lundgren, you need my help," Kesterson said, his voice grating like it had been rolled around in a can with gravel.

"Yes."

Thick, bushy eyebrows rose, lifting stacked lines on his forehead. "With what, pray tell?"

Chase looked at Sadie, but before he could continue, Kesterson turned his attention to her.

"Who's your lady friend?"

She cleared her throat. "Um. Sadie Powell."

"She's part of the reason we're here," Chase added.

Kesterson steepled his fingers and waited.

Now or never. Chase suddenly held a fear that this man could've been compromised, too. Maybe that was why he felt so uneasy. But he was already here, already on Zimmerman's radar as a possible problem, and he was not an idiot. He'd come in armed, knew he needed to be prepared for anything.

"What do you know about Lazlo Zimmerman?" he asked.

Kesterson didn't react. But Chase remembered the man's poker face, even this many years later.

"He's a white-collar mob type, isn't he?"

Chase nodded, weighing Kesterson's tone and body language. No warning bells went off, but he was already wired, and his eyes shifted to open doorways where anyone could jump out at them.

Kesterson's eyes glittered with understanding. Or was it satisfaction? He was likely reading Chase's nerves incorrectly.

"You in over your head with him?" Kesterson asked, unbelievably relaxed about the situation.

Chase grimaced and sat forward, resting his elbows on his knees. "Yes, but not in the way you might think."

The eyebrows quirked.

Chase sighed. "Yes, I've been working for him. But in an undercover capacity for the FBI."

Kesterson sat forward now, eyes zeroing in. "If that's true, then what do you need my help with? I'm retired."

"I'm counting on that fact."

Kesterson shook his head. "I'm old, kid. I don't have skin in the game, and I don't much care about a mobster that came to power after my time."

Desperation burned in Chase's gut. "Does it matter to you that he's got his hands *in* the FBI?"

Kesterson stiffened. "What do you mean?"

He'd gotten him. Now he had to reel him in. "I have some evidence that he not only has my boss under his thumb, but a couple of higher-ups as well."

Kesterson's lips pursed, skepticism bringing those heavy lids low over his eyes. "Who?"

"Jared Gibson. Hank Jeppesen. Larry Fink."

Kesterson sat back with a low whistle, worry etching an extra line under the crags in his forehead. "That's a pretty serious allegation. Your proof has to be irrefutable if you're going up against them." The muscles around his eyes tightened. "Unless. . ."

Chase's mouth twitched into a grim smile.

"That's why you're here. Well, shit." He pushed himself out of his chair, rubbing a hand over his stubbly chin. "And what does the girl have to do with it?"

Sadie's hands twisted in her lap. "My ex-boyfriend is mixed up in it, and—"

"Let me guess," Kesterson interrupted dryly. "He dragged you into the toxic cake mix. What did he do? Blackmail you?"

She shook her head, pink blossoming in her cheeks. "He dumped some of the evidence on me."

"Glad he's an ex, then. You got mobsters on your tail, I'd bet."

"Yes. The only reason I'm still alive is because of him." She jerked her thumb toward Chase, a shy smile ghosting across her face.

Kesterson's gaze sharpened as he analyzed how close she sat to Chase, though they weren't touching. Not that he didn't want to. The way Chase's skin craved hers was not something he could deny anymore. Especially after the way she'd kissed him in the car.

He'd experienced every bit of her body, her words, her hands the night before. But that kiss had seared him like a brand, and he knew there was no going back. It was more than what it had done to him physically. Because with that kiss, she'd sealed what her words had already done—made him feel seen. He'd said there was no after, but he wasn't sure he could commit to that now.

Kesterson said nothing about what he'd clearly figured out was going on between them. "So what evidence you got?" he asked instead.

Chase bared his teeth, watching the older man pace across the room. "Not enough to nail them. But enough to make somebody nervous."

Kesterson stopped in front of the window, staring out. He must have been immersed in his own thoughts because there wasn't much of a view besides the brick of the next row of townhouses on the other side of his fence.

"So you either need hard evidence. . ." he mused, rubbing his chin again. "Or." He turned around suddenly, and despite the wrinkles on his face, he seemed younger. Like he'd just needed to get back in the game to bring himself back to life.

"Or what?" Sadie asked.

"You have to get them to incriminate themselves."

"How are we supposed to do that?" Chase heard the edge in his own voice. He was grasping at straws, and even if Kesterson had an idea, desperation was crawling under his skin.

"You gotta make them think you have the hard evidence. Nothing like a little poisoned sugar water to bring out the creepy crawlies."

Chase shot to his feet, the unease becoming too toxic and heated within him. "Yeah, and what's the bait?"

Kesterson looked at Sadie. His expression made it clear the man knew what he was asking and how Chase would react. But Chase couldn't help the explosion inside of him anyway.

"No fucking way." The words snapped on the air like a whip. "She's already been in enough danger, roughed up too many times by these assholes."

"Listen, kid. You're at the end of the road for this. You gotta do what needs doing, or you disappear. By choice or because Zimmerman's guys take you out."

Chase threw his arm out in her direction. "But she has nothing to do with any of it."

"I get it. You feel all responsible for her because she's got a pretty face and a nice ass. But you have to remember the *job*."

It wasn't a conscious decision, though the rage roared inside of him, that dragon bursting to life. It wasn't until Sadie was screaming in his ear to let Kesterson go that he even realized he'd shoved him up against the wall, his hands fisted around the guy's shirt.

"Chase, stop it! Let him go!"

Kesterson didn't look fazed, though his words were strained. "Use that, kid. You gotta make her the bait then use that instinct to protect her and keep her alive. It's your only shot."

"I'm not putting her at risk for this." Chase almost spat the words in the guy's face. And admittedly, there was a part of him that felt some kind of latent anger that this man represented what had taken his father from him, too.

"Chase." Sadie's hand landed on his forearm, and a slow-moving balm soothed over his frayed nerves. "He's right. It's worth it if we can bring this whole thing down. I'm not safe until they're all behind bars anyway."

He hated that it was true, hated that they were both right. It was exactly the reason he'd come here—to get advice, an idea, a direction to go. Some part of him had known this was the only answer, but he'd hoped that Kesterson would have another option. That maybe he had some connection Chase didn't.

With a deep breath and very deliberate concentration, Chase released his grip on Kesterson. Heat still cascaded down his arms, but he stalked away.

Sadie followed him belatedly like she was still too stunned to move at first.

Chase was already reaching for the doorknob when she caught up to him, and Kesterson's voice chased them out the door.

"Be careful, kid."

43

The Next Move

Sadie could feel Chase seething. The anger flowed off of him in radiating waves that kept her silent on the drive to who-knew-where. She didn't dare ask where they were going. The silence was way too fragile, fissures made by his rage and her own fear at what was going to happen next weakening her resolve.

Not that it was clear what was going to happen. She just knew they'd be walking a very thin line between life and death. And so she understood his anger, especially after witnessing the lengths he'd gone to protect her. He'd literally killed to keep her safe.

A shudder ran through her unbidden, and she turned toward the window. Would this lead to more deaths? And would that somehow be her fault? Was she partially responsible for the men whose lives Chase had taken?

She couldn't find it in herself to feel remorse about that. Not after the way they'd treated her, the way Travers had violated her, and the things she suspected they'd done to others.

"What's the plan?" she asked, not looking at him. She couldn't face the way his expression would be hard and cold from his anger, like smooth glass.

"Get a hotel and some rest."

She turned to him then. His black mood was still palpable, but he managed to wrestle it back. It made sense to focus on the small details of what they could control first. Isn't that what she regularly taught her students?

"How about food?" she suggested, listening to the call of her gurgling stomach. They had only eaten the random gas station food they'd picked up on the run, and she needed something more substantial.

His expression softened, lines forming in his forehead as concern replaced his anger. He ran his hand over his face, sighing loudly. "Shit. I'm sorry, Sadie. I didn't even think about that."

She offered a small smile. "It's okay. It's been a lot over the last few days."

He shook his head, some of the anger sparking in his eyes again. But neither spoke until they drove through a fast-food place—a Mediterranean place she knew was decent with ingredients—and got dinner, then silence reigned again until they reached the hotel. It was a step up in comparison to the motel they'd spent the previous night in. They'd been found there anyway, so it didn't seem to matter.

They made their way to their room through a plush hallway, dim sconces illuminating the gold filigree in the wallpaper. Sadie's eyes fell on the black duffel bag Chase carried, and she swallowed against her anxiety. Of course, he wouldn't leave it in the car, but it represented everything that had taken place over the last week—had it only been a week?

Was anyone worried about her? Had anyone called the police? Checked her house and found it ransacked? Fiona would have noticed her silence. But would she panic? Or would she think Sadie had dipped town for some nature retreat as she had been known to do in the past?

Maybe she should have checked in with someone, called to say that she was alive and well and safe. Ish.

Safe as long as she was with Chase.

But that was probably going to end whenever they set things up to use her as bait like Carl Kesterson had suggested. Nerves danced in her stomach, but it was the most logical way of bringing this whole thing to an end.

Chase slipped the key card into the slot on their door and pushed inside, holding it open for her to go in first.

She walked straight to the king-size bed and threw herself back onto it, staring at the ceiling. Her heart beat raucously against her ribs, but she tried to quiet her mind.

Chase set the bag against the wall next to what would be his side of the bed and frowned down at her.

She patted the bed beside her. "Lay with me?"

His expression didn't change as he debated for a moment. Maybe he was still in the grip of his anger, unable to dispel the rage their conversation with Kesterson had ignited. But she didn't want that to define their last night together.

Finally he exhaled and relented, climbing onto the bed with her, lying on his side with his head propped on his hand while he stared at her. After one more hesitation, he reached over to brush his hand down her face.

She rolled onto her side to face him, nestling in, and pressed her face into his chest as his arms went around her. She inhaled the familiar scent of him, her heart slowing with the comfort.

"Sadie," he said softly.

Something stirred within her—something entirely foreign, beyond just the desire that also came alive at his proximity. It was more. More because of the kiss they'd shared before they'd gone to Carl Kesterson's. The desperation she'd felt in herself had been matched by his, and something had shifted between them.

"Sadie, I don't think I can do this." It was just a whisper.

Her heart plummeted, and she stiffened. "Oh."

Of course, he couldn't. Maybe the shift she'd felt had been only one-sided. That made sense. Things had changed for her because of what they'd shared and her heart had made a leap alone.

His arms tightened around her when she tried to pull away. "That's not what I meant."

Confusion swirled through her. This time, he let her pull back a little so that she could analyze his face.

He shut his eyes briefly, cutting off her access to whatever might have shown in his gaze. He was a hard read, but maybe, just maybe, he would've let her see this time.

"I can't bring you in on this, put you in this position. I'm afraid of what might happen." He took a breath and opened his eyes, laying bare the emotions that raged within him. "I'm afraid I'm going to lose you."

Her heart squeezed, almost painful, at his words. Hope stirred at the thought that he might reciprocate her feelings. Her mind grappled to stay with the conversation, though—what his words told her, not what she hoped he meant behind them.

She traced her finger along the seam of the collar of his shirt. "What would happen if we don't do it?" She looked up in time to catch his brows coming together over his eyes.

"What do you mean?" he asked, wary.

"What would happen to me if we *don't* do this."
He drew back a little. "Sadie."

The intensity of the situation was like a fire in her chest. "Chase, you tell me if I can go home right now and be safe."

His chest heaved with the force of his breathing. The recognition of what she was getting at was clear in his eyes as his lips pressed into a line.

"And if I'm not safe to go home now, what's left for me?" Her voice hitched as that came crashing in with full force. Some part of her had known this truth—that she *couldn't* go home until this was done. But she hadn't considered the ramifications and how final they would be.

Would she see her family again? Her brother, her sister, her dad? Her students?

"And what's left for you?" she asked, even as the tears filled her eyes. "You're locked into protecting me, and for how long?" She didn't add that eventually he might grow tired of her, of running to keep her safe, and then where would she be?

What kind of life was that for either of them, anyway?

His thumbs brushed the tears that rolled down her cheeks, and his expression softened. "I'd run forever, protect you for however long it takes," he murmured.

She shook her head because there was no way it was true. He'd hate her one day, when they were both tired and worn down. Because protecting her would take him away from the life he'd built, even if he was tired of undercover work. And maybe she would resent him too, even if it wasn't his fault.

She'd never see her students again, probably never be able to teach, and she didn't know how to exist without that part of herself.

She met his gaze, even as her eyes swam with more tears. "You know what the answer is, Chase." The words came out a whisper, all sound choked out by her emotions.

The stubborn set of his jaw showed how badly he wanted to argue with her, but he said nothing. Because he did know. There was no denying the truth of the situation.

"I trust you." She pressed her lips to his. "I know you can make this work, that you can keep me safe. You already have, and I can't thank you enough for everything." She kissed him again, trying to convey the depth of her gratitude, to dispel the extent of her fear.

"I'd do it a thousand times over," he breathed between kisses, sliding his hand behind her head to cradle it gently. His other hand went to her back, pressing her body against his.

He hadn't admitted it yet, but he hadn't denied the truth of her words either. Which meant that they needed to plan.

But maybe not just yet. Because there was a desperation that buzzed between them, an electric current that sizzled, that made their touch a frenzy that drove her to push him to his back and climb on top of him.

His hands traveled under her shirt to the skin of her back and up, unhooking her bra, and she sat up for him to yank her shirt over her head and toss it away. The bra straps slid down her arms, and she slung that across the room as well.

When she removed his shirt, she ran her fingers over the ripple of his ridiculously chiseled abdomen to the button on his jeans as his mouth devoured the skin along her throat and shoulder, sucking and nipping along her flesh as every inch of her cried out for more, faster, now—before the entire world came crashing down around them.

The need was so strong inside of her she couldn't stop panting like a wild animal as he flipped her onto her back, his hands grabbing and pulling at her. Her own fingers speared into his hair, gripping as he feasted on her flesh, sending zing after zing through her.

He slowly pulled the rest of her clothes from her body, standing to remove his own, then climbed back onto the bed, prowling like a jungle cat, his eyes so dark and molten that she felt more heat building inside of her. He brushed his lips along the inner part of her leg, then up her thigh, placing strategic nips along her skin that made her buck against him.

"Chase," she panted as he settled between her legs, using his mouth to tantalize her. And she suddenly couldn't speak anymore, not with what he was doing to her.

Her hands gripped the bedspread beneath her of their own volition, holding on for dear life as the pressure built inside of her body, crying out for release. She was filled to the brim with need, like a dam ready to burst.

Higher and higher she rose, winding tighter and tighter until she finally crashed over the edge. She cried out, completely shattered, lost to logic, to understanding as she shuddered through wave after wave.

He moved back to roll on a condom while she was still riding them, sliding into her so that he could move in a rhythm perfectly in sync with the rushes.

His scruffy cheek slid against hers, the roughness of his beard a welcome reminder of where she was and who she was. She was so undone, she barely registered any details as he thrust into her hard and fast, eliciting soft cries of pleasure from her.

"Oh, Sadie," he breathed into her ear, his voice strained from the effort of controlling himself. His control didn't last long, and his whole body tightened when he came.

44

The Setup

The rush of what they'd just shared—like their kiss earlier but on steroids—didn't stop even as Chase rolled to his side of the bed. He listened to the sound of her heavy breathing in syncopation with his while his heart hammered against his ribs, threatening to break through the bone. His skin tingled with the electric current that had only begun to abate.

"Wow," Sadie panted from beside him.

She shifted, her palm landing on his chest just over his heart.

"It's beating as hard as mine." She laughed.

He couldn't quite muster the energy to laugh with her, couldn't bring himself to find any of it humorous—not with this new seismic shift within him.

She lifted herself up, placing her hands on either side of him to bring her mouth to his in a sweet kiss. When she pulled back, she smiled, and it twisted his heart to see it. Because something about that desperate and wild act of connection had somehow eased her stress and worry. But it had amplified his.

Abruptly, he flipped her onto her back, laying lightly over her, nuzzling into her neck. She squirmed and squealed, which finally drew a laugh out of him, and a warmth spread through his chest.

This, he thought. This was what he wanted. And so he needed to make it possible, fight to make it a reality.

"I need to make some calls," he murmured against her throat, and she stilled, her pulse jumping erratically against his lips.

When he pulled back to stand, she sat up, her brows pulling over her eyes in concern.

"I need you to stay here while I get everything set up."

She sucked in a breath, the fear in it slicing through him. "How long will you be gone?"

He grimaced. "Not more than an hour, I hope."

He wasn't sure how well or how long he could protect her, but if he could keep one step ahead, he would do it. Setting it up sooner rather than later was the safest option.

She grabbed his hand, her soft, slender fingers sending tingles along his already overheated skin. "Be careful."

He leaned down and took one last taste of her lips, unable to communicate what her words meant to him—what *she* meant to him. He just hoped she could tell, that she would feel it.

He wordlessly got dressed and grabbed his wallet, the keys, and his duffel bag before he headed out.

He couldn't scrub the image of her from his brain as he rode the elevator down and out to the parking lot. The way she watched him from the bed, still undressed, looking more than just physically naked and vulnerable. But maybe he shouldn't get rid of that image because it tightened his focus as he approached the doors.

Waiting in the vestibule, he scanned the parking lot for unusual activity, lingering people in vehicles who might've been staking the place out. He was pretty sure no one had followed them, though he gauged they had about twenty-four hours before that changed. Hopefully, the showdown would be set up before that window of time closed.

Deciding it was clear, he made his way out to the stolen Lexus, casting another glance across the lot as he put the duffel in the back seat. His lips formed a thin line of determination as he reached for the driver's side door handle and climbed into the car.

He drove fast. Faster than he should have, but urgency danced with unpleasant energy through his body. It was unlikely given how cautious he'd been, but he still wanted to be careful about a possible tail, so he wove through a complicated route that brought him to the weathered and sturdy brownstone.

He kept his head low as he knocked, felt the way his shoulders sloped downward in contrition.

Kesterson's door swung wide, and one side of his mouth turned up in a satisfied smirk like he'd known Chase would return.

"Son of Lundgren. Welcome back."

He had to get far enough away, into a bigger city so that he could throw off any attempts at triangulating his location, and by extension, where he and Sadie were staying.

Part of the reason he'd picked the hotel he had was because of its proximity to several other large towns with multiple options for motels and hotels. Hopefully, that would keep Zim's guys busy enough that they wouldn't immediately locate them.

Once secure in the distance, he pulled into the parking lot of a large shopping center, settling in toward the back where there was less activity. He got out, casting his eyes toward another brewing summer thunderstorm in the distance, feeling some kind of kinship with the turbulence that roiled within those dark clouds.

He pulled out the phone he'd gotten from Kesterson, steeling his nerves before dialing.

"Gibson," the voice barked.

"I've gotten a hold of some interesting information," Chase said, taking satisfaction in the measured tone in his own voice.

There was a pause, and then: "Lundgren," spoken like a curse. "I knew this kidnapping situation would come back to bite me in the ass," Gibson muttered.

The man's agitation gave him an inkling of hope that this whole thing would play out the way he needed it to.

His lips formed a grim smile. "If you want the evidence to disappear, it's on my terms."

"I'm not an idiot, Chase. I won't negotiate with you. And if you do what I think you're implying, that puts you on the wrong side of the law."

Chase snorted. "That's rich coming from you. If you don't want to play by my rules, I can see if Stackhouse is so eager to dismiss me. Are you willing to chance it?"

"Lundgren, I swear if you—"

"None of this is going to look good if I go straight to the top," Chase interrupted.

Gibson laughed, but the edge in the sound let on that he was nervous. "You think you have this whole thing figured out? Let me guess: you want to walk free with your new little girlfriend."

Chase refused to rise to that bait. "We take down Zimmerman, make sure she's on nobody's radar, I'm willing to work out whatever you need. I won't go to Stackhouse, and you can keep your job."

"No dice, Lundgren. This has been a lucrative business for me. I'm not looking to cash out."

"Got it." Chase hung up on him. It was just to make him sweat and lure him out. As if Chase wouldn't go to Stackhouse and the top brass, anyway. He needed to get to the end of this list if it cost him his job, his reputation. . . even his life, if it came to it. He couldn't abide the lies and the corruption. And he couldn't have Sadie stuck in the middle for the rest of her life.

The phone rang.

He hit answer but said nothing.

Gibson's ragged breathing was the only sound for a few seconds.

"What do you want from me?" he asked.

Chase almost smiled, but the thought of using these tactics on someone he'd once trusted made his stomach twist. "Tomorrow at ten a.m." He rattled off an address. "I will have the evidence. You call off the dogs, we take down Zimmerman, and I want Sadie to walk free. No one touches her."

"You better not be fucking with me, Lundgren." Gibson's voice was a low growl.

Chase hung up instead of offering any sort of reply. He had more phone calls to make.

Pulling Zimmerman in was his next move. If he could get Zimmerman and the others to take each other out, he and Sadie might get off scot-free.

It gutted him to do exactly what Kesterson had suggested, but Sadie was his bargaining chip. Santiago had already laid the groundwork for that, touting Sadie as the key to Greg, so Chase just had to lean heavily into that.

And even though he was so good at shoving his feelings down deep, the disconnected and cold tone of his voice as he laid it out for Zim's guy chilled him on a level he'd never experienced before.

Then all that was left was to trust that Kesterson would do his part.

45

Ache For You

It was dark before Chase came back.

In the time he was gone, Sadie had taken a long soak in the tub, trying to ease her mind. But until she had him there with her, worry over his safety continued to stew inside of her. She'd even ordered some food, but it remained untouched.

Despite the shower in the motel, she couldn't shake the sense that a layer of grime hadn't washed fully away. But that feeling was soul-deep and not something she could scrub off.

She was flipping through channels on the TV when the lock clicked, and she startled, turning toward the door as it swung open.

The shadows clung to Chase's features, carving the lines and edges of his handsome face deeper, making his eyes glimmer as they shifted to her.

As soon as the door clicked shut, he strode toward her, pulling her against him before she could even react. His mouth took hers with a force almost equal to the one he'd had when he'd devoured her body earlier. That new level of connection glowed with the nearness, and she felt his need as intensely as she had before.

He pulled back, breathing hard with his eyes shut, and his hands cradled her face. "It's the worst being apart from you."

She took a breath, shocked into silence by the fact he was able to put words to what she'd been feeling. The fact that he felt it as fiercely as she did floored her. She'd thought it was her natural tendency to get overly attached. But here he was, declaring something she'd felt and not yet voiced.

"Is everything settled?" She heard the tremble in her voice and swallowed against it.

A sigh slipped between his lips, and his eyes opened. "Every-thing's set up. Settled will have to come after." He kissed her again then pulled away.

His absence was like a physical pain, but she reassured herself that he wasn't going anywhere. Not yet, anyway. And maybe this change, the thing that had grown between them, had shifted things for after. If they made it through what would come next.

He walked back toward the door to retrieve something—a bag—from the floor. She hadn't even noticed it when he came in. It had blended with the ubiquitous duffel, but it was clearly a shopping bag. So that was why he'd taken longer than he'd said he would.

"What's that?"

A soft little smile curved his lips as he glanced at her, walking toward the bed where he set the bag and nodded for her to come over. "I got some things for you."

Trapping a lip between her teeth as she approached, she peeked inside the bag to find her favorite toothpaste brand, some jojoba-infused moisturizer, and a bar of organic, free-trade chocolate. When her fingers met red lace, she narrowed her eyes at him.

"And some stuff for me," he said, arching a brow.

She laughed, the tension constricting her chest loosening.

"When you sent me to town before, I was taunted by this little bit of fabric, and I haven't been able to get the image of what you'd look like in it out of my head."

She rolled her eyes. "Such a man."

He chuckled and moved the duffel back to its spot against the wall, his muscles shifting and contracting, and she felt that pull of desire again. He caught her gaze and smiled, the desire in his own eyes obvious. Now that they'd been connected the way they had, he was easier to read. But he'd also let his guard down, intentionally inviting her to the inner world he'd kept so well hidden before.

She took a breath, knowing she'd need to redirect the conversation. This wasn't some kind of honeymoon, and they couldn't spend all their time having sex.

"So, do I get to know the plan for what's next?"

His expression darkened as he frowned. "You sure you want to spend time dealing with the nitty-gritty?" He sat on the edge of the bed.

"If we get all of that out of the way, we can just focus on our last night together."

She came to stand in front of him, placing her hands on his broad shoulders. His landed on her waist, and for once, they were eye level.

But his troubled expression remained entrenched. "I called and set up a meet. Each of them thinks they're the only one involved, and I'm giving them the only piece of evidence. That's how I'm securing your safety."

Her chest tightened again, and a knot formed in her stomach. "But we don't actually have any hard evidence."

He sighed. "It doesn't matter. The plan is that they all take each other out. Meanwhile, I've got Kesterson and his line inside to help incriminate everyone. If everything goes to plan, it will be quick. In and out."

The air grew thick with her worry. "And if it doesn't go to plan?"

He didn't answer right away. Instead, he reached up to brush the hair out of her face, trailing the backs of his fingers down her cheek. "I'm good at thinking on my feet."

She raised a brow as the knot in her stomach tightened. None of it made her feel better or safer.

He picked up on her strain. "Please stop worrying," he murmured, the sound of his voice a low rumble.

She studied the lines that fanned out from his eyes, a road map of expression, and noted that there were flecks of gold in the mossy depths of his irises. "I don't know that I can stop."

He took a slow breath, half-smiling. "That would be a permanent thing."

Her heart stuttered as her brows crashed over her eyes. "A permanent thing?" she repeated.

"Sadie, I. . ." He looked down, his fingers flexing along her waist. "Things are different. Do you feel it?"

Her breath caught when he lifted his head.

"Yes," she whispered.

He met her gaze with an intensity she felt down to her toes. "I thought I could just walk away. To keep you safe, I was prepared to take you home and leave with no backward glance."

She trapped the oxygen in her lungs, keeping it captive to the words he had yet to say, that she wanted to hear.

"I know I can't now. I'm going to make sure this whole thing ends for good, and then, if. . . if you want to see where this goes. . ." He looked down, his face actually flushing with embarrassment.

She put her hands against his cheeks, bringing his eyes to hers again. "I do, Chase."

He grimaced. "If we do this, I can't promise you a worry-free life."

The pieces clicked into place then. That's what he'd been getting at—that she would always wonder if he was safe. And he was telling her she'd have to make peace with that if this was going to become something.

She wanted to dive headfirst into it, promise that it didn't matter. But she also knew enough about herself to recognize how often she made rash decisions, how impulsive she'd always been. And she wanted to be sure, wanted him to be sure. She didn't want to mess this up with her thoughtless words and actions.

"I'm willing to give it a try," she said, her voice solemn.

It sounded foreign, so at odds with what was shouting inside of her. But this was still so new, still so influenced by their circumstances, that it could easily be something that fizzled as soon as the dust cleared.

He nodded, his expression stoic, the knowing there in his eyes. His gaze traced over her face in such an intimate way that she felt the heat blossom low in her body.

That tug was always between them, something she might never get used to. It was hard to tell. She'd had a handful of serious relationships, and she didn't dole out this kind of physical intimacy quickly or easily. But it was almost like her body had a mind of its own.

So when she lowered her face, bringing her lips to his, it wasn't a surprise—though she didn't understand how or why this felt so urgent all the time—that she'd broken her own rules so readily. As his hands wended around her waist, pulling her closer, bringing her flush against his chest, she wondered at the fact that they had known each other a mere few days.

But no one had ever made her feel so much herself, so accepted as she was. No one had devoured her the way that Chase had, the way she knew he would now as he slipped her shirt off.

"I want you so badly," he whispered against her collarbone, brushing his lips along her skin, while his hands skated up and down her back, just caressing her for the heck of it.

She tipped her head back and slipped her hands into his hair, gripping. His lips made a languid trail across the swell of her breasts threatening to spill from her bra, back up to her collarbone, across her shoulder, up her throat, and back down again.

"It never stops. This ache for you," he breathed across her ribs, peppering kisses across and down to her stomach.

Words wouldn't form; she couldn't communicate that she felt the same way, not while his mouth did these things to her, not when her body was screaming so loudly she couldn't think straight.

It was possibly the last night of their lives. So she wanted to drink deeply of his devotion to her body, fall as far as she could into the abyss of his strength, his hands, his mouth, his tongue.

And so she did, long into the night.

46

Turning Tables

The literal physical pain of sliding out of bed was agonizing. Sadie was curled up against Chase, every inch of her soft skin exposed. His fingers begged to feel her yet again.

Another taste of her had done nothing to sate him. He constantly wanted to experience her, feel her, hear her breathing and saying his name. Never enough. And yet, he had a job to do. If he wanted to have her in his arms, be with her freely, he had to bring the whole thing crashing to the ground.

So he rolled out of bed as quietly as he could, dressed, and made his way downstairs to pound through a rigorous workout in the hotel gym to center his mind. Then he came back up, checked his phone, showered, and made plans for what would happen next, all before she even stirred. The meet wasn't for a couple more hours, but he was too keyed up to settle, even after his workout.

And so he sat on the edge of the bed as the morning sun blazed through the crack in the curtains, casting one finger of light across Sadie's sleeping form. Her hair was spread over the pillow, one bare arm thrown over her eyes.

He couldn't help himself as he leaned forward, brushing his nose along the smooth skin of her arm, and she shifted, releasing the sweetest sleep-laden moan.

Cracking one eye open to find him looking at her, she tucked her face under her arm shyly.

"Morning," he said, cursing the time and their situation for stealing a moment he wanted to bask in.

She yawned and stretched, eyeing his clothes. "You already showered?"

He brushed a loose hair from her face. "Mmhm."

She squinted at the bedside clock. "You look like you've been up for hours."

He couldn't help his smile. "Only two."

"Two?" She pushed herself up, the blanket falling away from her naked body. "It's only seven!"

He lifted a shoulder. "I'm a morning person."

She scowled at him. "Ugh. I am not." Her expression softened, taking on a serious edge that told him she remembered what the day had in store for them.

He hated what that did to her, how she shrank, pulling the duvet over herself. Her eyes darted to the window as if the bogeyman would be right there, though they were on the third floor.

"We have some time," he assured her, despite the urgency simmering in the air. "You can get dressed; we can eat breakfast. Let's just pretend it's a normal day."

"I don't even know what a normal day for us is," she muttered.

He would have laughed if it hadn't been something he'd already been picturing. "A normal day would start with me making your organic, free-trade coffee with grass-fed, full-fat half-and-half."

She stared at him in amazement, her face cracking into her beaming smile, giving him a shot of the sunshine he needed. And damn it, if it was in his power, he'd give her that normal day.

He watched her dress and memorized the way her hands deftly braided her thick hair, the way she lightly brushed moisturizer over her smooth face. He hadn't seen her apply make-up once, and yet she glowed, her big, round eyes searching for him often, and her pillowy lips parted into a sheepish smile when she caught him staring at her.

But soon enough, his eyes shot to the clock, every minute passing like a hammer against his mind. Despite his intention to pretend the day was easy and innocuous, neither of them could fully commit. They ate their room service meal silently. Chase barely tasted the food as he repeatedly checked out the window for any unusual activity. Sadie jumped at every little noise, her body held so tightly that he worried she'd knock something over.

He made no comments, couldn't find any words to reassure her.

Finally, the time came.

What he really wanted was for her to stay at the hotel and out of harm's way. But she was the bargaining chip. If the situation called for a show of good faith, she had to be there. It twisted him up, but it couldn't be helped. So they packed up in silence and made their way downstairs.

They arrived at the meeting spot early. But even though they'd arrived well ahead of time, it was likely the others were scoping it out as well. His undercover training was taking over, and he felt the armor, the detachment, the darkness sliding into place.

He turned to Sadie, trying to soften his expression and tone. "Don't get out of the car, no matter what happens. You hear me? Not unless I come get you myself."

She wound her hands in her lap, round and round, tighter and tighter. "Chase—"

"Please, Sadie." The desperation was there, and he let it bleed from inside of him to infuse his words. "I need you to stay in the car."

She caught her lip between her teeth then nodded. "Okay."

If only it gave him some relief. He couldn't release the worry until everything was over. Right now, all he could do was wind tighter as they sat, his eyes going from the clock to the view out of their windows and back again.

"Stay here," he said, reaching for the door handle.

She lurched forward, slapping her hands onto the dashboard as he stood from the car. "Chase—"

"Stay here!"

She sat back as if by the force of his voice.

He wanted to apologize, but he couldn't, didn't have time, didn't have the capacity. Not when he'd gotten out of the car and was exposed to whoever might be there watching.

He shut the door against her shocked expression and felt his waistband for his gun, just to be sure. Only after he heard her lock the car door did he walk between the abandoned buildings, cutting through the alleyway to the open space behind the cluster of brick edifices.

47

Snatched. Again.

The man snuck up on her.

Chase had disappeared, and the air had grown so tight against her skin as time slipped by. Her eyes tracked the minutes, her heartbeat marking each one as they marched onward. Three. Then five. Seven.

Without warning, the window beside Sadie's head shattered, and she screamed, jerking her face away as the glass rained over her. Then the muzzle of a gun pressed into the back of her skull, and she froze.

He yanked her head up by her braid, pulling so hard she thought he'd rip her hair out, then stuffed the barrel of the gun under her chin, effectively keeping her from screaming again. It came out more like a whimper.

"Keep your mouth shut," her captor growled in her ear as he pressed the unlock button and opened the door.

She almost fell onto the concrete, but he caught her and jerked her back to her feet. As he dragged her down the alley, he pressed the gun so hard under her chin that she had to keep her head angled up. It made her stagger and lose her balance a few times as he tugged her along.

And all she could think was she'd already gotten her tenth life. She was now on borrowed time.

48

Meet-Cute

The skin along the back of Chase's neck prickled with awareness, his fingers itching to go for his weapon. But good faith and all that bullshit. He couldn't look like he was up to something.

There was no denying that his body longed to turn around and get back to Sadie. His fear told him they should take their chances out on the road. But he wouldn't relegate her to a life on the run. He didn't want to live that way either.

It wasn't long until the first of the men showed up, slinking along through the shadows, his loping walk familiar. They'd met in covert places before—when Chase had to check in and couldn't let anyone know he was FBI. A strange coil of regret unfurled within him, like he was deceiving—not a friend, exactly—but someone he'd relied on, trusted with his life. The wrath rose just as suddenly, and Chase had to shove it down, ignore the sting of betrayal as it festered so he could bring this whole thing down.

Gibson was the strong-jawed, hard-staring type, the stack of lines in the corners of his eyes not from smiling. His gray hair was thinning, but he kept it close-cropped to hide it.

"Shit place to meet," he said. The way his gaze danced around the space belied his nerves.

The comment made the anger spike inside of Chase as he glared at the other man. His own nerves died away, some part of him acknowledging how messed up it was that he felt so sure now, so used to this kind of pressure.

"Gotta pick somewhere no one else would think to come," he replied.

Gibson's top lip curled back in disgust. Were his kickbacks from Zimmerman so good that he'd turned into some pretentious prick? "You have what I need?"

"You going to give me what I want?" Chase shot back.

"Isn't this a nice little meet-cute?"

Gibson spun, giving away his anxiety as he pulled his weapon and pointed it at Zimmerman.

49

Cue Me In

The man pressed back against the brick wall, trapping Sadie against him with his free arm even as she jerked against his hold.

The gun dug harder into the underside of her chin, and no matter how high she lifted her chin, she couldn't pull her mouth open enough to get any sound out but a few grunts. As soon as she tried to take a breath, the man crushed the air from her lungs, smashing her against his body.

The faint sound of voices reached them, but she only caught snippets.

". . . nice to finally meet you in person, Gibson." The voice was so smooth, it might have been a recording.

Probably Zimmerman. The man holding her stilled, his breathing going softer. Panic lit upward from her toes, igniting her body because that wasn't a normal reaction. Unless he was listening for something.

She made the mistake of thinking his stillness meant he'd relaxed, and she tried to pull from his grasp again. The gun bit into her flesh, the sting of breaking skin making her hiss.

"This was your idea of a trick, then?" Another man's voice, tight and nasal. Gibson, then?

"Not a trick," Chase said, and she almost jolted. "Mr. Zimmerman has been wanting to meet you."

Hearing his voice, despite knowing he was still in danger, flooded her with a relief so deep her knees almost buckled. Her captor held her tighter against him, keeping her upright.

The men spoke quieter, just a soft rumble of male voices with no distinct words, and her nerves ramped up again. She wanted to know, needed to see what was happening around that corner.

"She must mean a great deal to you." The first man's voice, smug and confident, rang out louder.

It was a cue, she realized, as the man holding her jerked into motion, shoving her forward.

50

Satisfaction Not Guaranteed

Zimmerman was not a big man. Nor was he particularly intimidating at first glance. He was as bald as a baby, his face lightly lined. It made his age hard to guess. But the power lingered around him like an aura. He'd been commanding minions long enough to feel secure in whatever situation he found himself.

Chase would have to be careful, play his cards right. Gibson might mess the whole thing up with his nerves. He moved constantly, always on the balls of his feet, and he didn't lower the gun he'd pulled when Zim showed up. A sheen of sweat glistened on his forehead.

Zimmerman's black eyes darted to Chase's face, narrowing. "So where's the girl? And where's the drive?"

Chase didn't respond, clamping down on any reaction.

Zimmerman gave a slow smile. It wasn't friendly. "Well-played."

Gibson looked between them, gawking. "So it *was* a trick. You've got nothing."

"She had the flash drive," Chase said, voice even. "That wasn't a lie."

"Doesn't matter." Zimmerman waved his hand dismissively. "I have what I need. Chase has obviously been playing me this whole time." He shifted his attention to Gibson. "And you've been lying to me as well."

Gibson swiped at his brow. "I put him in place to make sure I could keep the Bureau off my back and out of your hair."

"You mean spy on me?" Zimmerman snapped.

Chase felt the shift, just like he'd hoped. Their attention turned to each other. So where the hell was Kesterson and his guys? Getting Gibson and Zimmerman to meet had been the clincher they needed to prove that they both were up to no good. They didn't have hard evidence, but Gibson's presence was self-incriminating.

"Please," Gibson scoffed, his nerves steeling a bit. "This was supposed to keep the operation going, so it looked like I was doing something without actually bringing it down."

"And yet, here we are," Zimmerman said, his eyes sliding to Chase again, expression darkening.

And he felt the shift again, the direction of the blame had moved back to him, and danger crackled on the air.

"My fault for picking someone who wasn't in on it," Gibson growled, his gun hand moving so that the barrel pointed at Chase.

Shit.

The first inkling of uncertainty hit him as a chill shimmied down his spine, but he kept his face and voice neutral, holding up his hands. "Hey, I'm not turning anyone in here. If I was out to get you guys, I would've gone above Gibson's head."

"But you lured us both here. What exactly were you hoping to accomplish?" Zimmerman asked, tipping his head to the side, that danger infusing his voice.

Against his will, Chase's heart started to hammer against his ribs, and the skin along his back tingled with awareness of the gun burrowed there. If he reached for it now, it would confirm exactly what they were accusing him of.

Maybe going with a little bit of truth would help. "I want out."

"I knew it was more than just protecting the girl," Gibson said, realization dawning in his leathery features. "You want out so you can be with her."

Zimmerman laughed, the sound threatening to punch through Chase's resolve. "That much was obvious when he took out Santiago and his men. Bravo, by the way. One man taking out five is pretty impressive. She must mean a great deal to you."

Zimmerman's satisfied grin sent another set of chills racing down his spine. And then he heard the shuffling of feet behind them.

No.

Chase spun.

51

Through-and-Through

From the corner of her eye, Sadie caught the way Chase lurched toward her, then halted as if jerked by a string. The gun bit into her skin again, and she gasped from the pain, lifting her head higher to relieve the pressure.

"So, tell me, Chase. What do you really have for us?" Zimmerman asked, his voice ominous, and she knew they were in deep trouble.

"A flash drive. With names." Chase sounded less confident than usual, the words coming faster. This wasn't going the way he'd planned.

Her eyes shot to his face, hope that it was just an act scoring her from the inside.

"Ah. So you really don't have the information I need." The man almost sounded bored. Unsurprised.

There was a pause, hesitation heavy in the air.

"No."

Zimmerman laughed, and the hair along her body stood on end. They weren't going to make it out of this alive. Chase might've been good at thinking on his feet, but if they were backed into a corner, it wouldn't matter.

"Drop your weapons!"

The words pelted her body with fear, and the man holding her jerked just as she did. This was an unexpected development for him, too. She heard the shuffling of the others, felt the ripple of confusion and fear that bounced between everyone there, ricocheting against the enclosed space like a pinball.

"FBI! Weapons down, hands up!"

The tactical team flooded the area, and the gun came away from her throat. She thought she was free, but the man holding her didn't release her. The panic in his movements poured into her as he dragged her back into the alley. She stumbled along, jerking against his grip, terror lighting through her bones.

Chase's eyes were huge as he was thrown to the ground like one of the criminals, his hands being yanked behind his back.

"I'm FBI!" he shouted, his gaze never leaving her even as the man dragged her away, kicking and flailing.

She clawed at his hands as Chase disappeared from view. The man grunted, trying to flatten her arms to her sides as he moved back into the alley.

"Release the girl!"

The man fired off several wild rounds toward whoever gave the shouted command, and a scream ripped up her throat as the strength left her legs. Dropping to the ground was what she should have done in the first place because he lost his grip on her as she went down.

Returning gunfire rang out from the mouth of the alley, and the man abandoned her entirely as he ran for the other end.

Scrabbling toward the nearest wall, she curled in on herself as bullets screamed back and forth. She cowered against the brick, pressing herself so tightly, the rough texture bit into her exposed skin, scraping like nails on her flesh. She focused on the sting because it kept her from losing her fizzing mind.

The ricocheting sounds of bullets stopped abruptly. She breathed once, twice, then lifted her head from under her shaking hands to look around, finding Zimmerman's guy sprawled on the asphalt several feet from her. His glassy eyes stared into nothingness, and a stream of blood dripped from the corner of his mouth.

Bodies crowded into her periphery, and she flinched away from reaching hands, zings of terror shooting through her.

"I'm FBI, ma'am," a man said, his smooth, tan face swimming into her view. He was in full-on riot gear, black from head to toe.

But you're not Chase, she wanted to say, but there was no strength left in her to say it. All she could do was try to look behind him for the one person she wanted to see.

"Are you hurt?" the man asked.

She blinked and met his eyes, his question shuffling through her head like a riddle in another language. Then her mind unraveled it, and she shook her head. The man slipped his hands under her arms to hoist her to her feet.

Now that she was standing, she tried to crane her neck to look through and over the bodies that crowded the space. There was shouting and frenzied activity, but only the kind that came after a high-stress situation, not during. And if they'd come for her, the immediate threats must have been taken care of. Her heart began to slow its hard rhythm, but she wouldn't be able to rest until she saw Chase.

Above the din, she caught a couple of words: "Ambulance" and "gunshot wound."

A knot formed in her stomach, and the adrenaline pumped again, shoring up her strength. "I can walk," she finally said.

The man gave her a skeptical look, but he let her take more of her own weight, keeping a gloved hand wrapped around her arm just in case, even as she sped up.

People parted, tides moving in a flow of specific directions like ants around their hill, and she caught a glimpse of Chase's disheveled golden hair. But he was on the ground, and the knot pulled tighter.

"Chase!" His name burst out of her, and she took off before the man holding her arm could react, crashing painfully to her knees in front of Chase.

There was blood, and his face contorted in pain. He was sitting up, though he held a hand against his side, crimson leaking between his fingers.

"Oh, crackers. What happened?" Panic stole the volume from her voice as her hands fluttered over him, fear of hurting him keeping her from touching his body.

"Shot," he said through his teeth.

"Chase!" she cried, panic shooting through her renewed, and the shaking in her hands started again as she touched his face.

He grimaced. "Got any of that arnica handy?"

She scoffed, the mirthless laugh a little watery as the tears gathered in her eyes. "Not for open wounds, remember? How bad is it?"

"It's a through-and-through."

She jerked to look at Carl Kesterson, who'd come to stand over them, his hands on his hips.

"Looks like you got the identity thing cleared up," he added.

Chase glared up at the older man. "Not that it would matter. Gibson was FBI, too," he said through his teeth.

It was absurd that they were having this casual conversation when he was bleeding this much.

"Can't this wait?" she snapped, narrowing her eyes on Kesterson.

He looked Chase up and down, then took in her expression. He gave a tight nod and moved away to speak with another man clad in black protective gear. He held a serious-looking weapon loosely in his hands, the muzzle pointing toward the ground between them. Kesterson, by comparison, looked like a middle school science teacher in his khaki pants and argyle-patterned polo shirt. But he was entirely at ease in the chaos of what was happening around them.

"Are you okay?"

She whipped around to take in Chase's concerned expression. "Me? Are you serious?"

He just stared at her.

She rolled her eyes. "I'm fine."

Chase's brows crashed together. "You sure? Shock and adrenaline can keep you from recognizing injuries."

She shook her head and touched his cheek, just under the healing slice from his fight a few days before. "Will you be okay?"

He grimaced as he shifted to lean against the wall at his back. "Yeah. Like Kesterson said, it's a through-and-through. A graze through my side. That's why no one's in a rush to get to me while they deal with Zimmerman and Gibson."

He nodded toward the crowd of agents swarming two vehicles with flashing lights. They watched as the two men were shoved into their respective transports. Seeing it didn't make the knot in her stomach release.

"Sadie."

She looked at Chase again, and the words shot out of her. "I didn't get out of the car on purpose. I promise."

He huffed a laugh, then sucked in a breath. "Don't make me laugh."

She winced. "I'm so sorry." Her hands fluttered above him again. She wanted so badly to touch him, check him over physically, do something. She felt so useless while he bled and ached.

"Hey," he said, his voice lower.

She met his gaze, tears gathering in her eyes again, threatening to spill over.

He hooked his free arm around her waist and pulled her closer.

She gasped, gripping his shoulders. "Doesn't that hurt you?"

"I don't care," he growled, his face drawing near to hers. "I just need to feel you, to know that you're here. Alive."

The comfort felt so good, so she curled herself around him, holding on for dear life until the paramedics came and forced her away.

She held herself, her eyes glued on the medics as they checked him, carefully loaded him onto a gurney, and wheeled him to the ambulance that waited. All the while, the crowd of law enforcement teemed around her like a mass of black ink swirling in her periphery.

52

Revelations

Only stitches. Chase figured that was all he'd need, and though the needle filled with the numbing agent had hurt like a bitch, he was feeling pretty decent, considering.

But anxiety crawled through him knowing Sadie was back at headquarters for questioning and separated from him while he was being doctored. He wanted to take her back to her apartment himself and hoped she'd still be at the office when he arrived. Not that he'd want her to have to wait around for him. That could be hours. But he still hoped.

It perished slowly as they took the time to address the slice in his cheek and check his ribs to be sure they weren't broken, running him through x-rays and CT scans, making him sit and wait for each in turn.

He tried to rush the process, eyes sliding endlessly to the clock as the urgency burned in his bones. They didn't care how badly he needed to get to headquarters, that he still had to debrief, fill out and file reports, do all the legwork required of him. The fact that there was a list of corrupt Bureau agents Chase needed to help bring in meant nothing to them.

Dropping his credentials did nothing to speed the process.

After way too long, bruised was the confirmed diagnosis for his ribs. Chase could barely contain his impatience, and every answer he gave was serrated.

The doctor's eyes flashed to Chase's face, the tablet in his hand. "Now, you need to take it easy. Because of location, those stitches could easily pop, and I'll tell you now it'll hurt like hell."

"Duly noted," he snarled, hiding his wince as he slipped his shirt back over his head, the fabric falling over the white bandage on his side.

"I mean it, son," the doctor said, his mouth carving a downward slope on his face. "You were damn lucky. With those ribs and that gunshot."

Chase merely growled and flew out the door.

With a growing sense of unease, he stalked through the cubicles, between rows of desks, moving straight back to interview rooms. He found the cluster of agents working the case, Kesterson among them.

"Where is she?" he demanded.

They all looked at him as if they had no idea the absolute panic wasn't lighting him on fire from the inside.

"Someone took her home after she gave her statement," Kesterson said, moving away from the group to put his hand on Chase's shoulder. "I knew you might be upset about that, but it's better if she goes home, and you work with us here on the last details of this situation. Then you can go to her, or whatever the hell you want to do."

His voice had started mild, but it ended on a tense note, like censure was veiled behind his words.

Chase stiffened, gritting his teeth, but he nodded, knowing that he was on some thin ice after going off the rails, even if doing so had brought them to the conclusion of everything he'd been working toward for the last two years.

If he'd known it would be so many hours—hours of aching muscles, stinging pain in his side once the numbing stuff wore off, and the absolute exhaustion that came with the waning adrenaline rush from earlier—he would have told everyone to fuck off.

But because of his connection to the case, he had to give his statement, answer questions, and have his story probed to depths he was borderline uncomfortable with when it got to the topic of Sadie—"*Yes, I did sleep with her.*" "*Yes, I understand this is a breach of protocol.*"

By the end of that session, he was in a foul enough mood that everyone gave him a wide berth as they all focused on the aftermath that bringing Gibson and Zimmerman incited.

The two agents who'd been on the list had outed themselves, scrambling when one of their own rank had been taken in, almost negating the need for the other information Greg Calloway had. More than likely, it would be financial records proving they were either complicit or had been blackmailed into Zimmerman's pocket.

Gibson rolled over easily, admitting to willingly jumping into bed with Zimmerman's operation. It wasn't clear if Hank Jeppesen and Larry Fink had been as eager to join ranks or if they'd been coerced, though there was evidence that they had a hand in keeping Zim from getting nailed by the Bureau for a while.

Chase couldn't find the energy to be shocked or angry, though the uncomfortable murmuring of the other agents was indicative of the general feeling about the news.

When they finally got to interviewing Zimmerman, Chase had little capacity to follow what was happening. Shrouded by dim light in the hidden office inside the interview room, Chase sat in one of those god-awful chairs in the corner, his hand pressed over the agony in his side, fighting to stay alert enough to catch what was going on in the other room.

"Tell us, Mr. Zimmerman, what role did Greg Calloway have in the organization?"

Chase sat up at the question. They'd dug in on so many other topics, things he'd provided information on, evidence for, that they probably had Zim for many years to come. But Greg had been the connection point with Sadie, and even though he was some peon in the organization, anything connected to Sadie would pull Chase's focus.

He grunted as he stood, and the other agents in the room shifted uncertainly as he joined them, casting wary looks in his direction.

Zim waited a beat. His attorney nodded his go-ahead.

"He was a finance guy," Zimmerman said, eyes dancing away for a split-second. His clasped hands tightened on top of the table.

Chase's skin tingled. Something was off. There was more to it than that. It hadn't seemed like it went deeper when Chase started investigating him, but now, something in his gut was firing off warnings about those small tics in Zimmerman's body language.

"Was he aware of your other dealings?"

The attorney shook his head, and Zimmerman remained silent.

But a tension pulsed in the room, and it was obvious to Chase, even from the other side of the glass. If Greg was just a low-level pawn, there wouldn't be any reason for Zimmerman to clam up about him. If anything, he would throw the guy under the bus.

"Do you know where Calloway is now?"

Zimmerman smirked, leaning back ever so slightly. Then his eyes shifted slowly to the two-way mirror like he knew Chase was standing there. That was a message if he ever saw one.

Chase stiffened.

"Not sure," Zimmerman finally answered, slowly bringing his attention back to the agent interrogating him. But he was smug now. "Calloway is a little unpredictable, but I think there are some people he might attempt to visit again."

All the oxygen in the room was sucked right out, taking the breath straight from Chase's lungs.

"*Son of a bitch,*" he whispered, pushing away from the window to sprint from the room, ignoring the other agents as he ran toward the elevators, mentally calculating how long he'd been there and how long Sadie had been alone.

He stabbed the down button over and over until he muttered a curse and booked it down the stairs. Injuries be damned.

53

Fizz You, Greg

Sadie's apartment was still a mess when she arrived home, and the disappointment that caused after the week she'd had was heavy.

She blamed her heaving sobs on that and not the fact that she'd been at the FBI headquarters for two hours and didn't get to see Chase after he was treated at the hospital.

She cried her way through the longest and hottest shower she'd probably ever taken in the dead of summer, continued to weep as she finally got dressed in her own clothes and braided her wet hair just to keep it out of her face.

Her eyes were puffy by the time she shuffled into her living room, squeezing a sigh out as she bent down to pick up her eviscerated pillows. At least the tears had stopped.

She went in search of her laptop to video chat with her dad to let him know she was all right. He was convinced he needed to make the two-hour drive to be with her, but she assured him that she was fine and wasn't in the mood for company.

Apparently, the FBI had been to his house when she'd gone missing and informed him that someone had gone through her apartment. It took her a long time to reassure him that she would be fine alone and hung up with a promise that she would ask Fiona to come over just to get him off her back.

She promised Fiona the same thing when she called her next, lying about her dad being on his way instead of asking her best friend to come over. It took a lot of convincing and half the story about what had happened to her—kidnapping by an undercover FBI agent and subsequent takedown of a major criminal, minus the sex part—before Fiona let it go. Sadie was too exhausted to go through every detail of the question mark that was her relationship with Chase, which she would have to do if Fiona was there. She could handle that tomorrow, after a good rest. And maybe—hopefully—after some clarity from him.

She shut her laptop with an increasing sense of uncertainty. He'd been clear about his feelings, but it was less clear what it all looked like from the perspective of his job. And what were they going to do from here on out? His cabin in the woods was his sanctuary away from chaos, but she lived here. She couldn't very well abandon her students, and she'd never ask him to give up his solitude. The distance made it impractical during the school year for her.

But his remote cabin had begun to feel like her own refuge after everything that had happened. Summers there, then? School years here? She shook her head, getting ahead of herself. They had only decided to see how it went.

Going to the kitchen, she downed two full glasses of water to clear the sandpapery feeling from her mouth, then frowned at her sad sourdough starter after a week of neglect. She could probably revive it. But after she cleaned the rest of the apartment.

It took an hour to clean the broken things scattered across her living room floor and stuff everything into the trash bag leaning against the kitchen island. The place still felt dismal and out of sorts. But it was more than just the fact that her stuff had been messed with. *She* was out of sorts. Her home felt wrong, like an ill-fitting outfit. She'd been irrevocably altered by what had happened this week, and life as usual didn't seem within her grasp anymore.

She went through her fridge to see if there was anything to eat and deemed all of it either expired or unappealing. It was one of those rare occasions she decided it was worth just ordering something as unhealthy as she wanted. 80/20, right?

After ordering the biggest, most loaded pizza for delivery, she settled on her couch with a glass of wine. Even though she wasn't a big wine drinker—or alcohol in general, for that matter— she decided it was a night for indulgence.

Her wine was half-gone by the time the knock came on the door. A little sooner than she'd expected, but she was ravenous and wouldn't hate having her pizza sooner than anticipated. Plus, she felt the slightest bit loopy from her wine on an empty stomach.

Stopping at her purse on the way to the door, she grabbed her wallet to pull out her cash. Her smile was genuine as she opened the door, ready to compliment and tip extra for the fast service.

The smile turned brittle and shattered when her eyes landed on Greg with a gun in his hand.

"Honey, I'm home," he murmured, shoving his way inside.

She dropped her wallet in her haste to back away from him. But a twinge of heat flashed through her. She was getting real tired of having guns pointed at her.

His eyes danced around her apartment as he shut the door, checking if she was alone. He craned his neck to look into the guest room, then jerked the gun for her to precede him toward her bedroom.

"What are you doing here, Greg?"

He tipped his head to the side, like he was trying to figure out why she sounded more pissed than scared. She wondered that herself. Maybe she'd been juiced on the fear for too long, and she had no energy to dredge it up again. Or it was the wine. Or it was just that someone as pathetic as Greg wasn't all that scary.

"You have something I want," he answered, waving the gun for her to sit on the end of her bed.

She obeyed because she wasn't a fizzing idiot. Her eyes never strayed from the gun that was trained unwaveringly at her. "I already turned the flash drive over to the feds."

He snorted. "That will keep them busy for a while. But that's not what I'm talking about."

The first cold finger of fear trailed down her spine. This didn't fit her image of Greg, nor did it match what she'd understood about his role in this whole fiasco. He was absolutely calm and collected. Downright cocky, if she had to name it.

She grew very still as she tried to understand what was happening. "I don't have anything else."

Greg smiled, his devilish grin that meant he was feeling pretty good about himself. "Yes, you do. You just don't know it."

Her breaths came in shallow spurts as the terror that started to manifest made his smile grow.

"What did you do?" she breathed.

He laughed. "What does it matter, Sadie? You didn't want any part of this life I was building."

"But you dragged me into it," she said softly. "Why?"

His smile dropped away, and the first glint of anger flashed in his eyes. "You really want to ask me that question?"

Heat sliced through her, and the sting coating her tongue infused her words. "Seriously? Because I wasn't living up to your expectations of what you wanted for a flashy life? Seems a little juvenile to me."

His expression darkened, and he moved toward her. "It doesn't matter what you *think*, Sadie."

She drew back, fear rising up from her core, little flashes of cold that spread through her.

"I wanted you to see what your rejection cost you."

She said nothing this time, not sure what words might set him off or not. But part of her wanted to scream what exactly it had cost her. Did he know what Travers and Santiago had done? Did he know it had nearly cost her her life?

What was the point of putting her through it if she'd been killed before he could boast about his victory?

He stepped closer again when she remained silent, and she flinched. This time he laughed, and goosebumps rippled across her body from the chill.

He snatched her arm and yanked her to her feet, dragging her toward the wall behind her bed.

"Reach behind the headboard," he commanded, all pretense gone. His expression was hard and unyielding.

She stared at him, debating the virtues of resisting. She could test his resolve, see how serious he really was about this whole thing. Her reward for hesitating was a pistol-whip across the cheek.

She cried out in surprise, her hand going to her face where it throbbed. She never would've guessed he was capable.

It was gratifying to see that he was a little shaken by his own reaction. There was the slightest tremble in his hand now as he raised the gun higher. "The headboard, Sadie."

This time, she did as instructed, groping along rough wood until she felt the shape of the flash drive under her shaking fingers. It took a couple of yanks to get the tape to give, but it ripped off and fell onto the floor, taking her stomach with it.

She released a tremulous exhale. "I dropped it."

"Get it." The irritation put a tightness in his enunciation.

She lowered herself slowly and reached around, feeling along the carpet until she found it.

As soon as she stood up, he snatched it from her hand, expelling a sigh of relief.

"Okay, you have it. Now leave." She was proud her voice didn't shake, but as his eyes came back to rest on her, she could see that wasn't part of his plan. But what did he want with her now?

Her heartbeat kicked into overdrive as she flipped through possibilities, each one worse than the last. He took a step toward her; she took a step back.

And then a knock sounded on her front door, and Greg's head jerked in that direction.

A jolt shot through her as she recognized the opportunity in that split-second. Desperation made her bold; wine made her heedless.

Using his distraction, she threw herself into him with every ounce of strength she had, ducking low enough that when the gun went off, its bullet missed her.

This time.

He grunted as they both went down, and he lost his grip on the weapon. It thudded on the carpet just out of his reach, and she scrambled to get off him and lunged for the gun.

He yanked on her shirt, the soft cotton ripping as she pulled against his grip. He managed to strong-arm her off-path, and she fell back against the unyielding frame of her bed, a scream of agony shooting up her spine.

Panic flashed through her when he went for the gun, and she kicked out at him, narrowly missing his head with a bare foot. Ignoring the pain in her back, she speed-crawled toward him, clawing at his arms and face like a wild animal, her desperation edging into madness. She released every ounce of rage she had as it bubbled out. Rage because he'd put her through hell when they were together; because he'd made her feel less-than; because he had put her into the path of psychopathic criminals; and because he had more plans for her.

Everything she had went into the effort, and a sick satisfaction poured through her when he screamed as her nails scraped along the skin of his face. He was pulled from the effort of reaching for the gun and knocked it further from reach. Whirling around, he turned his own fury on her, shoving her to the floor, straddling her middle as his fingers grappled for her throat.

She bucked and flailed at him, and his face twisted—teeth bared, nostrils wide, and those eyes filled with a rage that went beyond the depths of hell.

And then, suddenly, he was gone, an inhuman yell coming from somewhere above her. Then she heard the thud—a body against the wall.

She pushed herself up to her elbows, air punching in and out of her. She didn't understand, couldn't make her mind comprehend when Greg slid to the floor across the room from her and didn't get up.

"Sadie."

Every part of her melted at that voice. "Chase?"

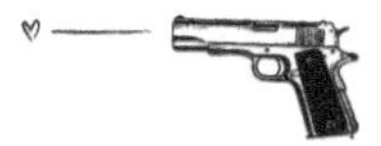

54

Hold My Heart

Chase lifted Sadie from the floor and brought her to the bed, setting her down on the edge. He knelt in front of her, wedging his body between her knees so that he could be as close to her as possible. Brushing all the wild, loose strands of hair that stuck to her sweaty face, he checked her over with frantic attention to detail.

Her eyes were glazed over like she couldn't believe he was there. Or like she was about to pass out.

There was an angry, swollen mark along her cheekbone, and he was careful of it as he cradled her face.

"Breathe, Sadie."

She flinched as if his voice was a blow against her skin. And then she took a breath, more even than he'd expected, and her eyes flashed to Greg's unmoving form in the corner.

"Keep your eyes on me."

She obeyed, her head swinging back to him. "What if he gets up?"

"He won't. Not for a while, anyway."

Not after Chase had thrown him across the room with enough force to knock him out.

The swarm of people was just as chaotic as it had been earlier in the day, though it felt worse because the space was smaller, and his tenuous grip on control was slipping.

It reminded Chase how much he hated crowds, hated feeling boxed in. It was one of many reasons he'd chosen the house he had—isolated and distant without being so far there was no civilization to be found. He wasn't a complete hermit.

But crowds always made him jittery.

As the last of the feds left Sadie's apartment, she leaned against her counter with her arms wrapped around herself, looking so small and alone. Her left shoulder was exposed through the rip in her shirt. Smooth, tan skin peeked out of the thin gray cotton, and anger stirred inside him to think about how it had happened. Not as enraged as he was about what had left the mark on her cheek.

By the time she'd gotten to that part of her story, the other agents had filed into the room and taken Greg, who'd only begun to revive.

Lucky break for that bastard because Chase would have gone full berserker on the guy, and being thrown across the room would be the least of his worries. The sizzle of the fury still spiked Chase's blood.

The rage dragon would sleep for now, though, calmed enough by her presence and the fact that she was alive and unharmed.

Mostly. His eyes shot to her again, his gut twisting at what could have been.

The whole situation hadn't been his fault, but the weight of the guilt settled into his bones because she'd been at the apartment alone, and it took so long to make it there once he'd figured out Greg was more of a threat than anyone realized.

He wouldn't blame her if she held him responsible for all of it. If she wanted to call the whole thing off, tell him to get out and never contact her again, Chase would do it if she asked.

But until she said those words, he couldn't bring himself to walk away from her. Not with the way his body, his hands, his heart sang for her.

He went to the kitchen, making sure she knew he was there before he touched her, and she practically melted into his arms, nuzzling against him like she wanted to meld their bodies into one. He winced in anticipation, but she managed to miss his stitches.

His eyes landed on the pizza box sitting on the counter. "Breaking some rules?" he asked with a smirk.

"I was hungry and didn't want to cook," she said against his chest, voice muffled. "It's probably cold by now."

"We can reheat it," he offered, attempting to pull away to do just that, but she gripped him tighter. That did slice him with pain, but he'd rather pop his stitches than make her stop.

"Don't let go," she whispered. The words nearly broke him, the fear in her voice creating little fissures in his heart, stirring the rage. "I don't want to be here anymore."

He took a deep breath, a glimmer of hope igniting in his chest. "Where should I take you?"

She tipped her head up, tears in her eyes, but she was smiling. "Take me home?"

He sucked in another breath. Did she mean *his* home? Like she saw it that way, too? Not a prison? Not a reminder of all the bad things that had happened to her?

"It's where I feel safe," she said when his surprise kept his words captive. "It's where you are."

Her words sent a slow warmth through him that shored up those cracks in his heart. He smiled, taking her into his arms without a thought for his injuries or his pain because it all disappeared in the light of her. He brought his mouth to hers, the kiss gentle at first, and then she pressed herself more fully against him.

He hated that they would have at least an hour's drive ahead of them before they'd arrive, before they could actually rest and recuperate, before they could explore what exactly came next for them.

But he wanted that as soon as humanly possible and so. . .

"Let's go home, then," he said against her lips.

Epilogue

END OF AUGUST

The trunk sagged with the load it held, cradling all the things that represented her summer adventure at the cabin. Thankfully, it had never known the weight of a clown suit or taxidermied animals. And hopefully, its one experience with a human was its last.

Plants, containers of homemade deodorant, shea butter lotion Sadie had tried her hand at making, a basket of freshly baked sourdough, and the cartons of eggs from the neighbor's chickens filled every available space. Then there was Sadie's and Chase's respective suitcases. Her clay and tools she'd lugged from her place to Chase's were sprinkled in any extra nook she found.

She turned to look at the beginnings of the garden she'd started as soon as they'd gotten back from her last night at her apartment. It had been her coping mechanism, her therapy. She'd clawed at the earth with her bare hands at points, infusing every ounce of her residual terror and anger into the process.

Her garden had been tilled with rage. But, next year, she'd sow it with love. Who knew—maybe fury made a great fertilizer.

While she'd tried to force Chase to rest on the couch—a losing battle, really—she'd also drawn up plans for a chicken coop. He'd done more of the work than she'd wanted him to in building it. But it was solid and pretty and ready for the day she could get her own hens. It was the future plan. Like in a year or two. Except she wanted to turn his secluded oasis into her crunchy lady Disneyland, ready to go full homesteader on it. Cows, goats, chickens, greenhouse. The works.

But she had to ease into that, even though Chase had taken everything in stride. He said nothing as his conventional products and food slowly disappeared and were replaced with locally-sourced, homemade, and minimal-ingredient items. Her plants had taken over the house—the ones that helped clean the air and brightened the space. He hadn't even complained when she made herself a little space in the extra room to work on her pottery and subsequently took over.

It had been a dream summer as the two of them learned the ins and outs of what being together looked like. Roberta had been surprisingly chill about letting Sadie abandon the library for the second half of the summer. Apparently, getting kidnapped made a *very* good excuse, and she even promised Sadie the job for next summer.

Fiona came out for a visit, giving full best friend approval of Chase's doting habits, despite him being particularly taciturn during those few days. To be fair, it wasn't long after they'd gotten back, and his gunshot wound had given him more trouble than he'd anticipated.

But those six weeks had passed. It was just enough time for him to heal, go to mandated (but necessary) therapy to work through the undercover job, and jump through disciplinary hoops so he could earn his place back in the office, this time as a desk jockey until he was cleared for field work again.

And now, their little vacation was over. She had to get ready for the new school year, and Chase was officially back on duty at the Bureau starting Monday. There was a lot of setup to do for her classroom and a lot of clean up for him to do on the case against Greg and Zimmerman, including tracking down the last of the people on the list.

She twisted her hair and secured it with the claw clip she had clamped onto the waistband of her shorts, chewing the inside of her cheek. Now they would transition from his cabin to her apartment, co-existing and taking on the stress that life brought, try their hand at being a couple in the real world instead of their little bubble in the woods.

Her eyes swept the expansive forest that surrounded the house. Already a pang of homesickness stabbed through her at the thought of leaving. She was ready to see her students, though, and there was a level of excitement for what a new year would bring. She took a breath and turned.

"Chase!" she called, her footsteps crunching on the gravel as she walked toward the porch.

He appeared in the doorway as if summoned by a spell, the mythical god of protection to beat back any darkness that threatened. Sunshine burst inside of her at the grin that flashed across his face as soon as he saw her. He had a bag slung over his shoulder and a jar in his hands, which pulled her attention.

"Ah!" She floated up the porch steps, then danced toward him. "My darling! The love of my life!" She snatched the jar from him, jostling the sourdough starter inside as she pressed it to her chest.

He rolled his eyes as he turned to lock the door. "If it was the love of your life, you wouldn't have left it on the counter."

"*She*," Sadie corrected, clutching the jar tighter as if to protect it from a bully. "I wouldn't have forgotten my beloved Meadow."

He yanked his keys from the lock and raised a brow at her. "You set *her* on the counter, then were distracted by getting the two little plants from the bathroom. Then you wanted your coffee, which you remembered you'd already put it in the car." He looked pointedly at her hands, which were only occupied by the sourdough starter. "And looks like you got distracted looking for your coffee."

Her cheeks warmed, though he was giving her an affectionate smile that sent a tingle up from her toes. "I was worried about the plants getting too hot with the sun beating down on them."

He leaned forward to press his lips to hers. "And then I brought Meadow."

She grabbed the front of his shirt to keep him from pulling back. "And then you brought Meadow."

One of his brows lifted. "I also brought your gun."

She sighed, her dismay pulling the corners of her mouth down. He'd been teaching her how to shoot for the last month and even went so far as giving her one of his Glocks so she would always have protection if anyone ever tried to hurt her again.

"You mean Harold?"

He grunted and pulled back, walking to the driver's side of the car. "What is it with you and naming everything?" he muttered.

She pressed her lips together to keep from grinning as she cradled Meadow and went to open her own door. She'd named his punching bag too. But he didn't think Big Pharma was as funny as she did.

He started the car once she was settled and took her free hand, bringing it to his lips so he could kiss it. "Ready?"

She nodded once, the warmth that started in her chest spreading to the smile on her face. "Let's go."

About the Author

Tracey began writing at age 13, when there wasn't much for kids who were mature, loved adventure, and weren't into the drama of everyday teenager-hood. She has always loved mystery and romance, and she has a hard time writing anything else. She really likes to read it too. *Kiss, kiss, pew, pew* and all that jazz.

In January 2022, she took a leap of faith and published her first book, *The Alternate End of Cassidy Marchand*. Since then, she's published the full trilogy, a side novel, a co-written book with C.H. Lyn, and now *Love Undercover*. And she ain't stopping. Except when she has to teach her kids during homeschool. Or when she has to answer her 800th *why* question. Or when she has to break up a fight between her two kids. But, you know, when she's not doing those things… she's not stopping!

Check her out on socials @authortraceybarski (honestly, she mostly does stuff on Instagram) to find out what shenanies she's up to, like book info, new releases, sneak peeks, and weird reels.

Go to traceybarski.com for all other info, to sign up for her very infrequently sent newsletter, and see what events she might have set up. Feel free to contact her with crunchy lady questions, too. Which came first: Sadie the crunchy teacher, or Tracey the crunchy mom?

Acknowledgements

YOU! You beautiful, lovely reader, you—this is a love note I must write in your honor. If you've read anything by me before, you know this was a little bit out of my usual. Or maybe not. I do like my romance with a little danger. But the fact that you gave me a chance with new characters and a new genre means the world to me.

I cannot convey how amazing this author journey has been because of the fans I have and the support my readers give me. I literally wouldn't be here without you all.

Shiny, my wonderful, amazing, genius, motivating, and giving writing friend—you are amazing and played such a huge role in getting this baby out there. Christina, your feedback was invaluable, you romcom queen! To my other llama ladies, Mandy and Lucy, I wouldn't be where I am without you both. Lucy, your feedback and eyes on this helped to make it what it is! Iris, you're a doll for jumping right in and helping me see this story through your eyes.

Danielle and Meredith, my forever fans and friends, I cannot express what your support and help has meant to me. I do this for you guys!

Mom, as always, one of my favorite people and best friends, you're amazing. You deserve so much more than words in the back of a book. You give and give and give. I want to hand you a million dollars.

Brandon, my love. MY LOVE. The man who inspires all the romance, all the sweet gestures, all the tall love interests. You are still the best decision I've ever made.

Alyssa, my bestie for the restie. My soul sister. I love you so much. I couldn't do this without your unwavering support. I couldn't do much without you, honestly. I don't want to, anyway.

To my babies: thank you for sharing your mama with her passions. You are my joy, my heart, my soul, and I love you forever and always. You can do big, scary things because I did.

To my community, those on Instagram, my friends near and far, my writing partners, my church, my mom groups, my family… You're all amazing, and I owe you so much.

And finally, Jesus. I love you.

Also By Tracey Barski

The Alternate Chronicles

The Alternate End of Cassidy Marchand
Resurrecting Cassidy Marchand
Cassidy Marchand Unraveled
Heart in Parallel

Written with C.H. Lyn

Love is Murder

9 781961 707153